Also by Patricia Scanlan

Apartment 3B
City Girl
City Woman
City Lives
Foreign Affairs
Mirror, Mirror
Promises, Promises
Finishing Touches

Published by Poolbeg

PATRICIA SCANLAN

FRANCESCA'S PARTY

POOLBEG

Published 2002
by Poolbeg Press Ltd.
123 Grange Hill, Baldoyle,
Dublin 13, Ireland
Email: poolbeg@poolbeg.com

13 5 7 9 10 8 6 4 2

A catalogue record for this book is available from the British Library.

ISBN 1 84223 075 1

Cover designed by Slatter-Anderson
Printed by Cox & Wyman Ltd, Reading, Berkshire

www.poolbeg.com

F177,062

Acknowledgements

'Why are ye so fearful, O ye of little faith? All things are possible to him that believeth.'

For sustaining my belief and making all things wonderfully possible, especially this novel and the ones to come, I thank you, Lord.

A reader wrote to me and said how much she enjoyed reading my acknowledgements and telling me how lucky I was to have so many friends. Dear reader, my family, friends and loved ones are the greatest blessings in my life and it is my honour to thank them. So, huge thanks to: my mother, father, Donald Hugh, Paul, Dermot and Mary; to Yvonne, Lucy, Rose, Catherine and Henry; and to my darling nieces and nephew, Fiona, Caitriona, Patrick, Laura, Rebecca, Tara and Rachel. Thanks for all the love and laughs and cherishing. And to my godmother, Maureen, whose talents cannot be counted.

Thanks to the dearest of friends who have been with me through thick and thin, especially to Joe, who has turned my gardens in Dublin and Wicklow into the most perfect, peaceful and beautiful havens ... there aren't enough thanks.

To the Wicklow Gang who feed and water me and celebrate with me under starry skies overlooking a corn field when a book is finished: Breda, Kieran, Gillian and Alison, Caitriona, Mark, Emma and Lorna, Helen, Liam and their gang ... here's to summer!

To Deirdre Purcell, Anne Schulman, Sheila O'Flanagan (and Drenda), Gareth O'Callaghan and all my writing friends who are only a phone call, and lunch, away.

To Annette Tallon, Debbie Sheehy, Anne Jensen, Margaret Neylon, Julie Dwane and John Carthy for all the love and light and encouragement they send my way.

To Catherine MacLiam and all my art class for our lovely Wednesday mornings.

To Aoibhinn Hogan, Anne Wiley and Margaret Daly whom I don't see enough of . . . my fault.

To Sarah Lutyens, Felicity Rubinstein and Susannah Godman, more precious than rubies.

To Alil O'Shaughnessy and Tony Kavanagh, the best mates you could wish for. And to Terry Carroll who told me all I needed to know and *more* . . . about international bankers.

To two new readers, Sinead O'Flaherty and Linda Maher . . . keep reading!

To Ciara Considine, Edwin Higel and all in New Island Publishers, who do it so well and so professionally. It's a joy to work with you.

To Sinead Burke of Marsh Financial Services and Eamon Leahy and Mary Burke of Leahy & Co, for all the sound business and financial advice.

To all in Transworld who have been exceptionally supportive and encouraging. The new adventure is just beginning. I look forward to it!

To everyone in the book trade who has helped my writing career all the way, a big thanks.

To all in Nikki's Hair Studio, Mack's Gym and Powerscourt Springs who spoil and pamper me.

To all the wonderful readers who wrote me such inspiring letters, especially Ronald Brown in Essex and Amella Sullivan in Hampshire, thank you so much: they make all the hours at the computer well worth while. Keep writing, they make such a difference. And to all who bought my books, I hope you enjoy this one.

I dedicate this book to Francesca Liversidge, whose
constant encouragement, support, kindness,
professionalism and integrity make her not only an
exceptional editor but also
a very dear friend.
Dearest Francesca, thanks for everything.

When one door closes, another opens . . .

FRANCESCA

invites you to her party in

THE COTTAGE
Cedar Road, Monkstown, Co. Dublin

Last Thursday in December
Dusk 'til dawn!!

RSVP

1343432

Chapter One

'Idiot!' Mark Kirwan swore and pressed his fist on the horn as he accelerated the BMW and overtook an ancient Volkswagen that was crawling along at a snail's pace. 'Stupid doddery old fool,' he snapped as he glanced in the mirror and saw an elderly man behind the wheel.

'Don't be so aggressive, Mark. He looks as if he's lost,' Francesca remonstrated with her husband. She hated driving with him. He was terribly impatient.

'If he doesn't know where he's going, he shouldn't be driving in rush-hour traffic, holding everybody up. I've a flight to catch! It was bad enough with the damn taxi not turning up. I've had it with that lot. They've screwed up once too often. I'm giving the account to someone else.' He drummed his fingers impatiently against the steering wheel. 'For God's sake, would you look at the traffic up ahead? I'm going to miss the damn flight, I'm telling you.'

'You'll catch it,' Francesca soothed. 'Have you ever missed a flight yet?'

13

'There's always a first time!'

'Well, today's not that day.'

'How do you know?'

Francesca scowled. 'There's no need to be so tetchy, Mark!'

'Sorry. Sorry. I feel a bit under pressure.' Her husband flashed her a quick smile but she could see as he turned away from her that it was merely automatic. His eyes were focused on the airport roundabout. He was miles away.

Francesca sighed. What was it about men that made them feel that life revolved about them and them alone? Her two sons, Jonathan and Owen, displayed the same traits – to a far lesser degree, but it was there, despite her best efforts. It was an inbred trait in males and in Mark's case it was more pronounced than most.

He got it from his father. Gerald Kirwan was the most selfish, cranky, self-centred old buzzard that ever existed and Francesca loathed him. He had been part of her life for the past twenty-two years and he was the bane of her existence. She shopped for him, often cooked for him, endured his company for a lengthy sojourn Christmas after Christmas, and for two weeks every year when he came on holiday with them. His own daughter, Vera, would have nothing to do with him, which was very convenient for her, Francesca thought wryly as Mark turned left into Dublin Airport and inched along in the heavy traffic.

'Don't forget to collect my suits from the cleaners, and when you leave the car into the garage tell Ed that I'd like him to check out the air conditioning. There's a slight knocking in it that shouldn't be there. And

14

don't forget to ring Lulu Kavanagh and tell her that we'll come to their dinner party.' Mark rattled off a list of instructions as he pulled up outside Departures. 'I'll ring tonight.' He leaned over, kissed her perfunctorily on the cheek, got out and took his luggage from the back of the car. He didn't look back or wave as he strode towards Departures, his black Burberry flapping in the wind.

He'd overdone the aftershave a bit, Francesca thought as she eased herself over to the driver's side and adjusted the seat to accommodate her shorter length. Mark spent more time on planes than he did at home. She shook her head. The joys of being an international banker.

This hadn't been the plan at all today. She'd miss her book-club morning at this rate. By the time she drove home through the rush-hour traffic and took the car into the garage for its service and got a lift home from there, she could wave goodbye to at least two hours. And Mark hadn't been a bit gracious about her giving him a lift. He could at least have said thank you, she thought crossly. She indicated and slid out into the lane of traffic. It had started out as a bummer of a day; she hoped it would improve.

Mark glanced at his watch as he hurried towards the automatic doors to Departures. His lips tightened. He was late. Of all the mornings to be late. He'd nearly done his nut in the traffic. That bloody taxi firm had cocked up *again*. They were history. He loosened the knot of his tie a fraction as he held up his luggage for scanning. Stress like this wasn't good for him. Dick Morris at work had had a heart attack the previous week and he was only forty-one, four years younger than Mark.

The airport was manic. It didn't matter what time of the day you went there now, it was always bedlam. His eyes raked the monitors looking for his flight number. Delayed. Mark heaved a sigh of relief . . . there was a God. For the first time that morning he felt his tension ease. He was here now. He hadn't missed the flight. He hurried over to the information desk to collect his ticket, anxious to get to Check-in.

'*Would Mr Mark Kirwan pick up a courtesy telephone, please. Mr Mark Kirwan please pick up a courtesy telephone.*' The Tannoy message echoed through Departures.

Mark grinned. He knew *exactly* who was at the other end of the phone.

Francesca leaned across the dashboard to switch the CD player on and cursed as she saw Mark's mobile phone plugged into the recharger. He'd go ballistic without his phone. He'd been in such a tizzy this morning. It was most unusual for him, he was usually so organized about things.

She sped back in a semicircle. Maybe, if the security man was sympathetic, she could park on the double yellows outside Departures and catch Mark before he went airside.

'Come on, come on,' she urged a green Fiesta dawdling up the ramp ahead of her and taking the only available parking spot. A silver Volvo pulled out ahead and Francesca shot into the vacant space, grabbed Mark's phone and jumped out of the car. She gazed frantically around looking for someone to explain her predicament to. The last thing she wanted was to be clamped. She saw an airport policeman and breathlessly explained the problem to him, waving Mark's phone to emphasize the urgency of the situation.

'That's OK, go on. Try not to be too long,' the policeman said kindly as a Tannoy announcement declared that Departures was a set-down area only. Francesca gave a wry smile and ran.

She gazed around frantically at the passengers hurrying to and fro. She didn't know his flight number. But he was going to Brussels. What was the Check-in-desk number for Brussels? She was about to stand back to look up at the big monitors when by chance she glanced over at the escalators and saw her husband's tawny head disappear from view. Relief flooded her. Great! She called his name but he didn't hear her. What on earth was he going downstairs to Arrivals for? she thought, perplexed, as she made her way over to the escalators. She could see Mark at the very end and was about to step on the escalator herself and call his name when her eyes widened in shock and her voice caught in her throat.

A young woman had stepped forward to greet him and, to Francesca's absolute horror, Mark wrapped his arms around her and kissed her ardently.

Chapter Two

Francesca felt the blood drain from her face. Her heart lurched sickeningly. It was as though someone had just punched her hard in the solar plexus. She couldn't breathe. She stepped back involuntarily and bumped into a man who was waiting to go down the escalator. 'Sorry, sorry,' she apologized, her voice seeming to come from a long distance as she moved out of the way.

You're dreaming, she told herself, incredulously. She looked down again. No! It was no dream. Mark and the young woman were moving away, talking and laughing animatedly.

Fear gripped Francesca. What was going on? She vaguely remembered the glamorous brunette. She worked in the Acquisitions and Mergers department of Mark's bank. She'd seen her at a few functions but hadn't taken much notice of her. She couldn't remember her name.

Hesitantly, she moved towards the stairs that paralleled the escalators. She took a few steps down and saw Mark and the woman striding purposefully along. They weren't checking in for a flight to Brussels. They seemed to be heading for Area 9, the Check-in area for domestic flights.

She shadowed them, loitering in O'Brien's Sandwich Bar until they had checked in and sauntered towards their boarding area, obviously now in no rush.

Francesca walked past the small queue at the desk and looked at the flight destination.

Cork.

Mark and the woman were on their way to Cork and she knew exactly where they were going.

How could he? How *could* he have an affair and bring his tart to the hotel that he'd taken Francesca to, just a few weeks ago, to celebrate her fortieth birthday?

But he couldn't be having an affair. It wasn't possible, she thought frantically, not knowing what to do. Should she follow them and confront them? She felt sick. She started to shake as shock set in. Taking a deep breath Francesca turned and retraced her steps. She needed to get to the car, needed to be alone to try and make sense of this nightmare that her life had suddenly become.

'Did you find him?' the airport policeman asked as she emerged shaken and stunned through the exit doors. He noted the mobile still clutched in her hand. 'Oh, you didn't.'

'No. No, he'd gone through. Thanks anyway,' Francesca replied. She was surprised at how normal her voice sounded, but her fingers shook as she went to put the key into the ignition.

Tears welled in her eyes as she drove off the ramp and she blinked frantically to try and clear them. Her throat was so constricted she could hardly swallow and in desperation she drove into the hotel car park, stopped and put her head in her hands. Then she cried her eyes out.

Why was this happening to her? To them? How could one's life be flowing along smoothly one minute and the next be an absolute catastrophe? How long had Mark been seeing this woman? Did he come from her bed to Francesca's? The thought made her feel nauseous.

How had he been able to keep it from her? What did this mean for their marriage? How could she tell the boys that their father was a philanderer? What was she going to do?

The questions whirled around her head, thick and fast like a blizzard swamping her, smothering her. She couldn't think straight, not sitting here in an anonymous car park with rain pelting against the windows and the roar of planes taking off filling the air.

Francesca took a tissue from her bag and wiped her eyes. Mark's phone lay on the seat beside her. No doubt he'd called *her* on it many times and made plans to meet, while lying through his teeth to Francesca.

She felt a hatred and rage bubble up inside her, so strong that she could almost taste it. She'd make him pay for what he'd done to her. She'd given him twenty-two years of her life and what had it meant to him? Nothing! He was a deceiving, lying, despicable bastard. She had always looked up to him, respected him, admired him. She'd thought that her husband was a man of honour. How wrong she'd been.

'I was beginning to get worried. Thought you weren't going to show. Thought you were going to be a wuss.' Nikki Langan slanted a glance up at Mark as they sat sipping cappuccinos in the coffee dock of the boarding area.

'Don't be daft! Of course I was going to show. Of all the days for the taxi not to turn up. That's really pissed me off. Are they mad or what? That's a lucrative account and they've lost it through sheer carelessness,' Mark retorted. He eyeballed her. 'So you think I'm a wuss, do you? Let's see if that's what you think when I get you into that big double bed down in Oaklands.'

Nikki slid her hand up his thigh and pressed lightly with the tips of her fingers.

'Stop it, Nikki.' But Mark couldn't suppress the pleasure that shot through him.

'You *are* a wuss,' Nikki taunted as her hand moved higher.

'Nikki!' Mark's hand shot down and caught hers. She giggled.

'Party pooper!'

'You're incorrigible. People will see.'

'They'll just be green with envy that I'm sitting with a gorgeous, sexy man dying to have my wicked way with him. Did you ever do it on an aeroplane?' She arched a perfectly shaped eyebrow at him.

'You're plain wicked.' Mark grinned at her.

'You've just led a sheltered life, darling. Just as well I'm here to change that,' Nikki drawled.

21

A Tannoy announcement called their flight for boarding and Nikki uncoiled her long legs from the bar stool. 'At last. If we don't do it soon, I'll explode. The sooner we get to Cork the better,' she purred.

'Me too,' Mark said huskily as he followed her to the gate. He still couldn't believe that a beautiful, bright, sexy, sensual woman like Nikki Langan would even give him a second glance, let alone be consumed with desire for him. Happiness filled his heart. He felt young and carefree and eager and horny. He hadn't felt like that in a long, long time.

They ran across the rain-splattered tarmac, laughing as he sheltered her within the confines of his coat. As he looked down at her he felt that he was the luckiest man alive.

'Don't forget to turn off your mobile,' she reminded him as she switched off her own phone once they had settled into their seats.

Mark reached into his inside pocket and a frown crossed his face. 'Shit!' he said. 'I forgot the bloody thing.'

'You can use mine if you need to,' Nikki said airily as she buckled her seatbelt.

'I hate being without my mobile. I'll need to call Francesca and tell her to take the phone out of the car before she takes it into the garage. I don't want any of those rip-off merchants ringing Australia.'

'Well, you'd better call her now before we take off. Here.' Nikki handed him her phone.

Mark grimaced. He didn't want to call Francesca with Nikki sitting beside him. He was as guilty as hell about having an affair, so he tried not to think about it. It was the easiest thing to do. He supposed that he loved his wife, they'd been together a long time. But this was the best thing that had ever happened to him and he was going to make the most of it.

He dialled her mobile but it rang unanswered until it went into divert. She obviously hadn't got it with her. Irritation swamped him. Typical Francesca. She was always leaving her phone behind or forgetting to turn it on. What was the point of having the damn thing if she didn't bother to carry it with her? He left a curt message on her line, clicked off and handed the phone back to Nikki. He scowled. For some reason the incident had punctured his good humour. It was stupid of him to forget his mobile. What could he have been thinking of? If Francesca needed to contact him she could start ringing Brussels and that could lead to complications. Why didn't she have her bloody phone with her so that he could reach her and nip any problems in the bud? There were times that Francesca drove him mad. Right now was one of them.

Chapter Three

Driving focused her mind. The traffic was heavy and the pelting rain had started to turn to flurries of snow and sleet. Francesca turned up the heating. She felt desperately cold despite the warmth of the car. Her hands and feet worked the gears and brakes automatically: her life had just been destroyed, yet she could still do something as normal as driving. In the distance she could hear a jet roar up into the sky. Was it their plane? Were her husband and his mistress sitting together up there, hand in hand, giggling and laughing like teenagers?

Francesca shook her head. It was incredible. Mark having an affair. He couldn't be. They weren't the kind of people this type of appalling thing happened to. They had a good marriage.

Of course there were couples in their wide set of acquaintances where the husband or wife was playing away. Francesca had seen it happen, often. But they were 'other people'. Never in a million years had she thought it would happen in *her* marriage.

An Audi cut in in front of her and she had to brake sharply. She jammed her thumb on the horn and kept it there. 'Bastard!' she swore savagely, cursing not only the anonymous driver but all men and especially her husband. 'Bastard! Bastard! Bastard!'

She knew she had to keep focused. Collins Avenue junction at rush hour was no place for a driver who hadn't her wits about her. 'Concentrate!' She gripped the wheel tighter in an effort to pay attention to her driving.

Twenty-five minutes later she drove into the circular drive of their big detached red-brick Victorian home, which nestled into a secluded hillside overlooking Howth. She fumbled in her bag looking for her keys. Tears welled and spilled down her cheeks again. When she entered the hall Trixie, her beloved cocker spaniel, bounded up to greet her.

Francesca knelt and buried her face in Trixie's soft white pelt. 'Oh Trixie, Trixie, why? How could he do it to me? I'll never get over this,' she cried, the pain in her heart so intense she could hardly breathe. Her little dog whimpered, gazing at her with perplexed melting brown eyes.

'Oh God! Oh God! What will I do?' She had never known fear until this moment but now she was in its grip. Her stomach clenched and unclenched, knotted, painful. Waves of panic washed over her as her heartbeat raced and weird fluttery sensations made her feel as though everything inside her had turned to water.

From a great distance, or so it seemed, she heard the tinkling of 'Für Elise' and knew that her mobile phone was ringing. She didn't want to answer it. She didn't want to do anything except stay curled up on the floor with her arms around Trixie.

The ringing persisted but she ignored it and let it ring out. She couldn't talk to anyone right now. She stayed where she was as her grief poured out of her while Trixie licked her frantically and snuggled in close in an effort to comfort her distraught mistress.

The main phone rang and she cursed it. 'Leave me alone,' she shouted. 'Just leave me alone.'

She heard the answering machine cut in and the voice of Owen, her youngest son, echoed cheerfully around the hall. 'Mam, I won't be home tonight. We're playing an away match and going for a few pints afterwards so I'm going to stay with Sean in town. See ya, Mam, and could you take my jeans out of the washing machine and stick them in the tumble dryer. Thanks, Mam.'

Owen was such a carefree soul. He breezed through life full of optimism, enjoying it to the limit, unlike his older brother Jonathan, who was more serious and intense. Jonathan was working as a systems analyst in a big American corporation in New York and had already been promoted in his first year. Like his father, he was hard-working and ambitious. Owen was more like her.

Francesca and Mark had flown to New York to visit Jonathan just two months ago and had had a wonderful trip. Bitterness swamped her as a memory came flooding back. Mark had been on his mobile phone one day when she had walked in on him in the bedroom. He'd been speaking softly, smiling as he listened to the caller at the other end of the phone. When he'd seen her he'd become brisk and businesslike and quickly ended the call. Francesca hadn't taken much notice except to think that he'd terminated the call very quickly. But then he was always on the phone: always taking and making calls even when he was supposed to be on his holidays.

He'd been talking to that woman, Francesca was sure of it now. And he'd been so eager to get back home. When they got home from the airport he'd had a shower and gone out immediately after. Said he was going to the office for an hour or so. He must have gone straight to her.

Now she knew that Mark was unfaithful, there were so many indications, so many little pointers that she hadn't picked up on – until now. The phone calls telling her that he wouldn't be home until later and not to keep dinner for him. Going back to the gym and losing half a stone. His renewed interest in his clothes and appearance. His concerns about his greying hair. And, of course, she thought contemptuously, remembering his off-hand kiss earlier, his new aftershave.

Classic signs. She remembered a discussion during one of her book-club sessions when there had been much shock and speculation regarding one of their members whose husband had walked out and gone to live with a younger woman. Collette Davies, an outspoken, gregarious blonde who'd been around the block a couple of times, declared that a man who went out and bought new underpants was a prime suspect. Francesca and the others had laughed heartily. The idea of *any* of their husbands going to buy their own underpants was ridiculous.

Francesca's lips tightened. Last Easter Mark had

come home from Brussels with a dozen Calvin Klein briefs saying that he'd got them at a very good price in the duty free. She'd teased him, and called him a pretty boy and insisted he model one. They'd made love spontaneously, which was rare, and it had been good. She remembered wishing that it would be like that more often, rather than the usual Saturday night half-hour, after which Mark would fall instantly asleep, snoring rhythmically, while she lay drowsing beside him feeling vaguely dissatisfied and unfulfilled.

He had been seeing that woman since Easter or before, she deduced. Leading his double life with apparent ease. Coming from her bed to Francesca's with no visible qualms of guilt. It was incredible. This was a Mark she truly did not know and after all their years together she'd felt that she knew her husband inside out.

She shook her head wearily, gave Trixie a hug and stood up. She was damned if she was going to take his car in for a service. Fuck him! She wasn't his personal assistant, his wee slavie. She was his wife and that had obviously meant nothing to him when Miss Career Sex Pot had come on the scene.

A nagging, throbbing ache at her temple sent her to the kitchen in search of some codeine. She filled the kettle and switched it on. She could do with a good strong cup of coffee. Her mobile was lying on the kitchen counter and she saw the envelope icon signalling that she had a message. She wondered if Mark had missed his phone yet. Probably not. He was most likely gazing into that bitch's eyes ... or down her cleavage. Phones would be the last thing on his mind.

It could be Owen who'd tried to reach her, or perhaps her only sister and best friend, Millie. Francesca gave a wry smile. Millie would be gob-smacked when she heard about Mark's carry-on. Millie was mad about Mark. They were always teasing each other. She thought he was the bee's knees.

Millie was a games teacher in a girls' secondary school in Clontarf. She had two young daughters and Francesca was crazy about them. She had always longed for a little girl and had tried desperately to get pregnant again after the birth of her two sons but it had never happened and tests had shown that her tubes were blocked with endometriosis. She'd been very lucky to have the two children she had, she'd been told. Endometriosis was a major cause of infertility.

Mark hadn't been half as upset as she'd been. He was happy with his sons. Two children made a manageable family, he consoled her. They could give them much more attention than if they'd had three or four. But Francesca had nursed her grief for years and would still feel, at times, a moment of longing and disappointment when her period arrived.

Now, though, she was very glad she didn't have a daughter. Hard as it would be to tell her sons that their father was with another woman, it would be a nightmare to have to tell a young girl that her father was a shit.

Suddenly she longed for Millie's strength and steadfast presence. She dialled the number on her messaging service but instead of Millie's effervescent tones Mark's voice came tetchily down the line.

'*Francesca, it's me. I wish you'd bring your phone*

with you and keep it switched on. I've left mine in the car, make sure to take it with you before you leave it in for a service. I won't be able to take calls and I'll be late getting back to the apartment so I'll call you later. Bye.'

Francesca stared at the phone in disbelief. How dare he leave a message like that for her? How dare he rebuke her for not having her phone, he who had left his own phone in the car, and then how *double* dare he lie to her? *Late back to the apartment.* The apartment was in Brussels and he was phoning her on his way to Cork!

'That's it, Mark Kirwan. You've played me for a fool once too often. By God, that's the end of it.'

She raced upstairs in a fury and pulled two large suitcases from the top shelf of the walk-in closet. Suits, jumpers, tracksuits, underwear, including the giveaway Calvin Kleins, went higgledy-piggledy into the cases. Shoes, trainers, anything that she could find, were dumped in until the cases were bulging at the seams. She struggled to close the zips, but her anger gave her strength and finally the cases were fastened. She inhaled deeply like a runner who has just finished a gruelling race. Her jaw jutted with a determined set. Her eyes were uncharacteristically hard. Her anger was mounting by the minute.

It was time her husband found out that their marriage was well and truly over. And he was going to find out personally, from her, before this day was out.

Chapter Four

The traffic had eased as she made her second journey to the airport in less than an hour. A quick phone call to the Oaklands Hotel had elicited the information that yes, Mr Mark Kirwan was booked in but had not yet checked in. The receptionist very obligingly gave her the room number when Francesca said that she'd call later. Another call to Aer Lingus strengthened her resolve when she learned that there was availability on the lunchtime flight to Cork and on the early-evening return flight. She could pay for her tickets by credit card and collect them at the airport. Francesca conducted the transaction in double-quick time. She was anxious to get under way. Now that she had decided on her course of action she was determined to carry it through.

She parked the BMW in the short-stay car park, took note of the bay number and made her way to Departures. It was still sleeting; she shivered as a sharp breeze whipped her coat around her as she crossed the ramp from the car park. Her hair blew across her eyes and she brushed it away impatiently. She'd look a right sight by the time she got to Cork, she thought glumly. She hadn't given any thought as to how she was dressed and what she looked like now. Maybe she should have changed into something more glamorous than the black trousers and lilac chenille jumper that she was wearing under her grey trench coat. Her face darkened. She wouldn't give Mark the satisfaction of thinking that she had dressed up for their confrontation. She looked very smart anyway, she always did. He'd always expected her to look good and had never queried what she spent on clothes.

It was just that her hair was between cuts and she could have done with an eyebrow and eyelash tint as her last one had faded and she'd meant to book an appointment. She'd nip into the loo if she had time, redo her make-up and use an eyebrow pencil and mascara. Anyway, what did she care what Miss Glamour Puss thought of her? Francesca would never see her again. She was looking forward to seeing the bitch's face though when she appeared at their hotel room. At least Francesca would have the satisfaction, hollow though it was, of catching them completely off guard.

Mark would be completely thrown. He hated scenes. He always liked to be in control of situations. Well, this was one situation he wouldn't be in control of, Francesca thought grimly as she queued to pick up her tickets.

A thought struck her. Maybe she was making things easy for him? Maybe she was giving him the chance to leave her? He might have wanted to leave and live with that woman but felt duty bound to stay. If she threw him out, it could be playing right into their hands. But what was the alternative? Go back home and pretend that she knew nothing and live full of anger and resentment? Or confront him at home and tell him to give his tart up? She'd still have to live with the knowledge that he'd betrayed her. Things could never be the same between them. There was no way she'd ever have sex with him again. Her anger surged once more. Mark had ruined their marriage. She hated him and she'd scratch his eyes out when she saw him.

She blinked away the tears that came to her eyes. She was next in the queue. She couldn't go up to the girl at Check-in blubbing. She managed to compose herself and even made polite chit-chat as she hauled the two suitcases onto the conveyor belt and was allocated her seat. She still had twenty-five minutes before boarding. As soon as she got to the gate, she went to the loo to do a repair job on her make-up. Mercifully she was alone. Her hand shook as she took out her mascara wand and attempted to brush it along her lashes. She smeared it and cursed aloud as a black streak appeared at the top of her cheek. She ran some water over a tissue and wiped it off and began again. This time she was more successful and she worked on her eyes and eyebrows until she was satisfied with the result. A defiant extra sweep of blusher to highlight her cheekbones completed her task and, after running a brush through her bobbed chestnut hair, she stood and surveyed her reflection in the mirror.

Two big, grey, troubled eyes stared back at her. A full mouth usually curved upwards in a smile was uncharacteristically down-turned. High cheekbones, her best asset in her opinion, were even more pronounced thanks to the blusher. She looked elegant, sophisticated, younger than her forty years. But not young enough, she thought bitterly. Motherhood had filled out her body. She used to be terribly thin and scrawny. Now she was a good stone overweight although she carried it well because of her height.

The woman he'd been with was petite and toned and youthful. Toned or not, Francesca would never be youthful again and at five feet seven petite was not an adjective that had ever been used to describe her, she thought bitterly.

She took a deep breath, sprayed some L'Air du Temps on her wrists and temple and went to wait for her flight to be called.

It was a bumpy ride as gusts of wind buffeted the small commuter plane and the 'Fasten Seatbelt' sign remained on for the duration of the flight. Her fingers curled in her palms as they hit a particularly nasty bit of turbulence and she didn't know whether to be grateful or not that her mind was occupied with something other than the forthcoming confrontation with her husband and his mistress.

The landing was rollercoaster scary and she thought how ironic it would be if she were to die in an air crash and make her cheating skunk of a husband a widower. Wouldn't that be convenient? she reflected as the plane lurched from side to side making her feel faintly queasy. The relief of feeling the thud of the wheels hitting the runway lasted until

34

the plane taxied to a halt, but then her stomach tightened again at the thought of what lay ahead.

Nikki looked stunning in an emerald-green bikini. Her tanned, toned body made a perfect arc as she dived into the warm sparkling waters of the hotel's pool. She was so fit, so vibrant. Mark loved being with her. Her energies rubbed off on him. He never felt middle-aged with her. He glanced surreptitiously at the tell-tale grey hairs threading the brown tangle of chest hair that Nikki liked to run her fingers through. He wondered, was it possible to dye them? Still, at least he was fit and muscular thanks to his renewed membership of the gym.

He dived in after her, enjoying the feel of the water against his body and sliced along the middle of the pool until he caught up with her. She splashed him playfully and he caught her to him and kissed her passionately. They had the pool to themselves and they lingered in the embrace, the decadent feeling engendered by taking two days off work, mid-week, adding to their enjoyment. They swam and kissed and kissed again until Mark thought he was going to take her there and then.

'Come on, let's go back to the room. This is driving me crazy,' he said huskily.

'I love driving you crazy.' Nikki nuzzled his neck and slid her hands down over his hips.

'Come *on*, Nikki.' Mark grabbed her by the wrist and waded to the side of the pool.

'Big boy!' Nikki giggled, eyeing his crotch.

Mark gave a sheepish grin as he climbed out of the pool and grabbed his robe. He wrapped hers around her and propelled her towards the door. 'Please behave until we get to the room, then you can be as bad as you like,' he exhorted as he led her along the corridor.

It seemed to take for ever to get to the lift and then to their room, but once the door shut behind them they kissed hungrily, their passions heightened by their lovemaking in the pool. Mark couldn't get enough of the woman in his arms. She was magnificent. He had never felt so alive.

Nikki lay nestled in the curve of Mark's arm listening to his steady breathing as he slept. She was drowsy and sated. Mark was a virile and demanding lover and she revelled in it.

She smiled. She loved the power she had over him. She loved turning him on and driving him crazy. He had been a great challenge from the start. She had noticed him early on when she had joined the Acquisitions and Mergers department of Eurobank Irl. He was serious, intense, completely wrapped up in his work. He spent a lot of his time in their Brussels office and she always looked forward to the times he was back in Dublin.

He had never seemed to notice her. This was a new experience for Nikki. She was used to being noticed by men. She was working her way up the corporate ladder and she was getting there because she was highly intelligent, ambitious, and very, very good at her job. Nikki had no time for the flirty, giggly nonsense of some of her female colleagues. She despised that type of behaviour. Certainly she would share jokes and tease her male colleagues when it was appropriate, but she demanded respect and would settle for nothing less. She wasn't universally popular, she knew that, especially since she had jumped several rungs on the ladder and been promoted over several guys who had come in at the same time as she had. They called her a ball-breaker behind her back. Nikki didn't care. That was their problem. Let them deal with it. They were looking up at her and she was looking down at them.

She was thirty-one. She was a manager in her division. She had her own apartment in Blackrock and drove a nifty Saab coupé. And now she was in a relationship that was challenging and satisfying, unlike any previous one that she'd had. The only thing was, she wanted more. Nikki sighed and snuggled closer to her sleeping lover. She knew that to show any sign of neediness or want would be disastrous. She kept Mark interested by *pretending* to be uninterested. Sometimes she would even tell him that she had an engagement and couldn't see him, when she'd be *dying* to see him and spend precious hours with him.

She wanted to make herself so desirable, so indispensable to him that he would leave his boring, middle-class wife, with her book club and charity functions and silly dinner parties. Their kids were practically grown up, one son was working abroad, so it wasn't as if she was taking him away from his children. There was nothing to feel guilty about there. His sons were starting to lead their own lives. He'd more than fulfilled his parental duty to them. Mark was so duty bound. She was trying gently to tell him that it was permissible for him to *enjoy* life.

She'd known almost immediately that he had never played away in his marriage. He wasn't a 'lad'. That was one of the traits that attracted her to him in the first place. He wasn't like some of the flash gits that she worked with, all ego and arrogance. He took his work very seriously, as did she, and that was how they'd made their first connection.

After she'd worked with him for some months, she'd asked his advice about investing in share capital in a company controlled by the bank. He'd offered to go through the draft proposal with her and she agreed only on the condition that he let her take him to lunch.

He'd looked surprised at her invitation but had agreed and they'd fixed a date when they were both free. She'd booked a table in a quiet little Italian restaurant, forgoing the swanky A-list eateries that she usually took clients to. She wanted something more intimate and less showy.

He'd been all businesslike, going through the draft paragraph by paragraph, discussing the investment strategy and the risk factors with great thoroughness.

Although she had gone through the draft pretty thoroughly herself, and had more or less decided to invest, she let him talk on. Men always liked giving advice. It was a great ego-stroker and a strategy that had worked to her advantage many times. Mark Kirwan was no different. He was sexy though, Nikki couldn't deny that. She found that she was becoming very attracted to him. Over the following months they'd continued to have regular lunch dates, getting to know one another, enjoying each other's company, and Nikki realized with a firm certainty that she was going to go all out to capture him. Mark was the man she wanted. Mark was the man she would have. She could sense his restlessness, his boredom with his marriage. He was stagnating and he wanted more from life. She was just the catalyst for change. They had been walking under a windswept Merchant's Arch on their way to lunch and she'd been laughing at one of his witty observations when he'd suddenly stopped and kissed her passionately, taking her completely by surprise as passers-by hurried past them. The hunger in him had startled and then excited her and she'd impulsively suggested that they get a taxi back to her apartment and have an extended lunch . . . in bed.

His desire for her had made it the most satisfying sex she'd ever had. As she lay close against him, in bed in their hotel suite, remembering that first wild afternoon, Nikki wondered how much longer it would be before he finally decided he wanted to be with her for good.

She'd never suggested that he leave his wife, she was much too subtle for that. That would have to come from him. But it was an effort to hide her impatience sometimes and keeping up her façade of indifference to their situation was getting more difficult to sustain.

He'd been very sharp on the phone to his wife earlier when he'd borrowed her phone. Nikki had pretended that she wasn't listening and hadn't noticed but it had given her immense satisfaction to overhear his obvious annoyance. It made her feel better about their own relationship.

Maybe things might turn around this week. Maybe all would change and he'd take the final step that would make him hers.

Chapter Five

'Are you on holiday?' the taxi driver was chatty as he drove out of Cork Airport and headed in the direction of the city.

'Just overnighting before flying to London,' Francesca fibbed. That would give a reasonable explanation for the two large, bulging suitcases in the boot. 'In fact I'd like you to wait for me while I check into the hotel, if you wouldn't mind. I want to go directly on into the city.'

'Certainly, ma'am,' the rotund little man said cheerfully. 'I'll take you wherever you want to go. Terrible cold weather, isn't it?'

'Mmmm,' murmured Francesca, wishing that he would shut up. She felt extremely tense. Her palms were clammy and her heart was thudding against her ribcage at a rate of knots. She felt like throwing up. Imagine if she disgraced herself by barfing in front of Mark and that woman. She slipped a Polo mint into her mouth. It helped a little.

'So, are you going on holiday to London?' the taxi

driver persisted, determined to get conversation going.

'Yes.' Francesca hoped her monosyllabic answers would give him the hint that she was not interested in conversation.

'What part?' he cocked an eye at her in the rear view mirror.

'Aaahh ... er ... Kensington.' This was crazy. Francesca bit her lip. Here she was on her way to catch her unsuspecting husband betraying her with his mistress, and to end their marriage for good, and she was engaging in the most inane, surreal conversation she'd ever had, with an absolute stranger. She had an urge to giggle hysterically.

'You must be going to stay for a long time with all that luggage. Those cases weigh a ton,' he commented.

'My husband will carry them, I'm meeting him at the hotel,' she said weakly.

'Aah ... that's good. You could do yourself damage lugging them around.'

I'll do you damage in a minute if you don't bloody well zip it, Francesca thought viciously. *No tip. Definitely no tip*, she decided.

'You'll probably do a bit of Christmas shopping in Oxford Street when you're over there. Harrods and all of that.'

'Probably,' she agreed, curling her fingers into her palms. She had a mad urge to grab his grey wiry hair and pull hard.

By the time they pulled up outside the hotel she was hopping mad and fit to be tied.

'Now let's get those cases out.' The taxi driver

eased his plump frame out of his seat and took a deep breath in preparation.

I hope you give yourself a hernia, Francesca fumed as she watched him struggling.

A doorman came down the steps to help. Francesca took a deep breath. This was it. There was no going back.

Mark leaned across the table and fed Nikki a fat, luscious prawn. They were sitting, relaxed and happy, dressed only in luxurious white towelling robes, enjoying a tasty room-service lunch.

'This is the life.' Nikki stretched languorously. 'We should do this more often.'

'We've got to be careful. If we take too much time off together, people might suspect something.' Mark expertly eased the top off the Moët and filled her glass with sparkling champagne.

'Hmm. But we're very discreet at work. No-one would ever guess.'

'Yeah, I suppose no-one would ever think that a beautiful woman like you would be bothered with an old fogey like me,' he teased.

'Don't be silly, darling. You talk as if you were ninety. You're my sexy older man. *And* you're in your prime. Twice in half an hour, I know thirty-year-olds who couldn't do that!' Nikki smiled seductively and stroked her foot along his leg. 'It's so nice having time to spend together. I could get used to it.'

'There's an international bankers' conference coming up in Malta, in February. If you came out on the last day, which happens to be a Friday, we could stay until Monday. How about that?'

'Sounds lovely,' Nikki enthused. 'But what about Francesca? Doesn't she want to go?'

'I haven't said anything to her about it,' Mark admitted.

'Oh!' Nikki was delighted at this news. This was real progress. This delightful interlude and now a possible weekend in Malta. She felt her heart lift and soar. She was starting to feel very, very happy. Things were getting better and better.

It was amazing how calm she felt after her nerves during the taxi journey. Francesca smiled at the receptionist. 'Hello. I'm just dropping my boss's luggage up to him in room 311. He's expecting me. He's checked in. Mark Kirwan?' She looked expectantly at the smartly groomed redhead.

'Yes, indeed. Mr and Mrs Kirwan checked in earlier. John can help you there.' She nodded towards the young porter who was hefting the cases onto a luggage trolley. 'John, suite 311, please,' she instructed.

Suite 311. Flash bastard, Francesca sizzled. He'd only booked a room for them when he'd brought her here for her birthday.

As she followed the young man to the lift, Francesca couldn't believe how well her bluff was working. If Mark wasn't in his room she'd get the porter to let her in and she'd be waiting to greet Mr and *Mrs* Kirwan on their return. The nerve of Mark! How dare he call his trollop Mrs Kirwan, how dare he dismiss Francesca's right to the title so easily? she raged as she followed the porter into the lift. It glided silently to the third floor and her heart pounded in her chest as they walked along the carpeted hallway to her husband's suite. Her little window of calm was disappearing fast. *God, please don't let me disgrace myself. Don't let me burst into tears when I see them*, she prayed, steeling herself for the ordeal ahead.

'Just open the door, please, and put the cases inside,' she said briskly, handing the young man a fiver.

'Certainly, madam.' The porter was delighted with his tip and inserted the key into the lock without further ado. With youthful vigour he deposited the cases in the hall, then departed swiftly, whistling to himself.

Francesca eased the door shut and surveyed the scene. How fortunate that the suite door led to a narrow entrance passage off which were two white painted doors. One no doubt was the bedroom, the other the lounge area. She could hear a woman's laughter behind the door on the left-hand side. She and Mark were obviously in there and they hadn't heard the main door being opened. All to the good for her purposes, she thought grimly. The woman laughed again, a happy, chortling sound. Francesca hated her. Then Mark's familiar deep chuckle followed. They were certainly enjoying themselves. Pain and hurt ripped through her. Didn't Mark care about her at all, that he could be so carefree? She took a deep breath, swallowed and opened the door. Mark and the woman looked over from where they were sitting, surprised.

Surprise gave way to shock as Mark recognized Francesca. He paled and jumped to his feet as she walked over to the table. The woman's eyes opened wide and her hand went to her mouth.

'*Francesca!* Francesca, what are you . . . I mean . . . Francesca, how . . . how did you know?' Mark stuttered as he pulled his robe tighter around him and tied the belt.

Francesca stared at him. He looked so handsome and relaxed in the white towelling robe, his hair, still damp from his shower, curling against the collar. Up until now she hadn't really believed what was happening. Had hoped against hope that it was all a big mistake. But there was no mistaking their intimacy. She was the outsider here.

The shock was very physical. She felt quite dazed. It was an effort to pull herself together. But she had to. For her own pride. Pride was all that would get her through this.

'You are the lowest of the low, Mark Kirwan.' She spoke in a cold, clear voice. Surprisingly strong. It took her husband by surprise and he lowered his gaze, unable to meet her contemptuous stare. 'I hope our sons haven't inherited any of your sly, lying, cheating ways. How dare you treat me like dirt? How dare you come from that slut's bed to mine?'

She turned to Nikki and said icily, her eyes full of scorn, 'Did he tell you that our marriage was over? That we weren't making love any more? He lied. Or maybe he didn't. Maybe you just don't mind sharing a man. Well, I do. I have some self-respect. So you can have him . . . with pleasure. He's obviously found his level in life and it's pretty low.'

'Now just a minute.' Nikki stood up, eyes glittering. She turned angrily to Mark. 'I won't have her say things like that about me.'

'Francesca, stop that,' Mark snapped.

She turned on him furiously. 'You. Don't *you* tell me what to do. You liar. You sly shit. When she says jump, do you say how high? How pathetic at your age. Your clothes are in two cases in the hall. Here's the keys to your car. It's in the car park at Dublin Airport with your bloody mobile phone in it. I never want to see you again.' She dropped the keys of the BMW onto the white linen tablecloth and turned on her heel and walked out.

The lift was still open and as the doors closed silently behind her, she exhaled a long breath. 'Bastard. Fucking bastard,' she whispered. The hurt and grief and pain were so intense, she thought she was going to pass out. She started to shake. Francesca bit her lip hard. She had to get control of herself. She couldn't give in to it yet. She had to get herself home before she could give way to the anguish that threatened to engulf her. Then, if she wanted, she could collapse in private and crawl into her shell and never come out.

The lift stopped at the first floor and a couple got in. They smiled at her and she managed a weak smile back. Seconds later the doors opened onto the foyer and Francesca had to restrain herself from running out of the hotel. She nodded towards the receptionist, who looked up as she passed, and kept on walking.

Her little plump taxi man jumped out, beaming, and opened the car door for her when he saw her, and her heart softened at his gallant good manners.

'Now, ma'am, whereabouts in the city?'

'Patrick Street, please. And thank you so much for waiting,' she said as pleasantly as she could.

'Not at all. I hope you didn't rush.'

If only he knew, she thought drily.

He chatted away for the rest of the journey into Cork and she responded as best she could, ashamed of her earlier ungraciousness. His garrulity helped to keep her thoughts at bay and gave her a chance to regain her composure. Making the effort to respond to his conversation temporarily blanked out the memory of the scene that she knew would haunt her for a long time to come.

She tipped him a fiver, and endured a flow of effusive thanks that caused her to feel irritable again; she half wished that she hadn't given it to him. It was a relief to watch his taxi disappear into the flow of traffic on Patrick Street and to feel the sharpness of the sleety wind against her cheeks. It was almost two-thirty and her return flight was at four-thirty-five. She'd have time for a cup of coffee before getting a taxi back to the airport.

A great weariness enveloped her. She hadn't eaten all day, but the thought of food made her feel faintly nauseous. Every cloud had a silver lining – maybe she'd lose a stone. Didn't all women lose weight when they found out they were being cheated on? she thought sourly as she trudged along the gaily decorated street, with signs of Christmas everywhere.

She wouldn't be celebrating Christmas this year and Mark's father could go and spend it with Mark and his tart, because she'd never cook a meal for that old buzzard again, she vowed as she opened the door into a small, crowded self-service café and took her place in the queue.

If that woman wanted Mark in her life so badly she

could take his baggage too. And Gerald Kirwan was excess baggage that Francesca had carried for far too long. Goodbye and good riddance, she thought as she ordered a cup of coffee and a scone. She'd try and eat the scone. The last thing she needed was to faint from shock and hunger. She had a lot to do when she got home and first on her agenda was changing the locks!

Mark Kirwan had just forfeited the right to come and go as he pleased in *her* home.

Chapter Six

'God Almighty! How the hell did she find out?' Mark paced up and down the room, his jaw set, his forehead furrowed as the enormity of what had just happened hit him.

'Well, she knows about us now, Mark. We have to go forward from here,' Nikki said calmly. Now that Francesca was gone, she was trying hard to disguise the bubble of elation that was threatening to burst out of her. The wife knew and had kicked him out. Perfect! Mark was all hers now.

'Did she have a private detective on me? What else is she going to do? Remember that guy whose wife split on him about his offshore accounts? It was all over the papers and TV. I have offshore accounts. I could be in deep shit if she knows about them,' he blurted out, completely rattled. 'We'd better get home. I have to talk to her. Calm her down.' He raced into the bedroom and began to dress.

'Mark, will you take it easy?' Nikki soothed, following him into the room. She knew she had to play this very cool. 'I don't think you should see Francesca tonight. She's obviously very upset right now and that's understandable. She'll be calmer tomorrow. She'll have had time to adjust a bit. There'd only be a row if you went home straight away.'

'This is a fucking catastrophe.' Mark sat on the bed and put his head in his hands. 'She'll never forgive me for this. My life will be a fucking nightmare.'

This wasn't what Nikki wanted to hear at all. She didn't want to hear about Francesca's forgiveness. That sounded as though he intended to remain with his wife. She allowed it to pass unchallenged. This wasn't the time to put her spoke in.

'She was so cold.' He shook his head in disbelief. 'I've never seen Francesca like that.'

'Well, how would you expect her to be?' Nikki probed gently.

'I know, but she usually loses her cool and rants and raves for a while. She's never like she was just now. She made it sound so final.'

'Well, Mark, we *have* been having a relationship for nearly a year. Didn't you ever think that she might find out about us? And didn't you ever wonder how she'd deal with it?' Nikki's tone had an edge to it.

'I never thought that she'd find out about us actually,' he muttered. 'I suppose I didn't want to face it.'

'Well, you have to face it now, darling, and you have to deal with it. It's happened and there's nothing you can do about that.' She wanted to say, *and you have to make a choice between her and me now. And I don't like being made to feel that I was only your bit on the side.*

51

'I know that, Nikki,' he snapped. 'You don't seem to understand the implications here. I have a lot to lose. I have children, a certain lifestyle, my reputation at work.'

'And me if you're not careful,' Nikki bristled. 'Don't lay the blame at my feet, Mark. It's not *my* fault. You have to take responsibility for your own actions. I didn't bulldoze you into this relationship.' She marched into the bathroom and slammed the door behind her.

'This is a bloody nightmare,' Mark swore. He didn't know what to do. Seeing Francesca standing in the doorway had been the most horrific moment of his life. He felt a cold sweat wash over him at the memory. God! The way she had looked at him, with such contempt. He cringed in humiliation. He'd always liked the way Francesca looked up to him. It had made him feel good. She was a very straight person. If she knew about his offshore accounts she'd be horrified. She'd always asked him to play by the rules and keep inside the law with his investments and he'd always assured her that he would, just to pacify her. Now she'd caught him having an affair and kicked him out. If she found out about his tax evasion there'd be hell to pay. His life was in ruins.

He didn't want his marriage to end. He liked being married to Francesca, even if she got on his nerves a bit. She was a good wife. She entertained well, and looked after his father and the boys so that he could concentrate on providing for them. He'd been happy having the affair with Nikki, but he hadn't planned to leave Francesca for her. And he'd never got the impression that Nikki wanted him to leave his wife. She was far too wrapped up in her career and social life to want to be domesticated. And that had suited him down to the ground. He'd had it every way. Now the ball game had changed, the goal posts had shifted and he didn't know which way to turn. He glared at the bathroom door resentfully. A sulking woman was the last thing he needed right now. Couldn't Nikki understand how traumatic all this was? He could hear running water. What the hell was she doing having a bath? She'd only had a shower an hour ago. She was being very selfish and unsupportive, he thought angrily. She had no commitments to anyone. No family unit to disrupt. She had nothing to lose. Unless he could make Francesca see sense and assure her that the affair meant nothing, he had *everything* to lose.

Nikki eased herself into the foaming water and lay back in the bath. She was furious with Mark. He was taking it out on her as if it was all her fault. She'd got such a shock when the wife walked into the room. It was like something out of a film. Nikki shivered in spite of herself. Francesca was more youthful than she remembered. But then she'd only seen her a couple of times at banking events, where she'd been dressed up to the nines.

She'd been damn insulting though, the sharp-tongued cow. And the way she'd turned on Mark. Bossy wagon. No wonder he'd gone elsewhere. Nikki knew she had to play her cards right. It was vital not to antagonize him. Otherwise he might dump her and beg his wife to take him back. She got out of the bath, wrapped a towel around her and went out to the bedroom.

'I'm sorry, darling,' she said contritely. 'I didn't mean to snap. I guess I got as much of a shock as you did and the last thing I want is to be a source of unhappiness for you.' She put her arms around him and drew him close.

'What am I going to do, Nikki? What am I going to do?' he groaned.

'Look, let me ring Aer Lingus and change our flights to tomorrow morning. We'll take your cases to my place for the time being. You hardly want to stay in a hotel, do you?' She arched an eyebrow at him.

He shook his head.

'OK. Then go home and talk to Francesca and see what she has to say and we'll see how things pan out from there. All right?'

'OK.'

'Now, why don't we get dressed and go for a walk in the grounds to clear our heads? Otherwise we'll sit here moping and that won't do us any good at all,' she said tenderly, stroking his head gently.

He nodded despondently. 'OK.'

'And then, when we come back, why don't I book us in for an aromatherapy massage? It would help de-stress you a little. It's been a tough day on you.'

'Yes, it has,' Mark agreed sorrowfully. 'It's been the worst day of my life.'

Oh, for God's sake stop being such a wimp. Things couldn't have worked out better for us. It was almost on the tip of her tongue to say it. She wanted to shake him. He was making her feel so unwanted and

54

unimportant. She forced herself to ignore her anger and resentment.

'I know, pet, I know. But it's happened now and there's no use in crying over spilt milk. Don't worry. Things will sort themselves out. And I'll be with you to help.'

'You're very kind, Nikki.' Mark held her close and her heart lifted momentarily. This was more like it.

'Sure I love you, darling,' she whispered softly. 'I love you very much.'

It worried her that he didn't respond.

It took Francesca almost as long to get home from the airport in the rush-hour traffic as it did to fly to Dublin from Cork, and she was weary to her bones as she paid the taxi driver and let herself into the darkened house. She switched on the porch light and the lamp in the hall and picked up the *Golden Pages*. If Mark came home on a later flight she was damned if he was going to get into the house. She found a locksmith in the area, phoned him, told him that her bag had been stolen with her keys in it and that she needed her locks changed urgently. He promised to be there within the hour.

How easily she had lied, she thought in disgust as she put the phone down, but needs must. The sob story would get him here quicker. And she wanted those locks changed badly. She wanted to have *some* control over the situation.

She went into the kitchen and plugged in the kettle. Trixie kept looking at her with puzzled brown eyes, sensing that something was up. She gave a little whine every so often. Francesca switched on the small portable TV and saw the end of the news. She couldn't concentrate. She was wound tight with nerves, half expecting to hear Mark's key in the door. Still, if he got a flight back to Dublin, it would take him ages to find his car because she hadn't told him the parking number, and the BMW could be anywhere in any of the three huge car parks, she thought with vicious satisfaction. Once the locksmith came and was finished, she could go to bed and cry her eyes out. It was a comfort of sorts, Francesca thought as she made a pot of tea and nibbled at a slice of tea brack.

The red light on the answering machine was flashing furiously but she ignored it. She didn't want to have to deal with calls. She was too numb.

It was an hour before the locksmith finally came and by then she was up to ninety. She kept imagining that she heard Mark's car in the drive and was up and down like a yo-yo, looking out of the sitting-room window. As the time passed she began to get angry that there was no sign of him. How dare he? she thought irrationally. How dare he not rush back up to Dublin to throw himself at her feet and apologize profusely and beg her forgiveness so that at least she would have the satisfaction of telling him to get out?

She forced herself to appear composed as she informed the locksmith that she needed him to change the locks on the front, back and garage door for her.

'That's a terrible thing to happen to you, missus,' the middle-aged man said as he took his tools out of a grey satchel.

'I still have a terrible headache after it. I'll just go

56

in and lie down if you don't mind,' she said apologetically, unable to summon up the energy to make polite conversation.

'You do that. I'll be as quiet as I can,' he said kindly. She felt like bursting into tears.

She sat, tense and unhappy, listening to the sounds of him working, waiting for Mark to arrive, and furious when there was no sign of him, nor even a phone call from him.

She couldn't believe how callous he was being. Was he dining with his fancy woman tête-à-tête without a thought for her? Had the scene earlier in the day had so little impact on him? Had he no feelings for her at all? Didn't he know that she would be devastated? Didn't that matter to him one little bit? Was she of so little consequence that hurting her didn't bother him? Was this the real Mark? Did she know her husband at all?

The questions whirled around in her brain, tormenting her, grieving her until she couldn't stand it and the tears welled up and spilt down her cheeks and she had to bury her face in a cushion to muffle her sobs.

I want to die, she thought. *I want to die. I do not want to endure this pain.* She could take tablets, paracetamol mixed with brandy. Then he'd feel guilty for the rest of his life, she thought bitterly, and it seemed like such a satisfying solution. She wouldn't have to endure the agony that was flaying her and he would spend the rest of his life in misery. Then again, perhaps he wouldn't. If she committed suicide it would leave him free to marry that woman. Francesca took a deep breath and sat up straight. No way. Under no circumstances would she facilitate them so easily. And she'd refuse to get a divorce. He could go fuck himself. No, she'd get through this and she would give him as much grief in the process as possible. Mark Kirwan would be the sorriest man alive that he had betrayed her and taken her for a fool. And that woman would rue the day that she had ever crossed Francesca's path!

Chapter Seven

'*Gerald M. Kirwan here. I've been trying to get you all day, I need you to get a prescription for me and cook me a bit of dinner and I need some honey and lemons to make a hot drink. I've got a very nasty chest infection. I had to call the doctor. Tell Mark I need to see him. Over and out.*'

Francesca's lips tightened as she listened to her father-in-law's irritable tones. Unable to relax as the locksmith worked on the locks, she'd played back her phone messages. Gerald Kirwan's crotchety voice boomed through the hall. He always announced himself with his full name. Pompous old goat. He hated leaving messages on the answering machine. He sounded hoarse.

Tough, Francesca thought stubbornly. Gerald Kirwan was no longer her concern. She was damned if she was going to cook meals for him and run around doing his errands. Let Mark look after his father. Or Vera, Mark's sister. Vera had turned her back on Gerald a long time ago. Understandable, knowing Gerald,

Francesca conceded. But it was very convenient, all these years, for her sister-in-law to have had nothing to do with her father. Vera never had the burden of him.

Well, Francesca wasn't going to have the burden of him any longer, she decided grimly. Why should she? She wasn't a blood relative and she was sick and tired of being used. As of now, she was no longer the Kirwan family's doormat.

She picked up the phone and dialled Vera's number. Her sister-in-law answered in her usual breathy whisper. 'Halloo, Vera Darmody speaking. How may I help yooouu?' Her standard greeting to all callers. It never varied.

Francesca didn't see her sister-in-law that often. She and Mark weren't close. It was left to Francesca to make contact at Christmas or Easter. Quietly spoken, with that soft, breathy voice, Vera gave the impression of being a helpless female, but over the years Francesca had come to see that whatever Vera wanted, Vera got. She lived her life very much on her terms. She was, although she would completely deny it, extremely like her father.

'Vera, it's Francesca.'

'Francesca, what a surprise,' Vera cooed. 'How are yooouu?'

'Fine thanks, Vera. I'm just ringing to let you know that your father has a chest infection and needs a prescription. I can't get it, I'm tied up. Mark's away so I'm ringing you.'

'Oh, but *Francesca*, you know that I haven't spoken to my father in *years*!' Vera's voice rose a couple of octaves in dismay. 'Why are you ringing *me*?' she added indignantly.

'I'm ringing *you* to let you know the position. He's not my father after all, Vera, he's yours. I'm not taking responsibility for him any more. I'll give you Mark's mobile number, you can leave a message and sort it out with him,' Francesca retorted, unable to keep the edge out of her voice. Typical Vera. Me. Me. Me.

'But, Francesca, I don't have anything to do with him. *Yooouu* know that,' Vera protested.

'Vera, that's your problem, deal with it. Here's Mark's number.' Francesca was getting more furious by the minute. For years she'd had to look after her father-in-law, while Vera went hill-walking every weekend and gadded around the country with her choral group and had a holiday in the Canaries every Christmas. She'd offloaded her father onto Francesca and got away scot-free. How nice for her. Well, the worm had just turned and Vera was being called to account.

Francesca called out Mark's mobile number in a clipped, tight voice.

'But why can't Mark look after it when he gets back? I can't go near that horrible man. You know that, Francesca. I'm *very* surprised that you phoned me. It's rather insensitive of you,' Vera whined.

That was the final straw. Francesca's face turned a dull shade of puce. 'I'm sorry if your sensitivities are hurt, Vera, but right now they're of no interest to me *whatsoever*. Mark's in Cork with another woman. You can discuss it with him. I won't be looking after Gerald any more, Vera. In fact I've no intention of seeing him or you again. I've had just about enough of the Kirwans, believe me. I'm just letting you know that your father is sick. You can do what you like about it. It's no skin off my nose. Bye.'

She heard Vera's sharp intake of breath as 'the other woman' titbit landed like a bombshell. She wasn't going to protect Mark from the consequences of his actions. Let him take responsibility for the break-up of their marriage. She was the innocent victim.

She hung up, none too gently. Truly, if she never saw Vera or Gerald again it wouldn't bother her one whit, she acknowledged crossly. She'd only put up with her in-laws through loyalty to Mark. That loyalty had been roundly abused. She didn't have to be saddled with them any more. Let Mark look after his family's affairs now. Let Miss Toned Pointy-Boobs do Gerald Kirwan's shopping for him and wash his cacky underpants when he stayed with her and Mark this Christmas.

Christmas would be interesting, Francesca thought grimly. What would Mark do with his father? What would *she* do for Christmas? Her face crumpled. Owen was going out to his brother in the States for ten days. She'd be on her own. It was frightening. She'd never been on her own before. How would she cope?

She picked up the phone and rang her sister's number. Millie answered in her usual brisk, no-nonsense style.

'Hi, Millie, it's me,' Francesca managed before bursting into tears.

'God Almighty, Francesca! What's wrong?' Millie demanded.

'Mark's having an affair,' Francesca blurted between sobs.

'Of course he isn't, don't be daft—'

'He *is*, Millie,' Francesca snapped angrily. 'I'm not stupid. I caught them together in a hotel in Cork. In their dressing gowns,' she added for good measure.

'Oh my God!! I'll be over. I'll be right over,' Millie exclaimed hastily. 'See you in a few minutes.'

Francesca hung up and tried to compose herself. The locksmith was working on the garage door; he'd finished the front and the back. She didn't want to be all tearstained and red-eyed when she was paying him.

She went up to the bedroom and brushed her hair and dusted a bit of powder onto her cheeks. She put her brush back down on the dressing table and saw a pair of Mark's gold cufflinks that she'd given to him as an anniversary present, years ago. 'Oh Mark,' she whispered. 'Why? Why did you do it?' She swallowed hard as she heard the locksmith call to her. Just this one thing to deal with and then she could fall to pieces, she promised herself as she hurried downstairs with her chequebook.

It was a relief when he'd gone and the silence of the house wrapped itself around her like a mantle. She felt some of the tension ease out of her body. The house was secure now. She had taken back control. Mark would have to knock at the front door to gain entry. See how he liked that, she thought bitterly, remembering the cosy intimate scene that she'd walked in on in Cork.

They'd seemed so at ease in each other's company, so lighthearted and happy. She couldn't remember the last time she and Mark had had an intimate evening together. Generally after dinner, if they weren't going out socializing, they'd watch TV and Mark would usually fall asleep. There had been a time when they used to take a stroll around Howth to exercise the dog, but as he began to travel more in the job, the task had fallen to her and he rarely walked with her now. But she still looked forward to his homecoming when he'd been abroad and always liked to hear the news and gossip from Brussels. She'd cook a favourite meal for him and fuss over him, knowing that he worked hard. He always brought her a present home: perfume, confectionery, a piece of crystal to go in her collection. Their marriage was easy. No wild ups and downs. Just steady and comfortable, if a little dull and unexciting. Nothing had prepared her for the shock she'd had today. As far as she'd known, their marriage was rock solid.

She heard Millie's car in the drive and went to open the front door. Her sister, tall, rangy, the epitome of vibrant good health, crossed the drive in a few long strides to embrace Francesca, who promptly burst into tears yet again.

'Come on in, Francesca. Have a good cry, get it out of your system, and tell me what happened,' Millie ordered, taking charge in her usual capable manner. She led her weeping sister into the lounge, sat her down on a sofa and began handing her tissues. Francesca bawled her eyes out as the events of the day finally caught up with her and she gave in to the luxury of grief. It poured out of her in great, gulping, body-shaking sobs, much to Millie's dismay.

After a while Francesca wiped her eyes and composed herself. 'Sorry,' she murmured, giving her sister a watery smile. 'I've been keeping it in all day.'

'I bet you have.' Millie grimaced. 'For God's sake, what happened? Are you absolutely sure? How did you find out? Could there be *any* mistake?'

Francesca sniffed and shook her head. 'There's no mistake. I caught the two of them together. I don't know what to do, Millie. My marriage is over.' She started crying again.

'Tell me what happened,' Millie urged, handing over another wad of tissues.

As best she could, Francesca told her sister the whole sorry saga and watched as Millie's expression became ever more shocked and incredulous.

'I don't believe it,' she murmured. 'Mark! It's incredible. God! Francesca, I don't know what to say.'

'I don't know what to say either. It's so unreal. I have to keep pinching myself to make sure I'm not dreaming.' Francesca sat up straight and pushed her hair out of her eyes. 'I've had the locks changed on the doors. He can bloody knock to get in here from now on.'

'That's a bit drastic!' Millie murmured.

'Fuck him, Millie. He's not going to waltz in here just like that and carry on as if everything's OK,' Francesca retorted indignantly.

'No, of course not,' Millie soothed. 'It's just that you're angry at the moment and you're not thinking straight. You've a lot to lose here, Francesca. You've been married for over twenty years.'

'How would you feel if you caught Aidan with another woman?' Francesca demanded.

'I'd cut his goolies off,' Millie said unequivocally.

'Would you take him back? Would you sleep with him again?'

'I don't know, Francesca.'

Francesca scowled. 'Well, there you are.'

'I know. It's horrible,' Millie admitted. 'I suppose you don't know how you would react until it happens to you. I just couldn't imagine Aidan having an affair. But then I couldn't imagine Mark having one either,' she added wryly. 'What are you going to tell the boys?'

'I don't know. Owen's staying with a friend tonight. It's just as well, I suppose.'

'Well, you can't stay here on your own,' Millie declared. 'Come on home with me and let's get pissed.'

For a minute Francesca was tempted. The idea of getting as drunk as a skunk and falling into bed in a stupor was somewhat appealing. At least she'd sleep, and it would be nice to have Millie's comforting presence about. But she couldn't drink herself into oblivion every night. She had to get through this. And she had to do it on her own. She might as well start now.

She shook her head. 'This is my life now, Millie, I'd better get used to it. Running away is not going to solve anything, and besides I don't want to have a raging hangover if Mark comes home tomorrow. I need to have my wits about me.'

'I suppose so. Look, I'll stay here. I'll give Aidan a ring and tell him that you're a bit under the weather.

I'll get up early in the morning to get the girls off to school.'

'Ah no, Millie. That's not fair, you have your hands full,' Francesca protested.

'Of course I'm staying. This is not any old common-or-garden trauma, Francesca. This rates pretty high on the scales.'

'You think so?' Francesca managed a smile.

'A top-notch drama. I mean, I think at least one stiff drink is called for. It's just so weird. I can't take it in. What was Mark thinking of?' She saw the stricken expression on her sister's face. 'Oh, sorry, me and my big mouth.'

'It's all right, Millie, I've been asking myself the same question over and over,' Francesca said miserably.

Millie gave her a hug. 'Sit over there by the fire and I'll get you a brandy. I'll just give Aidan a ring to tell him I'm staying.'

Francesca went over and curled up in the soft cream leather armchair by the fire. To tell the truth she didn't particularly like the leather suite, which had cost an arm and a leg. But Mark had loved it the minute he'd seen it. Its expensive opulence was affirmation for him of how far he'd come from their first small semi-detached house in Santry.

What would happen when he came home tomorrow? *If* he came home tomorrow. What was he feeling now? Did he feel guilty or was he relieved that it was all out in the open? Had she given him an easy way out so that he could go and live with his lover? Had she played right into his hands? Francesca stared into the flickering flames and felt a knot of fear. Millie was right. She had a lot to lose. Everything that she knew, her identity as Mark's wife, her place in society as his partner, her home, her lifestyle, all that she had taken for granted had been undermined in the blink of an eye. Now she was going to have to fight for what she considered rightfully hers. Now she was a woman on her own. Unless of course she looked the other way and pretended that Mark's fling was something she could get over.

It would be the easiest path to take, she thought ruefully. Be mad at him for a while, give him the cold shoulder, make him eat humble pie for months to come and eventually try and pretend that it never happened.

'But it has happened,' she argued with herself viciously. 'It *has* happened and you can't change it and life's never going to be the same.'

Millie poked her head around the door. 'Did you say something?'

'Just thinking aloud.' Francesca leaned back in the chair and took the proffered brandy goblet. 'What would you do if you were me?' she asked curiously.

'It's different for me.' Millie sank onto the sofa, curled her long legs up under her and took a sip of the fiery amber liquid. 'My circumstances are quite different. The girls are very young. I'd have to think of that. Your two are reared and on their way. That makes a hell of a difference. I know it's going to be hard for them to know what's happened but they're adults, they'll cope easier than two young children would. I don't know, Francesca, I just hope it never happens to me.'

'At least you've got a job. You're financially independent,' Francesca interjected.

'Look, see what happens tomorrow when he comes home. Maybe he'll be crushed and full of apologies—'

'And maybe he'll see it as an excuse to get out. They were totally relaxed together, a real cosy unit,' Francesca said bitterly. 'She was so fucking perfect looking, all long legs and pert boobs. I felt so frumpy and middle-aged beside her.'

'Don't be ridiculous, Francesca, you're the height of elegance,' Millie consoled.

'*Elegance!*' scoffed Francesca. 'It makes me sound so middle-aged. She was young, Millie. *Young.* I hate being goddamn forty. It's all downhill from here. Why is this happening to me? What sort of a life am I going to have? I'm past it, Millie. No man's ever going to give me a second look now.'

'Stop that nonsense right now, Francesca Kirwan. I won't have you downing yourself like that just because that total idiot of a husband of yours let his dick get the better of him. I'm telling you, six months of living with Miss Teen-Queen and he'll be on his hands and knees begging to come back. Trust me on this one, Francesca. And you'll be the one with the upper hand then and by God you use it.' Millie's eyes were hard with anger.

Francesca felt warmed by her sister's loyalty. She knew it was pathetic but she wanted everyone to hate Mark right now. She wanted them to despise and condemn him for all the hurt and pain he was causing her by his callous rejection of their marriage. He was the one who would end up ostracized and alone.

Family and friends would support her through this ordeal. Then he'd be sorry, she thought viciously. She hoped he'd suffer. She wanted him to suffer. She *hated* him. Her resolve hardened. She'd make Mark pay for the rest of his days for what he'd done to her. She was going to make sure the whole damn world knew what he'd done to her. He'd be mortified. Mark was an extremely private person. If he thought people were gossiping about him at work he'd be horrified. His dignity would be in tatters. By the time she was finished with him, he wouldn't have a shred of dignity left, she vowed, her grip tightening on the brandy glass as she stared into the flickering flames, oblivious to her sister's concerned gaze.

Chapter Eight

'Francesca, pick up the phone please. I'm at Dublin Airport. I need to know where you've left the car,' Mark growled down the phone. It was the following morning. He and Nikki had arrived back in Dublin Airport, tired and stressed. There were three huge multi-storey car parks plus an open-air one. The car could be in any of them. He hadn't a clue where to start looking.

The silence at the other end was deafening. His wife had the answering machine on but he was sure she was in the house. 'Francesca, pick up the phone, now!' he ordered. Silence. 'Francesca, if you're not there and you come in and get this message, call me on this number immediately.' He reeled off Nikki's phone number and hung up.

'There's nothing for it but to go through the car parks, I suppose,' he said irritably to Nikki who was flicking through a magazine in the book shop.

'I suggest we start with number C, it's usually the one where you have the most chance of getting a space,' she said calmly.

'OK, come on,' he agreed. He was as mad as hell. Francesca could have told him where the car was parked. She was being a vindictive bitch. Life was going to be fairly gruesome for the foreseeable future. She was probably going to insist that he stop seeing Nikki. He didn't know if he could. Maybe they could ease off for a while and when the heat had died down, get back together again. They trekked in silence to the furthest car park, each lost in their own thoughts. How on earth had Francesca found out about him and Nikki? Mark asked himself for the hundredth time. They had been extremely discreet. No-one knew about them at work, he was sure of it. It would have got back to him one way or another. It was mystifying. 'I'll do the first level,' he said as they reached the car park.

'OK,' Nikki agreed. They split up and began the search for Mark's BMW.

Nikki took the lift to the second level and tried to stay calm. She felt extremely agitated. She couldn't understand Mark's consternation at being found out. As far as she was concerned it was a liberation. It meant that Mark could now choose to be with her. They could be a couple. Francesca knew about them now, surely she wouldn't want him back.

She strode along the gloomy grey, cold car park, scowling. It seemed increasingly clear to her – from his behaviour since Francesca had barged in on them – that Mark saw her as mistress material, but not as a potential partner. That was extremely distressing. She'd had enough of being a mistress. She wanted a proper relationship with all the frills, she thought tiredly as she scanned the parked cars. She wanted a commitment from him. She'd never put pressure on him, knowing that it was the worst thing that she could do, but everything had changed now. The goal posts had shifted.

He was going to have to choose. It was as simple as that. Mark was going to have to make a decision either to leave his wife and move in with her, or stay with Francesca and risk losing her. And it was a big risk the way she was feeling right now. She felt very unloved and very unwanted.

Stay calm, Nikki told herself as she walked down yet another aisle. *He's in shock. He's not thinking straight. He's not himself. Of course he wants to be with you. He adores you. Don't let him see that you're feeling needy and vulnerable. He'll run a mile. Don't put any pressure on for a while. See what way the whole situation pans out. Don't let him see that it's getting to you.*

'Easier said than done,' she muttered as she traipsed the length of the second-floor car park with neither sight nor sign of Mark's car.

She was just about to go to the next level when he drove up alongside her. 'Hop in,' he said. 'I'll bring you to your car.'

'Where was it?' she asked as she got into the car beside him.

'The third level. I suppose it wasn't too bad. We could have been here until tomorrow.'

'What are you going to do?' she asked casually.

'I'd better go home and face the music,' he groaned. 'I'm not looking forward to it. God, Nikki, this is a nightmare. How the hell did she find out?'

'Give me a call and let me know how it goes. Keep your cool and don't get into a row if you can help it,' she advised as he pulled up beside her car. 'And, darling, don't worry too much. Maybe it's all for the best.'

He didn't look too convinced as he leaned over to kiss her. 'I'll hang on to the cases for the time being. See you, Nikki, I'll be in touch,' he said heavily.

'Whenever,' she said lightly. She got out of his car and got into her own and roared out of the parking bay.

I'll be in touch. That didn't sound as though he was going to leave his wife. In fact it didn't sound too promising at all. Why had he kept his cases? Was this the end of the road for them? Fear gripped her. She loved Mark more than she'd ever loved anyone. She didn't think she could face life without him. What would she do if he ended it? Nikki drove home more worried than she had ever been in her life.

Mark drove fast once he got onto the M50. The sooner the ordeal was over, the better. He felt apprehensive. He hadn't a leg to stand on. He had no defence. Francesca was perfectly within her rights to feel betrayed and angry, but, damn it, he hadn't fallen in love with Nikki on purpose. His wife would never understand his point of view if he tried to explain why he'd gone into the relationship with the younger woman.

The best thing to do would be to take his medicine and say nothing, he decided. Least said soonest mended. There was no point in getting into a full-scale row. It would make things worse. That was if they could get any worse. Things were about as bad as they could be, he thought agitatedly as he accelerated to pass a juggernaut. He hoped that Francesca wouldn't say anything about all this to Owen. It would be impossible to look his son in the eye. He felt sick even thinking about it. Both his sons admired and respected him. That respect was important to him. Now it was in total jeopardy.

'Oh, what a bloody mess,' Mark muttered, wishing he was a million miles away.

Francesca replayed Mark's message. She was incandescent with rage. How dare he speak to her like that? The *nerve* of him. Anybody would think that she was in the wrong. She hoped it took him hours to find his car. She shut off the answering machine. At least she now knew that he was in Dublin.

Would he come back home or would he go off with his tart to wherever she was living? She didn't know. Everything she had ever felt secure about had crumbled away. She felt lost, bewildered and frightened. What would she say to him when he came home? *If* he came home. She prayed that she wouldn't disgrace herself by bursting into tears. That would be *so* undignified.

Francesca hurried upstairs and ran a brush through her hair. She stared at her face in the mirror. She looked a sight. Big black circles under her eyes, pale skin tinged with the grey of shock combined with a sleepness night. She dithered, wondering whether to go the whole hog and slap on the war paint.

Why should she bother? she thought distractedly.

What did she care what she looked like for him? She wanted him out of her life. She didn't care if she never saw him again.

She was like a cat on a griddle, up and down every five minutes to peer out of the window. She went downstairs and made herself a cup of coffee and carried it into the lounge, but her stomach was tied up in knots and she couldn't drink it.

She went upstairs again and glanced out of the landing window. Her breath caught in her throat as she saw the car turn into the drive. She felt faint.

Francesca inhaled deeply and stood at the top of the stairs waiting for his key to go into the lock. When it did, she nearly threw up. She heard him take the key out and put it back in the lock and try again. She could imagine his impatience. The bell rang and she jumped, even though she was expecting it. It rang again and again, loud, insistent. And then continuously, setting her teeth on edge. Who the bloody hell did he think he was? she raged.

Chapter Nine

For a minute or two Francesca was sorely tempted not to answer the door. He didn't know whether she was in or not. Her car was in the garage. It would be good enough for him to let him stew. But as the shrill ding dong of the chimes kept ringing, her temper got the better of her and she flung open the door.

'Don't be so bloody rude,' she snarled. 'One ring was enough. I'm not deaf—'

'What the hell is going on here? Why won't my key fit in the lock?' Mark demanded, shoving his way into the hall, glaring at her in fury.

'Because I've had the locks changed, Mark. This is no—'

'You can't do that!' he interrupted, incensed.

'Excuse me, Mark. I can. And I have. You're not living here any more—'

'I'll live where I damn well like. This is my house,' he roared.

Francesca slammed the front door shut. 'Let's not let the whole of the Hill of Howth know that we're

77

having a row,' she said coldly. 'This is my house too. My home. You're no longer welcome here. You can go and live with your trollop and do whatever the hell you like.'

'You cut that out, Francesca. Nikki is not a trollop or anything like it. And she's not bloody petty like you, either.'

'Mark, I'm not interested in . . . *Nikki*' – her voice dripped contempt – 'I just want you to get out of here. You disgust me!'

'Well, you're disgusting me with your behaviour,' he retorted. 'I never thought you were vindictive.'

'It seems we don't know each other at all, doesn't it?' Francesca spat. 'I'd never have taken you for a lying two-faced cheat. You've been with her for nearly a year, haven't you? You lying bastard.'

Mark couldn't hold her gaze. He stalked into the kitchen.

Francesca followed him. 'Haven't you?' she repeated.

'Yes,' he muttered.

'Why? Why did you do it? What was wrong with our marriage that you had to go and sleep with someone else?' Francesca demanded.

'It isn't all about sex, Francesca,' he said heatedly.

'Oh, isn't it? Well, it didn't look like that to me when I saw you snogging her in the airport and when I walked in on you down in Cork,' she sneered.

'The sex side of our relationship is very good, as it happens,' he lashed back, knowing that it would hurt her. 'But there's much more to Nikki than that. She's a highly intelligent woman—'

'And I'm not? Is that what you're saying? I'm a

thicko who's no good in bed, is that it?' she shouted, utterly wounded by his defence of his mistress.

'I'm not saying that, Francesca,' he growled. 'Stop putting words in my mouth.'

'Well, what *are* you saying? We had a good marriage, didn't we? We reared two sons and made a nice home. Why have you turned your back on it? What was so wrong with us that you've gone and ruined everything?'

'Oh God, Francesca, I was in a *rut*. I was bored. Middle-aged. Fed up being responsible. Didn't you ever feel that there had to be more to life?' He banged his hand on the kitchen table. 'When she came into my life I started to have fun again. She made me feel that life could be different. She made me feel young—'

'You idiot, Mark! You're not young any more,' Francesca yelled. 'You *are* middle-aged, whether you like it or not. Deal with it. Do you think I like being forty? I don't. I hate it. But I didn't go out and start looking for a young toy boy to make me feel better. I felt bored and in a rut too, you know. Don't you think that I get pissed off looking after you and the boys and the house and your damn cranky old father? I do. Believe me. But I didn't go out looking for a quick fix with some . . . some passing fancy just to make me feel better . . . *younger* . . .' she raged.

Mark gritted his teeth. 'Well, maybe you should have, Francesca.'

Her sharp hard slap to his jaw shocked him.

'How dare you, Mark! I made vows on our wedding day and so did you. How dare you say such a thing to me?'

'Oh for heaven's sake, Francesca, get down off your high horse,' he said wearily, rubbing his jaw. 'That was over twenty years ago. We were kids. What did we know about life? People shouldn't be allowed to marry until they're in their thirties. What had we ever done or experienced? We went with each other from school. Didn't you ever wonder what it would be like to be with someone else? Didn't you ever feel that life was passing you by and that you'd experienced very little of it? Well, I'm sorry but I did. I do. And I can't help the way that I feel.' He glowered at her, exuding anger and resentment. 'I know this is going to hurt you but at least I'm being honest. I'm sorry that I got married so young and there's nothing I can do about that. That's the truth of it.'

'Why did you marry me then? You told me that you loved me. *You* asked me to marry you.' She was completely bewildered. Where was all this stuff coming from? Why did he make it seem like he was blaming her? Was this all her fault? It couldn't be. Hadn't he ever loved her? 'I thought you loved me. You told me often enough, Mark. I don't understand this at all.' She shook her head in disbelief, stunned at what she'd just heard.

'I did love you, I do still, in a different way. I married you because you expected it of me. Our parents expected it—'

'Are you telling me you felt *trapped* into marrying me?' She was incredulous.

'Kind of,' he muttered. 'That was the way it was then. Our mothers were always at us to "give them a day out". All our friends were getting married, it just seemed the next step to take.' He shoved his hands into his pockets and stared out of the kitchen window. 'And of course we couldn't have decent sex because we were too scared. Too conditioned to think it was a bad thing to do before marriage.' He turned to face her accusingly. 'I was only a young fella and I was as horny as hell all the time and you kept saying no.'

'I was scared, for fuck's sake. I was petrified of getting pregnant. It's really mean to blame that on me,' Francesca flared indignantly.

'It was the way we were brought up, and there's loads of unhappy marriages out there because of the way our generation, and generations before us, were reared and the pressures we were put under to conform. I hope our sons live with women before they marry them,' he said defiantly, his face puce with resentment.

'Oh, how convenient to blame our upbringing,' she flared. 'That's a real cop-out. All of this is such a load of crap—'

'Look, Francesca, if you don't want to hear what I have to say, fine. I'm trying to explain how I feel.'

Francesca stared at him. 'But you seemed happy; we had fun. I never felt that you didn't want to be married to me.'

'I was happy a lot of the time, especially at the beginning, and we did have fun, but I always felt I didn't have time to sow my wild oats and live a bit.'

'So you're doing it now,' she said bitterly.

'Probably,' he acknowledged flatly.

'Don't I mean anything to you?' she asked, her face crumpling as tears sprang to her eyes.

'Oh Francesca, try and understand it's not about

you or how I feel about you. It's about the way I'm feeling at the moment. Lost, resentful, angry that I'm getting older . . . I dunno.' He shrugged.

'It never has been about me, Mark.' She wiped away the tears, angry with herself for showing weakness. 'Just listen to yourself. Me. Me. Me. And I don't feature at all. As long as I kept the house going and looked after you and the kids and your father, that was all you cared about. You never bothered to ask if I was happy or fulfilled. Did you care that I might be lost, or resentful, or angry?'

'I looked after you well. You lacked for nothing,' he snapped irritably.

'You looked after me materially, and yourself too. But emotionally it's always been about *you*. *You* do what *you* want at the end of the day, Mark, you always have. Well, you've broken up our marriage to be with that woman so don't let me stand in your way. But I won't divorce you and I won't move out of this house and I want maintenance. I worked hard at our marriage. I'm not going to lose out just because you've lost the run of yourself and are having a fucking mid-life crisis.'

'Now wait a minute, Francesca' – he took her by the arm as she brushed past him to walk out – 'there's a lot to discuss here.'

'Let go of me, Mark. I've told you what I'm doing. I'm staying here and I'm not divorcing you and I want maintenance. That's all the discussion that you'll get from me. Oh and by the way, would you kindly ask your father to stop ringing here from now on, or else I'll get the number changed. I won't be looking after him any more, and you can get Nikki to do your Christmas shopping because I won't be doing that either.' She marched out of the kitchen, head held high, picked up her keys from the hall stand and walked out of the house.

Mark followed, somewhat at a loss. 'We need to talk, Francesca!'

Francesca ignored him, opened the garage door and reversed her car out of the garage. Then she confronted him once more. 'Take whatever stuff you need and put the alarm on when you leave and from now on phone me before you come over. If it suits me to be here, fine, if not, tough. I'll be talking to a solicitor.' She got back into the car and opened the window.

'For God's sake! Francesca, be reasonable—'

'Be reasonable!' Her voice hit the high notes. 'Get real, Mark. You're not the only human on the planet. It's not *all* about you!'

'Look, we have to talk. There're financial implications here that we have to take into consideration. And what about the boys?'

'Don't give me that. The boys were the last thing on your mind when you started "feeling young" again,' she jeered.

'Don't be a bitch, Francesca. It doesn't suit you.'

'Fuck off, Mark,' she swore at him and drove out of the drive like a bat out of hell.

Mark stood still, shell shocked, as it suddenly began to dawn on him that his life was never going to be the same again. He'd never thought that Francesca would find out about Nikki. He'd preferred not to think of the consequences. Well, the consequences were whacking him in the chops right this minute and all that he could foresee as long as Francesca was in this frame of mind was a long road full of hassle ahead of him.

He groaned and went back into the house to gather some papers and files that he needed. He stood in the hall looking around. The house felt different. Unwelcoming. It had to be his imagination, he told himself irritably. Houses were inanimate objects. Nevertheless, the atmosphere *was* different. Or maybe it was him. With a sudden certainty that brought a vague feeling of dread, Mark knew that this house would never be his home again.

Chapter Ten

Francesca drove towards Clontarf in a state of such anger and confusion that when she looked back on the journey she couldn't remember ending up in the car park opposite Casa Pasta. It was a miracle that she hadn't killed anyone, she thought shakily as she sat staring at the angry green sea surging relentlessly, mirroring her own turbulent emotions.

People walked up and down along the popular seafront walkway engrossed in their thoughts. Were any of them going through anything like she was enduring right now? The pain and hurt and sheer fury and resentment she felt towards Mark were unspeakable.

Why? Why? Why? Over and over the question tormented her. Why had he ever married her if he hadn't been sure. *She'd* been sure. She'd loved Mark from the very moment she'd met him at Mick's, a teen disco they'd frequented every Friday night when they were growing up.

He'd always been a bit reserved, less outgoing

than the other boys, much less pushy and in-your-face. She'd liked that. He'd asked her to dance one night and that was that. He was the one for her and she'd never looked at anyone else. She hadn't wanted to either.

Had she made him feel pressurized into marrying her or was that just an excuse? Her memory of her engagement was a blur. Planning the wedding and making sure everything went all right on the day had been the main considerations. Mark was right about one thing, she acknowledged, she hadn't given any real thought to marriage or what it entailed. She hadn't really looked beyond the wedding day. Marriage was what came next on the agenda after leaving school and getting a job. Then it was getting a house and a mortgage. She never remembered sitting down and thinking that she was committing herself to one man for the rest of her life. Or wondering if their marriage would last. She'd taken it very much for granted that it would. Why get married otherwise?

It was only after they'd married and lived together that she'd really got to know Mark. His neat and tidy ways. His need for time alone. His drive to succeed at work, compulsive at times. She'd driven him mad with her carefree untidiness and her desire to be with him all the time.

Francesca grimaced. Over the years she'd become tidy, she thought wryly. It was easier than listening to him giving out about the state of the house. When the kids were born and growing up, their toys and accoutrements were always tidied away before he came home. As he progressed in his career and they entertained more and more, she conformed to his idea of how she should look and how their house should be decorated, because it was easier than living with his subtle disapproval.

She stopped wearing jeans and tracksuits, adopting well-cut tailored trousers instead. She stopped shopping in chain stores and bought clothes that she knew he'd like in small exclusive boutiques. She'd become the perfect corporate wife, she thought bitterly, and lost her own identity in the process.

Francesca was shocked as this unwanted nugget of self-knowledge dawned on her. Had she really done that? she asked herself in dismay. Become the person he wanted her to be rather than be the person that she was? What kind of woman would she be if she hadn't married Mark and had two children? What kind of a career would she have pursued? Would she have travelled? How different would her life have been? And why was she sitting here feeling that she had sacrificed everything only to have that sacrifice flung back in her face?

Why did she feel like such a fucking martyr?

'Oh, for God's sake!' she muttered. 'This is ridiculous. He's the one having the affair. You've done nothing wrong.'

Yes, you have. You put him and his needs first. You made him your first priority; now he's left you and you've nothing to fall back on. You've nothing of your own. Her inner voice was so strong she actually thought she'd heard someone speak aloud.

This was crazy. She wasn't going to sit in the car chastising herself when everything was Mark's fault, she decided furiously as she got out and locked the doors. The wind blew fresh and cold in her face, heavy with sea salt and the smell of seaweed. She walked along trying to calm the turmoil raging within her. *It's not your fault. It's not your fault.* The mantra played in her head, but deep down Francesca knew that she was going to have to face up to realities that she'd far prefer to keep buried deep. Was it partly some failure on her part that had caused Mark to go looking outside their marriage for something he obviously felt that he wasn't getting in it? Had she taken far too much for granted and not put in enough effort pandering to him and his needs?

But what about *her* needs? He hadn't pandered to her in any way out of the ordinary, she thought resentfully. He had taken her for granted too. But wasn't that part and parcel of what it was all about? A couple couldn't spend their whole time navel-gazing their relationship, she thought irritably.

She walked as far as the Alfie Byrne road and back, reluctant to go home until she felt sure that Mark was gone. Hunger gnawed at her stomach. She hadn't eaten properly in thirty-six hours. Maybe she should ignore it. She'd lose a stone in no time. Look at Vanessa Feltz. When her husband had left her, she'd lost five stone in an effort to get him back. It hadn't worked.

Francesca scowled. She wouldn't give Mark the satisfaction of losing weight to try and get him back. What a sop to his ego that would be. He'd love it! She wasn't that needy or pathetic, she thought defiantly. And besides, she didn't *want* him back. The damage was done. He could go and fuck off with himself.

There was a chipper across the road. A nice hot portion of fattening chips and a batter burger would do very well indeed, Francesca decided purposefully and felt a little frisson of pride. *You're not at all pathetic*, she assured herself as she pushed open the door of the chipper and joined the lunchtime queue. She ordered a portion of garlic mushrooms for good measure. Vanessa Feltz, eat your heart out, she thought derisively. Slimming to get a man back indeed! What nonsense. Slimming to feel better in yourself, yes, she could cope with that, she thought as she watched the assistant behind the counter select a big batter burger and drop it into the hot fat. Why would she want to slim to get Mark back after what he'd done? It was like saying that he'd started an affair because she was heavier than she should be. Even she couldn't accuse Mark of being that shallow and she wasn't even going to take that notion on board, because if she did she'd go crazy altogether. If she had to take some of the blame because of the failure of her marriage, she was damned if she was going to blame it on being a stone overweight.

To her surprise, she actually enjoyed the rare take-away treat. Mark wasn't into junk food, he far preferred posh restaurant fare, or fresh salads and fish when she made lunch at home. And since he'd started taking care of his figure again he'd gone all finicky about what he ate. Somehow she couldn't see the svelte Nikki eating chips from a chipper, Francesca thought ruefully.

She sat in the car, eating her chips and licking her fingers, as she looked out towards Dublin port. A thought struck her. She could do this any time she wanted to now. She could do exactly as she liked, she no longer had to work her life around Mark's. It was a scary yet exhilarating thought.

From now on she was going to have to live a life that did not include her husband. What sort of a life would it turn out to be? Did she have the resources within to stand on her own two feet?

Well, you're not really going to be standing on your own two feet. You have the house. He'll be paying you maintenance. You'll just be making a new existence for yourself, supported by him, that horrible niggling little voice taunted.

'Oh, shut up!' she said exasperated as she bunched the white chip paper into a ball and started the ignition. She'd be a bloody basket case if she kept arguing with herself, she told herself as she slid out into the traffic and headed for home. She wanted to be there when Owen got in from college. Her heart sank at the prospect of her son finding out that she and Mark were in crisis. How was she going to deal with it? How would she tell him that his father was seeing someone else?

Hell! Why should *she* have to tell Owen? Let Mark do that. After all, he was the one who had destroyed their marriage. Let him look Owen in the eye and tell him just that. Francesca's jaw jutted stubbornly as she decided she was not going to let Mark off facing up to his obligations and taking responsibility for his actions. Owen would need a new set of keys too. Poor Owen. He'd get the shock of his life. He idolized his father. They had a great relationship. How was this split going to change that? Had she been too hasty in kicking Mark out?

But what other alternative did she have? she thought angrily. She wasn't a goddamned doormat – as her cheating husband had just found to his cost.

Mark sat in his BMW and looked over from Howth Summit clear across to Wicklow. It was a blustery day of dark tranches of clouds interspersed with sunlight. It felt very strange to be sitting aimlessly in his car in the middle of a working day. He felt agitated. Unfocused. What was he to do? Where was he to go? Should he go straight home and tell Francesca that he had no intention of moving out? She had an awful nerve changing the locks on the doors. That had really rattled him. It was his house too; after all, he'd paid the damn mortgage on it for long enough. He scowled. He wasn't used to being outmanoeuvred. Francesca had certainly not let the grass grow under her feet. She'd said something about seeing him and Nikki kissing at the airport. Kissing in public had been a big mistake. She must have come back to the airport to give him the damned phone, seen them and followed them to Check-in. Imagine following them to Cork! He'd never imagined that Francesca could be so impetuous. She'd dumbfounded him. It was surprising the lengths people were prepared to go to when pushed. But he hadn't expected it from her, she was normally quite passive.

Maybe he should go and stay at a hotel for a few days until she had calmed down. *If* she calmed down. Perhaps he should find a place to rent for the time being. His heart sank at the prospect. He could go and stay with Nikki, he mused. From the safety net of his marriage he'd often fantasized about living with Nikki and visualized the wonderful life that they'd lead. Now that it could become a reality, he wasn't at all sure. It was all happening so fast . . . and not on his terms. He felt events were very much out of control. This whole episode had taken on a dynamic of its own and he was being rushed along, helter-skelter. He didn't like it.

Mark sighed, leaned back against the headrest and closed his eyes. He hadn't slept well last night and he was knackered. The memory of Francesca's pale, ravaged face surfaced and he promptly opened his eyes again.

He'd really hurt her. That had been the worst thing. She couldn't make head nor tail of where he was coming from. The bewilderment in her eyes had been hard to take. A lump rose to his throat and a tear slid down his cheek. He didn't know if he was crying for Francesca or himself. For both of them really, he supposed. He was so utterly and completely pissed off. He'd made such a mess of things. All of a sudden his life had turned into a horrific nightmare.

Maybe he would go and stay with Nikki. She seemed to love him, for some weird and wonderful reason. It would be much nicer to be with her – for a while at least – until he sorted something out. He glanced over at the seat beside him piled high with paperwork and files and felt deeply unsettled. He was effectively homeless, he thought sorrowfully. Forty-five years old and his life in chaos. And he had no idea what the future held. The tinny ringing of the phone startled him. He cleared his throat.

'Hello,' he said warily.

'Hello, Mark. I've been leaving bloody messages

for you all over the place. Are you going to get me my prescription or not? I can't get in touch with Francesca. Bloody woman's always gadding about,' Gerald brayed down the line.

Mark groaned. This was the last thing he needed. He threw his eyes up to heaven as Gerald gave a theatrically chesty cough and launched into a tirade of moans and whinges.

'I'll be with you in twenty minutes,' he snapped, mid-moan, and hung up, much to his father's astonished annoyance. Then he punched in Nikki's mobile number.

'Hi, darling,' she answered cheerily and his heart lifted slightly.

'Can I do B&B with you for a while?' he asked heavily.

'I'm a strict landlady, and I don't spend my time slaving at the kitchen sink, and I'm very demanding in bed! Can you cope with that?'

'I think so.' Mark managed a smile. 'Where are you?'

'Work,' Nikki answered casually.

'What time will you be home?'

'Around four.'

'OK, I'll see you then.'

'OK, Mark. Take care.' She clicked off.

Mark stared at the phone. Nikki was something else. She'd gone straight to work after the episode they'd been through. It hadn't seemed to affect her at all. Her career was all important. It wasn't *her* marriage that was on the rocks, he thought a tad resentfully. Nor was she rushing home to give him sustenance. It was only lunchtime. He'd have to hang around for another few hours until she was home. He sighed again, a deep, depressed sigh that came from his toes. He'd better go and see his father and get him sorted. What was he going to tell Gerald about Francesca and his marriage problems? Gerald was old-fashioned and rigid in his beliefs. In his eyes marriage was for ever. Come hell or high water. Divorce and separation were wrong in the eyes of the Church and adultery was the greatest sin invented, according to him. Many were the lectures he'd given over the dinner table about the rapid decay of revered institutions such as marriage and the Church.

Today was not the day to tell Gerald that Francesca had kicked him out because he was having a relationship with another woman, Mark decided tiredly as he switched on the ignition and reversed out of his parking spot.

Would he and Francesca ever get back together? Did he want to go back or was this the start of a whole new life? Wasn't this what he'd wanted for so long? Freedom. Well, he had it now. And, somehow, having wasn't the same as wanting.

Nikki sat on the edge of her desk, one leg swinging nonchalantly as she ignored the flashing red light of her voice-mail. She was so exhilarated she wanted to run down the corridor shouting *Yes! Yes!! Yes!!!*

Mark was coming to stay with her. They were going to be a proper couple. What joy. What bliss. No more rushed furtive hours together. Time to relax and enjoy each other's company. Time to be themselves. This was truly the best thing that had ever happened to her, she assured herself. To be with a man who stimulated her mentally, who turned her on physically, who didn't feel threatened by her career, indeed who actively encouraged her in the pursuit of it, was a dream come true. None of her previous relationships had been even half as satisfying, Nikki thought happily.

She was rather pleased with herself that she hadn't gone rushing home just to be there for him. She wanted to, of course, but now was not the time to be too eager. It was better to play it cool and keep Mark on his toes. Besides, the worst thing in the world for him just now would be to feel smothered by her. The encounter with Francesca had really shaken him. Ending a marriage of over twenty years must be very difficult psychologically, she reflected, no matter how ready you felt you were to do so. There'd be rocky days ahead, but she and Mark would weather them. Of that, Nikki had no doubts whatsoever.

Francesca felt a flicker of apprehension as she indicated to turn into the drive. Just say Mark had decided to refuse to move out and was still at home. What would she do then? Short of physically throwing him out, which she wouldn't be able to do anyway, she couldn't force him to go. It could end up that she might have to move herself. Her stomach lurched as she swung into the shrub-lined drive. His car was gone. She didn't know whether to be glad or sorry. She was being so irrational, she chastised herself. One minute she was as mad as hell with him, the next she wanted him to at least *want* to make amends and stay with her. He hadn't put up much of a fight to save their marriage, she thought glumly. In fact he hadn't put up any fight at all. Bastard! He'd gone galloping off into the arms of his mistress. Just what he'd wanted to do all along probably.

Anger returned.

She stomped upstairs to see what he'd taken. His files. His golf clothes. Her heart sank. That seemed pretty final. Obviously he wasn't going to let a little thing like the break-up of his marriage interfere with his game. She burst into tears and flung herself onto the bed and howled like a banshee into her pillow.

Her chest felt so tight with grief she could hardly breathe. She felt so belittled and used and worthless. How would she ever get through this? Was this the way she'd feel for the rest of her life? For the first time ever she could understand suicide. The future seemed so empty and dark, full of despair and struggle. She hadn't the heart for it. She remembered a song from *Jesus Christ Superstar* that she'd sung many times, years ago when she'd been a member of her local parish folk group.

'Take this cup from me,' she whispered. 'Oh Jesus, please take this cross from me. I cannot endure it.'

But you have to. It's your time, her inner voice said and Francesca knew that no matter how much she prayed and begged and pleaded she would have to get through this one way or another. Eventually she fell into an exhausted sleep. It was dusk when she woke, chilled, from lying uncovered. She shot up on the bed and ran her fingers through her dishevelled hair.

Owen would be home from college soon. He'd be hungry. She'd better get her skates on and prepare dinner for him. Although he'd probably lose his appetite when he heard that she and his father had split up. How could she protect him from the pain of it? At least Jonathan was in America and had cut the ties to a degree. He had his own life to live; they were only on the periphery of his now. Owen was still her baby, still living at home. His life would be much more disrupted.

Francesca got up from the bed, switched on the lamp, pulled the curtains and brushed her hair. If what had happened during the last thirty-six hours had been bad, it could only be equalled by telling her beloved son that his family life as he knew it was going to change for ever. She'd have to keep an eye out for him coming up the drive. She didn't want him putting his key in the lock and not being able to get in. It had given her immense satisfaction when Mark had fiddled with the lock. *That* had been power, she thought with fierce satisfaction. *That* had given the arrogant bastard something to think about. She remembered the expression on his face when he'd barged his way into the hall. Angry, stupefied. But for an instant there'd been a flash of something akin to admiration ... respect even. He never thought she had it in her. Had she been such a wimp in her marriage? she questioned, dismayed. Was that how he saw her? A soft touch, a no-accounter. Was it because he had so little respect for her that it obviously hadn't cost him a thought to betray her? Would these questions ever cease rattling around in her brain and give her some peace? she thought dementedly. The idea that Mark didn't respect her was profoundly disturbing and it wouldn't go away.

'You *will* respect me, Mark Kirwan. By God, you will respect me by the time I'm finished with you and you will never humiliate me again,' she vowed aloud as she left the bedroom and went downstairs to make a shepherd's pie for her son. It was his favourite dish. A thought struck her as she prepared the ingredients. She must be very careful not to burden Owen with her problems or in some way use him as a substitute for her husband. She'd seen marriage splits where children were used as buffers, or, even worse, as pawns in the break-up game. Was making Owen a shepherd's pie a subtle way of beginning the nice parent/nasty parent scenario? If she were scrupulously honest with herself, wouldn't she admit that she wanted Owen to be on her side, and be disgusted with his father? She wanted Mark to cringe before his son's accusing blue-eyed gaze.

Was Mark right? Was she being very petty and vindictive? But what the hell did he want her to be, a bloody saint, for God's sake? she argued with herself as she chopped onions and sliced carrots.

For crying out loud, Francesca, it's only a blooming shepherd's pie, there's no need to go into shagging psychotherapy yet, she told herself crossly as she peeled the potatoes. It was dark outside and she pulled down the kitchen blind, acutely aware that Mark would not be coming home tonight or any other night. He was probably relaxing in Nikki's pad with not a care in the world. Her heart twisted in pain. How come she was the one suffering? Mark and Nikki were happy together and she was here crucified with anguish. Where was the justice in that?

98

She was a decent person. She'd never deliberately hurt anybody. Why had this punishment been inflicted on her while Mark seemed to be reaping most undeserved rewards?

Was there a God? she asked herself bitterly. If there was, she certainly didn't think much of his sense of fair play or compassion. Why had he picked on her when the world was full of truly evil and greedy people who seemed to get away with all their wickedness?

'I don't believe in you!' she shouted, distraught, looking up to heaven. 'You have deserted me.'

Chapter Eleven

Francesca heard Owen's banger chug up the drive. She'd been listening out for it for the past half-hour and her nerves were in shreds. She swallowed hard as she hurried to open the door before he got to it.

'Hiya, Mam,' he greeted her cheerfully as he barrelled into the hall in his usual effervescent way. 'We won yesterday! It was a great night.' He sniffed the air. 'Dinner smells nice. What is it?' He turned his bright blue gaze on her, his healthy handsome face still retaining an endearing smattering of freckles across his nose, his wiry chestnut hair still ungovernable.

'Shepherd's pie,' she managed. The sight of him and his youthful exuberance was almost her undoing. She bit her lip as he threw his bag and duffel coat under the stairs.

'My favourite. I'm starving,' he announced. 'I hope you made loads.'

'It's all for you. I had lunch out today so I'm not hungry.'

'Oh, great.' He loped into the kitchen and sat down. 'Feed me, Mother of mine.' He grinned.

In spite of her anguish she grinned back. Owen was such a breath of fresh air. Let him have his dinner and enjoy it before she said anything about Mark.

She dished out a generous helping of pie and heaped his plate with veg.

'Thanks, Ma.' He tucked in with gusto. She busied herself around the kitchen as he ate, responding to his chat about his day as normally as she could.

'Aw, Mam, that was delicious,' he declared twenty minutes later, as he scraped the remains out of the pie dish, having cleared his plate. 'I really feel sorry for some of the lads in digs. They get poxy food.'

'Just as well you live at home then,' she said brightly. Too brightly. He looked at her.

'Ma, are you OK? You look terrible. Like you were on the piss or something.'

'Thanks very much.' She made a face at him. 'I can't look ravishing all the time.'

'I didn't mean that, Ma. You just look a bit grey or something. Is it the unmentionables? Should I barricade myself in my room?' he teased, referring to her occasional episodes of PMT when she was like a briar and best avoided.

Francesca felt her stomach lurch and her palms go sweaty. It would be better to get it over and done with. There was no point in postponing the ordeal.

'Come on into the lounge with me, I need to talk to you,' she said quietly.

'Crikey, are you preggers?' Owen asked in sympathetic horror.

In spite of herself, Francesca had to laugh: 'No, I am *not* preggers,' she expostulated.

'Whew.' He wiped imaginary sweat off his brow as he threw an affectionate arm across her shoulders and walked with her into the lounge. 'Worse than that?' He cocked an inquisitive eye at her and she could see the beginnings of fear lurking in their blue depths. 'You're not sick or anything?'

'No, no, nothing like that,' she hastened to assure him. She turned to face him and her mouth went dry. 'Owen . . . I . . . Your . . . ahh . . . that is—'

'Mam, please, just tell me,' he pleaded, all youthful teasing replaced by concern and apprehension. 'What's up. Is Dad OK?' He grabbed her arm. 'Dad's OK, isn't he? You'd have told me straight away.' He blew his cheeks out in relief. 'It's Granddad, isn't it? Has he snuffed it?'

'Owen!' she reprimanded.

'Sorry,' he apologized insincerely. 'What's wrong with him?'

'It's not your granddad, Owen. It's . . . well . . .' She took a deep breath.

'Your father and I have separated.'

'*What!*' He stared at her uncomprehendingly.

'Your father and I have separated,' she repeated quietly.

'Since when? Why? I left home yesterday and everything was normal. What's going on, Mam?' Anger and confusion played across his boyish features.

'Look, Owen, I'd like you to talk to your father and let him explain to you—'

'No! You tell me,' he demanded. 'Why have you separated?' His voice rose an octave. 'What's going on? Whose idea was it?'

'It wasn't mine,' she said flatly, sitting down on the sofa.

'Well, why does he want to leave? You're happy together. What's his problem?'

'Owen, please. Phone him and arrange to meet him and let him explain it. To be honest with you it's just as much of a shock to me,' she said wearily.

'When will he be home from Brussels?' Owen was pale with shock.

'He's not in Brussels. He's in Dublin,' Francesca replied weakly.

'Where?'

'I don't know.'

'I'm going to ring him right now and get to the bottom of this. This is all wrong, Ma,' he blustered. 'This is all wrong.' He lifted the phone on the side table and dialled.

Francesca, unwilling to listen to the conversation, slipped out of the room and closed the door. She heard Owen say brusquely, 'Dad, what the fuck's going on here? Mam says you're separating. I want to know why. I want to meet you now, Dad.'

Francesca raced into the kitchen and closed the door and leaned against it. She actually felt faint. She heard Owen open the lounge door and braced herself.

'I'm going to meet Dad off the Dart in Sydney Parade. Will you be all right until I come back? Jeepers, Mam, you should go and lie down or something. You look like you're going to keel over. Will I bring you a cup of tea?'

'No thanks, love. I might go up to bed. It's been a very long day.' A thought struck her. 'Owen, I have to give you a new set of keys. I had the locks changed.'

'God, Mam! He wasn't hitting you, was he?' Her son's shock was palpable. *Fuck you, Mark, for doing this to him*, Francesca raged silently as she saw Owen's obvious distress.

'Nothing like that, no, no, I just overreacted a bit,' she said hastily.

'To what?' he probed.

'Owen, just go and meet your father and remember that whatever our differences are, we love you and your brother and nothing changes that.'

'Aw, Mam, this is terrible.' Owen hung his head but not before she could see the tears in his eyes. He looked so young and vulnerable with his hair hanging down into his eyes, it grieved her.

She put her arms around him and felt his tighten around her. 'If Dad's done anything to hurt you I'll break his fucking neck,' he muttered brokenly.

'Ssshhh, don't say that, and don't curse, love,' she chided. 'I don't want you taking sides. Remember he loves you as much as I do and he's your father. The new keys are on the desk in the hall; drive carefully to the Dart station and I'll see you when you get back. Oh, and get me a litre of milk, would you? I forgot to buy any today.'

'OK, Mam,' he muttered, subdued. She watched him leave and wondered if there was any other way that she could have handled it that would have made it easier on him. Maybe she and Mark should have told him together instead of making him travel halfway across the city in an appalling frame of mind. What kind of a mother was she to put her child through that misery, just to score a point with her husband?

Although it was only gone seven, she switched off the lights in the lounge and kitchen and went upstairs to bed, where she curled up in a ball and tried not to imagine the encounter between Owen and his father.

Mark sat at Nikki's black marble kitchen counter top with his head in his hands and cursed his wife roundly. Nikki, wisely, refrained from comment.

'She's so fucking vindictive. She's so spiteful. I can't believe it. She just couldn't wait to tell Owen that we've separated and she won't tell him why. She's leaving that to me. Bitch!' He shook his head in disbelief. 'What the fuck am I going to say to him without looking like a right bastard? Oh, she's playing a blinder all right. She'll rub my goddamn nose in it as hard as she can. And she'll come out smelling of roses.'

Nikki said nothing. She came and stood behind him and expertly massaged the back of his neck.

'It's so out of character for her. I've never seen her like this. I know this isn't easy for her but there are limits.' Francesca's behaviour had shocked him to the core. 'I'm not a total bastard, sure I'm not?' He twisted around to look at Nikki.

'Of course you're not,' she said vehemently. 'You didn't plan for this to happen and if Francesca hadn't found out no-one would be any the wiser and no-one would have got hurt. Relationships change, pet. *People* change – as they get older. Not every marriage is cut out to last for ever. People who think that are living in fantasy land. OK, it's tough on your son, I agree. But he'll get over it in time and carry on with his own life and there'll come a time when you'll hardly feature in it at all – when he's experiencing his own relationships. I know it's very important to take kids' feelings into consideration but you can't not live your own life and make changes in it just to protect them from feeling hurt. That's a recipe for disaster, Mark.'

'You might feel different if you had kids of your own. It's tough, Nikki. I'd rather lose that new French acquisition than go and face my son tonight,' he said heavily.

'Oh, Mark.' Nikki shook her head, at a loss for words. If he felt that way, it was bad, he'd worked his butt off over that take-over. 'Look, let him blow his top and say whatever he has to say and get it off his chest and don't try even to defend yourself, because in his eyes at the moment there's no defence for what you've done. Just take it on the chin and smile. You've got to tough this one out, love. He'll calm down in time,' Nikki advised.

'Will he?'

'Yes, he will. Darling, millions of people go through what you're going through and they don't all stay mad at one another. Things will work out.'

'I suppose you've got a point.' He turned to face her and put his arms around her. 'Are you sorry that you got involved with me?'

106

She silenced him with a kiss. 'What do you think?' she asked demurely when it was over.

'Witch!' He laughed, and kissed her hard. 'I'd better go and eat humble pie before my son,' he sighed. 'That crashing sound is me tumbling down off my pedestal,' he added wryly.

'Ah, Mark, don't be so hard on yourself. You're only human,' Nikki urged as she stroked the back of his head.

'That's not what Francesca thinks at the moment. She thinks I'm the devil incarnate.' He nuzzled her neck, inhaling the delicate perfume she wore.

'She'll get over it too, in time, Mark. Life moves on whether we like it or not. I've been through enough broken relationships to know that much.'

'I didn't want to hurt her. I didn't do this on purpose but I can't be totally responsible for her happiness or unhappiness. She has to take some responsibility for her own life too. I can't carry her on my back all my life. Especially the way I feel right now. I don't want to. Is that so awful? It is awful, isn't it? Especially after twenty years of marriage.' He groaned.

Nikki sighed and kissed the top of his head. 'You're not a saint. Stop trying to be one.'

'You can say that again,' Mark said as he stood up. 'Better go. Say a prayer for me.' He walked into the narrow hallway and took his coat off the hall stand. 'Thanks for being here for me,' he said gruffly.

'You're welcome.' She closed the door gently behind him. Mark jammed his hands into his coat pockets and took the stairs instead of the elevator. He needed to calm himself. Owen had been so uptight on the phone. His heart contracted. His son would hate him. He wouldn't remotely understand what his father was going through. The best thing to do was, as Nikki suggested, let him get it off his chest and not react.

Nikki was very good at seeing things from a detached point of view. And her advice was pretty spot on, he thought admiringly as he let himself out of the foyer and walked over to the car. It was a cold, clear night. Frost crinkled underfoot. A sprinkling of stars shone overhead. A crescent moon etched sharply against the inky blackness of the night sky. An ordinary winter's night that would never be forgotten by him or his son as long as they lived.

He'd had a turning point in his relationship with Francesca, earlier in the day. Now he was going to have one with his son. Where would it lead? He'd have to talk to Jonathan too. Another ordeal to be faced. The price for trying to be true to himself was turning out to be extraordinarily high, he thought disconsolately as he turned left out of the apartment complex onto Mount Merrion Avenue and headed for Sydney Parade Dart Station. He'd chosen Sydney Parade because it was close to the car park on the Sandymount seafront. They could talk in private in the car. It was hardly appropriate to ask his son to go for a drink and try and discuss this most private of matters in the noisy environs of a bar. Mark felt the weight of dread on his chest. He could quite honestly say that this was the worst day of his life. It didn't help to know that it was all his own doing.

Owen sat on the hot, stuffy, swaying commuter train, his hands clenched in his lap, his stomach tied up in knots. He felt like crying but it was so unmanly to cry. Imagine if he started bawling in front of all these strangers. He looked at some Spanish students jabbering away in their native tongue as they sat on the seat opposite him. Imagine the expression on their faces if he suddenly started blubbering.

What was up with his folks? Everything had seemed so normal when he'd left home the previous morning. Where had this bombshell come from? Why was his ma being so reticent? Why was she so insistent that he talk to his da? She'd said something about being as surprised as Owen was. It must be his da that had initiated things. But why? And why had she changed the locks? That meant she truly did not want to have his da in the house.

Owen gazed out at the cold tiled platform of Pearse Street Station as the train discharged dozens of passengers, including, to his relief, the youths opposite him. He hoped no-one else would sit there. He needed time to compose himself for the meeting with his father.

Only a couple more stops and then he'd know what it was all about. He saw a man and woman kissing on the platform, before she got on the train. The man was older than the woman. He picked up his briefcase and strode away. She looked sad as she sat down on the seat across the aisle from him. Maybe they were having an affair, he thought idly. He sat bolt upright in his seat as awareness dawned.

His father was having an affair. He had to be. Why else would his mother have kicked him out? Owen felt sick to his stomach. How could his dad do that to his mam? Poor, poor Francesca, he thought, full of pity for his mother. By God, when he met his father, he'd let him have it. He really would, Owen thought grimly as the train trundled out of the station towards the southside suburbs.

Chapter Twelve

Two trains passed through the station and there was no sign of his son. Mark wondered whether he had changed his mind. He was tempted to phone Owen on his mobile but decided against it until one more train had pulled in. The longer he waited the more agitated he got. He saw the barriers go down and heard the dull clickety-clack of an incoming train. He sat, tense and apprehensive, watching a dribble of passengers come through the exit gate, and then experienced a thud of recognition as he saw the familiar gangly lope of his youngest son. Owen looked uncharacteristically serious as he scanned the street looking for the car.

Mark tooted the horn and waved as Owen looked over in his direction. His son did not wave back. Mark took a deep breath. It was ridiculous but he felt like he had when he was six years old and Gerald was berating him for some childish misdemeanour.

'Hello, son.' He kept his tone even as Owen opened the car door and sat in beside him.

Owen did not return the greeting. 'What's going on, Dad?' It was clear that he was very angry.

Mark ignored the question and switched on the ignition. 'Let's drive to the car park overlooking the sea. I'm on double yellows here.'

'Fuck the double yellows. No-one's going to do you at this hour of the night. You're seeing another woman, aren't you?' Owen accused belligerently.

'Is that what your mother said?' Mark said flatly.

'Mam said nothing, Dad. Nothing! You're seeing someone else, aren't you? Some silly blonde bimbo with big tits and her skirts up to her arse who flatters you and makes you feel good and lets you spend a fortune on her 'cos you're a fucking vain idiot who's lost the run of himself.' Owen spat out his accusations with a ferocity that took Mark aback.

'It's not like that, Owen,' he protested. 'Nikki is not a bimbo. And it's not what I wanted to happen.'

'You're pathetic, Dad,' Owen shouted, his face twisted with contempt. 'You're just a middle-aged git trying to get his leg over some bit of stuff until she dumps you for some other sad idiot.'

'Owen, don't judge someone until you've stood in their shoes.' Mark tried to keep his temper in check. 'You don't know any of the circumstances.'

'It's enough to know that you've treated Mam like shit and to know that I'm ashamed to call you my father.' Owen jumped out of the car and slammed the door behind him. He ran across the road and disappeared into the Dart station.

Mark sat immobile as his son's shaming, accusatory words replayed in his brain. A pathetic, middle-aged, sad git. You couldn't fall much lower than that, he thought dispiritedly. Each cruel slur hurt in a way that he hadn't thought possible. He felt wounded. Owen hadn't even wanted to listen to any explanation he might have given. He'd simply taken Francesca's side and jumped to her defence. That was painful. Much more painful and guilt-provoking than he'd been prepared for.

Nikki had been right about Owen's anger, he thought wearily. It might be a long, long time before he and his son could salvage what had been a very loving relationship. Mark heard a northbound train come in and the barriers went down once more. Minutes later the train moved out of the station and, very clearly, for a moment he saw his son sitting gazing into space with a look of immense sadness on his face.

It was Mark's undoing. Memories of his birth, his first tooth, his first steps, childhood milestones, passed through his mind and he buried his head and cried as he had never cried before. *I'm sorry. I'm sorry. I'm sorry*, he called silently as the train slowly disappeared from view and the red and white barriers lifted and strangers in their cars gave him peculiar looks as they flashed by.

Owen was trembling as he sat on the northbound train. What a bollocks his father was. He despised him beyond belief. The memory of his mother's drawn, tired face made him clench his hands into fists and he was suddenly sorry that he hadn't clocked his father one. It would have given him immense satisfaction.

Thinking of him with another woman was revolting. Owen gave a shudder. It was bad enough to think of your parents having sex anyway without thinking of them having sex with strangers. What was that woman like? That Nikki. Didn't she know that his father was married? Had she no morals? he thought indignantly, forgetting completely about the time he'd had the hots for a mate's sexy mother and for months had thought of nothing else but doing it with her. Another thought struck him. He was supposed to be going to America for Christmas. He'd been saving like mad from his part-time job in a local printer's and he'd been looking forward to it mightily. He just couldn't go off and leave his mother on her own at Christmas. She'd need all the support she could get, he thought glumly. His life had just turned upside down and it looked like one disaster after another was heading his way, he reflected as the train sped towards home.

'Under no circumstances are you cancelling your trip to see Jonathan,' said Francesca firmly when Owen told her of his plans to stay at home. He'd come in, pale and exhausted-looking, and declared that he was not going away for Christmas.

'I'm not leaving you here on your own. What sort of a son do you think I am?' he demanded indignantly.

'I think you're a wonderful son, my love,' she said gently. 'I couldn't wish for better. But I'd feel far happier knowing that you and Jonathan were together supporting each other, especially as he's so far away from home. When he finds out what's happened he's going to need a bit of support too.'

'But what about you? What will you do?' He brightened. 'Why don't you come too?'

'No, Owen. I know that you've planned to go skiing and it's only a couple of months since I was in the States. And anyway . . .' She paused, unsure. 'I suppose I'll have to start cutting down a bit until things are sorted.'

'But what will you do? You can't stay here on your own for Christmas.' Owen was aghast.

'Of course I'm not staying here on my own for Christmas,' she said briskly. 'I've arranged to go to Millie and you know how I love being with the girls, so that will be nice for me.'

'It's going to be a bummer of a Christmas,' Owen blurted out.

'Owen, it will be what we make it and my life will be much better and happier if I know that you're having a good time with your brother.'

'He's a bollocks, Ma! Da's a bollocks.' The tears came to Owen's eyes and he cried like a baby, great gulping sobs that broke her heart as she wrapped her arms around him. The youthful, musky scent of him brought the tears to her own eyes.

'Don't say that, Owen. He's your father,' she whispered.

'Well, I wish he wasn't after what he's done to you,' he said brokenly.

She couldn't answer and they held each other for a long time, crying out their grief for what would never be again.

Chapter Thirteen

She could honestly say it was the worst Christmas of her life, Francesca reflected as she ironed Owen's shirt and added it to the growing pile under the ironing board. Owen was packing for his trip to America and his bedroom was in a state of absolute chaos. She didn't have the heart to nag him about it. He had enough to contend with, she thought guiltily.

The phone rang. She was loath to answer it. She didn't want to talk to people. The answering machine clicked in. She heard her oldest son's deep voice begin a message. Hastily she snatched up the receiver of the kitchen extension.

'Hi, Jonathan. I'm here. Hold on until I switch off the machine.' She hurried into the hall, switched off the answering machine and picked up the receiver. 'Hi.'

'Hi, Mam. How are you feeling?' Jonathan asked awkwardly. He'd been totally shocked when his father had phoned him to say that he and Francesca had separated and that he was with someone else.

He'd phoned Francesca immediately and offered to come home, but, touched as she was by his concern, she wouldn't hear of it.

'I'm OK, Jon, I'm just ironing your brother's shirts. If he was left to his own devices he'd come over to you looking like a ragamuffin,' she said lightly.

'Are you sure that you won't come with him? Or are you sure that you wouldn't like me to come home?'

'No, love, to tell you the truth I'm looking forward to a bit of time on my own to think things out and see where I go from here. I'm really glad that Owen's going out to you. It's been very tough on him here. It will do him good,' Francesca said firmly.

'Well, if you're sure. We'll ring you at Millie's on Christmas Day,' Jonathan assured her.

Francesca smiled. 'I'll look forward to it.' They chatted briefly and she put the phone down reluctantly, wanting to maintain the contact.

It had all been extremely difficult, especially when she'd had to explain to her parents why Mark and the boys would not be visiting on Christmas Day. Francesca groaned as she ironed a particularly stubborn crease on a pair of jeans remembering her mother and father's shock when she'd initially told them that she and Mark had separated.

'But why? We all go through difficult times. We have to get over them. That's what marriage is all about. We can't just turn and run when the going gets tough,' Maura Johnson said bossily. 'Your father and I had to tough things out. This divorce thing has made life far too easy for people. You can't run away from problems, Francesca.'

Francesca gritted her teeth. 'I'm not running away, Mother.'

'Well then, tell Mark to come home and stop this nonsense and sort it out. You have two children to think of, after all. Poor things. What about them?' Her mother was clearly not at all impressed and certainly felt no sympathy for her.

Francesca held her tongue. She couldn't bear to tell her mother that Mark was with someone else. Her mother was dreadful for interfering, and she still treated the boys as if they were five years old.

Several phone calls later, with Maura demanding to know if Mark was back home and had they sorted themselves out for Christmas, Francesca flipped.

'Mother, I've told you, we've separated. There isn't going to be a family Christmas this year. Owen's gone to spend Christmas with Jonathan. Mark's with another woman, so for God's sake will you leave me alone!'

'He's with another woman?' Maura's voice went into orbit. A brief silence followed as she digested the news. Then: 'Why is he with another woman? Were you refusing him his . . . his marital rights?' she demanded.

Francesca thought she was going to explode. 'No, Mother, I was not refusing to have sex with him. You'll have to ask him why he's seeing someone else. Goodbye.' She slammed down the phone in a temper. Her mother was still so old-fashioned about marriage and sex. She'd led a very sheltered life as a young girl and had grown up with the notion that sex was a duty, not a pleasure. No wonder Francesca had been terrified of sleeping with Mark before their

118

marriage, she thought resentfully, remembering his complaints about having to get married to have decent sex.

'Well now, Francesca, you hardly expected any different? Poor Ma,' Millie laughed a few days later when Francesca conveyed this latest nugget. 'You know you've disgraced the family by separating. What on earth is she going to tell "the Relations"? You don't think Mother's going to change at this stage in her life, now do you?' Millie added quizzically.

'As if I haven't enough on my plate.' Francesca scowled. 'Thanks for having me stay with you over Christmas. I'd go loony otherwise.'

'Well, what would you be rattling around the house for on your own now that Owen's gone?' Millie declared.

Owen had left for New York the previous day, still protesting that he wanted to be with Francesca for Christmas. She'd made a supreme effort and put on such a façade that she was coping and looking forward to a flop time with her sister that he'd half believed her, but his eyes studied her intently as he prepared to go airside.

'Are you sure, Mam?'

'Honest, I'm positive.' She grinned. 'Now have a ball, Owen, and for God's sake don't break your neck on the ski slopes.'

'I won't, Ma, don't worry. Are you *sure* you don't want me to stay?'

'Scoot.' She gave him a playful shove. 'And give Jonathan a huge big hug and a kiss for me.'

'I will,' he promised. And she knew it would be a

relief for him to get away and be normal and not have to consider her feelings and state of mind. Sometimes she felt the trauma of the break-up was hardest on him. She could see him watching her carefully as if he were afraid that she would crack up; sometimes she found it difficult to keep a show of normality going for his sake when all she wanted to do was to stay in bed all day and cry and feel sorry for herself.

Nevertheless, it was the loneliest moment of her life as she watched him disappear from view amidst all the festive glitter of the airport.

Mark had returned home several times before Owen went away. He'd always phoned her first to make sure that she'd be there. He'd had to collect bits and pieces and Francesca wished that he'd come home some day and take everything that belonged to him so that he would no longer have an excuse for dropping by.

Owen had always remained in his room until he had gone, ignoring requests to talk or go for a drink. It gave Francesca some satisfaction to see that Mark didn't appear too happy himself. He looked grey and strained and uncomfortable and their conversations were clipped and polite.

Gerald had not phoned again and Francesca was agog with curiosity to know what Mark had told him, but her pride wouldn't allow her to ask. She was still using their joint account; money was not a problem. Mark, whatever his faults, was not mean, but Francesca knew that she would feel much better when their financial situation was ironed out.

'There're the Christmas cards that have arrived so far. I'm not sending cards this year,' she'd informed him curtly on his last visit to the house.

'That's a bit rude,' he'd remarked coolly.

'What do you want me to do? Write and say, "Happy Christmas, love Francesca, Mark, *Nikki* and family"?' she drawled sarcastically.

'There's no need for that,' he snapped.

'Look, Mark, it might come as a surprise to you, but I won't be celebrating Christmas this year and when Owen is gone, I won't be putting on a good face for anyone. And if that doesn't suit you, tough.'

'What are you doing for Christmas?' he asked diffidently.

'As if you care.' She couldn't keep the bitterness out of her voice.

'I do care. If you want me to, I'll have lunch with you, so that you won't be on your own.'

'How ... kind ...' she said scornfully. 'Don't worry about me, Mark. I've made my own arrangements, thank you very much.'

'Look, I'm just trying to make this a little bit easier all round,' he said heatedly. 'Let's at least try and be civilized.'

'"*Try and be civilized*,"' she echoed. 'Of course. Why not? Much *easier* to pretend we're civilized, much easier for *you* than for me to behave like a wagon that right now just hates your guts. Stop treating me like an idiot, Mark, and at least acknowledge that I've a right to my feelings no matter how uncomfortable they make you,' she stormed, turning on her heel and walking out of the lounge.

He didn't follow and shortly after she heard him

leave. It was the last time she saw him before Christmas.

She spent the two days following Owen's departure ensconced in her bed, drained and exhausted, unable and unwilling to make an effort to see or talk to people. She turned the phone down, unplugged the extension in her bedroom and when it rang, as it did constantly, didn't answer it. She knew that friends were phoning to make arrangements to meet over Christmas as they usually did but she could not bring herself to talk to them or to tell them of her new circumstances. When Millie called to see her, concerned, she simply said that she had a bit of a cold and she was staying in bed to shake it off and that she'd see her on Christmas Eve. With just the faithful Trixie for company she shut out the world and wallowed in her misery.

It was a relief not to have to make the effort even to dress herself. She lay in bed replaying every key scene between herself and Mark and when she got tired of that she fantasized about meeting a wealthy, gorgeous, handsome man who would sweep her off her feet. She visualized with pleasure Mark's horror when he realized that he'd lost her for good and had no hope of getting her back. An even better fantasy was of him coming to the understanding that it was she, not Nikki, that he wanted to spend his life with. She spent hours creating and polishing the scene where he begged her to take him back, telling her what a fool he'd been, and she telling him that she didn't want him. She had a new life to lead.

In between her fantasies, she drowsed and tried to read, but she couldn't concentrate on her book, her thoughts invariably returning to her own far more consuming trauma.

By Christmas Eve she was heartily sick of herself and desperately lonely. She went to the hairdresser's for an appointment she'd booked weeks previously and managed to get a manicure as well. It lifted her spirits somewhat and gave her enough of a boost to finish the Christmas shopping that she had left until the last minute.

Look at me, I'm shopping. I'm being normal even though my life is destroyed, she thought in faint astonishment as she flicked through racks of little girls' outfits in Adams. Two hours in Grafton Street and Wicklow Street were all her frayed nerves could take and she scurried back to Duke Street car park and inched her way home in the chaotic Christmas Eve traffic.

The house was mausoleum silent. Francesca stood in the hall, cuddling Trixie who came scudding out to greet her. It was the weirdest Christmas Eve that she had ever spent, she reflected as she flicked through the last-minute post. Usually the house would be alive with the sounds and scents of Christmas. She'd be up to her eyes preparing for the champagne and smoked salmon supper they always had for friends and neighbours before going to Midnight Mass with Mark and the boys and, of course, Gerald. A big bedecked tree would grace the lounge, the open fire would be blazing and the house would be decorated with enormous arrangements of holly, poinsettias, azaleas, roses and chrysanthemums.

This year, not one festive flower arrangement, glittering bauble or otherwise decorated the house.

There was nothing to indicate that it was anything other than an ordinary day. It was like the house of a bereaved person, which she was in a way, she acknowledged. She didn't want to be here, she thought despondently. The phone rang; she ignored it. When Christmas was over she'd write a note to all her friends telling them that she and Mark were separated. It would be the easiest thing to do, she thought wearily. Right now she was like the proverbial ostrich and the more sand she could bury her head in the better.

Throwing a few clothes into a case, she gathered together the champagne, smoked salmon, pâtés, cheeses and other foodstuffs that she was taking to Millie's and packed up the car. Ten minutes later, with the house locked up and alarmed and Trixie on her rug in the back seat, she drove down the drive and didn't look back. The sooner Christmas was over and life was back to some semblance of normality the better. Although Millie had told her that she could be as miserable as she liked, she knew that she would have to make some effort not to ruin their Christmas. The thought of it daunted her.

I hope that Nikki bitch chokes on her turkey drumstick, and Mark too, she thought savagely as she closed the wrought-iron gates behind her and headed off to her sister's house.

Chapter Fourteen

Mark stood frowning in front of a jeweller's window in Wicklow Street. What on earth was he going to give Nikki for Christmas? He should have bought something the last time he was in Brussels instead of leaving it until the last minute. Shopping on Christmas Eve was a nightmare. He studied the contents of the window intently. He didn't want to send the wrong message. A ring would be far too personal. Women had a way of getting the wrong idea when you gave them a ring. Earrings, even though she wore them all the time, were a bit too wishy-washy as a gift and very much a matter of personal taste.

It was strange to be standing outside a jeweller's and not to be looking for a gift for Francesca. He would have liked to exchange Christmas presents with her. Just because he was with Nikki didn't mean that he no longer had feelings for her. Francesca had been part of the tapestry of his life for so long, and always would be, if she wanted to. But right now she didn't want to have anything to do with him. Women were so intense about these things, dwelling on imagined slights and affronts. Seeing insults where none was intended. Why did she have to take it all so personally? Couldn't she understand his point of view at all? It wasn't as if he'd cut off her cash and cancelled her credit cards. He'd behaved in a most generous manner, he thought, aggrieved, as he moved along to where the watches were displayed.

You'd think he was a murderer or something the way Owen was treating him. At least Jonathan had been a bit more civil, if very shocked when he'd phoned him with the news.

'I think you're making a big mistake, Dad,' he'd remonstrated. 'Maybe you and Mam should go and have counselling.' How American, Mark had thought, but he'd given some non-committal answer and had told Jonathan that he would keep in touch. He hadn't been half as judgemental as Owen. But then he was living in a culture where marriage break-up was a way of life. He was obviously more of a realist about it all. Owen had gone to America without even saying goodbye. That had cut Mark to the quick. His own son had disowned him.

He straightened his shoulders and walked into the shop. He'd seen the watch that he would buy for Nikki. That was one task to cross off his 'to do' list. It was a Swiss timepiece, a Corum Padlock watch, inlaid with tiny diamonds. Very Nikki. He was sure she'd like it.

Later, as he sat sipping a latte that he didn't really want, he knew that he was going to have to go and visit his father. He'd told Gerald that Francesca was very under the weather – woman's trouble, he'd lied – and said that she was unable to have Christmas as usual this year. He'd told Gerald to contact him on his mobile if he needed him and not to phone the house under any circumstances as Francesca's nerves weren't the best and the phone was driving her mad.

His father had been most put out and had promptly set about foisting himself on a first cousin that he played bridge with for Christmas lunch. He'd have to tell Gerald the truth in the new year, Mark decided glumly.

He hoped Nikki liked the watch. He hadn't seen much of her in the past few days, he thought ruefully. She had a hectic social life and she was partying like mad. She'd asked him to accompany her but he'd balked at the idea.

'Let's wait until next year,' he'd suggested. 'As soon as I tell people at work about the separation.' She wasn't happy at his dithering. She wanted them to appear at functions as a couple, but he was reluctant to go public yet. He didn't want people knowing about his private business.

He'd told his colleagues at work that Francesca had a very bad flu and he wouldn't be going to the big Christmas party that was held every year. He'd said the same to friends who'd issued invites to this do and that. It was a strain lying to people and then trying to remember what lies he'd told. Nikki was losing patience with him. He felt pressurized.

Didn't she realize how difficult it was for him right now? He had so many new sets of circumstances to adjust to, not least living in the apartment with her.

He missed his house, he thought sadly. He missed

the gracious elegance and spaciousness of it. He missed the gardens. Not that he ever did anything to them, except mow the lawn occasionally. He had a gardener to tend to it once a fortnight or so. But he liked walking or sitting in the large, private, shrub-filled back garden, reading the paper or doing the crossword.

Although he wouldn't say it to Nikki, he felt trapped sometimes in her first-floor two-bedroom apartment. Although it was bright and spacious as apartments went, he still felt like he was living in an egg box. There was nowhere to get away and be alone. He missed his space. And the noise of the traffic, although masked somewhat by the trees in the landscaped gardens, was a never-ending, intrusive, dull roar that he couldn't get used to. He wasn't sleeping well at all. Nikki was a fidgety, twitchy sleeper, unlike Francesca who conked out once she hit the pillow and rarely changed position. She was sex mad too. He was exhausted trying to keep up with her. He was petrified he'd wilt on her some day and disappoint her. How Francesca would laugh at that, he thought wryly. So much for feeling young again.

The whole bloody thing had turned into such a nightmare since Francesca had found out about them. Some men got away with it for years. How had he been so bloody unfortunate? he thought sorrowfully as he picked up his parcels and emerged into the hordes of last minute shoppers.

He and Nikki were going to have a candlelit supper, prepared by him. They shared the cooking. He still had to go to Marks & Spencer's food hall to get dill and baby potatoes. He was doing salmon in cream and wine sauce. It was the easiest dish that he could think of at the moment but when he saw the queues and the big trolley loads at the check-outs, he turned on his heel and hurried back towards Stephen's Green where his car was parked in the bank's underground car park. He'd call into Superquinn in Sutton, it was on his route home.

Mark was halfway down Dawson Street before he remembered that he didn't live in Howth any more and Sutton wasn't on his route home now. It was a very forlorn moment. He'd never felt as lonely in his life.

Nikki put the finishing touches to wrapping the luxurious terry-towelling robe she'd bought for Mark's Christmas present. In one pocket she'd put the latest Terry Pratchett novel, in the other a pale yellow and grey silk tie that he'd admired one day when they were out shopping and an expensive Grand Cru that he particularly liked. She'd spent time deciding what to buy him. She wanted him to like his presents.

She sighed. Mark was terribly unsettled. Moody even. It was very frustrating. She could see that it had been a great upheaval in his life but it was time that he faced facts. His marriage was over, he had to get on with it. Every time he went home to Francesca he'd come back in a ferociously bad humour. It disturbed her that his wife still had such an effect on him. Why couldn't he just get on with enjoying life with her? It could be so good if only he'd relax and let go of the past.

It hurt that he wouldn't accompany her to any of the Christmas parties she'd attended. It *really* hurt that, to all intents and purposes, no-one knew about their relationship at work and people still thought that he was happily married to Francesca. But she was afraid to put pressure on him in case he upped and left. That would be a fatal mistake. At least they were going into a new year and things might move forwards, she consoled herself as she placed an elegant red bow on the crisp gold paper she'd used. She surveyed the parcel. It looked mysterious and sophisticated and not a bit garish, she thought with pleasure. Just like the image she liked to portray. If the hot shots at work who thought she was such a cool bitch could see her now, wouldn't they gloat, she thought wryly. She who had always said that no man was more important than her career. She'd believed it once too, in her late twenties. Until she'd got involved with Mark, relationships had certainly played second fiddle to her career. But this was different. She loved Mark. He was a complex, challenging man to love, but she'd relish the undertaking much more if she knew there was going to be a positive outcome. Maybe they should get a place together and move. It might feel more like his place. This apartment had her stamp firmly upon it. But she liked it. It represented the sum of her achievements and financially it was her biggest asset.

She looked around the sitting room. It was stylish and minimalist. No clutter. Polished floors. Pale cream walls. Muted dusky pink and grey patterned drapes that picked out the colours in the expensive hand-woven rugs that she'd bought on a trip to Egypt. A pale grey sofa and two chairs that she'd bought in O'Hagan Design. A coffee table with an expensive candle on each corner stood in the centre of the room. An antique sandalwood chest and a glass shelf unit to house her collection of Louise Kennedy crystal were her only other pieces of furniture.

Patio doors led out onto a small tiled balcony. She had one cordyline and some pots of long grasses, for effect. Plants were not her forte.

Her apartment had appeared in a homes and garden feature in a supplement in one of the week-end papers. Everyone in work had bought it. There'd been a lot of envious glances in her direction that week and she'd felt delightfully superior. She'd been complimented on her exquisite taste by Sonia Grimes, the MD's wife. Praise indeed! She *did* have good taste, she affirmed as she straightened a candle that was slightly crooked.

Her only concession to the festive season were masses of slim elegant red tapers and a delicate set of white lights entwined in a stunning red and white floral arrangement of bare branches, red berries and white lilies that she'd had made to order in an exclusive florists off Stephen's Green. It lent an extremely stylish air to the room. Nikki could not stand gaudy baubles and tacky glitter.

She was looking forward immensely to their supper tonight. It was definitely going to be her nicest Christmas ever. She was going to visit her family with their presents and get that out of the way right now. It would be lovely, then, to come home knowing that there was a tasty meal prepared for her by the man she loved. And afterwards . . . Nikki felt a tingle of pleasure shoot through her. She was feeling horny already.

Chapter Fifteen

New Year's Eve

'Yoo hoo, Francesca, Francesca, where on earth have you been? Is everything all right? We've been wondering, as we haven't seen you around? You didn't have your usual Christmas Eve bash, and we couldn't get in touch to invite you to our soirée.'

Francesca's heart sank as she heard Viv Cassidy hollering at her from her car window. Viv lived in a big house on the opposite side of the road. She was a nosy cow, and Francesca didn't really like her. She loved boasting about the exotic locations she and her husband, Desmond, a barrister, travelled to several times a year. She was an out and out snob, a member of this yacht club and that golf club, friendly with this celebrity and that politician.

Francesca took a deep breath as she pushed open the gates. It was now or never, she decided. She couldn't keep putting it off for ever. 'Viv, hi.' She turned to face her neighbour, who had pulled into the kerb, all ready for a chat. 'We haven't been here for Christmas and we didn't have our usual do because Mark and I have separated.'

'Oh my God!' Viv's blue eyes got rounder and rounder. 'Oh, I'm so sorry,' she squeaked. 'I had no idea.' *What a simply glorious piece of gossip*, she thought delightedly. *Wait until I tell the girls!* 'You poor, poor dear. Is there anything I can do?'

'Not a thing, Viv. Thanks,' Francesca said evenly. She knew that Viv was dying to race off to spread the news.

'You poor darling. No wonder you look so shattered. And how are the boys taking it?' Viv oozed sympathy.

'These things happen, Viv. They're coping.'

'But you and Mark seemed so . . . so compatible.' Viv tutted. 'Er . . .' she *had* to ask – 'is there anyone else involved?'

'Viv, I'd love to stop and chat but I'm in a bit of a rush. I'll catch you again.' Francesca slid into the car and revved up the engine and shot into the drive, leaving Viv open-mouthed at the abrupt ending of their conversation. Francesca hadn't gone ten yards before Viv was on the car phone to Eva Collins, her bosom buddy.

'Guess who's separated? You'll never believe it,' she burbled excitedly.

'Who? Who? Tell me right now or I'll hang up,' Eva demanded. This would be good: she knew Viv of old.

'It's Francesca and Mark. Isn't that something? I just can't believe it. Darby and Joan! And when I asked her if there was anyone else involved she got into the car and whizzed off like a bat out of hell. One of them must be having an affair and I bet it's not her. She looks dreadful. Big bags under her eyes and awful black circles. I never thought he had it in him. He's so serious. It's the quiet ones you have to watch, Eva. Still waters run deep. If I find out anything else I'll let you know.'

'Hang on, Ed plays bridge with Mark's father. I'll get him to suss it out when he phones him later on to make their arrangements. There's a big game next Tuesday for some charity or other.'

'Oh, get Ed to ring now,' Viv urged. 'And call me back the minute you hear anything.'

'I will. I will,' Eva twittered excitedly. 'Talk soon.'

Francesca heard Viv drive off and cursed her roundly. 'Nosy, snobby old bitch,' she swore as she let herself into the house. She knew fine well that the news would be around the entire neighbourhood and their circle of acquaintances before the evening was out. They'd be the talk of many a party tonight, she thought grimly as she punched in the numbers for the alarm.

She shivered. The house was freezing. She'd turned off the heating for the week that she was staying in Millie's. She should have come home and put it on and then gone grocery shopping instead of doing it the other way around. She flicked on the master switch and heard the heating come on. She might as well unpack the shopping instead of hanging around shivering, she told herself crossly, annoyed at her lack of forward planning. It was bad enough coming home alone on a New Year's Eve without coming home to an igloo.

Millie had begged her to stay, but Francesca badly needed to be alone. She couldn't face the party that her sister was hosting. The thought of singing 'Auld Lang Syne' at midnight was enough to crack her up. She didn't particularly like New Year's Eve at the best of times but tonight was going to be the pits.

She'd filched two of her mother's sleeping tablets when she'd called to see her parents earlier in the day. By nine p.m. she'd be in a drugged stupor, she promised herself as she lugged her shopping out of the boot.

She was just sitting down to some tea and toast when the phone rang. She ignored it. It wasn't the boys. She'd phoned them earlier to wish them as happy a new year as they could have under the circumstances. Moments later her mobile rang.

'Tsk!' she muttered, annoyed with the unwelcome intruder. It might be Millie trying to change her mind, she thought ruefully as she rooted in her bag and found the phone.

Her heart leaped when she saw Mark's name up on the screen. For a moment she was tempted not to answer, but curiosity got the better of her.

'Yes, Mark?' she said coolly.

'For fuck's sake, Francesca, what the hell do you mean by telling Ed Collins that we've separated?' Mark barked. 'He asked my father about it and of course Dad knew nothing because I hadn't told him. I've just had him on the phone doing handstands. You'd no business telling people without my permission.' Mark's fury was palpable.

'I don't need your goddamn permission for anything, Mark Kirwan, and I never said a word to Ed

Collins. I'd know better than to discuss my private business with that old idiot,' she ranted. 'But if I want to tell the world and his mother that you and I are apart, I reserve the right to do so and tough if you don't like it. Your feelings are of not the slightest interest to me any more.' She hung up in fury and switched the mobile off completely.

'The nerve of him,' she muttered, pushing her toast away, her appetite gone. The only thing that gave her any satisfaction was imagining Gerald's lockjaw when Ed Collins had broached the subject. It hadn't taken long for Viv to get the jungle drums rolling, she thought grimly. She'd have loved to be a fly on the wall when her father-in-law rang Mark. She wondered if Mark had admitted to being with another woman. She drank her tea and surfed the TV channels but she was too agitated to concentrate on anything. Mark had made her so mad, she hoped her anger would not prevent the tablets from taking effect. The last thing she needed was a sleepless New Year's Eve night, listening to the sounds of revelry at midnight. She thrust the tablets into her mouth and took a slug of tea and marched upstairs and undressed. It was seven-thirty.

She got into bed, switched off the light and waited for oblivion.

Mark was so angry he felt like driving over to Francesca and shaking the living daylights out of her. How disloyal of her to blab to the neighbours without even warning him. When Gerald had phoned demanding to know what was all this about a separation, he'd nearly died. His father had lectured him long and loudly about the sacrament of marriage and about the binding vows he'd taken in the sight of God the day he'd married Francesca. In the end he'd hung up on his father with a brusque, 'It's really none of your business.' Gerald was in a foul humour anyway, having had to look after himself over the Christmas season. He'd had a very cushy number all these years coming to stay with them and eating them out of house and home. For the first time, Mark realized just how much Francesca had had to put up with. And he could quite understand her resentment of Vera for ducking out of it all.

Nevertheless he was as mad as hell with her for her complete disloyalty. Now it would be all over town and he'd have to tell his colleagues at work. If it weren't for the fact that Nikki truly loved him life wouldn't be worth living, he thought angrily as he waited for Nikki to come down to the car. They were heading to West Cork for New Year and he was looking forward to getting out of Dublin for a few days.

When they came back he'd tell them at work that he and Nikki were living together. Might as well get it all over and done with. It might not be so bad then. They could start the new year afresh. Francesca could go her way and he would go his and they'd work out some sort of financial package. At least the house was paid for, he thought with relief. He'd paid off the mortgage on it years ago. It would grieve him greatly to be paying a mortgage on a house he wasn't even living in. It was in their joint names. Francesca could live in it and at least he'd know it was there to return to if things didn't work out with himself and Nikki. He could live upstairs and Francesca could live downstairs . . . and if she didn't like it: tough.

He saw Nikki coming out of the apartment. She looked stunning. She wore a three-quarter-length ribbed black jacket over a cream polo neck and tailored cream pants. She smiled when she saw him looking at her and his heart lifted. She was beautiful and he loved her. Nikki deserved his love far more than Francesca did. Nikki would never treat him in the shabby way his wife had. Well, as far as he was concerned the marriage was over and he and Nikki were going to have a good life.

'You look beautiful,' he said as she slid into the car beside him.

'And you look very distinguished, darling. All the women will be riddled with envy when they see the gorgeous man I'm with.'

They kissed tenderly. Mark felt more lighthearted. The news was out; there was nothing he could do about it. He was free to be with Nikki without being overcome with apprehension and guilt. It was a good feeling and, he hoped, a very auspicious start to the new year.

Nikki leaned her head on Mark's shoulder as they danced closely together after a most delicious meal. The quartet of musicians were playing soft romantic music that suited her mood completely. This was the most perfect New Year's Eve of her life. Thinking of all the frenetic forced gaiety of the previous year's Millennium Eve when she'd been lonely and without a partner, she shuddered. Who would have thought that she would end up with the man of her dreams after all? Mark had told her that he was going to tell their colleagues that his marriage was over and that they were a couple. It was the greatest gift he could have given her and she was ecstatic. It couldn't get any better than this, she thought happily as Mark nuzzled her ear and whispered, 'Let's go to bed.' Nikki didn't need to be asked twice.

Francesca's phone rang and rang. Viv frowned as once more she got no answer. She could see through the trees from her bedroom window that there was a light on in the hall of Francesca's house across the road. There was one on in the bathroom too. She was ringing to do the neighbourly thing to tell Francesca to come over to the party that was going on down-stairs. The world and his mother were at it and Viv felt that it would be very good for Francesca to pop over for an hour or so and forget her woes. She'd spent a thoroughly delightful afternoon phoning friends and acquaintances with the news – as well as checking that they were coming to the party, of course. It would cause quite a stir if Francesca walked in, now that everyone knew. She tried once more and reluctantly hung up as the phone just kept ringing and ringing.

Francesca lay curled up in bed, fast asleep, thanks to her mother's pilfered sleeping tablets. As the old year slid away and the new one arrived, not even the rowdy gaiety of Viv's party across the street, as revellers whooped and hollered and beeped car horns, disturbed her peaceful slumber.

Chapter Sixteen

A mournful whine and a damp tongue on her cheek woke Francesca. Trixie stood on the bed gazing down at her anxiously between licks. Francesca patted her on the head and, bleary-eyed, tried to focus on her alarm clock. Shocked, she saw that it was almost quarter past eleven. She'd really conked out, she thought groggily. Those sleepers worked. Her head felt light and clouded and she was tempted to lie down again and drift off. But Trixie was impatient to be fed. She pushed back the duvet and shivered. The bedroom was freezing. The heating couldn't have come on, she thought irritably as she dragged on her dressing gown and fished her slippers out from under the bed.

Trixie barked in anticipation of a tasty breakfast.

'Shush! Be quiet, Trixie,' Francesca chided. She had a dull throbbing headache from sleeping too heavily. The phone rang as she reached the bottom of the stairs. It was Millie.

'I'm just up,' Francesca confessed. 'How did the party go?'

'Very well . . . I think, if my head is anything to go by,' her sister groaned. 'How are you? Are you sure you won't come and spend the day with us? What are you doing over there all by yourself?'

'I'm fine, honestly, Millie,' Francesca lied. 'I'm going to take Trixie for a long walk and wash the cobwebs away. I feel like some fresh air.'

'But it's pissing rain out,' Millie retorted.

'I don't mind. I'll wrap up well.' A walk in the rain would suit her mood perfectly. She could weep in peace and no-one would know she was crying. It had been difficult trying to keep going over Christmas when all she wanted to do was bawl her eyes out.

'Well, if you change your mind do drop down, won't you?' Millie urged.

'I will, honest. Now I'd better go and feed Trixie. Thanks for everything, Millie. We'll talk soon,' Francesca promised.

Millie was a great sister, she reflected as she prepared Trixie's food. She was lucky. She had two great sons and a stalwart sister. Why then did she feel so utterly and completely alone? Tears trickled down her cheeks into Trixie's food as she placed the dish on the floor. She sat down at the table and buried her head in her hands and cried, great shuddering sobs of grief, until her eyes hurt and her head ached even more.

The doorbell chimed and she froze. She couldn't let anyone see her like this. It rang again and Trixie barked.

'Shush!' she snapped. Trixie gave her an indignant glare, unused to such a sharp tone from her mistress. After a minute or two Francesca peered out of the kitchen door and could see no outline at the front door. She hurried upstairs to Owen's bedroom just in time to see Viv disappear out of the drive.

'Nosy wagon,' she raged, knowing that Viv was not calling out of genuine concern. The house was eerily quiet. It was getting on her nerves. She had to get out of here. She shivered again as she went into the bathroom, and remembered that she hadn't checked the heating.

Her heart sank to her boots when she saw the oil gauge and realized that she had run out. She had been so distracted over the past weeks she'd completely forgotten to get her oil refill.

She cursed long and loudly knowing it was pointless even to consider ringing her oil company on New Year's Day. What a way to start the new year. Dopey-eyed from sleeping tablets, grief-stricken, and bloody cold. What an omen for the next twelve months.

She decided against a shower and washed her face and teeth before pulling on a snug black body hugger, a pair of warm socks and a fleece. She grabbed a pair of chinos from the wardrobe and scowled as she struggled with the zip. To add to her woes, she was piling on the pounds. Soon nothing would fit her. Defiantly, she marched into the kitchen and buttered a slice of Vienna roll and smeared it with blackberry jam. She ate it standing up, waiting for the kettle to boil. By the time she'd made herself a cup of coffee she'd demolished three more slices and a muffin.

Trixie was ecstatic to be going on a walk with her beloved mistress. The dog scooted out of the door ahead of Francesca and in spite of herself she had to smile. Trixie was such a lovable little thing. If it weren't for her Francesca would have gone straight back to bed and stayed there.

It was a wet, cold, blustery day as Francesca drove to Howth Summit. She pulled on her wellies, buttoned her jacket up to the neck and pulled up her hood. No easy, civilized walk on the pier today. She was going to tramp along the mucky pathways that weaved around the summit; maybe if she was lucky a gust of wind would blow her onto the cliffs below and that would be the end of her misery, she thought forlornly as she set off in the teeth of a howling gale. It would be so easy to end it all. To not have to face the sorrow and uncertainties that were Mark's legacy to her. If she didn't want to throw herself into the sea she could take tablets and alcohol, she mused. Much easier.

But then she'd be leaving Jonathan and Owen, and Millie and her family, a legacy of grief and guilt and sorrow that would ravage *their* lives. Could she do that to them? She started to cry again as the sleety rain whipped into her face. She felt very frightened. What was she doing thinking of suicide? Surely she was strong enough to cope with this crisis?

But was she? She didn't feel at all strong. She felt scared and trembly and full of panic. She was such a disaster she'd even forgotten to order central heating oil, she thought wildly.

Should she beg Mark to come back to her and try and forget the nightmare of knowing that he didn't love her any more, that he loved someone else. A young, smart, independent woman that she couldn't compete with?

Humiliation swamped her. Could she sink so low? Was she that pathetic? How Mark and that woman would despise her and hold her in complete contempt.

'Don't even think of it,' she muttered as she tramped through murky puddles, head down to her chest, hands jammed into her pockets. A man on a horse appeared around a bend on the upper path and she called Trixie to heel until he passed by. She wasn't the only mad person in the world, she thought wryly. A couple ahead of her were walking briskly hand in hand, their laughter floating back on the wind. Even though she and Mark had followed this route many times, it was a long, long time since they'd walked hand in hand. They'd got so used to each other, those important little touches had somehow been lost in the familiarity of everyday life.

She wondered if the same thing would happen to him and his new woman when the first flush of romance had died away. They were probably having mad passionate sex right this minute, she thought bitterly as she paused for breath and stood gazing out at the turbulent pewter sea, which seemed to merge with the leaden sky until all around her was grey and grim.

Maybe he'd have a heart attack from over-exertion, she thought viciously. That would be good enough for the pair of them. And she was damned if she'd go to his fucking funeral.

Agitated and unhappy, she walked the round of the summit and came back to the car along the road, watching the twinkling Christmas trees in house windows and wishing that it was 6 January, when the festive season would end and life could get back to whatever was normal from now on.

She drove home, switched on the electric blanket and was just about to get undressed and retreat to bed when the phone rang.

'Halloo, Francesca, it's Vera.' Francesca's heart sank as she heard her sister-in-law's tones. '*Sooo* sorry to trouble you. I'm trying to get Mark. His mobile is turned off. Do you happen to know where he is?'

'Haven't a clue,' Francesca said grimly.

'Oooh, dear. I got a call from the Kennedys, Father's neighbours, to say that he's locked himself out of the house and is trying to break in through the back door. I mean, it's outrageous. Why are they ringing *me*?' Vera bleated. 'They tried you but there was no answer.'

'I was out,' Francesca said crossly. 'What did they want me for?'

'Well, they thought that you might have a spare set of keys that you could pop over with.'

'Are you serious, Vera? Why the hell should I have to drive across the city to give your father a set of spare keys? What exactly do you think I am? A doormat? Why can't *you* do it?' Francesca exploded resentfully.

'But, Francesca, I don't have spare keys. And besides I'm entertaining. I simply can't leave my guests. Couldn't one of the boys take them over?'

'The boys aren't here. They're in the States.'

'How inconvenient. Couldn't you just oblige me this once? You know I can't stand that old bastard,' Vera cajoled.

'Vera, get lost. If you want the keys, come and

collect them. If not, fine. Now you listen to me. I don't ever want another phone call from you about your father. He is not my problem any more—'

'Well *really*, Francesca, your rudeness is beyond belief. There's no need for your tone. I'll send Noel over for the keys and I assure you, you won't be hearing from me again. Under *any* circumstances.'

'Fine,' Francesca snapped. 'The keys will be in an envelope tucked into the trellis behind the climbing rose. I'm going out.'

'I don't think much of you at all,' Vera retorted huffily and hung up.

Francesca stared at the phone, raging that she hadn't had the chance to hang up first. Snooty wagon, she wouldn't miss her, for sure, she thought angrily as she trudged upstairs and began to undress. She was damned if she was inviting Noel, Vera's plump, pampered son, into her freezing cold house.

She wrapped her towelling bathrobe over her nightdress and snuggled into the bed, warmed by the blanket, but lay as tense as taut wire until she heard her nephew's car drive up to the front door half an hour later. Only when he was gone moments later did she begin to relax before falling into a troubled sleep.

Gerald Kirwan was fit to be tied. He had locked himself out of the house and had had to take refuge in his next-door neighbours' house while he tried to get the matter sorted. He couldn't remember Mark's new phone number or his mobile one.

There was no answer from Francesca's and in desperation he'd asked his neighbour to phone his ungracious upstart of a daughter to relay his predicament. Vera had been most unhelpful and eventually, unwilling to impose on his neighbours any longer than was necessary, he had gone around the back of his house and broken a pane of glass in the back door and let himself in that way. Now he was trying to hammer a piece of board over the broken glass and had whacked his thumb badly. It was too much. What sort of ungrateful, uncaring children had he reared that wouldn't even be with him on a New Year's Day? And that Francesca hadn't even had the decency to phone him to see if he was all right for Christmas. Not even a card. As for his grandsons ... He was changing his will, he decided furiously as he bathed his throbbing thumb under the cold tap.

Owen had phoned to say that he was off to America. Jonathan hadn't bothered to send a card either. Ingrates, the pair of them. Well, they were out of the will and that was final, Gerald decided as he poured himself a stiff whiskey to get over his trauma.

Two hours later, a fat, red-haired youth knocked on his door, thrust a grubby envelope at him, muttered something about spare keys and waddled back to a swanky-looking car. He had his mother's sharp nose and his father's elephant ears, Gerald thought spitefully. A sorry excuse for a man.

'It's a bit bloody late,' he said ungraciously and shut the door with a bang.

'Up yours, Gramps,' muttered Noel as he helped himself to a chocolate out of the box he'd taken with him to keep him going on the trek across town. He was starving. They'd been about to sit down to lunch when he'd had to go haring off to his aunt's house to get keys for old Grumpy. First and last favour he'd do for *him*. Noel scowled as he put the boot down and headed home for his ruined meal.

Gerald marched into the sitting room and flung the keys on the coffee table. A fat lot of use they were to him now. He felt old and tired. It was obvious he was only a nuisance to his family. Nobody wanted to be with him. He couldn't depend on any of them. What would happen to him if his health failed? He'd probably be turfed into one of those depressing, soul-destroying nursing homes for old people. The thought chilled him to the bone. Imagine having to depend on strangers to take care of him and feed and clothe him.

A picture of the Sacred Heart hung over the fireplace. His dear departed wife had always lit a little lamp in front of it. He'd got out of the habit. Suddenly it felt important that he follow her lead. He rooted in the drawers of the sideboard and found a packet of night lights. He placed one in the little red holder and lit it. It flickered to life, casting weaving shadows on the kind countenance of the Saviour. It brought a little comfort. Gerald found himself on his knees.

'Don't leave me on my own, Lord. Let me be able to look after myself until the end. I place all my trust in Thee,' he murmured brusquely in the deepening dusk, before blessing himself and struggling to his feet to pull the curtains against the gloomy wet night.

'Look, Vera, I can't and won't do everything. It's not fair. You're his child too whether you like it or not. You have to accept some responsibility for him,'

Mark raged down the line at his sister. He was back in Dublin and had had a furious and whining phone call from his father informing him of the whole sorry saga of New Year's Day.

'Mark, he can rot in hell for all I care. I'm telling you here and now I am having nothing to do with him. He made my life hell when I was growing up. Shouting and roaring if I was even five minutes late and creating a drama if I wore the tiniest bit of lipstick.'

'I know that, but he's old now. He's not as bad,' Mark retorted.

'Tough!' Vera was not to be swayed.

'You're very unforgiving, Vera. You'll regret it some day,' Mark warned.

His sister gave a dry, brittle laugh. 'Indeed I won't, Mark. Quite the contrary. He's all yours. And don't worry, I won't want anything when he's gone. You can have it all. That should make up for whatever hassle you have to put up with. Bye.' Vera hung up abruptly.

Mark scowled and ran his fingers through his hair. This was one problem he certainly hadn't envisaged when he'd started his relationship with Nikki. And it was going to get worse.

He logged on to his computer and began to key in an e-mail.

I wish to make it known that my wife and I have separated and I am now in a relationship with my colleague Nikki Langan. We would ask that you respect our privacy in the matter. Thank you.

Blunt and to the point, he thought grimly. He'd already spoken to Larry Grimes, the MD. Larry was shocked. He'd always had a soft spot for Francesca. Mark had wanted to tell him personally. He was sending the e-mail to key staff that he worked with. Everybody else could find out for themselves, not that it was really any of their business. But it had to be dealt with. His finger hovered over the keyboard. Might as well get it over and done with, he reflected. He took a deep breath and clicked *send*.

He picked up the phone and dialled Nikki's private line. 'Yes?' she said crisply.

'I've sent the e-mail.'

'Good, now let's get on with our lives, Mark. It's a great way to start the new year. Have to go, I've a meeting scheduled. Well done.'

Mark hung up and walked over to the office window. A flurry of snow swirled against the glass. Was it a good start to the new year? Right now he just didn't know.

'Did you hear about *the* e-mail?' Elaine, Nikki's secretary, bubbled excitedly to her best friend Imelda. They were standing at the photocopier pretending to work.

'I certainly did,' Imelda admitted. 'At first I thought it was someone playing a joke. But it's legit.'

'Can you credit it?' Elaine's eyes sparkled. 'Mark and Hot Shot Langan. How long has it been going on?'

'*You* should know. *You're* her secretary,' Imelda retorted.

'I swear, they never gave any indication. You never

see them together. I'm just gobsmacked.' Elaine shook her head. 'I never thought he'd be her type. He's too old, forty if he's a day. And he's very stand-offish.' Elaine removed Imelda's photocopy from the copier and inserted a recipe for salmon mousse that she was longing to try out.

'He might be past his prime but he has a certain something. I'd say he was a great ride in his day,' Imelda said wistfully. She'd always rather fancied the reserved Mr Kirwan. He was sort of Mr Darcyish, she decided.

'He obviously keeps Super Nicks happy so he must still have some tea left in his teapot,' Elaine giggled.

Imelda snorted as she gathered her photocopying together and hastened down the corridor to discuss the most gloriously delicious piece of gossip to have hit the office in a long time with her friend Brona in Foreign Exchange.

Nikki strode into the canteen and took her place in the queue. She knew all eyes were upon her as a little ripple spread around the typists' table.

Silly cows, she thought dismissively as she ordered a portion of chicken and a side salad. She had debated whether to eat in the canteen today, knowing that Mark had sent the e-mail, but she had no lunch meetings scheduled so instead of skulking off downtown she decided to grab the bull by the horns and get it over with. It had to be done sometime.

She paid for her meal and saw John McNally sitting at a table by the window. He was one of the dealers and she liked him. He wasn't a bullshitter like so many of them.

'Mind if I sit with you, John?' She plonked her tray on the table.

'Sure,' John said easily. 'I'll bathe in your reflected notoriety.'

'You heard about the e-mail then?' she said drily.

'Sure did. Caused quite a stir.'

'See WestAir went belly up.' Nikki deliberately changed the subject. 'Glad I didn't buy shares in them.'

'Me too,' John sipped his coffee. 'I knew a few people who've taken a hit. Lorcan Donnelley for one.'

Nikki whistled. 'Know-All Donnelley. Well, well!' She laughed, much to the chagrin of the typists who had hoped she'd have the decency to look just the tiniest bit mortified. They should have known better. Nikki Langan was made of sterner stuff.

Chapter Seventeen

Francesca read the kind and diplomatically worded letter from Alison Curtis and sighed. During the second week of January she had sat down and written to a few dear friends and told them of her separation. She'd been putting it off but Mark had phoned her to let her know that he had sent an e-mail to key people at work and that the news was out. It had made the break-up seem very final and she'd been so hurt, she'd just snapped, 'Thanks for telling me,' and hung up.

Larry Grimes, Mark's MD, had phoned the following day to say how sorry he was and to ask after her welfare. She knew she had to get down to the task of telling people. Writing was her preferred method. She'd kept the notes short but every time she wrote that she and Mark had separated and that he was with someone else she wanted to stab him. Her anger was unspeakable.

Yet, as angry as she was, fear was her strongest emotion. It had really hit her just how vulnerable she was when she'd written a cheque for the central heating oil. The price had increased by over £100 from the previous refill. She was at Mark's mercy financially and it was a most unsettling feeling. He wasn't mean, but nevertheless she was entirely dependent on him for money and she began to suffer from insomnia that left her exhausted. Night after night she would toss and turn, her mind a whirl as thoughts raced around her brain and she wondered what would become of her. Her stomach would clench into knots and her heart would start palpitating and it would often be dawn before she fell into an exhausted sleep.

She tried her best to hide her distress from Owen, who had come back from America full of enthusiasm about going to work there for the summer and beyond.

'You could come too, Mam. It would be good for you,' he urged.

'Stop worrying about me, Owen. You don't want me in America with you when you're sowing your wild oats, now do you?' she teased.

'I don't like leaving you here on your own,' Owen fretted.

'I might sow a few wild oats myself when you're gone, never you fear.' Francesca planted a kiss on his cheek and smiled at him.

He was a great son, she thought gratefully as she slid Alison's note back in the envelope and slipped it into the drawer of her desk. She stood up, agitated. She had to get out of the house. Owen was back in college and the long day stretched ahead of her. She had a few bits and pieces of grocery shopping to do.

It would get her out and about for an hour. She decided to drive down to Clontarf. She didn't want to bump into any of her neighbours in Superquinn. She just wasn't up to social chit-chat.

Francesca did a bigger shop than she anticipated in Nolan's and was grateful as she packed the boot that at least it wasn't raining. She pushed the trolley back to the bay and idly scanned the noticeboard. A small typed advert caught her eye.

Urgently required.
Temporary receptionist/clerk typist wanted for
maternity cover in busy accountant's office.
Start immediately. Good remuneration.

A mad impulse found her rooting in her bag for her mobile and before she knew it, she had dialled the number given. A harassed male voice answered and she explained that she was ringing in answer to the advertisement.

'When can you come for an interview?' he demanded.

'Now,' she blurted.

'Excellent. We're on Seafield Road, the Vernon Avenue end.' He gave her the number. 'My name is Edward Allen. Just ring the bell and announce yourself. What's your name?'

'Francesca Kirwan,' Francesca replied. Her voice quivered. Was she mad?

'Right. See you shortly.' Edward Allen clicked off and she was left looking at the mobile in astonishment.

She hurried to the car and got in. She flicked open

her compact mirror and brushed some bronzing powder over her cheeks and touched up her lipstick. Nothing could hide the suitcases under her eyes, she thought dolefully. Hopefully he wouldn't hire her for her looks. She was wearing black trousers, a tangerine roll-neck jumper, and her fawn winter coat edged with fur trim. Like all her clothes, it was a casually elegant outfit. Still the bank manager's wife, she thought drily as she ran a brush through her hair.

What was maternity leave these days? About three months? If she got the job it would be something on her CV and it would give her a taste of what it would be like getting back into the workforce.

Before she lost her nerve, she started the ignition and drove off. She was less than five minutes away from her destination. She pulled up outside the red-brick house and her heart began to pound. It wasn't too late. She could drive off and forget the crazy impulse that had set her off on this totally unexpected quest.

'Don't be a coward,' she muttered as she got out of the car and drew her coat around her. She pressed the intercom and said her name. The buzzer went and she pushed open the door and found herself in a shabby hallway. The red carpet on the floor and stairs was threadbare in patches and there was a faintly musty smell about the place.

A bespectacled plump grey-haired woman popped her head out of a door along the hall. 'Mr Allen's room is the one across the hall. He's waiting for you,' she said, and disappeared.

'Thanks,' Francesca murmured faintly, to thin air.

157

She knocked on the cream-painted door. The paintwork was chipped and cracked. It might be a busy accountant's office but it certainly could do with a lick of paint, she thought as she waited to enter.

'Come!' a voice said gruffly.

Francesca pushed open the door and her eyes widened at the chaos that surrounded her. Six filing cabinets groaned under the weight of box files and folder files. Bookshelves overflowed with tomes on tax and accountancy. Finance magazines littered the floor. Edward Allen sat at a big mahogany desk in the middle of the chaos. Computer and phone cables and extension leads snaked untidily across the floor.

The accountant had a gaunt lugubrious face that reminded her of a particularly sad-looking bloodhound. His hair was slicked over the side to cover his bald patch and his grey suit hung ill-fittingly on his bony frame. He stood to greet her, his handshake limp and uninterested.

'You must be Mrs Kirwan?' He had a slow, ponderous voice. Clearly they would not be on first-name terms, Francesca realized as she sat opposite him in the chair he indicated.

'Yes, Mr Allen,' she said politely.

'What experience of office work do you have?' He joined his fingertips in a steeple and peered at her through his bi-focals.

'Well, I can type, file, answer phones,' Francesca murmured.

'Hmm. What was your last position?'

She had a wild urge to say 'the missionary'. This

was ludicrous. Could she seriously see herself working for this dry old stick?

'I'm just coming back to the workforce. My children are reared and I want to get back to work, but I haven't actually worked outside the home for twenty years.'

'Hmm. But you can type?'

'Oh yes,' Francesca assured him. She could do a passable two-fingers style of typing, so she wasn't really fibbing she assured herself.

'We were badly let down by a young madam from one of the agencies. She stayed half an hour and left us completely in the lurch. Maybe an older woman would be more reliable.' He eyed Francesca up and down. 'January is a particularly busy time as you know. We have to have our returns in and the pressure is intense. Miss Carter, my assistant, works in the other room across the hall. Your domain would be the room to the front of the house. It is also the clients' waiting room. I would expect you to keep it tidy at all times and to make coffee for me as I require it, as well as attending to your clerical duties. The job is for three months' duration with a possibility of it becoming permanent if Mrs Sullivan decides not to return. The salary is two hundred pounds per week. When can you start?'

'Oh!' Francesca was so surprised to be offered the job she couldn't think straight.

'Tomorrow,' prompted Edward Allen.

'Fine,' Francesca stammered.

'Very well. Nine sharp. Punctuality is of the utmost importance, I'm sure you'll agree. I live upstairs so you don't need a key.' He picked up the phone and pressed a button. 'Miss Carter, could you come into my office please?' he instructed.

Moments later Miss Carter plodded into the room. About fifty, with a helmet of iron-grey hair, she wore a navy pleated skirt and a navy cardigan buttoned up to the neck. A pearl brooch was her only adornment. She wore no make-up.

'Miss Carter, this is Mrs Kirwan. She is our new receptionist. She is starting work for the firm tomorrow,' Edward announced.

'Pleased to meet you,' Miss Carter said tightly in a prim little voice. She held out a pudgy little hand that was withdrawn almost as soon as Francesca had extended hers. Her little brown eyes were hard and unfriendly as she studied Francesca from head to toe.

'Well, I'll see you tomorrow then,' Francesca said brightly.

'Excellent.' A hint of a smile hovered briefly on Edward's face. Miss Carter remained grim-faced as she surreptitiously studied Francesca.

'See you tomorrow then,' Francesca repeated as she backed out the door.

She let herself out of the hall door, pulling it shut behind her.

What on earth had she let herself in for? She shook her head in bemusement. Wait until Millie heard this. And Owen. She wouldn't tell Mark until she was good and ready.

She might not tell Millie or Owen for a while either, she thought doubtfully. Edward Allen & Co. wasn't exactly at the cutting edge of high finance.

She drove home and set to work on a marathon

cook-up. Feeding Owen was her number-one priority. All she'd have to do for the rest of the week was pop the made-up dinners in the microwave. She could have a bite to eat in Clontarf at lunchtimes and at least she wouldn't have too far to travel. Maybe it would work out very well. She heard her son's key in the door.

'Hi, Ma.' He raced into the kitchen, flung his bag under the table, gave her a kiss, divested himself of his coat and said, 'What's for dinner? I'm starving.'

Francesca laughed. He said the same thing every day. 'Roast stuffed pork steak,' she informed him.

'Oh yessss!' Owen rubbed his hands.

'Owen . . . umm . . . I wasn't going to say it for a couple of days until I see how it goes but I got myself a job today,' she blurted out as she busied herself serving their meal.

'A job! Doing what?' Her son was astonished.

'It's in an accountant's in Clontarf. It's clerical and reception work.'

'How did you manage that?'

'I'm not an imbecile, Owen,' Francesca said indignantly.

'I didn't mean that, Ma,' he assured her hastily. 'I was just wondering how did it come about?'

'I saw an ad in a shop window today and when I phoned about it they asked me to come for an interview immediately. They want me to start tomorrow.'

'Jeepers, that's fast moving,' Owen remarked as he demolished a succulent slice of meat.

'I'm not saying anything to anyone until I see how it goes.' Francesca sat down to eat her meal but she wasn't very hungry. Now that she'd told Owen it felt real. She couldn't back out.

'Well, go for it, Ma, and the best of luck.' Owen raised his glass of milk in toast.

'Thanks,' she murmured. She was having palpitations already at the thought of tomorrow.

She went to bed early and slept fitfully. She woke the next morning and lay snuggled in bed in the relaxed moments between waking and sleeping before suddenly realizing with a heavy lurching of her stomach that today was different. Today was the start of her life as a woman of independent means.

She was parked outside the redbrick office at five to nine. Across the road she could see Miss Carter sitting in a sporty red Honda Civic. She was surprised at Miss Carter's choice of car. Still waters run deep, she thought, amused.

At precisely half a minute to nine Miss Carter got out of her car and crossed the road. Francesca got out of her own car.

'Morning, Miss Carter,' she said cheerfully.

'Morning,' Miss Carter reciprocated primly as she glanced at her watch and rapped smartly on the door. It was opened moments later by Edward.

'Good morning, ladies,' he greeted them politely. 'Mrs Kirwan, if you would kindly bring me some coffee? Black, no sugar. Miss Carter, will you show Mrs Kirwan the kitchen area please?' he instructed.

'Certainly, Mr Allen.' Miss Carter gave a tight little smile. 'This way if you please.' She led Francesca into a gloomy, brown-tiled kitchen with an old-fashioned gas cooker. Mustard-coloured presses lay along one wall and Miss Carter pointed to one and said, 'China and coffee. Mr Allen likes his coffee in a china cup, as I do myself. I take my coffee at ten. You may have yours at ten-fifteen until ten-thirty when I'll answer the phones for you. Lunch is from one until two. I'll show you your desk when you've made Mr Allen's coffee.' The accountant clumped out of the kitchen in her serviceable brogues and tweed coat.

Francesca sighed as she took off her coat and filled the kettle. Scintillating conversation was not going to be the order of the day in Allen & Co.

She made her boss a cup of black coffee, knocked politely on his door and entered at his command. He didn't look up as his long bony fingers flew over a calculator. She placed the coffee on the desk in front of him and left him to it. This place was as dead as a morgue, she reflected as she knocked on Miss Carter's door. Miss Carter opened the door with a thin smile.

'I have some letters for you to type and some bills for you to send out. You should start promptly as we have fallen behind a little and that is not the way Allen & Co. do business. Here is your tape.' She handed Francesca a tiny cassette. 'Your Dictaphone is on your desk. Follow me, please.' She marched down the hallway to Francesca's domain.

A desk with an electric typewriter and a phone was positioned at right angles to the window. The phone was an old-fashioned model and Francesca hid a smile as she remembered how worried she'd been that it was going to be a complicated switch system, when, in fact, it was extremely basic.

'If you wish to put a call through to Mr Allen, push the first button. If you wish to put a call through to me, push the second one. Personal phone calls should be taken or made sparingly. Mr Allen is very strict about that.

'The typewriter should be unplugged each evening and the photocopier also.' She indicated a huge antique of a machine in the alcove beside the old-fashioned fireplace. Four hard dining chairs stood along the wall opposite the window and a coffee table held a few well-thumbed copies of *Business and Finance*.

'This is your appointment book. We have two clients calling this afternoon. Any VAT or income tax returns you direct to me. Mr Allen deals with all other business—'

The phone rang. Francesca almost leaped out of her skin. 'Answer it,' instructed Miss Carter.

'Hello, Allen and Co., how may I help you?' Francesca said politely.

'I'm after getting a threatening letter from those VAT people saying they'll send the sheriff after me in twenty-one days,' came a very irate voice down the line. 'I want to speak to Miss Carter.'

'Certainly, who may I say is calling?' Francesca asked calmly, aware that she was under Miss Carter's beady-eyed scrutiny.

'Tell her it's Francis Kelly.'

Francesca put her hand over the mouthpiece. 'It's a Mr Francis Kelly for you. Something about the sheriff calling in twenty-one days because of non-payment of VAT.'

Miss Carter flushed a deep red. 'Tsk. Put it through immediately,' she instructed coldly, much to Francesca's relief. Miss Carter was hard going.

She sat at the desk and switched on the typewriter and ran her fingers over the keys experimentally. The golf ball clattered noisily. Obviously the receptionist/clerk typist was not deemed important enough for a computer. She slipped the cassette into the Dictaphone, inserted her ear plugs and pressed *play*. Miss Carter's starched voice came tinnily into her ear. With a sigh, Francesca switched it off, inserted some headed paper into the typewriter, lined it up, restarted the tape and began to type slowly. She had just got to the last paragraph when she hit the wrong key and wrote assisyance instead of assistance. Groaning, she replaced the offending y with a t. Her next letter was more successful and it was ten-fifteen before she knew it and Miss Carter was standing at the door telling her that it was time for her break.

Francesca sat alone in the brown and mustard kitchen sipping her coffee. She must bring a book to work in future she decided, as chatty tea breaks were obviously not a feature of Allen & Co.

At ten-thirty precisely, Francesca was back at her desk. The phone rang several times. On one occasion she put a call through to Mr Allen which was meant for Miss Carter. On another she put one through to Miss Carter which should have been taken by Mr Allen. Miss Carter was quite snippy about it and Francesca had to resist the urge to tell her to get lost. She ploughed through her letters, pleased with her progress, and at twenty to one brought five completed letters in to Miss Carter to sign. The accountant's office was even more chaotic than her boss's, which surprised Francesca as she had assumed that Miss Carter would have a pristine office with a place for everything and everything in its place.

It was a relief to leave the building for an hour. The morning had gone quickly, she had to admit, but she had a tension headache that was getting worse. She hurried down to the seafront and slipped into Casa Pasta for a bowl of carbonara and a cup of coffee. It was strange not being her own boss, knowing that she couldn't go home and flop in front of the TV for the afternoon or take Trixie for a walk on the pier.

Miss Carter was waiting for her when she got back, her eyes glittering with antagonism. 'Mrs Kirwan, a word. We never send out Tipp-exed letters at Allen & Co. You'll have to redo two please,' she said triumphantly.

'Oh, I see. Did you ever consider getting a computer for your clerk typist? It would be much less time-consuming in the long run,' Francesca suggested.

'Our previous employee was an excellent typist, she didn't need one,' Miss Carter said snootily as she plonked the offending letters in front of Francesca. Fortunately a client arrived and Miss Carter scuttled back into her own office to prepare for her meeting.

At three-fifteen Edward made an appearance. He presented Francesca with a tape and requested that the letters be ready for the evening post. Francesca's heart sank. She'd have to work fast but carefully seeing as Tipp-ex was not permitted.

She had just completed the final, long and complex letter when she hit the wrong key accidentally and a line of x's appeared on her lovely neat type-script.

'Oh fuck, fuck, fuck,' she muttered. Now she'd have to do that last page again and it was ten to five.

Miss Carter's heavy tread sent Francesca's heart plummeting. 'It's almost five p.m. Mr Allen likes us to be prompt about leaving.'

'I've nearly finished this,' Francesca said tightly. *Just go away and leave me alone.*

'Well, don't be long.' She closed the door behind her and Francesca groaned. She finished the letter and picked up the rest of them for her boss's signature.

He perused them slowly before signing them, then franked the envelopes and handed them back to her. 'Thank you, Mrs Kirwan. I'll see you in the morning,' he said gruffly.

'Goodnight, Mr Allen,' Francesca said tiredly. She had a pounding headache and she was knackered. She couldn't wait to get home.

She was dozing by the fire when Owen got home. 'How did it go?' he asked eagerly. Francesca made a face and regaled him with her day's events as he made her a cup of cocoa.

'Don't stay there if you don't like it,' he advised.

'I'll see how it goes. It was only the first day. It would be good to get a bit of speed up in my typing. I should do a course, I suppose.' She yawned.

'You should do a computer course, Ma, you won't really get anywhere without computer skills now,' Owen said sagely.

'I suppose you're right. I'll do something in the

167

spring. I have to go to bed, Owen, I'm whacked. See you in the morning.' She dragged herself upstairs, fell into bed and fell fast asleep. It was the first time she'd fallen straight asleep in months.

The following day was almost a replica of the previous one except that she got a chance to do some photocopying and filing. The day passed quickly enough but she found Miss Carter's unfriendliness wearing and she saw little of Edward who remained ensconced in his office.

Her third day was a Friday and she was so looking forward to the weekend. It was a busy day, client wise. Miss Carter had two and Mr Allen three. The final client arrived at four and Edward asked her to bring coffee for both of them. She carefully made the coffee, poured milk into a china jug for the client and carried it into the office. She smiled at the elderly gentleman and then to her utter dismay caught her high heel in the cable of the computer and watched horrified as two cups of coffee, a milk jug and a bowl of sugar cubes described a graceful arc and landed all over Mr Allen's desk, splattering him and a file of papers with liquid.

'I'm *terribly* sorry!' she exclaimed in horror as Edward moved with more speed than she would have thought him capable of, gasping as the hot coffee hit him.

'How clumsy! Mop this mess up while I go upstairs and change,' he rasped.

'I'm so sorry, Mr Allen, Mr Walker,' she stuttered. She dabbed ineffectually at the sodden mess on the desk.

'Get a towel from the kitchen,' Edward barked as he hurried out of the office.

'Don't fret, love,' Mr Walker said reassuringly as he helped her put the coffee cups and sugar cubes back on the tray. 'Get a towel and we'll clear up this place in a jiffy.' Francesca felt like bursting into tears. She was mortified. More to the point she was terribly afraid that she'd seriously scalded Edward. She got a towel and a cloth and mopped up as best she could but she could see that Mr Walker's income tax form was sopping wet.

'There'll be plenty more where they came from,' the old gentleman chuckled as she tried her best to dry it out. 'Don't worry your head about it.'

Edward reappeared. 'You may go. We'll forgo the coffee.'

Francesca departed the office thoroughly chastened. She felt like a ten-year-old. What a completely gauche and uncool thing to do. She sank into her chair and cursed Mark. It was all his fault that she was stuck here, she thought irrationally as she tried to concentrate on a stack of bills that had to be typed up.

Half an hour later she heard Edward show Mr Walker to the door. She tensed as she heard her boss knock on her door and walk into her office.

'I suggest *flat* shoes in future. High heels are not suitable office attire,' he said curtly and disappeared back into his office. Francesca felt thoroughly deflated.

The traffic was bumper to bumper going home and Trixie needed to be walked. Wearily she changed into jeans and running shoes and pulled on her sheepskin jacket. A walk around the houses was the most Trixie was getting tonight. She'd take her for a walk on the pier on Sunday.

The following morning she luxuriated in her lie-in. It was bliss. She made herself tea and toast and went back to bed with *Vanity Fair*. Millie called an hour later and Francesca couldn't contain herself: she had to tell her of her experiences of the past three days.

'God Almighty,' giggled Millie. 'I wish I'd been there. The pair of them sound like two right oddballs.'

'They are, believe me. Miss Carter has the hots for Edward. She blushes if he looks at her. *He* can only think of his precious calculator. He never comes out of the office. And you should see the antique office equipment. The copier sounds as if it's going to expire every time I copy something and the type-writer is out of the ark.'

'Why don't you give it up and get something better if you want to work?'

'I'm not trained for anything, Millie. I'm too old.'

'Rubbish,' scoffed her sister. 'You're an intelligent woman, you shouldn't be content vegetating in that place.'

'Easy for you to say,' Francesca retorted.

'True,' Millie conceded mildly. 'Just don't limit your opportunities.'

Francesca thought of her sister's words as the following week dragged slowly by. On the Wednesday morning, Miss Carter presented her with a cassette. 'Please have these letters completed by lunchtime. They're quite detailed so take extra care,' she instructed.

Francesca took the cassette and inserted it into her Dictaphone. She listened to the letters once before typing them, to get their gist. She pressed the *replay* button and heard a strange whirring sound. She nearly had a heart attack as she pressed *rewind* and heard an even worse noise. Frantically she opened the Dictaphone. She couldn't believe her eyes as she saw the gobbled-up tape in ribbons.

'I don't believe it,' she muttered. 'Oh shit!' Miss Carter would have a canary. Francesca sat looking out the window. Her panic receded. She had enough crap in her life. She didn't need this. She was forty years old, a mother. What was she doing waiting to be chastised by Prudy Carter? She slipped her coat on and picked up her bag. She placed the tape in an envelope and wrote on the outside: *I suggest you update your equipment. I resign.*

She closed the office door behind her and let herself out as quietly as she could and felt the salt sea breeze on her face. Her first foray into the workforce had been a disaster. She wasn't going to repeat that experience in a hurry. Just as well she hadn't said anything to Mark. If he knew of her failure, her humiliation would be truly complete.

Joan Carter dropped Francesca's resignation note in the bin and smiled triumphantly to herself. She hadn't lasted long. Just as well. Francesca was a very glamorous woman. Joan had envied her from the bottom of her heart. How she longed to be tall and striking and confident and sophisticated, then perhaps dear Edward would take some notice of her. But she was small and plump and plain and it was

171

only in times of crisis, such as now, that her beloved realized just how much he depended on her. She would make him a nice strong cup of coffee just the way he liked it and break the news of Francesca's departure. And, until the next interloper arrived, dear Edward would be all hers. Today was a happy day indeed.

Chapter Eighteen

June

'I saw Mark and his new lady friend at the theatre last night,' Eva Collins prattled artlessly as the book-club group took a break from their discussion of Sheila O'Flanagan's delightfully bitchy novel, *Far From Over*.

'For goodness' sake, Eva!' Janet Dalton snapped, seeing the expression on Francesca's face.

'Oh, oh . . . sorry!' Eva realized that she had made a *faux pas*.

'It's OK, Eva. Don't apologize,' Francesca said coolly. 'You don't have to tiptoe around the subject. It's six months now, I *am* adjusting.'

'Of course you are, dear.' Eva flashed a triumphant look at Janet. 'You're doing very well indeed. You look much better than you did. That ghastly pallor is gone. What you need now is a nice holiday in the sun to bring a bit of colour to your cheeks. And who knows, you might even have a little holiday romance for yourself to perk your spirits up and give you back your confidence. Mark and his lady friend had wonderful tans. They must have been away.'

'Eva, would you pass me the sugar, please,' Janet growled and Francesca gave her a grateful smile. Janet was a dear and if Eva didn't shut up soon, Janet was going to let her have it. She could see Janet's annoyance on her behalf and it warmed her. Eva Collins was a gossipy old bitch and a plonkie as well, Francesca thought resentfully as she tried to keep her composure. She felt like crying. Hatred against her husband surged and swamped her like a tidal wave.

It was almost a physical blow to hear that Mark had been seen out and about with that woman. She felt wounded. And to think they had been on holiday together. Having fun. Making love. Did Mark ever think about her at all? Did he feel nothing for the pain he had caused her? Was she of so little consequence to him?

Her heart contracted with hurt and despair. She was lying when she said that she was adjusting. It was getting harder and harder, she thought in bewilderment. After her disastrous experience at Allen & Co. she'd become more reclusive than ever. Her self-confidence was nil. Every time she thought of the cowardly way she'd run from that office, she cringed. It was so unlike her. She'd changed so much since Mark had left her. She couldn't hack her marriage break-up even after six months.

Millie was always giving her pep talks, telling her to get out and about, but Francesca just didn't have the heart for it. She preferred to stay at home reading or watching TV rather than going out to meet people.

She'd kept on the book-club morning because she enjoyed it, but she'd given up her art class, mainly because Viv was in it and she was always pumping her for news and bringing up the subject of the separation. She hadn't been to the gym in months and she felt flabby and unfit. So much for losing weight, she thought wryly. She'd put it on.

In her fantasies of course she became slender and toned and looked a million dollars and swanned around on rich men's arms much to Mark's chagrin. If it weren't for her fantasies she would have gone round the twist altogether.

One day she would get it together, she kept promising herself. But not today. It was too much of an effort. It was far easier to wallow in self-pity and hug her suppurating wound to herself. No-one had ever suffered like she had, Francesca assured herself. *Her* pain and her grief were deeper than anyone else's. *Her* betrayal was the betrayal of all betrayals. The sharp, intense dart of anger and jealousy reminded her of just how betrayed she felt and how much of a shit Mark was. Would her emotions always be this intense? she wondered wearily.

'I'll tell you, Francesca, you're lucky that your boys are grown up.' Eva intruded on her thoughts as she nibbled at a cracker. Eva eyed Francesca slyly. She was watching her figure. She didn't want to end up looking stodgy and fat like the younger woman, although it gave her great satisfaction to notice the pounds creeping up on the woman she had always envied.

'Why is that, Eva?' Francesca responded politely, waiting for the next clanger with some anticipation.

'Well, at least they can deal with the break-up in some sort of mature way. Colin Doyle walked out on his wife for a twenty-year-old air hostess and he has two young daughters that he never sees. Do you know how he communicates with them?'

There was silence around the table as the six other women waited for Eva's next titbit.

'He e-mails them. Can you believe it? E-mail. Rita is going up the walls over it because they're becoming quite a handful. It's all emotional, of course. Feelings of abandonment and rejection, a child therapist told her. And *imagine*, that bastard wouldn't even go with her to discuss it. How selfish can you get?' she added self-righteously. 'I just don't understand it.'

'Eva, men come from a different planet,' interjected Frances Kelly caustically. 'They are a different species entirely. The trouble with men is that they're not women.'

Everyone laughed, even Francesca.

'Wait until I tell you about my fella,' Margo Williams declared ... Francesca sighed as the conversation eddied and flowed around her. Mark e-mailed Jonathan regularly, she knew that. They were civil to each other but Owen would have nothing to do with his father and that grieved her, although she was deeply touched by his loyalty. A father and son shouldn't be estranged. She was worried about Owen. He was doing his finals and he was as moody as hell. Apart from the stress of the exams, Francesca knew that he was worried about

176

her. He still wanted to go to the States for the summer but he felt guilty about leaving her, no matter how much she assured him that she would be fine.

She knew in her heart and soul that it wasn't right for her to be depending on him. He had his own life to lead. But she'd be terribly lonely without him. He was good at cheering her up. He teased her and made her forget her troubles for a while and he often bought her little treats out of the blue like a book by a favourite author or a CD he knew that she'd like. He'd drag her out for a walk with Trixie and tease her about how unfit she was. But as the exams had drawn closer, he'd had to buckle down and study, and as the pressure'd mounted he'd become tetchy and stressed. Francesca knew that he had to have his own space and she'd tried not to be needy.

Being alone was a nightmare though. Nothing had prepared her for it. She'd read articles about women whose husbands had left them and how they'd made new lives for themselves and discovered resources within that they didn't realize they had. They made her feel bloody inadequate, she thought resentfully. She didn't have any resources worth mentioning. She seemed to be living in a fog. Getting through one day after another, each one more or less the same as the last, with no objectives or goals to strive for. Nothing to give her life focus. She was simply existing. Mark had set up a separate bank account for her and closed their joint account. He paid a standing order into it once a month. He was still keeping her, supporting her financially, and part of her hated it.

She felt like a beggar with her hand out. But why should she feel like that? she argued with herself fiercely. She'd supported him emotionally, nurtured him, kept house for him, reared his children and looked after his father for the duration of their marriage. She had made her contribution to their life together, to their future, and he had gone and snatched that future from under her. She'd had no time to prepare for her swift and drastic change of circumstances. He could damn well support her, she raged.

She hadn't seen Mark for three months. In the new year, he'd come back a couple of times to collect further belongings and clear out his small study of personal papers. Each time he'd called she'd left him to it and taken Trixie for a walk on Howth Pier, telling him to put on the alarm when he was leaving. Otherwise all their business was conducted in terse, unfriendly phone calls.

The last time she'd seen him had been at a mutual friend's mother's funeral. They'd sat stiffly side by side in the church and she'd sneaked occasional little looks at him and was furious because he looked so well. His hair was cut short, tighter than he'd worn it when he was with her. It made him look younger, and somehow less of a banker type than before. He looked fit and lean and healthy, and she was extremely conscious of her extra pounds. She'd hoped that he might appear stressed and tired like she was so that she could comfort herself that he wasn't lying on a bed of roses either. It was absolutely galling to see him looking so well cared for. Francesca couldn't suppress her bitterness and had given short, clipped answers to all his polite queries about her wellbeing. He'd invited her to Roly's for lunch afterwards but she'd refused. Said she had appointments to keep and felt furious at him that he had the nerve to think that she would sit through a lunch with him making polite chit-chat as though nothing of consequence had happened to them.

She wanted to scream at him that he had ruined her life, and destroyed her trust. She'd wanted to call him every vile and vicious name that she could think of. She'd walked away from him in the graveyard struggling to keep her composure, determined that he would not see the tears in her eyes. She'd gone home, cried her eyes out and then eaten a packet of Jaffa Cakes to comfort herself. She hadn't tasted even one of them and had been disgusted with herself for her gluttony. It had been one of the worst days and nights she'd endured since their separation. And, incomprehensibly, as she'd lain in their big double bed and remembered how well he'd looked, desire had suffused her and she longed to feel his arms around her and his hard body on top of hers comforting her with the intimacy of loving, companionable sex.

The aching want enraged and terrified her at the same time. Would she ever have sex again? Would she ever feel safe and trusting within the shelter of a man's arms? Was aloneness her way of life from now on? Mark didn't have those fears or unfulfilled desires, she thought angrily, picturing him lying in bed with his chic, sexy, career woman who probably knew the *Kama Sutra* off by heart. His needs and desires were being taken care of. That was all that mattered to him. He probably never even gave her a thought these days.

He seemed totally unruffled by their separation. He'd gone seamlessly from his marriage to her, to his relationship with that bitch. It infuriated Francesca. How come that he wasn't *suffering* like she was? She knew that he wasn't having sleepless nights, his stomach knotted up in fear and tension, floundering about with no prospects of peace of mind ever coming his way again. That was the legacy he had dumped on her. Her despair was all his fault. She'd groaned as she pummelled the pillows into a comfortable shape and tried desperately to sleep. The harder she tried the more it eluded her until in desperation she'd swallowed two sleeping tablets. Anything for oblivion, she thought grimly, ignoring the niggling feeling of guilt that she was taking far too many sleeping tablets lately and that it really wasn't a solution.

Her bitterness and resentment ate away at her day after day. It was with her from the time that she woke up in the morning to the time she fell into restless, troubled, tablet-induced sleep in the early hours. She felt as though she was wrapped in a strait-jacket of darkness that she could not shift, no matter how hard she tried. She regularly cursed God for inflicting such a cross on her and to her dismay she even found that she could not be with Millie, Aidan and the girls for long without resenting their happy family life.

She hated the person she'd become but she didn't know what to do to change. Even as she sat with her book-club group, she felt like yelling at them all to shut up and stop their silly gossiping because she couldn't concentrate on her trauma.

Unthinkingly, she ate another biscuit, unaware that Janet was watching her with pity and understanding in her eyes.

Chapter Nineteen

Mark yawned as he sat in the bumper-to-bumper traffic as it crawled past the Merrion Gates. It was hot, he was tired and this gridlock was enough to send anyone's blood pressure up a couple of points. He'd had a long day. He'd flown back from Brussels that afternoon after a particularly gruelling round of meetings and gone into the bank to find out that his secretary was leaving to move to Cork with her partner. Jenny had been with him for the past ten years and she was the best secretary he'd ever had. She was organized, efficient, great at using her own initiative and he depended on her more than he'd ever depended on any woman in his life, he thought morosely as he waved a driver on the slip road to go ahead. Now he was going to have to get used to someone else and they were going to have to get used to him.

Today had been a crap day. His stomach rumbled. He was hungry. He'd had a plastic meal on the plane and that was it. A sudden longing for roast beef and mushy peas came into his head. Francesca cooked terrific roasts and her mushy peas were unlike anyone else's. Done to perfection, steeped overnight in the bicarbonate of soda, just the way he liked them.

Nikki was not the world's greatest cook, he acknowledged. She wouldn't cook mushy peas for him because she claimed they made him fart. If he farted in front of Nikki her pert little nose would wrinkle in disgust and she'd look at him very disapprovingly. It was difficult containing his farts sometimes. With Francesca he could fart in bed in comfort knowing all that she'd say to him was a laughing, 'Mark, you're rotten. Light a match.'

He missed Francesca sometimes. He missed the easiness of living with her. They were so used to each other's little foibles, likes and dislikes. He hadn't had to make much effort after the first couple of years, he thought a little guiltily. She hadn't demanded it of him like Nikki did. Mark yawned. He could do without making any efforts today. He was beat. He wondered idly what Francesca was cooking for dinner today. Maybe she'd barbecue because it was so hot. His mouth watered at the thought of spare ribs and chicken breasts, baked potatoes and a side salad.

Mark sighed. Francesca was still extremely bitter and antagonistic towards him. She had hardly been able to bear sitting beside him at Mona Cook's funeral. Suppressed anger had oozed from every pore. He frowned at the memory. Her anger always made him feel guilty and he hated feeling guilty. OK, their marriage had broken up. It happened to millions of couples but he'd treated her very well.

One guy he worked with in Brussels had been taken to court by his wife because he was so lax in paying maintenance.

Once when he'd bumped into Ann Mitchell, a friend of Francesca's, soon after Christmas, she'd lit into him and told him that he was an awful bastard. He'd indignantly replied that he'd let Francesca live in the house and that he was paying her a damn good allowance. She'd rounded on him in fury and said, Big deal, he could afford it. That was no hardship.

He'd been as mad as hell with her, because deep down he knew the accusation was true. There was no mortgage on the house. He'd paid it off long ago. It was a little goldmine now that property prices had soared. He was happy enough for Francesca to live in the house. It was a family asset and at the back of his mind was the knowledge that if things didn't work out with Nikki he could always go back to Howth and work out some sort of separate living arrangement, whether Francesca liked it or not. He pushed the memory of Ann's contemptuous barbs aside. The friends had definitely divided into two camps. His and hers. Most of them, after the initial shock on hearing of the break-up, had readjusted and eventually he and Nikki had been invited to dinner parties as a couple. Mark knew that a lot of their acquaintances stayed friends with him because of what he could do for them, loan-wise and business-wise. He was no fool. The ones he had most respect for were the ones who were polite to him when they met but whose loyalties lay with Francesca. At least they weren't users, he mused as the traffic inched past the Blackrock clinic.

He glanced at the clock in the dash. Six-ten. Nikki was probably somewhere in the traffic behind him in a taxi. She'd been to London for the day dealing with a new London-based acquisition. She'd been there for four days the previous week. Mark smiled. She thrived on it and she was damn good at her job.

The apartment was like an oven when he got in and he flung open all the windows and balcony doors to let a breeze whisper through. He poured himself a shot of whiskey and sat down on the uncomfortable sofa. He hated it with a vengeance. How he missed his soft leather one that you could sink into and relax. He must have dozed because the next thing he heard was Nikki's key in the lock.

'Hello, darling, you look wrecked.' She greeted him with a kiss on the cheek. She looked as fresh as a daisy in her favourite taupe Donna Karan business suit. She kicked off her beige high heels and sank elegantly onto the sofa beside him. 'Tough day?' she asked with a yawn.

'*Very!*' He groaned for added emphasis.

'Me too.' She cuddled in and gave him a proper kiss. He kissed her back, hoping she wasn't going to want anything more. He was knackered. The kiss deepened, her tongue flicking lightly against his, her mouth open wider inviting him to reciprocate. He sucked her tongue the way she liked him to.

'Sexy man,' she whispered, running her hand lightly over his crotch. 'I need a bath though, London was stinking hot. And Heathrow was *indescribable*. I hate that airport with a vengeance.' She stood up and smiled down at him. 'Darling, be a pet and pour me a glass of wine. There's a nice

Chablis in the fridge. And there's strip loins, salmon steaks, trout, and pork in the freezer. Any of them would be nice with a Caesar salad. And you could do some of your gorgeous garlic potatoes. I thought you would have started cooking already. I'm starving!' She sashayed out of the room and Mark's heart sank. He'd forgotten that he was on cooks today.

He hauled himself up from the sofa and went reluctantly to the kitchen. At the beginning it had been a bit of a novelty. He'd liked cooking to impress her. Having the candles lit and flowers on the table. The novelty soon wore off when he realized that Nikki expected him to do his share of cooking. He hated coming home from a hard day at work and having to turn around and rustle up a meal. Francesca had always had a meal ready for him, but then she'd been at home all day with nothing else to do. Nikki was working hard at her job too, he had to admit, and it wouldn't be fair to expect her to cook all the time. They could eat out, he supposed. They did regularly, but he wasn't up to showering and changing and driving into town or to Monkstown. Invariably they met business acquaintances or friends; tonight he just wasn't in the humour to talk to anyone.

The desire for roast beef and mushy peas assaulted him once more and his stomach rumbled loudly. With a sigh that came from his toes he threw two strip loins into the microwave and pressed the defrost button. In the background he could hear the sound of running water and Nikki humming to herself.

'Don't forget my wine, darling,' she called.

'Coming,' Mark said wearily as he took the chilled

bottle out of the fridge and got to work with the corkscrew.

Nikki lay in the scented bath and sipped the wine Mark had brought her. She held the cold glass to her cheek. It was refreshing after the humidity and air-lessness of London. She was tired. It had been intense but she'd been on top of her brief and had held up her end very satisfactorily. She was looking forward to telling Mark all about it later on.

She wriggled her toes. Her feet ached from wear-ing high heels all day. She wouldn't dream of wearing flat shoes though. They gave the wrong impression. You couldn't eyeball someone wearing loafers the way you could wearing three-inch heels. There was one particular guy that she hated. Clive Morton, an investment banker with the new lot. He was so damn arrogant. He'd practically ignored her at the first meetings until she had started asking him direct and well-researched questions. He'd brushed her off several times until she had called him on it and asked him if he had a problem dealing with her. Her blunt-ness had taken him aback. Now he afforded her polite, informative answers to her questions, but he disliked her. There was often a lot of negativity from the underdog during a takeover or merger and she was used to that, but Clive Morton had pushed her too far. She was glad that she was taller than Clive in her heels, she thought smugly, taking a sip of her chilled wine. And by God she would wear the highest of heels in her dealings with him. He'd look up to her one way or the other, while she would make it very clear that she was looking down at him.

Nikki smiled with satisfaction, remembering the hostility in the banker's lizard-like eyes. 'Tough,' she murmured and took another sip of wine.

The smell of sizzling steak wafted through the partly open bathroom door. Nikki inhaled deeply. This was the life, she thought happily. After a hard but satisfying day's work, dinner cooked by Mark – he was an excellent cook, better than she was – good wine, conversation about all kinds of things including work, and then delightful lovemaking in her king-sized bed. What more could a woman want?

I'd like to be married to him. The thought slithered into her head. It came every so often. They'd been living together for six months now and it was working out rather well, much better than she'd anticipated after the trauma of the initial break. They were accepted as a couple now, though there had been an enormous amount of shock at the office when they'd told colleagues that they were together. Some of the wives had taken it very badly and were quite snooty to her at functions. Nikki didn't give a hoot. That was their problem. She wasn't living her life to suit them. Mark had hated it all. It made him feel uncomfortable. His colleagues knew and liked Francesca and he detested being the subject of gossip. However, there had been nothing to do but grit their teeth and get on with it and, eventually, as time passed they were no longer a nine-day wonder. All in all it hadn't been as rocky as she'd expected and she and Mark had settled into a very nice life together. It was time to take the relationship a step further. Marriage was the next logical step.

Nikki frowned. Mark was adamant that he

wouldn't divorce Francesca. He wouldn't subject her to the trauma of it. It would kill her, he'd told Nikki when she'd light-heartedly broached the subject one night after a couple of drinks. That response had sobered her up pretty quickly. And Owen would never forgive him either, he'd added for good measure, much to her intense irritation. In her view, Owen needed a good kick up the ass for his childish behaviour.

'But he's not even speaking to you now,' Nikki retorted. 'So what difference would it make?'

'He'll come round,' Mark declared confidently.

Selfish little shit, Nikki thought privately. Mark was profoundly troubled by his son's rejection. It was one of the big drawbacks in their relationship. The other big bugbear was Francesca. It really annoyed Nikki the hold that woman still had on Mark. He'd been very upset after that funeral they'd been to, where she'd hardly spoken to him. It had thoroughly pissed him off and given him a dose of the guilts for a week. When Mark was in guilt mode he got moody and quiet and was very difficult to live with. It drove Nikki nuts and she had to try hard not to betray her irritation.

Francesca was an adult, for God's sake. Let her get on with her life and not be hanging on to Mark's coat tails. Marriages ended. That was a fact of life. And their marriage couldn't have been up to much, otherwise Mark wouldn't have got involved with her. It was bad enough that he was shelling out a fortune to keep Francesca. That big house out in Howth that she was mouldering away in must be worth half a million at least. All paid for because of Mark's hard work. She'd told him that he should sell and split the proceeds but Mark had said that it was Francesca's home. Nikki had little sympathy for her. Any woman who was so dependent on a man the way Francesca was deserved a kick in the backside to make her stand on her own two feet.

A gleam came into her eye. If Mark wouldn't bring up the subject with Francesca, she would. Woman to woman. She'd get her to see how unfair she was being. How needy and undignified she was being by not letting Mark move on and have a new life. Surely the woman had *some* pride. *Some* self-respect.

If Nikki wanted to be Mark's wife she'd have to be pro-active and that was one thing she was very good at. Little titch Clive Morton was testament to that, she thought contemptuously. She wasn't going to let a whingy, wishy-washy, clinging vine get in the way Nikki decided firmly. Francesca Kirwan would be getting a visit from her in the very near future and would be told in no uncertain terms to step aside and butt out of her and Mark's life. Enough was more than enough, reasoned Nikki as she drained her glass.

Chapter Twenty

'Oh hell! Is it that time of year again?' Mark flicked the gold-embossed invitation onto his desk and grimaced.

'Who is it from?' Nikki enquired as she sipped coffee and pencilled in a clue on the Crossaire. She and Mark had travelled into the bank together and were having coffee before starting the day's work.

'It's from Karen Marshall. It's her annual gala for Cancer Research. A couple of years back I arranged for the bank to give an annual donation so we were always honoured guests.'

'We?' Nikki arched an eyebrow.

'Francesca and I.'

'And is she included in the invite this year?' Nikki asked.

'No. It says Mark Kirwan and guest,' Mark admitted.

'Good, then I'll come with you,' Nikki said crisply.

'I was thinking of not going this year. Maybe I should find out if Francesca is going. It might be awkward,' Mark hedged.

Nikki smiled sweetly. 'I won't feel at all awkward, Mark.'

'Er . . . well, I was thinking of Francesca really.' Mark frowned. 'There'll be a lot of people there that we know.'

'So?' Nikki's tone held a hint of steel.

'Oh, come on, Nikki, don't be like that,' Mark retorted defensively.

'Don't be like what, Mark? I'm sick of this crap. Either we're a couple or we're not. I won't be shoved into the background when it suits you. We live together. I'm your partner and if you can't deal with it maybe we should split,' Nikki exploded.

'For God's sake, will you keep your voice down? Someone might hear,' Mark hissed, indicating the door to his secretary's office.

'I don't give a hoot whether anyone hears or not. I'm fed up with this, Mark. I'm fed up with being treated like a second-class citizen. Do you hear me?' Nikki's voice rose shrilly. 'We've been living together six months now. I will *not* be hidden away and ignored just because your ex can't let go of the past and get on with her life. That's her problem, not mine. OK?' She glared at him, her face thrust aggressively up towards his, her eyes dark with anger.

'OK, OK, calm down. We'll go to the bloody thing together,' Mark said agitatedly.

'Good!' Nikki retorted and swept out of the office as he looked at her retreating back in astonishment.

It was the first time he had ever seen Nikki exhibit temper. She was always very together. The last thing he needed was her on his back. Being stuck in the middle of two women's sensibilities was a nightmare.

He'd only been trying to do the right thing. Bloody Karen Marshall and her damn charity do, he scowled. He should have kept his mouth shut, sent his regrets and Nikki would never have known a thing about it.

Nikki marched down the carpeted corridor to take the lift to her own office two floors below. She was raging. Mark was still putting Francesca before her and it galled her. Her temper had erupted out of her, surprising her as much as Mark. But months of resentment at being second best had been too much to contain and the dam had burst. She couldn't believe that she'd suggested splitting. What if he'd agreed? Nikki gave a little shudder as she stepped into the empty lift and pressed the button for her floor. It gave her some satisfaction that he had backed down so quickly, but it was an issue that shouldn't have arisen at this stage in their relationship. She was going to have to do something about the huge thorn in her side that was Francesca Kirwan. Maybe this gala event would be just the place to have a quiet word, Nikki reflected as she marched into her office and dumped her elegant briefcase on her rosewood desk.

Enough was enough. It was time to sort Madame Francesca out for good!

'Hello?' Francesca sounded chirpy enough, Mark thought with relief as he heard her voice down the phone.

'Hi, Francesca, it's me,' he said evenly.

'Yes?'

Mark's heart sank at the instant frostiness. Wasn't she ever going to give him a break? He kept his tone deliberately up. 'I was wondering if you're going to Karen Marshall's charity thing this year? I just wanted you to know that I'll be going with Nikki.'

'Mark, there really is no need for you to phone me to tell me of your and Nikki's social diary. It's of supreme indifference to me, I can assure you.'

Mark could hear the contempt in his wife's voice. He felt his anger rise. He was trying to do his best, for heaven's sake. 'Look, I just wanted, out of politeness, to let you know that we were going, that's all, Francesca. I didn't want you to be embarrassed.'

'Mark, rest assured I won't be the slightest bit embarrassed meeting you and your new woman in public, if that's what you think. Why should *I* be embarrassed?' she added pointedly. 'Believe me, what you do with your life and with whom are no concern of mine any more. Is there anything else?'

'No, not really.' Mark sighed. 'How's Owen? When's he heading off?'

'He's fine. He's going soon.' Francesca kept the information to a bare minimum. He wondered why he bothered. He tried once more.

'Are you going to go to Karen's bash?'

'That's none of your business. Goodbye,' she said curtly and hung up.

Mark stared at the phone and shook his head. Francesca had not shown a scintilla of forgiveness since they'd parted. If anything she was even more condemning. Well, fuck her, Nikki was right. They were a couple now and if Francesca didn't like it she could lump it. Mark opened the Bergmann file on his desk. He needed to keep on top of things. One of his colleagues had been sidelined recently to make way for a new up-and-coming hot shot; Mark was determined that wasn't going to happen to him. He buzzed the intercom for his secretary. Rhona was youthful and fresh, in her early twenties. She made him feel ancient.

Her eager, Dart-accented voice answered immediately. 'Yaas, Mark?' He disliked the unmistakable southside cadence that was all over the airwaves these days.

'Get me a coffee, Rhona, please, and you didn't have the *FT* on my desk this morning. That's twice this week it hasn't been here, please don't let it happen again,' he said crossly.

'They were all gone,' Rhona said plaintively.

'Well, Rhona, just make sure that you get in in time to get my copy in future,' he retorted and clicked off.

How he missed Jenny. She'd always had all the papers for him and fresh coffee percolating and she'd known his humours as well as Francesca had. She'd known his job inside out, and always had her finger on the pulse. Poor Rhona was still only finding her feet, although she was quick, he had to give her that. Maybe he'd been a bit crusty. It wasn't fair to take his bad humour over Nikki and Francesca out on her.

'Sorry I barked,' he apologized when she arrived with his coffee five minutes later. 'Bit of a headache,' he lied.

'That's OK. I can get you some Panadol if you want.' Her helpfulness made him feel like a heel.

'No, no, I'm fine,' he said hastily. 'Just get me Anton

195

Chagall in the Paris office, will you? And book my flight to Brussels for next Tuesday.' He smiled at her and was relieved when she smiled back. He didn't want his new secretary thinking he was difficult to work for.

'Yaas, Mark, I'll take care of that straight away,' Rhona said smoothly.

Why couldn't she say 'yes' instead of 'yaas'. It drove him nuts, he thought irritably as he watched her leave. Women were the bane of his life, he decided as he reluctantly directed his gaze at the sheaf of figures in front of him.

His mobile phone rang and his heart sank as he saw his father's number come up. Gerald was being such a pain lately. He'd had a bad dose of indigestion and been convinced he was having a heart attack or angina. Mark had had to go over to him in the middle of the night and take him into Casualty. After a wait of six hours he'd been told to lose weight and sent home with a note for his own doctor.

It was only since he'd split with Francesca that Mark had realized just how demanding his father was. His wife had shouldered a lot of that burden and he'd taken it for granted, he acknowledged with a moment of remorse. The phone went into divert. No doubt there'd be a testy message for him. He'd listen to it later. It had been a bad morning so far; Gerald would only make him feel worse.

Francesca swallowed hard and her stomach clenched into knots as she hung up the phone. She was red-faced with fury. She shook her head at her reflection in the mirror over the hall table. 'What a cheek,' she raged. 'Arrogant, smug bastard!' Just where did Mark Kirwan get off, ringing her to tell her he was taking his fancy piece to Karen Marshall's annual bash? Why did he still think that she'd care? Did he think that she was sitting at home pining after him? He'd always had a big ego and this was pure proof of it.

A thought struck her. She hadn't received an invitation to the party. Karen had sent an invitation to Mark and Nikki and left her out. Tears sprang to her eyes as darts of hurt assaulted her. Karen Marshall had been one of the few to phone on hearing of the break-up, and offer kind words and solace. Obviously the donation from EuroBank Irl. was more important than friendship. Francesca felt betrayed. She'd known Karen for five years and had held coffee mornings for her various charities. She and Mark had moved in the same social scene as Karen and her husband Dennis, a client at EuroBank. They'd gone to the theatre and opera occasionally as couples. They weren't bosom buddies, Francesca acknowledged bitterly, but she'd expected more from Karen.

She went into the kitchen, switched on the kettle and stood looking out of the window. The tree peony was in full bloom in the flower bed nearest the house. Mark had bought it for Valentine's Day two years ago and she'd been thrilled. The rich reddish-pink blossoms were enormous, opening up to the sun. She felt like going out and pulling every single bloom off and mashing them into the ground. She hated him and every reminder of him.

Just when she'd be getting on some sort of an even keel after the break-up Mark would go and pull a stunt like this. He did it all the time. It grieved her to think of him and that woman swanning into Karen's party, while she'd been deleted from the scene as though she'd never existed. How come he was having such a wonderful life and she was as miserable as hell? Where was the justice in that? She made herself a cup of coffee and buttered several thick slices of Vienna roll and ate them smothered in blackberry jam. An hour later she parked the car at Clontarf Dart station and hurried to get a ticket, afraid a train would thunder into the station before she got upstairs to the platform. She need not have worried, the monitor told her there wasn't one due for another eight minutes, so she sat on the hard green metal bench and turned her face up to the sun. It was a warm, balmy day. She regretted wearing her black trouser suit. Francesca contemplated taking off the jacket, but the top she was wearing underneath was sleeveless and didn't cover her ass and she was far too conscious of her weight gain to reveal her unwelcome pounds.

She was meeting Owen for lunch and she wanted to buy some gifts for him to take to Jonathan in America. She frowned, thinking of Mark's enquiries about Owen. Her son had resisted all her urgings to ignore what was happening with herself and Mark and to make an effort to patch up their relationship.

'Mam, I just don't want to have anything to do with him, so just leave it, OK?' Owen had retorted angrily the last time she'd brought up the subject and the underlying hostility in his voice had dismayed her. If she was furious with Mark, Owen was twice as wrathful.

'It's my treat, Mam, let's go to Little Caesar's in Temple Bar,' Owen suggested as he met her off the Dart in Tara Street.

'Whatever you say.' Francesca smiled, her heart lifting at the sight of her beloved son. Remembering Karen's betrayal, she felt at least with Owen she had one staunch ally at her side.

'God, Mam, you'll be baked alive in that,' he remarked as they walked up along the quays. 'Take your jacket off.'

'I can't,' she murmured.

'Why not?' Owen glanced down at her, curbing his long, loping stride to suit hers.

'I just can't.'

He looked perplexed.

'I'm too fat,' she murmured.

'Don't be daft, Mam,' he said stoutly. 'Who cares if your ass wobbles a bit? That's what happens when you get to your age,' he teased.

'You want to go headlong into the Liffey, boy?' Francesca drawled.

'You and whose army, Ma?' Owen gave her a friendly poke in the arm.

She was breathless by the time they reached the restaurant. She'd got so unfit it was unbelievable. She was going to have to take herself in hand and do something about it. Maybe she'd join a gym, she thought unenthusiastically as she perused the menu and opted for nice, fattening garlic mushrooms for her starter.

'Are you sure you're going to be all right when I'm gone, Mam?' Owen said after they'd ordered.

'Don't worry about me, Owen. I'm fine. Honest,'

she assured him. 'It took me a while to get over the shock of it, but I'm getting by. I'd really freak if I thought you wouldn't go to America because of me.'

'I know. I just feel a bit mean about it. I'm afraid you'll be lonely in the house on your own.' Owen fiddled with the pepper and salt.

'I might get a part-time job or do something for a charity a couple of mornings a week,' Francesca said vaguely. 'To be honest I quite like pottering about doing my own thing.'

'Yeah, pottering about is OK for an eighty-year-old, Ma, for God's sake. You're only forty,' he burst out, concern written all over his face.

Francesca couldn't help but laugh. 'I'm just taking a bit of time out, Owen. It's nice to get off the tread-mill for a while. Life with your father was a little frenetic at times. All the social stuff, all the travel, taking care of his clothes and packing for him every time he went abroad. Looking after your granddad – and you know what a chore that was – not to talk about washing your filthy football gear,' she said in mock rebuke. 'It's nice having time to myself. I've never had time to get to know myself. That's what I'm doing now.'

'Oh! I suppose I hadn't thought of it like that. I just want you to be happy again, Mam. I know you cry at night. I've heard you.'

'Love, I won't deny I have rough days. I'm lonely sometimes. I miss what your father and I had. That's life, I'm afraid, and I just have to get on with it.'

'You could take in a lodger,' Owen suggested brightly. 'There's a huge shortage of accommodation.'

'Thanks but no thanks, Owen. I've got Trixie for

company. She's more than enough.' Francesca chuckled. 'Of course, I could always do a Mrs Robinson on it and seduce a younger man.'

'Who's Mrs Robinson?' Owen demanded. 'Never heard you talking about her.'

'You idiot. Did you never see the film *The Graduate* with Anne Bancroft and Dustin Hoffman, about an older woman who seduces a younger man?'

'Gee, Mam, that was in the dark ages, long, long before my time. Anyway, you're not old enough to be an older woman yet. Can I have one of those garlic mushrooms while you have one of my chicken wings?' The food had arrived and Owen was eager to tuck in.

'Help yourself.' Francesca proffered her plate, wishing that she could tell her son that she was dreading his leaving and that it was his love and support that had got her through the worst days of her life.

She was hot, sweaty and tired when she got home with her shopping later that afternoon. There was a pile of post in the hall but she left it on the table and hurried up to the bedroom to get out of her clothes and have a shower. It was only later, lying on her sun lounger on the deck, catching the evening rays, that she flipped through the bills and opened the slim cream envelope with her name on it.

Mortification shot through her as she read Karen Marshall's kind handwritten note and invitation to her gala evening. So Karen hadn't deleted her from the guest list despite Francesca's unkind thoughts earlier. And she'd written that as Mark had been invited to bring a guest she was more than welcome to bring one too.

Francesca sighed. How she longed to be able to waltz into Karen's party, a stone lighter, on the arms of a handsome hunk. Now that she was invited to the party she was going to have to get something new to wear. None of her posh frocks fitted her any more.

She could invite Millie as her guest, she supposed, but it did look a bit pathetic dragging her sister along as a companion when her husband would be with a glamour puss ten years younger than her. Maybe she just wouldn't go, Francesca dithered. She had a few days to think about it, she'd make a decision by the weekend, she thought drowsily as her eyes closed and she fell into a welcome snooze.

Chapter Twenty-one

'Bye, darling, I'll see you in Paris on Friday evening. I can't wait.' Nikki wrapped her arms around Mark and kissed him passionately. 'It'll be great, Mark. We'll have a real romantic weekend for ourselves. We deserve it.'

'Yes, we do.' Mark slid his hands into the opening of her silk dressing gown and felt the soft warmth of her body. 'I'll miss you,' he whispered. 'Five days is a long time.'

'I know,' Nikki murmured as she slid her hand down to his crotch.

'Ah, Nikki, we haven't time for this, the taxi's outside.' Mark drew away reluctantly.

'Five more minutes won't make any difference. He won't care, he's getting paid,' Nikki said huskily as she unzipped his trousers and slid her hand into his briefs.

Mark groaned and drew her tight against him again, pulling down her silk panties. He pushed her up against the wall and thrust himself into her, supporting her as she wrapped her slender legs around him. 'Oh Mark,' she muttered as he moved rhythmically, frantically, 'you're the best lover I ever had.'

'Nikki, Nikki, you'll murder me,' he muttered hoarsely when he'd come with a long shuddering sigh. They held each other, kissing tenderly.

'I have to go, I really have to go or I'll miss the flight,' Mark murmured against her hair.

'I'll miss you. Phone every night, won't you? We can talk dirty to each other.'

Mark laughed. 'You're incorrigible.'

'And you're dead sexy,' Nikki purred as she straightened his tie while he adjusted his clothing.

'Go back to bed, you still have a couple of hours before you have to go to work,' Mark said as he ran his fingers through his hair and picked up his travel bags. 'I love you.'

'I love you too,' Nikki assured him.

As Mark sat in the taxi on the way to the airport he felt invigorated. Nikki's sensual farewell made him feel ready for anything. To find a woman like her at his age was a real bonus and he was going to make sure he kept her happy, he vowed. OK, so they'd gone through a rough patch but all couples went through those. They'd had to adjust to living together under difficult circumstances and they'd come through well enough. If only Francesca would be a bit more civilized about things and Owen would step down off his very high horse, life wouldn't be too bad at all, Mark reflected, feeling more cheerful than he had in a long time.

He was looking forward to his trip to Brussels, he

had to admit. He could flop in the apartment after work, read and watch videos, and catch up with old friends. He liked having time to himself. Francesca had come to Brussels regularly with him when he'd first started commuting but as time had gone on it had been easier for her to stay at home with the boys and he'd grown to like his time alone.

Five days to do his own thing and then a glorious weekend of eating gourmet food, drinking fine wines and making passionate love to Nikki. In Paris. Mark stretched and yawned. Life was definitely improving.

Nikki lay in bed exhilarated. She felt the relationship with Mark was finally back on track. It had been rocky going now and again and she'd felt at times that Mark was regretting his involvement with her. There were times when he withdrew from her completely and got moody and silent and it freaked her. It was stressful to say the least and trying to hide her anxiety about the whole situation from him was draining. Nikki felt she was in limbo and it was starting to do her head in. The episode over Karen Marshall's charity do had been the straw that broke the camel's back but since she'd lost her temper Mark had gone out of his way to be nice to her: it had been his idea that they spend the weekend in Paris after his week in Brussels.

When he'd suggested it, it had given her such a lift she'd been on a high for the rest of the week. This was more like it should be, she thought dreamily. This was the way it could always be, if only he'd divorce Francesca and put the past behind him once and for all.

Nikki shot up in bed. Why not? she thought to herself. It was a perfect time to do it. Why wait until that party to confront Francesca and have to worry about whether Mark would overhear or not? He was out of the country. She could take the morning off and go and sort Francesca out once and for all. Then they could all get on with their lives. Mark was far too soft to deal with the issue. He allowed that woman to blackmail him emotionally and it was very unfair on him. Nikki felt extremely sorry for him sometimes. It was clear he wouldn't do anything about the matter. She would just have to sort it. She felt energized. Now that she had decided on a course of action she felt much more optimistic and in control.

'Bring a suit.' Francesca insisted.

'Mam, what do I need a suit for? I'm going to be working in a bar. I don't want to frighten away customers,' Owen explained patiently as his mother unpacked his jumbled suitcase and began to place T-shirts and sweatshirts into plastic bags. 'And what are you doing that for?'

'It helps to keep them from creasing and it's easier to sort them out when you're unpacking and putting them away. Now get your grey suit, you never know whom you might meet or what job interview might come up.'

'OK then,' Owen submitted with bad grace.

'Look, why don't you go into town and do your bits and pieces and I'll take over here.'

'Mam, I want to travel light now, right?' he warned.

'Right!' she agreed. 'Go on now and get out of my hair. You're interfering with my pottering.' She grinned at him. 'Oh, and by the way,' she added lightly, 'when I was speaking to your father the other day he was asking about you. Maybe you should give him a call before you go.'

'Leave it, Ma.'

'He is your father, love.'

'Unfortunately,' Owen said gruffly. 'I'm off. I'll see you later. Do you want anything from town?'

'Don't forget to get a couple of six-packs of Tayto for Jonathan.'

'He's e-mailed his list. Lion bars, Crunchies, crisps and Dubliner cheese. I'll be like a little corner shop,' Owen grumbled as he ran a comb through his hair and picked up his wallet and mobile from the chest of drawers. 'See ya, Ma.' He grabbed her in a bear hug, lifted her off her feet and swung her around. 'Love ya,' he said, exuberantly kissing her on the cheek before planting her on terra firma.

'I love you too, now get outta here.'

Francesca struggled not to burst into tears. It was the day before Owen was due to leave for America and she was dreading it more than she had thought possible. She heard him run downstairs and only when the front door had closed behind him did she sink down on his bed and bury her hands in her face as the tears overflowed. What would she do without him? The house would be so lonely and empty. It had been bad enough when Jonathan had gone to America, she'd missed him for months and felt an emptiness every time she went into his room that had unsettled her. But at least she'd had Mark and Owen to buttress her. Now with Mark gone from their marriage and Owen leaving for the summer, she felt utterly bereft. Her life had changed completely in the past months. The rug had been pulled from under her feet and all she could see ahead of her was an empty, lonely existence.

Francesca shivered. She was frightened. Her life had no focus any more. What was she going to do with herself?

Wearily she stood up and continued folding and packing Owen's case. She had just finished and was contemplating whether to have a cup of coffee or a shower first when the doorbell rang. She glanced at her watch: ten-thirty, it must be the postman. It could be a book-club selection parcel for her. She'd ordered several titles from a club they subscribed to. She ran her fingers through her hair and tightened the belt of her dressing gown and hurried downstairs to open the door.

'Hi.' She smiled, expecting to see the friendly face of her local postman. The smile froze on her face as she recognized the extremely glamorous, steely-eyed young woman who stood on the doorstep.

'May I come in?' asked Nikki Langan. 'We need to talk.'

Twenty-two

Francesca stared at Nikki, stunned. This was the last person she'd ever expected to see standing on her doorstep. Fear struck her. 'Is Mark all right?' she asked sharply, figuring that the only reason the bitch would come to her door would be to tell her that something had happened to her husband.

'He's fine,' Nikki said coldly. 'Well, not exactly fine. That's why I want to talk to you. I think I should step inside, if you don't mind. I don't particularly relish a discussion on the doorstep.'

Her self-possession so rattled Francesca that she found herself stepping back obediently to let the younger woman in. She caught sight of her reflection in the hall mirror and cursed silently, raging that she'd been caught looking like the wreck of the Hesperus. Her hair was unruly and unbrushed compared to the other woman's immaculate chignon. Her cheeks were blotchy and tearstained from her crying bout, her eyes red-rimmed. She looked an absolute disaster. Normally at this hour of the morning she'd be dressed and have her make-up on. Trust Miss Bloody Perfect to arrive the very morning she was in a heap.

She was wearing a superbly tailored tangerine business suit that suited her colouring to a T. Her make-up was faultless, and very professionally applied, Francesca had to admit. Her slim black briefcase was a very elegant accessory as well as being practical. She looked like one of those glam lawyers out of *Ally McBeal*, Francesca thought enviously, wondering what on earth such a superbabe had seen in her husband, when she surely could have had any man that she wanted.

'What's wrong with Mark?' she demanded truculently.

'He wants a divorce but he won't ask you for one because he's afraid that you'll go to pieces, basically,' Nikki informed her crisply.

'I beg your pardon?' Francesca was horrified. Mark had never mentioned divorce when they were discussing her financial arrangements.

'Mark wants to divorce you, but on past experience having seen how dependent you are on him he's reluctant to ask you for one.' Nikki eyed her up and down, contemptuously.

'But you're not?' Francesca gritted her teeth, seething at the other woman's utter cheek.

'No, I'm not,' Nikki declared. 'After all, you must know how unfair you're being to Mark, living in this enormous house on your own – now that both your sons have gone – and tying up a big asset. Expecting a generous living allowance every month and doing nothing to earn it. It's parasitical. Have you no pride?

Aren't you able to stand on your own two feet? Look at you,' she said disdainfully. 'You're not even dressed yet. Mark was up at five a.m. to go to Brussels to work like a dog so that you can be kept in the style to which you're accustomed. You should be ashamed of yourself!' Nikki's voice began to get shrill. Francesca, incensed as she was, could see that her unwelcome visitor was not as calm as her apparently cool demeanour implied. 'You can't free-load for ev—'

'Now just one moment,' Francesca interrupted, determined not to hear another word of abuse.

'No, *you* listen to me,' Nikki insisted angrily. 'Why *should* Mark have to carry you on his back? You're not helpless. You're not an invalid or disabled in any way. Isn't it time that you made a life of your own and stopped sponging—'

'Have you finished?' Francesca demanded icily, restraining herself with the greatest difficulty from clocking Nikki one in the kisser.

'No, I haven't—'

'Well, *I've* had enough of listening to *you*,' Francesca snapped. 'How dare *you* come to *my* home and lecture *me* on *my* behaviour. *I'm* not the one who muscled in on another woman's marriage and broke it up.'

'Excuse me.' Nikki gave her a withering look. '*I* didn't break up your marriage. You did that all by yourself. If your marriage wasn't in trouble, Mark would never have gone outside it looking for what he gets from me.'

'Get out of my house, you cheeky little tart,' Francesca thundered, drawing herself up to her full height as she flung open the front door. 'Under no circumstances will I divorce Mark and I think even less of him – if that's possible' – her voice dripped scorn – 'that he didn't have the guts to come and ask me for a divorce himself. You know something? You're welcome to each other. You've both found your own level.'

'Now just wait a minute—'

'Out. *Now!*' Francesca's tone brooked no further argument and Nikki quailed at the ferocity of the anger sparking from Francesca's grey eyes. 'Get out.' Francesca grabbed Nikki by the arm and roughly manhandled her out onto the front step. 'And don't you ever come knocking on my door again.'

Nikki blanched at being physically ejected, her mouth a round O of shock as the front door was slammed shut firmly in her face.

Francesca felt a surge of adrenalin. For the first time since she'd found out about Mark's affair she felt in control. So he wanted a divorce, did he? He could whistle for one. He and superbabe would get married over her dead body. She'd never give in. This was her home and she'd live out her days here, she vowed as she picked up the phone and dialled Mark's mobile number. She half expected it to be turned off as it often was when he was attending meetings but to her immense satisfaction he answered it with a note of surprise in his voice as her number came up.

'Listen, you,' she snapped, cutting off his greeting. 'You tell your little tart never to come knocking on my door again. If you want a divorce you ask me for one yourself, you cowardly, despicable asswipe. But I can tell you here and now that you won't be getting one from me, so go fuck yourself.' Francesca slammed the phone down and marched upstairs. When it rang moments later, she ignored it. She wasn't at his beck and call any longer. And she had just made very clear to Miss Nikki Langan that she was someone to be reckoned with. That tart wouldn't make the mistake of treating her like a nobody again.

Invigorated, she dropped her night clothes on the floor, stepped into the shower and stood under the bracing spray scrubbing herself with the loofah.

Once she was dressed she was going to go and get her hair cut. Karen Marshall's bash was coming up the following week and her hair always looked its best about a week after it was cut. After that, she was going to go for a brisk walk along the Clontarf seafront. She badly needed to start walking again, she was puffed after five minutes these days. Then she was going to buy a load of vegetables and make a huge pot of vegetable soup and live on that for a couple of days now that she wouldn't have to cook for Owen. Even if she lost half a stone it would make a difference, she decided firmly. She was going to look her very best at this do. That Langan wagon had put iron in her soul. Francesca was *Mrs* Mark Kirwan and that was a title that bitch would never have.

Humming, Francesca ladled on passionfruit gel and lathered it up into a satisfying foam all over. She inhaled the scent with pleasure. Odd though it seemed after such an upsetting encounter, she felt more alive, invigorated and purposeful than she had since the whole sorry saga had begun. Maybe Nikki Langan's unexpected and unwelcome visit had unwittingly done her a service. It was time to stop pottering and get on with her life, Francesca decided as she stood under the water and rinsed the frothy suds from her body.

Nikki felt uncharacteristically flustered as she drove back towards town. The encounter with Francesca had not gone at all as planned. Nikki had expected a short, sharp, ladylike discussion; instead she'd been called names and physically shoved out the front door. Practically assaulted. She could sue, she thought angrily. It was clear Francesca had no intention of being shamed into a divorce. And why would she be? Nikki thought sourly as she did seventy along the Dublin Road (she was in no humour for speed limits today). Francesca Kirwan had the life of Riley. A lady of leisure, content to slob around her big house. Why should she go out to work when Mark, the fool, was making it all so easy for her? Could he not see that he was being taken for a ride? Why didn't it infuriate him? Why was he carrying around such guilt? Francesca wasn't his child, for God's sake, she was his equal and being equal meant taking a share of responsibility, not abdicating it as she had done. It was so frustrating. Nikki bit her lip as she shot past St Anne's Park, one of Mark's favourite walking spots when he'd been with Francesca. Nikki's lip curled. Middle-aged, frumpy cow, she'd made Mark old before his time. Did the woman not want closure, for crying out loud? Had she no desire to move on? Nikki couldn't understand it. She'd never want to be financially dependent on a man. She could think of nothing worse.

Her father had been an autocratic tyrant, her mother meek and subservient, totally dependent on her husband for every penny. It had galled Nikki to watch her mother put up with the shit her father dished out. She might as well have been his servant. From the time Nikki had got her first summer job in the local supermarket and started earning her own money, she'd been determined to be financially independent. She'd worked her way through college and studied industriously. Everything she'd achieved since then she'd worked hard for and she had an extremely well-developed sense of self-worth. A financially independent woman she would always be, whether she married or stayed single, that was one certainty in her life, she thought grimly as she swung left onto the Alfie Byrne Road. A kept woman, like Francesca Kirwan or her mother, she would never be. Nevertheless it didn't mean that she didn't want to be Mark's wife. She'd just have to try another tack. But what that tack would be she wasn't sure yet.

Mark looked at the phone in complete astonishment. What on earth was Francesca's tirade all about? What was all this about a divorce? He didn't want a divorce. He was happy enough to be separated and nothing else. He dialled her number again but it just kept ringing. His mouth tightened in anger. He knew that she was there and not picking up. She'd been bloody rude calling him an asswipe, he thought angrily. There was no need for that. And what did she mean by saying to tell his tart not to come knocking on her door? Was she talking about Nikki? Surely Nikki hadn't gone calling on Francesca? He groaned. Nikki wouldn't be so stupid . . . or would she?

He frowned and dialled Nikki's mobile number. It went into divert. 'Damn!' he muttered. He dialled her direct line. No answer. What the bloody hell was going on? He dialled and asked to be put through to her office. Her secretary answered and informed him that Nikki had taken the morning off. She hadn't said anything to him about taking the morning off. With a deep feeling of unease, Mark went into a meeting of his European counterparts, all his earlier youthful vigour dissipated as a niggling thread of worry pervaded his thoughts, making it hard to concentrate.

Twenty-three

'What the bloody hell did you do that for, Nikki? You had no business going anywhere near Francesca. For crying out loud, didn't I tell you divorce would devastate her?' Mark raged down the phone as Nikki sat impatiently in traffic on the East Wall Road as juggernaut after juggernaut poured out of Dublin Port. The meeting was delayed so he had managed to get a call through.

'Look, I can't talk now, I'm driving,' Nikki said tightly, irritated beyond measure at his anger. He was always taking fucking Francesca's side. What about her, for God's sake? Didn't she rate at all in the bloody triangle? 'Phone me tonight and we'll talk,' she said curtly and clicked off. She turned her mobile off completely in case he phoned her back. She couldn't understand it. She'd thought that he'd be pleased that she'd made an effort to sort things out. After all, she'd done it for him. Instead it seemed as though she'd made a major strategic error going out to Francesca's house. It had got Mark's back up, and that was the last thing she wanted to do. But *why* did he not want things to move on? What was his problem?

'Shit! Shit! Shit!' she swore as the lights turned red yet again, leaving her tapping her thumbs impatiently on her steering wheel. There were times when she felt like throwing in the towel. Didn't Mark know just how bloody lucky he was to have her? What would he do if *she* kicked *him* out? He'd better bloody watch it or she just might, she thought sourly as the lights turned green and she managed to get through before coming to a halt as the barrier came down to let the toll bridge up. Nikki cursed long and loudly. Was nothing going to go right this day?

'Can you believe it, Janet? She actually had the nerve to come to my door and lecture me about being a parasite. Then she demanded that I divorce Mark. I told her where to get off in no uncertain terms, I can assure you,' Francesca told her friend Janet Dalton as they sipped coffee after having their hair done. She'd met Janet at the hairdresser's and when the other woman had suggested having a cup of coffee, Francesca had been delighted to accept. She liked Janet, and always enjoyed the lively discussions she had with her in the book club.

'God, I was so mad,' she confessed. 'I wanted to whack her one in the face. I nearly did.'

'I know, it's terrible, isn't it?' Janet gave a wry smile. Francesca looked at her in surprise. 'I've been in that place where you are now. I know all about what you're going through.'

'Really, Janet? I never realized.' Francesca was

astonished. 'What happened – or can't you talk about it?' she added, not wishing to cross any boundaries.

'Oh, it happened a long time ago. Twenty years ago. I was twenty-five, the kids were young, in primary school. I caught my husband with my best friend.'

'Your best friend!' Francesca made a face. 'That's pretty low. At least I don't know the bitch. Did you stay with him?'

'Oh no, I couldn't. And besides, Keith didn't want to stay. He wanted to be with her. So I more or less became a single parent. He provided for us, paid the bills and so on, but he wasn't there for the sick tummies, the homework, the hormony years, the exam angst. And don't even mention the teenage years. He wasn't there for any of the day-to-day stuff. I had to do that by myself and I hated and resented him for it. He went back to a life of being a bachelor with Una and they had a ball. I remember one Saturday, it was a hot sweltering day, I dropped Peter at football and Orla at her running and raced into town to buy their schoolbooks when I saw Keith and Una strolling hand in hand into the Kylemore for breakfast. The pair of them hadn't a care in the world. They'd just come back the previous week from a long weekend in Kerry.' Janet shook her head at the memory. 'I tell you, Francesca, I was so livid I waited until they were sitting down with their grub and then marched in and poured a jug of milk over the pair of them. It was a horrible time. I was eaten up with anger and bitterness. I was desperately unhappy.'

'I'm sure you were. That was horrible to be left

219

with young children. At least my boys are grown up,' Francesca said sympathetically.

'Yeah, well, in the long run Keith really was the loser. The kids got used to not having him around and they grew away from him. He has hardly any relationship with them now. And it wasn't any of my doing. I tried to keep my feelings about Keith to myself and not let it colour how they felt about him, but at the end of the day, when they got older, they saw him for what he was, a shallow, selfish, rather pathetic man. He taught me great lessons though, and I'm very grateful to him.' Janet smiled.

Francesca eyed her quizzically. 'You're *grateful* to him?'

Janet laughed at her tone. 'Believe me, Francesca, one day you could very well be saying the same thing to me.'

'I don't think so,' Francesca said caustically.

'Well, you know, you have the choice to let the anger eat you up and stay feeling as though you're a victim, or you can move on from it. I'm only sorry it took me a good ten years of bitterness until I realized, with the help of a lovely healer, what I was doing to myself.'

'Really?' Francesca was doubtful.

'Well, look at me now. Once I eventually took responsibility for my own feelings and stopped laying blame and saw that I ultimately had to take responsibility for my own life it was like a huge burden lifted from me. I was so fearful of the future I'd hung on to Keith's apron strings and all the negative energy that entailed. I couldn't let go and move on.

'After many healing sessions with Sam, I enrolled

in a back-to-work course and got a job as a legal secretary and then I did a computer course and moved into the IT sector. I job-share now so I've the best of both worlds. I'm independent, I've met loads of people and made lovely friends and I enjoy my life. Once I let go of the past doors opened for me.'

'But don't you hate Keith for what he did to you?' Francesca countered.

Janet shook her head. 'Not any more. Hating someone is exhausting. It took all my energy. I remember Sam saying very gently to me, how long was I going to give Keith free lodgings in my head, because it meant there was no room for anything or anyone else. I remember thinking, That's easy for you to say. You didn't go through what I went through. You didn't have a terrible injustice done to you. I was still in victim mode, you see. And some people carry their victimhood with them for the rest of their lives and never move on.' She laughed again, a deep throaty chuckle. 'I was very angry with Sam and swore to myself that I was never going back to him to listen to that bullshit because he was saying things that I didn't want to hear. I called him a quack and told myself he didn't know what it was like living in the real world, but something drew me back because part of me, deep in my soul, knew that he was right and I wanted to hear more. Going to him changed my life. Not overnight. I struggled with anger and lack of forgiveness for a long time after, but, Francesca, the day I realized Keith meant nothing to me any more and that I was in control was a great day for me. I knew no-one and nothing could ever hurt me like he'd hurt me, because I'd never give my control away again like I had with him. It was a powerful life lesson, Francesca, believe me, and as your friend and as someone who's been through it all I'd really like to help you the way I was helped. That's why I'm telling you all this and I hope you don't mind. Just don't give that pair all your energy.'

Francesca bit her lip. 'I don't think I could forgive. I want him to suffer the way I'm suffering. I hate thinking that he's happy while I'm miserable. Why should he get off scot-free?'

'No-one gets off scot-free, Francesca. In one way or another every deed and every action is accountable for. If you tie yourself up in knots hating Mark and that woman, there's no room for new and good things to come into your life. If you want to move on, you have to let it go and trust that it's all part of a bigger picture that we can't see.'

Francesca scowled. 'But I don't want to let go. It's the anger that keeps me going.'

'I understand that – more than you know, Francesca. I carried such anger for a long, long time. But it's only when you let it go that you realize just how exhausting it is.' Janet topped up their coffee cups.

'Do you believe in that bigger-picture stuff?' Francesca queried doubtfully.

'I do think one's life is mapped out to a degree,' Janet replied easily, 'although I wouldn't have said that ten years ago. When I went to Sam first, he gave me a little affirmation to say every day and I do say it. It's very simple really. I just ask for the Divine Plan of my life to unfold and so when things are happening to me where I feel I'm not in control, I just think of it as the Divine Plan and it helps. If you like I could give you Sam's number and you could make an appointment to see him,' she ventured.

'OK,' Francesca agreed, privately thinking that she just couldn't see herself going for a healing. She wasn't into any of that New Age stuff at all. And if this break-up of her marriage was part of a Divine Plan, she didn't think much of it.

Janet wrote the number down for her and Francesca tucked it into her bag and promptly forgot about it as their conversation turned to Owen and his imminent departure for the States.

'I'd better get home and cook something for him, he's going out with his pals tonight for a couple of drinks. At least his stomach will be lined.' Francesca stood up. 'Thanks for everything, Janet, it was great talking to someone who understands. I never knew you'd gone through all of that.'

'I have no need to talk about it now, unless it's to try and help someone see that there is light at the end of the tunnel. And believe me, Francesca, there really is, I promise,' she said earnestly.

'Thanks, Janet, it helped, honestly.' Francesca gave her friend a warm hug. 'See you at the book club, I've got a great new Madeleine Wickham, *Cocktails for Three*. You'll enjoy it.'

'And I've got Dermot Bolger's and Joseph O'Connor's latest, they're both terrific so we've some real goodies this week.' They smiled companionably at each other and Francesca felt warmed by Janet's friendship as she crossed the road to the car park. Today had been a very good day, all in all. The best since the break-up. Maybe after Karen Marshall's bash she might try the letting-go bit, but until then she was going to do her damnedest to look her very best and to pretend that she was getting on fine because it was quite clear from the encounter this morning that she was a thorn in Nikki Langan's side. She intended being one for a very long time, she thought grimly, remembering the tirade of abuse and insults that she'd endured this morning. Being called a parasite was something she'd never forgive that little bitch for. Janet might be saintly and forgiving, but she definitely wasn't.

Owen came home to a feast of roast beef, roast and creamed potatoes, mushy peas, baby carrots, broccoli and rhubarb crumble for dessert.

'Ma, that was mega. I'm really going to miss your home cooking. Jonathan can't cook for buttons.' Her son planted a smacker of a kiss on her cheek.

Francesca laughed. 'I'm sure you won't starve, Owen. The restaurants are great over there. You'll have a ball.'

'Are you really sure you don't mind me going?'

'Honestly, Owen, I don't. So don't worry about me. I'm fine.'

'You look different today. You seem much perkier. Has something happened?' he asked as he cleared his dishes from the table and put them into the dishwasher.

'Well, I got my hair done,' she said lightly. She had no intention of telling Owen about her unexpected visitor.

'Yeah, it's nice, Ma. That style suits you.'

'Come on, flattery will get you everywhere. Let's go to Millie's so you can say your goodbyes.'

Francesca smiled at her son. She was going to miss him terribly.

'The very woman I wanted to see,' her sister said gleefully twenty minutes later when they knocked at Millie's door.

'Oh, why's that?' Francesca asked.

'I've booked a week's holiday for us in the Algarve. Aidan's taking a week off to mind the girls. Francesca, we're going to take Portugal by storm.' She beamed delightedly from ear to ear.

Francesca looked at her, bemused. 'Wait a minute, what's all this about?'

'We are going on a girls only holiday. That's what it's all about. And I just can't wait. We deserve it, dearie, so go pack a few glad rags and prepare to boogie in three weeks' time.'

'Are you serious?' Francesca was gobsmacked.

'I certainly am.' Millie grinned. 'And if the Algarve's not posh enough for you, tough. It was the only place I could get at such short notice.'

'The Algarve's fine. I like Portugal. It's just so unexpected,' Francesca said faintly.

'Nice one, Millie,' Owen approved. 'It's just what Mam needs.'

'Exactly!' Millie agreed. 'I'll give you all the details in a minute. I'll just stick the kettle on and we'll have a brew.'

Ten minutes later Francesca was poring over a brochure, feeling about twenty. It was years since she'd been on a charter holiday with her sister. 'Oura Praia. It sounds lovely and the studio looks nice, and there's air conditioning. Excellent.'

'I could only get a studio,' Millie said apologetically.

'There wasn't a one bedroom to be had for love or money.'

'A studio's fine, Mil. This is going to be fun. What made you decide to book?'

'I thought it would do you good to get away for a week. It will certainly do wonders for me to get away from that.' She indicated the back garden where the kids were screeching and yelling in delight as Owen chased them up and down. 'I know it's not as expensive a holiday as you're used to but it will be like old times.'

'I think it will be brilliant, and thanks so much for thinking of it.' Francesca jumped up and hugged her sister.

'I'm only using your trauma to get a holiday for myself,' Millie giggled, 'so don't feel at all in my debt.'

'Nikki Langan called at my door today looking for me to divorce Mark,' Francesca informed her.

Millie's jaw dropped. 'You're joking!'

'Nope!'

'And?'

'I told her to get lost and shoved her out the door.'

'I hope you gave her a good kick up her bony little ass for good measure.'

'Well, I didn't quite go that far,' Francesca said regretfully. 'Although I felt like it when she called me a parasite and asked me had I no pride and was I going to sponge off Mark for the rest of my life?'

'She *didn't*!' Millie exclaimed. 'The unmitigated gall. How did you restrain yourself, 'cos I know your temper when you're riled.'

'With great difficulty,' Francesca said drily.

'Pity,' snorted Millie. 'You're totally intimidating when you're on the warpath. What a cheek though. And how cowardly of Mark to send her instead of doing his own dirty work.'

'To be honest, I'm not sure if he knew about it. He sounded surprised when I bawled him out over the phone.' Francesca nibbled on a chocolate digestive, forgetting her diet plans.

'Interesting,' declared Millie. 'Maybe he doesn't want a divorce because he doesn't want to commit, and she's getting desperate. Veerry, veerry interesting!'

'Oh! I hadn't thought of it like that,' Francesca admitted.

'Well, that's what it sounds like to me,' said Millie firmly. 'Little Miss Muffet is not happy on her tuffet and wants to get married and figures if he won't ask for the divorce, she will. I bet Mark's having a canary. Why on earth would he want to get married when he's got the best of both worlds as it is? Francesca, when divorce was introduced into this country an awful lot of second relationships broke up because the man's excuse for not being able to cut the ties from the first wife was no longer legitimate. You know Jill and Kenny? They split because he wouldn't divorce his wife and marry Jill. She just got pissed off at the idea of being second best and dumped him. She's with someone else now and he's on his own.'

'Really?' Francesca was surprised at this titbit. 'I didn't know that.'

'Ducky, if you told Mark that you were divorcing him, he'd have an absolute mickey fit, I promise you,' Millie retorted. 'It would be the worst thing in the world you could possibly do to him because then he'd have no excuses to make to Miss Pushy. His life would be absolute *hell*!' she drawled.

Francesca laughed. 'You raise bitchiness to a high art, sister dearest.'

'You'd better believe it. And I'm right in what I'm saying. If you don't want him to come slithering home ever again and you want to get your own back, you divorce the bastard and take him for half of everything he's got and then watch him squeal,' Millie concluded confidently as Owen came into the room with his young cousins and the subject was dropped.

That night as Francesca lay in bed having an early night, she reviewed the events of the day, remembering her anger at Nikki Langan's distasteful slurs. Although she found it hard to admit, she wasn't happy about being financially dependent on Mark. Now that they were no longer a couple living together, she felt the need to earn her own money so that she wouldn't feel beholden every month when his cheque was credited to her account. But she'd made such a mess of her first pathetic little job. The thought of trying to find another that she liked and that she could do was daunting. She grimaced. She couldn't imagine Nikki Langan being financially beholden to any man or being intimidated by any job. That crack about having no pride had touched a nerve.

Maybe she should do a back-to-work course like Janet had. Or some sort of a computer course. It seemed like her only option. But it had worked for Janet. It could work for her, she thought with a little more optimism. She'd look into it after her holiday. Definitely!

Chapter Twenty-four

'Look, I was just thinking of you, Mark. I was thinking of how hard you work and how much you have to pay out. Surely a divorce would be much more economical and easier on everybody in the long run.' Nikki put her point across as reasonably as she could. It was seven-thirty in the evening, she'd had a long and tiring day and she was doing her level best not to lose her temper. Mark had phoned in a foul humour. She reckoned it was better to act cool. If they had a row over divorce it could be the end of them and Nikki didn't want that. If this relationship ended it would be because she wanted it to and not because of Francesca bloody Kirwan.

'I appreciate that, Nikki, but it didn't help. You should have spoken to me about it first. I had Francesca on the phone giving me dog's abuse and, believe me, it was the last thing I needed,' Mark said wearily. 'Forget about divorce for the time being. It's too soon. I can afford to pay her the money so let's leave things to settle down for a while. We're fine the way we are. And please, promise me that you'll never get in contact with Francesca again. She's a proud woman, she won't take kindly to it.'

'OK, Mark, if that's what you want,' Nikki said crisply. 'I'm sure you're tired, I'll let you go. Talk to you tomorrow.'

'Night, Nikki.' She heard him yawn as he hung up. Nikki replaced the receiver and took a slug out of her G and T. If Francesca Kirwan was so goddamn proud how come she was sponging off Mark and how come he couldn't see it? It was damn infuriating. She scowled as she picked up the remote control and surfed the channels. She missed Mark around the place. It would have been nice to have a drink and a cuddle. She was getting domesticated, she thought in horror. She'd better nip that in the bud. She picked up her palmtop and scanned the screen for the number she was looking for. If her friend Ava was free they were going clubbing this very night, long day or not. Nikki had an image to maintain. She wanted to be able to tell Mark that she'd been out on the tear so that he wouldn't be under any illusions that she was sitting in pining for him, hoping against hope that he would divorce his shrew of a wife.

Owen groaned as he sat up gingerly and opened his eyes. Not too bad, he thought, pleasantly surprised. Just a dull throbbing in his temples. He'd had far worse hangovers than this. But then he hadn't gone completely overboard last night. Not with a long flight ahead of him. A shower and some grub and he'd be fine. He glanced at his watch. Nine-thirty: he'd need to get a move on.

'Morning.' Francesca eyed him in amusement as he sloped into the kitchen. 'What do you want for the last breakfast?'

'I think a fry-up might hit the spot nicely and after that I just have to hop into town for an hour or so.'

She raised her eyes to heaven. 'What have you to get? I thought you did all that yesterday.'

'Ah, just bits and pieces. Anyway, I've loads of time. The flight isn't until four.'

'I wish you'd have flown direct with Aer Lingus. I would have paid for the flight, Owen,' Francesca said as she laid strips of bacon on the grill pan.

'Ma, it was much cheaper to fly to Heathrow and get the red-eye and you need your money and I wasn't taking *his*.' Owen cut a chunk of brown bread and smeared it with butter and marmalade. Mark had wanted to pay for his flight but Owen wouldn't hear of it, much to his father's chagrin.

'It's nothing to do with me. I haven't discussed it with him one way or another,' Francesca had said coolly when Mark had tackled her about it. She knew that the rift between himself and Owen was cutting him up, but he'd made his bed and he could lie on it as far as she was concerned.

'I'm thinking of doing a computer course and trying for another job again,' Francesca said as she added sliced mushrooms to a pan of sizzling butter seasoned with salt and pepper.

'I think that would be great for you, Ma. Go for it. It means you won't end up pottering before your time.' He laughed as she flicked him with a tea towel. He loved his ma, she was the best in the world and if he could get his hands on his da, he'd hammer him.

Bastard! he thought angrily. They'd had a good family life until he'd gone muckin' about. Why had he thrown it all away for a bit of skirt?

'Why don't you have your shower? This will be cooked by the time you're ready, if you hurry,' Francesca suggested as she put the tomatoes alongside the mushrooms.

'OK,' he agreed. He didn't feel quite so worried about his ma now. She seemed a lot perkier in herself and he was delighted that she was going on holiday. It was time that she started having a bit of fun again. Whistling, he stepped into the shower. Things were looking up.

Nikki suppressed a moan as she bent down to pick up the pen she'd dropped. She had the mother and father of a hangover. She'd met Ava in the Morrison and they'd downed a bottle of champers and several cocktails before heading to Lillie's. It was after five when she got to bed and right this minute she felt like crawling home and staying under the duvet for a month.

She ran a comb through her hair. She'd worn it loose today, she couldn't face the effort of putting it up. She sprayed some Oscar de la Renta on her wrists and freshened her lipstick. She had a meeting in five minutes. She needed to be on top of things. She couldn't hit the sauce the way she used to, she thought ruefully, but Mark had been surprised when she'd told him about her night out. He'd phoned her at home but she wasn't there. She'd stayed over at Ava's and he hadn't been able to contact her until she got to the office. She'd kept her mobile switched off on purpose. It was good to keep him on his toes. One thing was for certain: she'd make damn sure that he never took her for granted.

Twenty minutes later, feeling rather queasy, Nikki sat listening to her colleague from Finance go through a list of figures in relation to their latest acquisition. It was a sad reflection on their relationship that she had to go to such extremes to keep Mark interested. She was beginning to think that he meant more to her than she did to him and it worried her.

Tears welled in Francesca's eyes as Owen leaned down and gave Trixie a belly rub before lugging his case out to the car. He shoved it into the boot then put his arms around her and hugged her close.

'Come on now, Ma, don't cry, you promised you wouldn't.'

'You're a great son,' she sniffed. 'You've no idea how much you helped me. I would have been lost without you.'

'I don't have to go. I can get a job with Art Breen, no problem,' he said stoutly.

'You get your ass on that plane, boy, or you'll have *me* to deal with,' Francesca chided, wiping her eyes. 'Come on, if we've time after you've checked in we can have a coffee.' She got into the car and started the ignition, determined that there would be no more tears. It wasn't fair on Owen.

The airport was jammers, and the queue for Owen's flight to Heathrow was daunting.

'We won't have time for that coffee, Mam,' Owen observed ruefully. 'I'll hardly have time to look

233

around the shops at this rate. I want to get a couple of bottles of spirits for Jonathan.'

'Go easy on the booze over there, won't you, and don't dabble in any illegal substances,' Francesca warned.

'Mam, you're talking to a finely tuned athlete here. I'm not interested in that stuff,' Owen said indignantly and Francesca hid a smile. 'I would be interested in her though.' He nodded in the direction of a pretty young blonde woman further up the queue. 'I wonder if I could get a seat beside her.' He gave a wolfish grin and, with a dart, Francesca saw how closely he resembled his father, now he was older.

'I think I'll just pop over to the bookshop,' she said easily. 'See you in a minute.' But instead of heading for Hughes & Hughes, she hurried into the nearest loo, bolted into a cubicle, put the lid down on the seat, sat down and buried her face in her hands.

'Get a grip!' she told herself fiercely as tears spilled down her cheeks. 'Get a grip.' Mark ought to be here with her to see Owen off. It shouldn't be like this, she thought bitterly. Her son should be able to join his brother in America with an easy mind and she shouldn't have to go home to a big empty house alone.

She eventually managed to compose herself and emerged from the cubicle red-eyed. She did a swift repair job on her make-up and hurried back to join Owen. He'd moved considerably closer to the top of the queue.

'Why don't you go home instead of hanging

around here?' Owen said kindly. 'I'm nearly through now.'

'Ah sure, I'll wait until you've checked in,' Francesca said lightly. 'Just to make sure you're really going.'

'But don't come over to Departures with me.'

'Will I not? Are you afraid I might burst into tears again?'

'It just might be easier,' he said gently.

'You just don't want me to make a scene in front of the blonde bombshell,' Francesca teased.

'Yeah, it would do my street cred no good at all,' Owen agreed as he hauled his luggage onto the conveyor belt. When he'd completed the formalities he took Francesca by the arm. 'Come on, I'll walk you to the car.'

'No, no,' she protested.

'Yes, yes,' he argued. 'Then I won't have to worry about you trying to find the car and bawling your eyes out at the same time.'

'It's not my fault I'm a softie.' Francesca tucked her arm into his as they walked briskly across the concourse. He was right, of course, she would have wept buckets watching him disappear airside. This way was easier.

He opened the car door for her when they reached the parking bay and dropped a light kiss on the top of her head. 'Drive carefully now and I'll ring to let you know I've arrived,' he said matter-of-factly.

'OK. Have a ball, Owen, and give my love to Jonathan,' Francesca said, easing herself into the seat.

Her last sight of him was of him waving vigorously

as she drove out of the parking space. Fortunately for her, she couldn't see the sudden biting of his lips as his eyes darkened with loneliness and worry and a lump the size of a golf ball threatened to choke him.

You're on your own now, she thought dolefully as she slid her ticket into the machine and watched the barrier rise. Owen, her dear and precious son, had been her buffer against aloneness. Now she was truly going to have to face up to it and deal with it once and for all.

She had just got in the door when the phone rang. 'Hello,' she said, dropping her car keys, house keys and bag onto the hall table.

'Hi, Mam, just phoning to see how you are. Thought you might be feeling a bit lonely after leaving Owen at the airport.' Jonathan's tones came clear as a bell down the line.

'Jonathan, you pet.' Her eldest son's thoughtfulness touched her deeply. He'd been very good about phoning and e-mailing her since the break-up and she sent a silent prayer of thanks heavenward for the gift of her two lovely sons.

'I suppose you were bawling,' Jonathan said fondly.

'I wasn't too bad, smartie.' Francesca smiled. It was so good to hear his voice.

'I was just thinking, why don't you come over for a week or two while Owen's here. I'll send you the money for the fare,' he offered kindly.

'Thanks, Jonathan, we'll see. And I can pay for my fare, love. I'm not a pauper.'

'I know ... I just wanted to treat you, Mam,' Jonathan said.

'Thanks, love, you're very kind and I really appreciate it. I'm off to Portugal with Millie shortly, maybe I'll come over after that. We'll play it by ear.'

They chatted for a while and Francesca didn't feel quite so alone when she put down the phone. They were only a phone call away and they were good at keeping in touch. She was glad Owen had Jonathan to go to. It would do him good to get away from her. He was young. The break-up of his parents' marriage wasn't his burden to carry. It was time he enjoyed his youth.

Poor old Jonathan, offering to pay her fare. He was a great old stick really, Francesca acknowledged as she rooted in her bag for a tissue. He was so responsible, so steady, but she didn't like the feeling of knowing that he saw her as financially dependent on Mark.

That was twice in the past two days that she'd been made to feel in some way helpless and inferior. Jonathan hadn't meant to make her feel like that, but Nikki Langan very definitely had.

She really should do something about getting another job. It was the only way forward for her, she admitted to herself. But employers wanted young, experienced employees. It was awful to think you were a has-been at forty, she thought, glumly studying her reflection in the mirror. The lines around her eyes had deepened perceptibly, and were there little lines along her top lip? Francesca puckered. And unpuckered just as quickly when she saw the result. Yikes! she thought in dismay, noting a few fine lines around her neck. Right! That was it, factor fifty on holiday, definitely, or she'd have a dried-up neck like an old wan, Francesca decided as she went into the kitchen to heat up a bowl of her vegetable soup. She was determined to have a half-stone lost by Karen Marshall's do. Mark and Nikki would see her looking nothing but her best, she vowed as she drank a glass of water, one of the eight she was drinking religiously every day. She'd slid as far down the ladder as she was prepared to go. The only way now was up. Snooty little superbabe would never look down her pert little proboscis at Francesca again.

Chapter Twenty-five

Francesca checked her appearance in the mirror once more as she waited for the taxi to collect her. She studied the reflection of the immaculately made-up woman in the black palazzo pants and lightly sequinned three-quarter-length jacket worn over a deep pink camisole top that highlighted to perfection the tan she'd got lying out on the deck. Black high-heeled sandals showed off her coral-painted toenails and gave her added height. She looked well, she thought without vanity.

She'd had her make-up professionally done and a manicure and pedicure to boot. Her hair was perfectly coiffed and highlighted, she'd lost the half-stone in weight and her cheekbones had made an appearance once more. She was getting there, she thought with satisfaction. She might not be able to compete with the toned and sculpted youthful Ms Langan, but she looked sophisticated and classy – the way Mark had always liked her to look, she thought wryly as she heard the taxi crunch up the drive.

As she sat back in the seat and tried to relax on the trip to the Burlington, Francesca felt butterflies in the pit of her stomach. She'd been to a thousand galas and the like, sometimes twice and three times a week in the hectic years when Mark had been climbing up the career ladder, but tonight she definitely felt nervous. It was the first time she'd gone to a function since the break-up of their marriage and it was certainly the first time she had ever walked into a party on her own. She was dismayed at how daunted she felt. Had she got so dependent on Mark during their marriage that her confidence disappeared at the thought of going it alone? That was pathetic, she thought in disgust. *You just get in there and strut your stuff with your head held high, you could do it blindfolded*, she told herself sternly, annoyed at her wimpish attitude. Nevertheless, her mouth was dry and she unwrapped a mint and sucked it in an effort to quell her nerves.

What would she do if she bumped into Mark and Nikki? Ignore them, knowing that everyone who knew them would be looking to see her reaction? It was difficult. She didn't want to talk to them, but she didn't want the gossips to have a field day either. The only comfort she had was knowing that Mark wouldn't be particularly comfortable either, it would have suited him much better if she'd stayed away.

By the time the taxi pulled up outside the Burlington, her heart rate had doubled and she felt sick. Her palms were sweaty and she was heartily tempted to tell the taxi driver to turn around and take her home.

This is ridiculous, she reproached herself irritably

as she paid the taxi driver and hurried into the hotel to find the nearest loo. She took several calming deep breaths, studied her reflection yet again in a sparkling mirror and was reassured to see that outwardly there was no hint of her inward turmoil. Squaring her shoulders, she turned and marched out to the foyer. She read the noticeboard to find out in which function room the gala was being held. Might as well get in there and see what was happening on the social scene she'd been away from for so long.

'Francesca, Francesca, hi,' she heard a familiar voice call and smiled with relief when she saw Monica Gill and her husband Bart crossing the foyer. Monica and Bart were old tennis partners of hers and Mark's and Monica had taken her to lunch and offered support when she'd heard about the split.

'I'm really glad you've come and you look stunning!' the older woman praised as she gave Francesca a warm hug. 'Doesn't she, Bart?'

'Million dollars,' Bart concurred, enveloping her in a bear-hug.

'You look pretty dishy yourself, Bart,' Francesca declared admiringly. 'You've lost weight.'

'You think so?' Bart beamed. 'Started hill-walking. It's exhausting but I love it. You should come with us sometime. You'd like it.'

'You should, Francesca,' Monica agreed enthusiastically. 'You meet loads of people, it would do you all the good in the world.'

'Sounds fun.' Francesca smiled. 'Maybe I just might.' They strolled into the function room, chatting and laughing, and Francesca began to relax.

To hell with Mark and Nikki, she had as much right to be here as they had and it was nice to see old friends again. Nevertheless, while she chatted and mingled, her antennae were up and a small knot of tension remained as she surreptitiously scanned the throng every so often to see if she could get a glimpse of her ex and superbabe.

She was talking to an elderly couple whom she'd often met on the circuit when Karen Marshall saluted her apologetically, 'Francesca, dear, I'm so sorry I wasn't at the entrance to greet you, there was a tiny crisis about the seating arrangements that I had to sort out. Well, actually' – she lowered her voice and threw her eyes up to heaven – 'the Dennings and the Kerrs had a falling out over some shares Dominic Kerr advised Leo Denning to buy. Seemingly he lost more than a couple of grand, and they're not talking. I didn't know this and I had them seated at the same table. Dreadful *faux pas*. It's so hard to keep track of who's talking and who isn't. My nerves are shattered.' She laughed good-humouredly. 'You look really well, dear, I'm so glad you came. You heard Mark cancelled?'

'Did he?' Francesca was surprised at the news and paradoxically half dismayed. Now that she was here and back on form she'd wanted him to see that she was perfectly capable of attending a function without him. All the effort she'd put into getting ready and he hadn't turned up. How irritating. 'Why, Karen? He rang me a while back to say he was coming.'

'He had to go away on business, he said, when he phoned me to let me know. Maybe he chickened out,' Karen suggested with a twinkle in her eye.

'What matter? You're here and I want you to enjoy yourself. I've seated you with Monica and Bart. They're always good fun and the Lloyds are at your table too so it should be quite lively. Oh, damn,' she muttered, 'here're the Clarks. Would you look at the get-up of her, she'll do anything for notice. Tacky, tacky, tacky.' Karen planted a smile on her lips as two of the city's most well-known publicity addicts swooped, air-kissing all round them as a photographer clicked busily.

'One more, darlings, just one more and you too, lovie.' He smiled cheesily at Francesca. She endured the photos and then edged away discreetly, grinning as Lisa Clark twittered in Karen's ear, lauding her gala and telling her how wonderful she was. Far better than Michelle Jenkin's pathetic effort for Alzheimer's. Lisa didn't lower her voice. She'd had a falling out with Michelle and the social knives were well and truly out. While she'd been in hibernation, Francesca had forgotten just how cut-throat the social scene was. Just as well she'd never taken it seriously. She knew couples who'd be on the edge of a nervous breakdown if their photos weren't in the social and personal columns following a function or if such and such a celebrity didn't attend a gala night, first night, opening or launch.

So Mark and Nikki hadn't come. Surprise, sur- prise, she thought a little triumphantly. He couldn't face her after his girlfriend's totally uncalled-for behaviour. And rightly so, she thought with satis- faction, hoping that her picture would be in the social pages of the weekend papers, so that he would see it. That *would* be satisfying, she mused. *You're as bad as the Clarks*, she chided herself, aware that she was being childish, but knowing she'd be at the newsagents first thing Saturday and Sunday morning buying all the papers to read over breakfast.

The fact that her husband wasn't there to bump into helped her relax and to her surprise Francesca thoroughly enjoyed the rest of the evening. It was so long since she'd dressed up and gone out, it was actually a bit of a treat. A lot of people hadn't seen her since her split with Mark and she knew she was under scrutiny. She made sure that she kept smiling.

She was sipping coffee after the meal, chatting to Monica, when the subject of her future plans came up. 'I want to get a job,' she confided, 'but I'm not really trained for anything. I can type with two fingers, file and answer the phone. But I need to do a computer course or something, I suppose.'

'They're dreadful things, aren't they? I wouldn't know one end of them from another.' Monica chuckled. 'But once you can type you can't go wrong.'

Can't I? Francesca thought, remembering her first fiasco.

Monica's eyes gleamed. 'You know, Francesca, I'm glad you told me that you're job-hunting. I think I just might have the very thing for you. Yes indeed. This is marvellous!'

'What is?' Francesca was agog.

'Look, just let me talk to someone tomorrow and meet me for lunch on Friday. I have a phone call to make but I think I know someone who has a job that would suit you down to the ground.'

* * *

'Lovie, she'd be perfect for you,' Monica assured her nephew, Ken Kennedy, who ran his own PR company and was in dire need of an assistant.

'No, Monica. But thanks for thinking of me,' Ken said firmly.

'Now, Ken,' protested Monica. 'At least give her an interview.'

'There's no point. I need someone who knows what she's about. Who can use a computer and who won't be going through the change of life or something,' her nephew said uncompromisingly down the phone line. 'I don't want to hurt your feelings, but a middle-aged, separated woman coming back to work after twenty years or so is very definitely *not* what I need.'

'Ken Kennedy! That's a dreadful thing to say. I'm ashamed of you,' Monica scolded. 'She's a very well-bred, sophisticated woman who knows how to behave in company. She's been on the circuit for years and has great contacts and she's just the kind of person you need to give your scutty little company a touch of class. You should be down on your knees begging her to work for you. Those silly little fluffy puffettes you tend to employ haven't a clue. If she can type she can learn to use a computer. I'm telling you you won't do better. She comes highly recommended. You know me, I wouldn't put someone your way unless I thought they were suitable. Go on, give her a try,' Monica wheedled. 'I've told her you would,' she fibbed.

'Oh, *Monica*!' Ken hissed in exasperation.

'Look, I'll phone you on Friday and see how you're fixed. Talk to you then.' She hung up without giving him a chance to reply. Ken really didn't know what was good for him sometimes, but she loved him to bits. He was her favourite godchild as well as nephew and Francesca was just what he needed – whether he liked it or not.

Chapter Twenty-six

'It's nice since they've refurbished, isn't it?' Monica remarked as they studied the menu in L'Écrivain.

'Very nice,' approved Francesca as she gazed around at the bright, airy, extended restaurant. She and Mark had often entertained his guests here in the past. She felt a pang at the memories. She wondered, did he bring Nikki here? *Forget it, you're moving on*, she told herself firmly as she took the menu from the waiter and began to study it.

'Let's be naughty and go the whole hog, will we? We've something to celebrate, I hope.' Monica was on top form, and her gaiety was infectious.

'Have we? I'm dying to know what you're up to.' Francesca laid aside the menu and stared at her friend, trying to work out what was going on. Monica smiled broadly and settled herself more comfortably in her chair.

'You remember my nephew Ken?' She arched an eyebrow enquiringly. Francesca nodded.

'Well, he was working for a PR company that was

247

run by a pair of crooks, as far as I'm concerned.'
Monica's nostrils flared in disgust and Francesca prepared herself for a tirade. She'd often heard her
friend giving out about Little and Large as she'd
nicknamed the two partners in the firm of
McDonnell & Lynn. Monica loathed them and
never lost an opportunity to express her displeasure
with them.

'They made him redundant, didn't they?'

'Indeed they did, the creeps, after he'd worked his
butt off for them. You know he had to work
Saturdays, Sundays, late nights, and he never got a
penny overtime. Pure exploitation, Francesca. I
remember him telling me one time that he'd taken a
musician they were doing a publicity tour for out to
RTE to appear on a late-night show. Afterwards he'd
taken him to the coffee dock in Jury's and by the time
he got home it was practically dawn. Well, five a.m.,'
she amended. Monica was prone to exaggeration.
'Anyway, he went into work half an hour late the
next morning and that little jug-eared consequence,
the older one with the loud jackets, said as smart as
you like, "I think someone needs an alarm clock."
Really, Francesca, it was abuse and bullying the
whole time he was there. No less.' She frowned.
'There's so much bullying in the workplace that goes
unheard of. Bart was telling me about this young
lad—'

'Tell me about him later. What's all this got to
do with me?' Francesca instructed firmly. Monica
was also notorious for getting sidetracked in
conversation.

'Oh! Right!' she said apologetically. 'Ken worked

his butt off for those two bastards for a pittance and got no thanks for anything he did. It was the best thing in the world for him when they let him go although it didn't seem like it at the time. Seemingly they had a cash-flow problem because they were buying property – under the company's name of course ... talk about chicanery, you've no idea. Anyway, to make a long story short – Oh, here's the waiter. We should order. What do you fancy?' Monica asked.

'Oh, the Caesar salad and go lightly with the dressing, and the rack of lamb, well done, for me, please.' Francesca smiled at the waiter, trying to curb her impatience. What did Ken's work problems have to do with her? They'd been in conversation for over twenty minutes and she still had no idea what Monica had planned for her.

'And I'll have the tiger prawns and my steak rare,' Monica was instructing the waiter, completely unaware that Francesca was in a tizzy of curiosity. She took a sip of her Chardonnay. Francesca did likewise. 'Anyway, where was I? Oh yes. Well, for the first six months he was out of work. Nothing! *Nada!*' Monica declared dramatically. 'His marketing degree, work experience, all for nothing, no-one was biting. It was soul-destroying. He was thinking of emigrating. But in the end one of the new independent TV companies asked him to do a bit of freelance work and then a record company asked him to organize a tour for one of their up-and-comings, then a couple of publishers asked him to arrange author tours and publicity and it all snowballed and he was doing so well he had to get

someone in to work with him. And that was grand.'
Monica took another sip of wine.

'And?' prompted Francesca.

'Well, he employed this assistant, a ditzy piece if
ever you saw one, all fluff and no substance, and she
went and fell in love with some musician and has
gone haring off to America after him,' Monica
explained.

'And where do I come in?'

'Francesca, you'd be perfect for her job. You bring
people to interviews and out to RTE and TV3 and
you wine them and dine them and pop them back to
their hotels or out to the airport. You'd have no
problem doing it. You've been doing that kind of
thing all your married life for Mark. You're great
with people. You know all the restaurants that count,
you know all the hotels. You can drive. Your time
is your own now. The salary is good and there's a
generous expense account and if you're interested,
Ken's willing to see you. He needs someone badly,
he's snowed under. He said if you were interested
would you pop in and see him this afternoon. It's just
what you need. A whole new career.' Monica sat
back, extremely pleased with herself, and waited for
Francesca's reaction.

'Oh, I don't know. It's a bit sudden,' Francesca
demurred, flustered.

'Well, you can always have a chat with him and see
how it works out,' Monica urged.

'I'm going on holiday for a week with Millie,'
Francesca declared. Now that she had the chance of
a job interview, she wasn't sure how she felt about it.

'Stop making excuses, Francesca,' Monica said

briskly as her tiger prawns and Francesca's Caesar salad were placed in front of them.

Francesca made a face. 'Is that what I'm doing?'

''Fraid so. Look, give it a try. At least you know of Ken, so he's not a complete stranger. Come on,' she encouraged Francesca. 'Just imagine Mark's reaction when he hears that you're working. Who knows who you might meet? It's better than sitting at home feeling sorry for yourself.' Monica dipped a prawn into her sauce and demolished it with relish.

'I'm scared, Monica. I've lost my confidence completely,' Francesca said quietly. She was tempted to tell her friend about her stint in Allen & Co., but just couldn't bring herself to.

'I know, lovie, and that is truly terrible. A fabulous woman like you. But believe me, all it'll take for you to get it back is to get out there, give it a bash and make a go of it. I honestly think it's perfect for you and you're exactly what Ken needs. Otherwise I would never have suggested it. Recommending people to relatives can be a bit tricky and it's not something that I usually do. But in this case I had no qualms whatsoever. He's really stuck. You'd be doing *him* a great favour, honestly. And besides, you wouldn't have too long to think about it. Sometimes it's best being thrown in at the deep end.'

'Oh, Monica!' Francesca groaned.

'Go on. Say yes. You can do it. It's *you*!' Monica said earnestly.

Francesca burst out laughing, touched and amused at her friend's confidence in her. 'All right then, I'll give it a go,' she declared.

'*Yes!*' Monica punched the air with her fist,

forgetting where she was. Other diners looked around in amusement.

'Oops. Listen, I'm just going to pop outside for a second to give Ken a tinkle on the mobile to tell him the great news. I'll tell him to expect you between two and three. He works in an office in Monkstown so it would be very handy if you wanted to Dart it on the days you weren't bringing clients around.' Monica jumped up and hurried out of the dining room leaving Francesca gobsmacked, apprehensive and faintly exhilarated.

Ken Kennedy put the phone down and gave a deep, deep sigh. What was Monica getting him into? He had no desire to meet this Francesca woman but his aunt was insistent and once she got a bee in her bonnet there was no stopping her. For the sake of peace he'd see her but if he didn't think she was suitable he'd make no bones about saying so, he decided crossly. She had the nerve to want a week's holiday almost as soon as she had started. Was the woman for real? Wake up and smell the coffee if you want to get a job, he thought irritably as he sorted out a pile of press releases he should have sent out at the beginning of the week at least. He could do with someone to sort out the office. It was a disaster. It really was an employee's market these days. They could pick and choose. Unfortunately they weren't choosing him. Well, he wasn't desperate yet. Francesca Kirwan was going to have to impress the hell out of him and he had strong doubts about her ability to do that.

* * *

Monica sat down excitedly. 'Right. It's all sorted. Ken's expecting you and he's delighted,' she exaggerated. 'Here's the address.' She handed Francesca a slip of paper. 'Now, let's make the most of your last day as a "Lady Who Lunches". Next time we dine it will be Francesca Kirwan, "Career Woman". To tell you the truth, I feel a tad envious. My life feels dull and predictable by comparison to the one you're going to have. Maybe I should have gone for the job myself.'

'Would you like to? Why don't you?' Francesca demanded.

'Don't be ridiculous, Francesca. First of all, I'm his aunt and it's fatal to mix family and business. Secondly, I'm on the wrong side of forty-five. Thirdly, I'm far too scatty. Fourthly, I don't have your style. Fifthly, Bart would have an absolute fit if he had to go home and get his own dinner. *And* I'd eat my way through the expense account and turn into a sumo wrestler. I could go on but you get the picture,' she said good-naturedly as she tucked into her fillet of steak with relish.

Francesca laughed. 'Don't say things like that about yourself.'

'All true, unfortunately. Oh look! No, don't turn around yet in case they see you. It's Marise Conway and her new toy boy. She's hitting the sauce really badly, I believe. Made a show of herself at Cora Lloyd's barbecue and, my dear . . .' Monica launched into a saga of delicious tittle-tattle as she brought Francesca up to speed on the goings on of their numerous acquaintances.

An hour and a half later, more than a little nervous, Francesca parked her car on the seafront at

Monkstown and followed the directions Monica had given her. Along a side street that led to the main road she found Ken's office building and with some trepidation buzzed the intercom.

'Hello, Francesca. It's the first floor,' a disembodied male voice crackled through the speaker as the door clicked open. She climbed up the green-carpeted stairs and noticed a plant holder with a drooping display of sad-looking plants on the landing beside Ken's office. The glass door opened and her new boss stood waiting for her, a mug of coffee in his hand, his tie loosened and his shirt sleeves rolled up.

'You need to water your plants,' Francesca informed him as she walked into his office. He was like an older version of Owen, she decided, not at all intimidating.

'Oh God, yes.' He rubbed his jaw ruefully. 'Sandra always looked after that kind of thing. Er . . . sorry about the mess, I'm up to my eyes and I haven't had time to file.' Why was he apologizing to her and where did she get off telling him to water his plants? He scowled. She was elegant, but much younger than he'd expected, he observed, surprised. She had nice twinkly eyes.

Francesca stared around the untidy office that had two desks piled high with folders and paper cuttings, brochures and press releases. *Yes indeed, Owen to a T*, she thought happily. This was so different to Allen & Co. This felt good. 'How about if you make me a cup of coffee, and I start trying to clear this lot away and familiarize myself with your . . . ah . . . filing system so that when I come in on Monday we'll have tidy desks,' she suggested briskly.

'You mean you're going to take the job and you don't even know the salary or what you have to do?' Ken was incredulous. This wasn't the way he'd planned it at all.

'Well, you can interview me as we tidy up and tell me what's involved. You obviously need a bit of sorting out at the moment. Monica said you needed someone to start immediately,' Francesca said matter-of-factly.

'Oh, I do,' Ken said, flustered, as he ran his hands through his unruly mop of black hair. 'I've had a few temps since Sandra left but it's very unsatisfactory. That's why the place is in such a mess,' he found himself explaining. 'I've got the publicity contract for the City of Light opera festival so I'm up to my eyes next week and I need someone to man the office and collect a science-fiction author from the airport, bring her to her hotel for a couple of interviews and then bring her to the SF convention out in Dun Laoghaire. After that to bring her for a meal, back to her hotel and out to the airport the following day. That's the kind of work I need someone for. It's probably not what you're looking for though,' he backtracked.

Francesca studied the gangly young man in front of her with the nice hazel eyes and the faintly harassed air and knew immediately that Monica had coerced him into seeing her. She felt sorry for him. She couldn't help it.

'Look, Ken, did Monica pressurize you into seeing me?' she asked.

Ken blushed. 'Er ... something like that,' he admitted sheepishly.

'And I'm not really what you're looking for?' she said kindly.

'Well, it's just . . . ummm—'

'It's OK, Ken, really.' Francesca laughed. 'We'll just tell Monica we didn't think it would work out.'

'Mmm . . . well, if you'd like to give it a try for a couple of weeks I suppose there'd be no harm in that,' Ken heard himself say. 'I could do with a bit of back-up.'

Francesca looked him squarely in the eye. 'Are you sure now?'

'Why not?' he said impetuously. This woman seemed like a bit of a sport. At least she'd copped that Monica had foisted her on him and hadn't taken umbrage. He'd liked the way she'd dealt with it.

'What's this science-fiction author's name? I should read one of her books so I can talk to her about it,' Francesca suggested.

'Good thinking,' Ken exclaimed, rummaging through a mess of papers on his desk. 'Here you go, I have one right here.' He handed her a slim paperback and a sheaf of notes. 'Her press releases and publicity material. Umm, Francesca, the salary would be in the region of fifteen K. That's around two hundred and eighty-five a week, and of course all expenses will be covered.'

'Fine. Will I have to travel much outside of Dublin? If it works out, of course.'

'It depends on the client's requirements. Generally publicity tours usually take in Cork, Belfast, and perhaps Galway. Arts and music festivals crop up every so often. I also have the CMD music chain store as a client and I do all their publicity nationwide. But I'll look after that. I need you to do the one-off type of thing plus mail out press releases, keep on top of press cuttings, mail out invites to launches and so on. All the addresses are on computer.'

'You'll have to show me how to use it, I'm not very computer literate,' Francesca confessed. 'In fact I haven't a clue.'

'It's a doddle really. You'll pick it up in no time,' Ken assured her confidently.

'Did Monica tell you I'm booked to go abroad for a week?'

'Yeah. Thank God it's not next week, I'll be OK the week you're gone, there isn't much pencilled in, but the week you come back is a bit hectic. I have a launch in CMD Grafton Street and an art exhibition in Chief O'Neill's, a celebrity chef doing a sushi night to promote a new hotel in Temple Bar and an MBS author for TV3 and Gerry Ryan.'

'What's an MBS author?' Francesca was unfamiliar with the term.

'Oh, it's Mind Body Spirit. It's a genre that's really taken off in the last few years. This one, Katherine Kronskey, is a spiritual healer and works on a cellular level with great success, seemingly. She sees past lives and all that stuff. It sounds a bit far out to me but her books always make the bestsellers and that's all I care about,' Ken admitted with a broad grin.

Francesca laughed. 'How very pragmatic of you.'

'Well, Francesca, in this business it's all bestseller lists and column inches, unfortunately, and if past lives and all that stuff does it, it's OK by me. Think you can cope?'

'I think I'd cope better if I had a tidy desk,'

she chivvied. 'And I'm still waiting for my coffee.'

'It's on the way,' Ken declared, disappearing into a small hallway. Francesca followed. 'Loo's to the right. Kitchenette to the left. Er . . . I'll tidy it up,' he promised, having the grace to look ashamed as she observed the overflowing waste bin, the milk cartons and the remains of burnt toast on a plate. 'There's a microwave and two-ring cooker and fridge, as you can see, if you want to stay in for lunch when you're in the office. But there's lots of nice little places around to go to for lunch if you prefer.'

'Great. You tidy up the kitchen and I'll start on the office,' she said briskly. Better to start as she meant to go on, and that was definitely not being a kitchen skivvy, she decided, remembering Edward Allen and his morning coffee.

'OK, boss,' Ken said wryly, sweeping the empty cartons into a refuse sack.

'I'll water your plants for you and I'll wash up when I use the kitchen and that's the extent of my domestic duties. I have enough of them at home.'

'Fair enough. Honestly, I'm not usually such a slob, it's just this week was manic,' he said sheepishly. 'Please don't say anything to Monica—'

'Ken, if I'm working for you what goes on between these four walls is between you and me. We'll give it a month and see how it goes. Agreed?'

'Agreed.' He held out his hand and she took and shook it. 'Welcome to Ken Kennedy Publicity.'

'It's a spoon of coffee, milk and no sugar,' Francesca informed her new boss as she walked back into the office and took off her jacket.

Ken could hear her moving about the office as he

boiled the kettle. He was a bit bemused, to say the least. It had been the strangest interview that he'd ever conducted, that was for sure. In fact he felt in a funny sort of way that Francesca had interviewed *him* and found him satisfactory. So much for being the boss! The next month was certainly going to be interesting. If she started bossing him around she'd be out on her ear pronto, he decided as he stirred in a spoon of coffee and rooted in the press for a few biscuits to serve his new employee.

Chapter Twenty-seven

Nikki slipped out of the apartment and took the lift to the foyer. Mark was still asleep, and she didn't want to disturb him. He'd flown in from Geneva the previous evening and had had to go straight out to attend a colleague's retirement function that had gone on until the early hours. He was whacked. He didn't normally sleep on and she'd twisted and turned beside him before deciding to get up and go out.

Normally they went out for brunch on a Saturday, but given that he'd been tired and cranky Nikki thought it might be better to have something at home on the balcony. Some torte or quiche perhaps, with pissaladière and a crisp salad, washed down with a nice Sancerre. Maybe that might put him in a good humour, she thought glumly. Although he had no business being in a mood. It was *she* that was entitled to feel miffed. The trip to Paris had been a disaster because he'd read her the riot act again for calling on his precious Francesca and he'd been as moody as hell all weekend.

Then he'd informed her that he had to go to Geneva unexpectedly and he wouldn't be able to make that Marshall woman's gala. That had been the icing on the cake. She'd flown home from Paris alone. Privately Nikki felt the Geneva trip had suited Mark down to the ground. It had given him a handy excuse for staying away from Karen Marshall's bash. She was still fuming over it. She'd bought a beautiful but very expensive Amanda Wakeley black halter neck the last time she was in London, especially for the occasion, and it galled her that it was still lying in her wardrobe, unworn. She'd so badly wanted to walk into that function on Mark's arm and eyeball that slobby wife of his. It would have been a perfect opportunity to show Francesca that the marriage was over once and for all. After their encounter, she was beginning to feel that Francesca's claws were in Mark for good and he'd never get his freedom.

Nikki sighed as she started the ignition and drove towards the imposing black wrought-iron gates that opened smoothly to allow her to drive onto Mount Merrion Avenue. Her apartment had been an excellent buy, she reflected. Bought just before the boom in property prices, it had trebled in value in the past three years. She'd been thinking about investing in another apartment, one she could rent out, but the last Bacon report had made her have second thoughts. The punitive stamp duty and other taxes plus the exorbitant property prices did not make for ideal investment. And the way things were going it looked as though being a landlord wasn't worth the hassle.

Perhaps she'd buy in Spain. She'd seen beautiful

beach-front apartments in Marbella advertised by Hamilton Osborne King for half the price of property here and the same estate agents had recently advertised attractive town houses in Nerja that included their own swimming pool. It would be nice to have a place abroad that would be relatively self-financing through rental income in the high seasons. Then she could take off to the sun for a week or so every spring and autumn to recharge her batteries.

Her dream of buying a home with Mark didn't look as though it was going to materialize, so it was best to get on with things, she decided. Her bonuses were bound to be pretty good next year, she could well afford to consider investing abroad. Besides, it would do Mark all the good in the world to know that she was a completely independent woman. He was beginning to take her too much for granted and she didn't like it. He wasn't dancing attendance on her like he had at the beginning of their relationship. That delightful first bloom, when it was all new and exciting, had worn off and she missed it, she thought sadly. He'd always been so glad to see her, been so hungry for her. Now sometimes she felt that he wanted to get sex over and done with. It was a chore for him. Maybe she should be realistic and face the fact that they seemed to be going nowhere fast. Maybe she should end it. Hastily she brushed the thought aside. She wouldn't think about ending it yet. She'd give it another little while and see how things panned out.

Disheartened beyond measure she got into lane and drove into Blackrock.

Mark yawned and stretched and reached over to cuddle Nikki. His eyes opened as he felt cold sheets. She wasn't there. He called her name. No answer. He lay on his back staring up at the ceiling. A little breeze blew through the open window and he could see from the bed that it was a fine sunny day. His stomach growled. He was hungry. He thought longingly of Francesca's sizzling fry-ups on a Saturday morning that the whole family had enjoyed. Nobody could cook fried bread like Francesca. Nikki rarely cooked a fry. It stank out the apartment and she hated the lingering smell of bacon. He thought of Owen and Jonathan in America, no doubt gorging on waffles and maple syrup on Saturday mornings. Owen had gone off without as much as a goodbye. That had hurt. Owen was obviously never going to forgive him.

Mark sighed. He knew there was a lot of disapproval among his older colleagues too. Francesca had been very popular. But fuck it, he wasn't going to live his life just to suit a few dry old codgers who behind all their disapproval were probably suffused with envy. If they had a chance to get involved with a woman like Nikki they'd jump at it.

Mark rubbed his eyes. It was hard on Nikki too. He was inclined to forget that. He hadn't been very nice to her in Paris, he conceded. If he wasn't careful she'd kick him out. She'd been highly annoyed at missing Karen Marshall's party. Personally he'd been relieved. He didn't want to be at a function that both Francesca and Nikki were attending. He far preferred to keep a low profile. Besides, he didn't want to rub Francesca's nose in it, he thought ruefully. Nikki was a woman in her prime, his wife had started on the slippery slope to middle age and from what he'd seen the last time he'd been with her, she was making no effort to halt it. There was no need to let herself go. It just took discipline and self-pride. He felt far better since he'd gone back to the gym and got fit again. And he should thank Nikki for not cooking frys for him and for keeping him on the culinary straight and narrow.

He admired her for the way she took care of herself. Her body was in tip-top shape because she worked out and ate well. Her eyes were bright, her skin clear, not like Francesca's dark circles and lacklustre skin tone. Nikki was a very disciplined woman and it showed. Francesca could learn lessons from her, he thought crossly.

He wondered if she'd gone to the gala. She hadn't been out and about much since their split. If she had gone, she'd probably taken Millie as her guest, he conjectured as he reached over to the phone and dialled Nikki's mobile. 'Where are you, honey? I miss you,' he said huskily.

'I'm heading into Blackrock. I'm going to Minsky's to get us something for brunch. I thought you might prefer to eat on the balcony instead of going out,' Nikki's voice came crisply down the line.

'Why don't we go to IdleWilde and go for a walk on Killiney Hill afterwards? It's a lovely day – I could do with some fresh air.'

'Oh Mark, that would be great. A walk is just what we need. I'll come home and change. Won't be long.' He could hear the lilt in her voice before he hung up and he smiled. They were going to have a nice day today. He was dying to tell her about the double-dealing that was going on behind closed doors in Geneva. Mark loved talking to Nikki about work. She was always so interested, far more than Francesca had ever been. Nikki loved the cut and thrust of banking and high-powered finance; in that they had a true bond, he thought happily. He was a lucky man to find a woman who was so intellectually stimulating and dead sexy with it.

He jumped out of bed and strode into the shower. He felt horny. Before they headed off to IdleWilde they could have a nice sexy interlude and afterwards he'd really be ready for a hot cup of La Scala and one of the café's most popular orders, the big breakfast roll. He'd have his fry-up after all, he smiled as he stepped under the hot jets of water, hoping Nikki would be home soon to join him.

Francesca sat on the deck and turned her face up to the sun. It was a glorious morning. After breakfast she would take Trixie for a walk along Howth Pier. She poured herself a cup of freshly brewed coffee and buttered her toast. What was it that made eating outside so inviting? she wondered as she bit into the crisp toasted bread smothered in melting butter.

The garden looked lovely with masses of trailing roses along the trellis and a profusion of colourful bedding plants and shrubs in bloom. The breeze sent a perfumed waft of lavender drifting under her nose and she inhaled it with pleasure. She wondered sadly if Mark missed the garden. He'd always enjoyed sitting out, reading his paper or doing the crossword.

There wasn't much privacy on a balcony, she thought derisively as she flicked to the back page of the *Irish Times* weekend supplement. She couldn't help the broad smile of satisfaction that creased her face as she saw the rather flattering picture of herself, with the Clarks, in the social column.

When she saw another picture and read the column in the *Irish Mail* she felt an even fiercer sense of satisfaction. 'Stick that in your pipes and smoke it, the pair of you,' she muttered as she reread the piece.

> Flying solo but flying high, after several months of absence on the social circuit, since the break-up of her marriage from dishy international banker Mark Kirwan, Francesca Kirwan looked radiant in sequins at Karen Marshall's cancer charity gala. Mark and his new squeeze, fellow banker Nikki Langan, were nowhere to be seen. Wonder why . . . as he has always shared the top table since EuroBank Irl. contribute generously to Karen's good cause. Rumour has it the two ladies are at daggers drawn. *Quelle surprise!*

Quelle surprise! indeed, Francesca thought triumphantly, *her* transformation and new life had begun in earnest and she hoped her husband was reading all about her wherever he and his 'new squeeze' were having breakfast.

Would she ever have someone to share breakfast with again? she wondered forlornly as her spirits sank at the thought of Mark and Nikki eating breakfast and gazing into each other's eyes in some 'in' eatery. All she had for company was Trixie. Since Owen had gone the house seemed dull and empty. She missed him sorely. Missed his unquenchable exuberance and sense of fun. The house was as quiet as a morgue. Big and empty and quiet. It unnerved her sometimes going from room to room remembering when the boys had been growing up and the house had been filled with their friends. She and Mark had often retreated to his cosy study to get a bit of peace and quiet. He still had books and magazines and golf trophies that he hadn't taken with him. Almost as though he had left part of himself in his study for the day when he might come back.

She didn't want him back, she thought fiercely. Their life together was finished. She should insist he clear out all his rubbish and take it over to Ms Career Woman's luxury pad on Mount Merrion Avenue. Mark had given her the address and asked her to redirect his post. She couldn't bring herself to write *her* address on the envelopes so she sent it to the bank instead, much to his chagrin. Maybe she might meet an interesting man in her new job, she thought wistfully, trying to cheer herself up. How satisfying it would be to be with someone just to show Mark that she wasn't past it.

'Oh, you're pathetic,' she muttered crossly. Such an attitude to have at her age. If she were sixteen it would be understandable, but to be forty and want to have a man just to give the finger to her errant husband was the pits. 'You're a sad old boot,' she told herself as she poured more coffee. Just as well she was starting a new job, things were really rock bottom when you started talking to yourself. She held out a bit of buttered toast to Trixie. Just as well, too, that the gossip columnist couldn't see her now. Far from 'radiant in sequins'. But she *had* started to get on with her life.

Francesca finished her breakfast and tidied up. She needed to sort out her clothes for the following week and get the car valeted if she was going to be collecting authors and the like from the airport. She took one last look at her photo and studied it intently, trying to view it through Mark's eyes. Not a hint of depression or trauma, thankfully. In fact she looked as if life were a bowl of cherries. And it will be, she assured herself. It was said life began at forty. She was more than ready to test the theory.

Mark bit into a mouthful of sausage and egg and took a long slug of hot coffee. IdleWilde was buzzing and the atmosphere was laid back and trendy. It made him feel young, part of a scene he'd missed out on, tied down as he'd been with family and career. He smiled at Nikki. She was beautiful . . . and *wild*. They'd gone at it hot and heavy in the shower. Just as well the apartments were thoroughly soundproofed. He slid his hand along her thigh. He felt eighteen again.

'How about we take a couple of days off and head down to Kinsale and spend a bit of time together?' he suggested.

'Oh Mark, I'd love to,' Nikki enthused. 'But I'll have to check my diary. I've meetings in London next week that I simply have to go to.'

'Oh! I was hoping we could go next week while the weather is so fine,' he said, disappointed.

'And what about your appointments?'

He shrugged. 'I'll reschedule.'

'Mark, we're at a particularly sensitive juncture in negotiations, I need to be there,' Nikki explained.

'Why? What's happening?'

Nikki set aside her cup and began to detail the nitty-gritties of their latest takeover. Mark listened intently, interrupting occasionally with a pertinent question. They ate and talked and ordered more coffee and then Mark told her about the goings-on in Geneva and as Nikki laughed heartily at some witticism he made, he felt really glad to be in her company.

His mobile rang and he scowled as he noted the number on the screen. 'Hello, Dad,' he said patiently. He should have known the day was going too well.

'Have you seen the papers?' his father demanded.

'No.'

'Hrumph. It's a bloody disgrace, that's what it is. Disgracing the family name. That wife of yours going to parties on her own and you being discussed in most disrespectful terms. It just isn't good enough, Mark. I'm damn annoyed. Thank God your dear departed mother isn't alive to see this.'

'Dad, the signal's very bad. I'll call you later,' Mark said firmly as he switched off the phone. What on earth was his father talking about?

'What's wrong with your father?' Nikki asked, half-heartedly.

'Oh, he's going on about something about me in the papers. Give us a look until I see what he means.' He held out his hand for a paper. Nikki took the *Irish Times* out of her sun bag and handed it to him. She turned to the back page of the *Irish Mail*.

Mark felt his stomach give a little lurch as he saw Francesca's familiar face smiling out at him. She looked very well, he thought in surprise as he read the caption. So she'd gone to Karen's do. Somehow he hadn't really felt she had the bottle to do it. And she looked as though she was enjoying herself too. Well, good for her, he thought ruefully as he saw Nikki's expression change.

'What does it say?'

'I'm your "new squeeze",' she said caustically.

'Let's see.' He read the piece. 'Sarky bitch. Take no notice. It's tomorrow's fish-and-chip wrappings.'

'I bet Francesca enjoyed it,' Nikki retorted.

'She's not really into gossip columns,' Mark said quickly.

'Why do you always defend her?' Nikki snapped.

'I'm not defending her, Nikki. I was merely making a statement.'

'You *do* defend her. All the time,' she persisted. 'She can do no wrong in your eyes. Get over your guilt, Mark, and take a good look at her picture. That woman is saying to you: I don't need you. I can do this on my own. She doesn't *need* you any more, Mark, so deal with it.'

'Will you calm down, Nikki? There's no need to get so agitated over a simple remark. Let's finish our meal and go for a walk,' Mark suggested. He really didn't need a scene about Francesca right now. Why did Nikki feel so aggressive towards his wife? It was illogical. 'Look, Bono's just come in,' he murmured, hoping to take Nikki's mind off the subject.

'Big deal,' she muttered, studiously refusing to gawk.

'I'd love to see his house. The views are stunning,' Mark continued evenly.

'Talking of property, I'm thinking of investing in the south of Spain,' Nikki said coolly.

'Oh!' Mark was surprised. This was news to him. 'Well, it's extremely important where you buy, don't forget. Location. Location. Location. Resale value, rental desirability and all of that.'

'I'm not a fool, Mark,' Nikki retorted snootily. 'I know all that.'

'Sorry! Of course you do,' Mark apologized. That had been a stupid and patronizing remark. Nikki would have all options covered.

'So where are you thinking of buying, and will you take me along for a dirty weekend?' he teased.

'Maybe.' Nikki relaxed a little. 'I'm thinking of Marbella—'

'Great golf courses there,' Mark interjected enthusiastically. 'Go for it, Nikki. You won't go wrong. And this is the time to buy. Property prices are rising in Spain and Portugal. Get in while the going's good.' Mark was delighted with Nikki's news. It was good to see her investing wisely. He really admired her. There was a lot to be said for independent women.

Nikki sat leaning against a tree on Killiney Hill looking out to sea. It was a stunning view, she thought appreciatively as she looked south over the sparkling sea towards the emerald green coastline that curved down to Wicklow.

Mark's head rested in her lap as he snored lightly. He had such long dark lashes and a mouth that was made

271

for kissing. It was a very firm mouth, a masculine mouth. Nikki was particular about mouths. She hated loose-lipped men who slobbered all over you.

It was a peach of a day: the sun warm against her face, a balmy breeze rippling the trees and keeping the air cool in the intense heat of the sun.

Why had she made such an idiot of herself over brunch? She was furious with herself. It was so stupid of her to get rattled over Francesca's picture in the paper, and to be affected by that silly gossip columnist's remarks. Where was her poise, her dignity? No wonder Mark had got irritable. Men hated needy women who were always looking for reassurance. It was something she'd noticed in her own and friends' relationships. She'd never felt the need for such reassurance before because she had always been in control. But this relationship with Mark was completely different. He was the one in control, although he didn't realize it, so successful was the façade she'd created. It slipped sometimes though, she thought despondently. Like this morning. Disaster! She was turning into a pathetic co-dependent that all those ridiculous self-help books were written for. She despised such women. Women like Francesca. How ironic that she was in danger of becoming one. *Never!* Nikki vowed. She was going to nip this in the bud once and for all. She just had to keep a lid on her feelings about Francesca. But it was so damn difficult.

Nikki traced her finger over the relaxed line of Mark's jaw and felt a wave of desire. He had taken her with some of the old hunger this morning and she'd revelled in it, arching and thrusting against him as the water sluiced over them until they could hardly see each other for the steam. She'd felt very cherished, wanted and loved and she'd been so looking forward to their brunch and walk. It had all been going delightfully until his bloody father rang whingeing about the piece in the papers.

And then *she'd* lost it.

Nikki exhaled deeply and looked down at the man sleeping in her arms. What did he truly feel for her? If Francesca hadn't discovered their affair would it have continued? Would he ever have left his wife for her? Deep down she was half afraid to think too deeply about such things. In her heart and soul she felt the answers might be no and there lay the source of her insecurity.

She examined Mark's handsome face, softened in repose, and felt a deep sadness. Were they going to make it as a couple or was she on a train to nowhere? He'd been genuinely delighted for her when she'd told him of her plans to invest. Was it because she was making her own plans for her future . . . a future that he wasn't planning on sharing, or was it because he thought it was a good financial investment? He'd teased her about going away for a dirty weekend and she knew that he liked to play golf.

Maybe he did see them being abroad together. Maybe she was just being insecure. It was all so uncertain. If that stupid woman would divorce him and go on her way so that he could make his own plans without living in this ridiculous limbo it would all be so different. Then at least she would know one way or another how Mark truly felt about her. As long as Francesca was in the picture he had the perfect excuse for not committing. Much as she loved him, Nikki wasn't at all sure that his feelings for her were strong enough to satisfy her. If she stayed with him would there always be this feeling of lack, this insatiable desire for more? Could she live with this driving need to be loved by him, day after day? Were the increasingly rare days of happiness worth the unrelenting misery that went hand in hand with her love for him?

A tear trickled down Nikki's cheek and she brushed it hastily aside. How Francesca would relish this, the cold bitch, she thought angrily. Knowing that the 'other woman' was so unhappy would be such a triumph.

Nikki took a deep breath. This was so unlike her and she was sick of it. She wouldn't give in yet. She'd stick it out until Christmas and if things hadn't improved, she'd start the New Year unattached. Although he didn't know it, Mark was on notice. A woman could only put up with so much, Nikki decided firmly as she raised her face to the sun and felt herself relax knowing that she had taken some control back over her future.

Chapter Twenty-eight

'Just explain who you are if they ask you,' Ken instructed as he drove past the security barrier in RTE with a wave to the guard, who clearly recognized him. It was Monday morning, the first day of her new job, and Ken was dropping material into RTE and giving her a guided tour at the same time.

'That's the TV Centre. The Radio Centre is further up. I'll show you around each of them but generally once you introduce yourself at the desk and give your contact name, someone will come and collect you and your guest and take care of you from then on. They're very good out here and in TV3 so all you have to worry about is soothing fraught guests' nerves,' Ken assured her as he pointed out parking areas which seemed to Francesca to be pretty full wherever she looked.

'There's a guest car park up there by the Radio Centre but just park on the double yellows if you're not going to be too long.'

Francesca stared around the huge complex as Ken parked the car. The grounds were beautifully kept.

She hadn't realized it covered such a large area. She'd never been in RTE before and she was curious as well as a little intimidated. Ken seemed so assured as he greeted people by name and knew exactly where he was going. It was exciting, she had to admit as she walked up the steps to the Radio Centre and saw Gareth O'Callaghan, the popular 2FM presenter, hurry past.

Ken took her around the huge open-plan office in the Radio Centre and then brought her to the small coffee dock where she tried not to stare as she saw newsreaders, presenters and celebrities sitting having coffee breaks, deep in conversation with producers, researchers and production assistants.

'This is where you can bring guests before or after a radio interview for a reviving cup of coffee. There's a small canteen in the TV Centre and of course there's the main staff canteen. I'll show you that too,' Ken said kindly. 'Don't be fazed, Francesca. You'll know it all like the back of your hand in no time. The first time I came here, I was petrified. I thought I'd never get to know the place. But you'll be fine after a couple of visits.'

'You see and hear all these TV and radio personalities on screen or behind a mike, it's strange to see them sitting having coffee just being normal,' Francesca remarked as Ken guided her to a vacant table.

'They're very normal, as you'll find out for yourself.' Ken laughed. 'Tea, coffee?'

'Coffee please,' Francesca said. 'And could I have a scone?' She'd been too wound up to have any breakfast and she was a little peckish.

Ken grinned. 'Thank God you're not one of these awful women who doesn't eat. They drive me mad. Scones coming up.'

Oh God, I wonder is he telling me that I'm too fat? Francesca thought guiltily, making a mental note not to eat goodies in front of him. Her mobile phone rang. She saw Mark's number on the screen. What on earth was he ringing her for? His timing was the pits, she thought irritably. Trust him to pick her first morning in her new job. Well, she wasn't telling him about it yet. Just in case it didn't work out.

'Hello,' she murmured. Behind her, the clatter of cups against saucers and the hum of chat made it difficult to hear.

'Hello, it's me. Where are you? I tried you at home first,' Mark asked curiously.

'It doesn't matter,' Francesca said hastily. 'Why are you ringing me?'

'Oh! I, ah . . . I just wanted to say how well you looked in your photo in the papers on Saturday. I hope you enjoyed Karen's do. I couldn't make it myself. Had to go to Geneva suddenly,' Mark said chummily.

'Really,' Francesca said coolly. 'You missed a good night. Look, I'm kind of busy right now, was there anything else?'

'Not really, I suppose.' Mark sounded deflated. 'We're going to Kinsale for a few days, if you're looking for me. I'll be contactable on the mobile.'

'Fine. Bye.' Francesca clicked off. She was furious. Patronizing bastard! How dare he ring her up and tell her that she looked well. As if he cared, she thought bitterly. So they were off to Kinsale, were they? How nice for them. He hadn't even had the decency to ask her if she was going to take a holiday this year. He had the life of Riley, swanning around the country with his fancy woman. Living the life of a bachelor. She felt betrayed yet again. It should have been her going to Kinsale for a few days. No doubt Mark would be taking Nikki to Ballybrit, to the Galway races in August. She and Mark had always spent a week of their holidays there. If she wanted to go to the races this year she'd be going on her own, she thought unhappily.

Fuck him. Why did he have to phone her this morning with his talk of Kinsale? She'd been doing really well, on a high about her new job, and now she was back on a downer again. How long would it take to get over it? Would she ever be able to look at Mark and Nikki's relationship with detachment? Or would it always be a red-hot needle in her heart? Why couldn't she be like her husband and get on with things? The break-up didn't seem to have knocked a feather out of him. But then he had a lover to cushion whatever emotions he felt. She was alone, dealing with it by herself. He had such a nerve, though, with his patronizing guff about how well she'd looked. If he'd been anyway near her she knew she would have clobbered him, she felt so angry.

She saw Ken weaving between the tables carrying a tray and composed her features. She certainly didn't intend for her private life to interfere with her work, especially on her first day. She pushed Mark and Nikki to the back of her mind and smiled at her employer. 'This doesn't seem like work in the slightest.'

'Believe me, Francesca, there'll be days when you'll go home and say to yourself: "Am I mad?"' Ken said cheerfully, munching on a thickly buttered scone. 'Enjoy it while you can.'

By the end of the day she was whacked. There was so much to assimilate, and even the commuting was an eye-opener. She stood swaying with the motion of the Dart, packed like a sardine in a crowded, stuffy carriage, envying the lucky ones who had a seat. This was something that would take some getting used to, she mused when a portly man trod on her toe as he shoved his way towards the door. Nevertheless, the day had flown by and she was reasonably pleased with the way she had handled herself. And Ken was nice and, despite his scatty air and laid-back style, extremely professional and good at his job.

She was so tired by the time she got home that she buttered some brown bread, cut a chunk of red cheddar, grabbed a can of Diet Coke and sank onto her sun lounger to catch the dying rays in her bra and pants. It was only as she drifted off to sleep later that night having pressed her clothes for the morning that Mark's phone call came briefly to mind but she hadn't the energy to sustain the anger and resentment she'd felt earlier in the day. For the first time in a long while she slept soundly and woke surprised that the night had passed so quickly.

The following morning found her standing at Arrivals in Dublin Airport holding a cardboard sign with her author's name printed in large letters, hoping that the woman would see it without difficulty. Magda Waldon was one of the most prolific science-fiction authors in the world and at fifty-four was still producing a book a year. She was the guest of honour at a science-fiction convention in Dun Laoghaire.

Francesca scanned the crowds pouring out onto the concourse. She'd studied the photograph in the publicity pack and knew that she was looking for a red-haired woman with deep-set eyes and a haughty stare.

'You there.' A stout little woman with a halo of flame-dyed hair cascading extravagantly down her shoulders poked Francesca in the ribs. 'I'm Magda Waldon and I need a drink badly. That bucket we flew in hit every air pocket going.'

Francesca's heart sank. From the fumes of brandy emanating from her it was obvious the woman had already been drinking. Francesca stared at her charge and tried to match the reality with the publicity photo. What a difference airbrushing makes, she thought drily. Magda looked every minute of her fifty-four years. Red-rimmed eyes stared out through silver bifocals. Bright red cheeks, veined and puffy, were a far cry from the peaches and cream complexion on her obviously retouched photos. The diminutive author wore black patent high heels and clinging black trousers; a low-cut top revealed a wrinkled, tanned cleavage and a scarlet-waisted jacket emphasized Magda's voluminous curves. Chunky gold jewellery dripped from ears, neck and wrists. She jangled as she walked. *Probably hides the clink of bottles*, Francesca thought uncharitably as she held out her hand.

'I'm Francesca Kirwan. I'm from Ken Kennedy PR and I'll be looking after you—'

'Yes. Yes. Take me to the bar.' Magda waved away the niceties, clearly not interested in the pleb who'd be looking after her.

'If you come this way,' Francesca said politely, leading her towards the bar area. Magda didn't waste time. She downed two double brandies in quick succession before Francesca said firmly that it was time to leave as she had two interviews lined up at her hotel before lunch.

'Bugger them,' Magda snorted derisively.

'I'm sorry, but they've been arranged and we don't want to let people down,' Francesca said smoothly. Inside she was quaking. This was her first test. What a disaster it would be if her author arrived pissed and cancelled the interviews. Trust her to get a lush for her first assignment.

'I need the loo and I'll be with you then,' Magda barked, annoyed at being thwarted.

When she disappeared into the Ladies, Francesca made a quick phone call to Ken. 'Hi, it's me. She's pissed,' she whispered.

'Don't worry. Her publishers told me about her. She always rises to the occasion. Just get her to the hotel as quick as you can,' Ken advised.

'Why didn't you warn me?' Francesca demanded.

'I didn't want you to be worrying. I'm sorry she's not the easiest first task but if you cope with her you'll cope with anything. Just think of it as a baptism of fire. Be firm with her, her editor said.'

'I'm resigning as of now,' Francesca announced.

'God, Francesca. Don't do that to me. We agreed a month's trial. I've grown dependent on you already. There'll be a bonus at the end of the year.' Ken's cheerful tones had disappeared. He sounded horrified.

'Just teasing.' Francesca grinned. 'So there's going to be a bonus, is there? It'd better be good,' she added. Magda tottered out of the Ladies on her impossibly high heels. 'Have to go,' she murmured, 'here she comes.'

'Are you sure we don't have time for one more?' the author demanded.

'Unfortunately not,' Francesca said firmly as she hoisted Magda's bulky overnight bag onto her shoulder and led the way to the exit.

'So much for Irish hospitality,' muttered Magda truculently in her wake.

By the end of the day, Francesca knew what Ken was talking about when he'd warned she'd end up asking herself if she was mad to be doing the job. Magda had insisted on changing her hotel room because she didn't like the view. She drank her way through several double brandies during her interviews. After a lunch of lobster she drew herself to her full height and said morosely, 'Better get this buggering ordeal over with. Lead the way, Frannie.' She'd taken to calling Francesca Frannie.

Francesca had watched in amazement as she held her adoring audience spellbound during her reading and question-and-answer session. Afterwards, to Francesca's immense relief, she had gone to her room for a nap in preparation for the dinner which the convention organizers were hosting in her honour. Francesca slipped off to her own room, had a shower, lay on her bed and tried to relax.

What a day, she thought drowsily. This time last

week she'd been sitting around at home feeling sorry for herself. She smiled, amused at the difference a week could make in someone's life. It might be a trying day but so far she hadn't had time to be bored or sorry for herself. This job was just what she needed right now, she thought gratefully.

At eight-fifteen, Magda appeared in the foyer, ready for action and a hard night's drinking. She was dressed in a clinging purple jersey dress that revealed every generous bulge and clashed alarmingly with her hair. Not even the cloying scent of Poison could disguise the smell of alcohol which oozed from every pore. As they sat in the taxi on the journey to the restaurant she took a silver flask out of her bag and took a long slug. Francesca discreetly pretended not to notice. Not that Magda gave a hoot anyway. Keeping up appearances was obviously not a priority. She immediately found fault with the restaurant because it had wooden floors and moaned that the noise was giving her a headache. *Not as much of a headache as I'll give you if you don't put a sock in it*, Francesca thought balefully as she smiled sympathetically at her and offered her an aspirin which was brusquely waved away.

Halfway through the Irish coffees, Magda's head slumped onto her chest and she started to snore. On top of her earlier intake, she had downed three aperitifs and a bottle of red wine during dinner, plus another brandy. Francesca and the organizer of the convention, an earnest young man called Des, hauled her out to a taxi and as Francesca got in beside her, Magda opened her eyes for a second. 'Take me to the bar,' she slurred, before conking out on her shoulder.

With the help of the night porter, who whooshed Magda onto a luggage cart, Francesca got her charge to her room. Between them they managed to unload the comatose woman onto the bed and turned her on her side. Francesca pulled her shoes off but decided against trying to undress Magda. She covered her with the quilt and slipped out of the room praying fervently that the author wouldn't puke and choke.

On tenterhooks, she called reception the next morning and asked to be put through to Magda's room. The phone rang unanswered for ages. Francesca started to panic. She was about to ask the girl on the switchboard to get someone to check that Magda had survived the night when she heard a distinctly grouchy, 'Bugger off.'

She was alive anyway, Francesca thought with relief as she hurried into the shower. All she had to do was get her through Check-in and that would be her responsibility for Magda Waldon, SF doyenne, completed.

The phone rang as she gulped down hot coffee. It was Millie. 'How's it going?'

'Don't ask. I can't stop to talk but I'll tell you all about it this evening.'

'Are you enjoying it?'

'Enjoying it might be a bit of an exaggeration,' Francesca grinned. 'It's certainly not boring. Talk to you later.'

Magda was not in good humour. She opened the door to Francesca's firm knock looking dishevelled and very much the worse for wear.

'Oh, it's you,' she grunted.

'Yes, it's me,' Francesca said cheerfully as she flung back the curtains.

Magda winced. 'What did you do that for? Get me a brandy immediately.'

'Right. You have your shower and I'll ring room service for a brandy.' The minibar was open, some of the bottles had been drunk, others stuck out of Magda's bag, so there was no point in rooting for a brandy there. 'Do you want breakfast?' she asked politely.

'Bugger breakfast,' Magda growled.

An hour later, Magda teetered out to Francesca's car. The brandy had revived her somewhat and she gazed blearily around. 'Never get to do much sight-seeing on these sorts of jaunts. Far too busy, you know. Pity. Looks quite interesting,' she muttered as they drove past the yacht clubs and then past a ferry docking. 'Sea looks nice,' Magda declared before subsiding into silence.

It was with enormous relief that Francesca watched her charge disappear through the departure gate later that morning.

'You're not the worst I've been with. Here. It's a signed copy,' she announced, thrusting a hardback of her latest novel into Francesca's hands. Then she was gone with a toss of her hair and a wave of her bejewelled wrist, wreathed in a mist of alcohol fumes. Francesca pitied the passenger sitting beside her on the plane.

'An experience not to be missed for any good publicist,' Ken laughed as Francesca regaled him with the events of the past twenty-four hours, back at the office. 'You did well, Frannie. I think I'll call you Frannie from now on,' he declared, po-faced.

'You do and I'm out of here big time,' Francesca warned.

The rest of the week was a doddle in comparison to Magda's shenanigans. A journalist cancelled an interview at very short notice and asked to reschedule, much to the annoyance of a young fashion designer who was making news with her far-out designs. She'd been highly snooty with Francesca, but had been as sweet as pie when Ken got back to her to calm her down.

The computer in the office terrified her. Ken had given her a brief tutorial on how to use it, but he was so proficient he took it for granted that she understood completely what he was showing her. As soon as she got back from Portugal she was enrolling in a computer class, she decided.

As she travelled home through the Friday rush hour after her first week at work she felt exhausted but exhilarated. The train sped past the Merrion Gates. Lines of traffic waited for the barriers to rise. At least she hadn't had to drive in today. Driving around the city and trying to get parking was the stuff of nightmares. Driving home through horrendous traffic on a hot Friday evening was not for the faint-hearted. Only a couple of stations to go; she'd be home in twenty-five minutes. If she were driving she'd be at least an hour and a half in the traffic.

She'd done well, Francesca comforted herself as the train pulled into Connolly and droves of weary commuters swarmed into the carriage. She'd put manners on the filing system and tidied up the office. She'd taken charge of her first author and ferried her around with a façade of confidence she'd been far from feeling. Magda had been a blessing in disguise. If she could cope with Magda she could cope with anyone. She hadn't wiped anything off the damned computer, although that was due more to luck than knowledge, she thought wryly as she shoved her way towards the door as the train eventually clattered into Clontarf Station.

A welcome breeze blew around her as she climbed the green iron steps to cross the tracks. The heat in the sun, warm on her face, lifted her spirits. She'd have her tea outside on the deck, relax for a little while and then pack her case. The week in Portugal couldn't have come at a better time: this time on Sunday she'd be sipping cocktails beside a pool. This holiday was just what she needed.

Chapter Twenty-nine

Francesca yawned. She was dead tired and longing to get to their holiday apartment.

'I wish those doddery idiots would sort out their problem and get on the bus,' Millie said irritably.

'Me too,' murmured Francesca as she looked down at the elderly couple outside the bus who were angrily remonstrating with the courier.

'What's wrong with them anyway?'

Francesca yawned again and nearly gave herself lockjaw. 'Something about damaged luggage.'

A baby at the rear of the bus squalled lustily. 'That's all we need,' groaned Millie. 'The next time I have a brainwave about going away for a week, deal with me severely. I'd forgotten the horror of the "charter flight holiday".'

'Me too,' admitted Francesca. 'How long does it take to get to the apartments?'

'About an hour. If we ever get going,' growled Millie, resisting the urge to rap smartly on the window. 'If they don't get a move on I'll go down there myself and manhandle them onto the bus.'

'Mammaay, Mammaay!' Another toddler launched into wails.

'Jeepers, Al Jolson would be proud of him,' Millie groaned in exasperation.

Francesca tittered. 'Stop it, Millie, you're awful. They're tired, God love them. It's after midnight.'

'It will be just our luck that all those kids end up in our apartments, then you won't be so magnanimous.' Millie sniffed.

'It was a brand-new Louis Vuitton and I'll be wanting it replaced,' the elderly woman in the pink catsuit reiterated loudly as she climbed the steps into the bus, followed by her red-faced husband. 'It's an absolute disgrace the way we're treated,' she declared to all and sundry as she plonked herself into a seat.

'What's that raddled old bag doing on a charter holiday if she can afford a brand-new Louis Vuitton?' Millie snorted.

'Millie, shush, they'll hear you!' Francesca chided.

'Good! I want them to.' Millie had had enough. The flight had been very delayed. It had been a tiring day and her patience had long since evaporated. The engine throbbed into life and the bus slowly pulled out of its parking bay. 'At last,' murmured Millie as the child's screeching and the baby's bawling subsided and they got under way.

An hour and a half later, Francesca and Millie lugged their cases into the reception area of Oura Praia apartments. They were the last passengers to be set down after a long winding journey that left them queasy. Thankfully, Pink Catsuit and the screeching children had got off at the first set-down. A nice young man behind the desk slid their registration forms across to them and took their passports. Two minutes later they had the key to their studio.

'I'm not happy about this,' Millie fretted as they took the lift to their designated floor. 'This lift is going down. I asked for a top-floor apartment.' The lift doors opened and the whiff of chlorine wafted past.

'Shit, we're on the ground floor. Francesca, this is not on. I specifically asked for top floor.' Millie was fit to be tied.

'Let's have a look and see what it's like,' Francesca suggested. She was longing for bed. 'I like the way they have carpet on the corridor. I've never seen that before in apartments,' she added approvingly as they pulled their cases behind them.

Millie slid the key in the lock, pushed open the door and switched on the lights.

'Let's see. It looks nice.' Francesca peered eagerly over Millie's shoulder. She'd only ever been abroad twice, with friends, before she got married; suddenly a vivid memory came floating back, of her excitement as she and two tipsy giggling friends had click-clacked their way down a marble-tiled corridor in Ibiza for their first glimpse of their tiny one-bedroom egg box of an apartment.

Millie wrinkled her nose as she marched over to the patio doors and pulled back the curtains. 'Definitely not, Francesca. There's a smell of smoke in this one and it's right opposite the pool. Can you imagine the noise!'

Francesca's heart sank as she backed out of the

studio. Millie was very good at making scenes and standing her ground. Much better than she was. If Millie had discovered Aidan entertaining another woman in a hotel room he would now be minus a limb at least, she thought glumly as she followed her sister back the way they'd come.

She hid a grin as she watched Millie stride across the foyer. The poor unfortunate at the desk had no idea what he was in for. Millie was not to be trifled with, especially in the early hours of the morning. Francesca puffed her way after her sister with her case. She was so unfit it was pathetic. Lugging her case around was making her breathless. Granted, there were at least seven large paperbacks packed in there, but nevertheless she was going to have to do something about her lack of fitness. It was ridiculous. She was forty, not ninety.

'But I *specifically* requested a top-floor studio,' Millie was emphasizing vehemently.

'I'm sorry, madam, all the studios are allocated,' the receptionist told her politely.

'This is *outrageous*—'

'Excuse me,' interjected Francesca, 'but do you have any top-floor one-bedroom apartments vacant?'

'Actually, madam, we do but they would be much more expensive. Let me see.' He tapped away at his computer and smiled at her. 'It would be forty-eight thousand, three hundred escudos more.'

Millie's jaw dropped.

'It doesn't sound too bad when you say it quickly.' Francesca grinned as she took out her credit card. 'Visa?' she enquired hopefully.

'Fine, madam.' The young man beamed, relieved

beyond measure that he didn't have to deal with the Amazon who looked as if she could flatten him with one punch.

'Francesca, how much extra is it?' Millie demanded.

'Who cares? I got my first pay cheque. And I can dump you out in the sitting room if you start getting on my nerves.'

Millie laughed. 'Mind your cheek.'

For the second time that night they stood in the lift, only this time it glided upwards to the sixth floor. 'Francesca, how much extra *did* it cost?' Millie asked. 'I can't figure out all those noughts.'

'It's about one hundred and sixty pounds extra, I reckon. It will be worth it to have a nice quiet apartment.'

'It better be, or I'm going to cause ructions,' Millie said.

Eagerly they hurried down the corridor and Francesca thrust the key into the lock, pushed open the door, switched on the light and smiled broadly. 'Yes! This is more like it,' she said with satisfaction.

'It's really nice,' enthused Millie as she stepped into the small entrance hall and looked around at the large, beautifully furnished lounge.

'The bedroom's huge and the balcony goes right along to the lounge. And the bath's like a swimming pool,' Francesca said happily.

'Oh Francesca, look at the view,' Millie urged.

She went to stand beside her sister on the balcony and gazed around in pleasure. Below her the huge floodlit turquoise pool sparkled invitingly. The lights of the resort twinkled beneath them and out to sea a full moon shone on a glassy sea in a sky full of stars.

'Let's have a cup of tea. I'm gasping for one,' suggested Millie. 'We'll sit on the balcony for a while and get our equilibrium back.'

'Good thinking, Wonder Woman. And there's a packet of Club Milks packed away in the supplies bag.' Francesca rooted in the pretty holdall she'd packed essentials in and triumphantly waved the packet of Club Milk snacks.

Twenty minutes later they were sitting gazing out at their kingdom for a week, munching chocolate snacks, with their unpacking done and six more days of lazy bliss beckoning. It was a nice feeling and Francesca felt almost young again as she sat laughing at her sister's witty asides.

Men! Who needed them when you had a sister like Millie? was her last conscious thought as she finally fell asleep beneath crisp white sheets a little while later.

Mark threw his eyes up to heaven as Viv Cassidy wittered on. 'It's just we'd love to have Francesca in the mixed doubles but I can't get my hands on her. I've phoned the house constantly but haven't got an answer. She usually has her answering machine on and I leave a message but not these past few days. Unfortunately I don't have her mobile number. Is she away? I haven't seen her around and I haven't heard Trixie barking, and of course our book club is finished until September so I don't see her at that,' Viv said breathlessly.

'Look, Viv, leave it with me, and I'll get her to give you a call. I've got a meeting now so I must go. Nice talking to you,' Mark said smoothly and hung up.

'Bloody inquisitive cow,' he muttered, stretching and yawning. Imagine going to the trouble of calling him at the bank. *And how are you? You must bring your new lady friend over for drinks*, she'd invited in that saccharine tone of hers that got on his nerves. He could imagine Nikki indulging in small talk with Viv. Or rather he couldn't. He chuckled at the notion. Viv would definitely not be Nikki's cup of tea. She didn't suffer fools gladly.

He frowned. He was damned if he was going to give the silly bitch Francesca's mobile number. Viv would pester her morning, noon and night if she had it. That was the type she was.

He dialled his old home number. It rang unanswered. It was unusual for Francesca not to have her answering machine on. Maybe she *was* away. But hardly. She'd surely have had the courtesy to tell him; after all, he'd told her about going to Kinsale, he thought self-righteously, forgetting the numerous other jaunts he'd taken with Nikki that he hadn't mentioned.

His secretary buzzed him. 'Charles de Fressange on line from Paris.'

'Fine. Put him through,' Mark instructed. He'd try home later in the morning and if there was no answer he'd buzz Francesca on the mobile. After all, he had a legitimate excuse. If you could call Viv Cassidy an excuse. It was awful to think that he needed an excuse to talk to the woman he'd shared his life with for twenty years, he thought sadly. Francesca really needed to grow up and let bygones be bygones. She'd held the grudge long enough.

'*Bonjour*, Mark.' The deep fruity tones of his French colleague came down the line clear as a bell and Mark turned his attention to matters that were far more pressing than Viv Cassidy trying to contact his estranged wife.

'This is the life.' Francesca turned over on her tummy and felt the sun's rays warm on her back.

'I was born for this.' Millie stretched luxuriously on her lounger. They'd just finished a tasty lunch at the poolside restaurant and were preparing to have a nice snooze under their gaily coloured yellow umbrellas.

'I'm going to sleep my brains out this week,' Millie declared.

'Do you miss the kids?' Francesca asked sympathetically.

'Nope. I'm delighted Aidan is having quality time with them,' Millie said firmly and Francesca laughed.

'It was good of him to take the week off and let you go away.'

'For crying out loud, Francesca, what are you on about?' Millie said irritably. 'He gets away for his rugby weekends and his fishing weekends. I'm *entitled*. If you'd have heard them in school. "Isn't he wonderful?" "Isn't he supportive?" "You're very lucky, my fella wouldn't do that for me." It's ridiculous. No-one ever tells me I'm wonderful or I'm supportive when I have them day in day out and when Aidan's away.'

'I suppose,' Francesca murmured.

'Well, it's true. Women are expected to do everything. Work, look after the kids and run the home and if the man mucks in now and again she's considered lucky.'

'Aidan is much more hands on than Mark was,' Francesca remarked.

'That's because I'm working outside the home. He has to be. If I'd stayed at home like you did I can guarantee you his contribution would be much less – and I don't mean that in a nasty way. It's just the way it goes. Deep in their hearts men still see women in the role of mother and nurturer and that's never going to change.' Millie settled herself more comfortably having vented her indignation.

'I wonder, does Nikki Langan want children?' Francesca rested her chin on her hands. 'She certainly doesn't seem the mother/nurturer type.'

'Mark would get some shock if she got pregnant. Wouldn't he?' Millie chuckled. 'The last thing he'd want is a baby.'

'They seem very happy though. It might happen in the future,' Francesca said glumly. 'They went to Kinsale for a couple of days.'

'That's nice for them,' Millie said drily. 'They might seem very happy but he isn't in any apparent rush to divorce you and marry her. I'm telling you, Francesca, he has the best of both worlds. Would you take him back if he came back to you?' she asked curiously.

'I don't know,' Francesca admitted. 'Sometimes I think I would. Other times I vow I wouldn't. It depends on the humour I'm in. I'm terribly lonely. I miss waking up on a Saturday morning and having a snuggle and making plans for the day. I miss having someone to talk to – you know, the "wait until I tell you" bit. The house is like a morgue. It's so quiet, it's eerie.'

'Sell it,' Millie retorted.

'Sell it?' Francesca echoed. 'Oh, I couldn't do that. It's the family home.'

'Francesca, my dear girl, Jonathan's in the States and what's the betting Owen won't stay there too? Mark's done a bunk. There's nothing to stop you and Mark selling the house and you getting half the proceeds and buying a smaller place of your own. Jonathan and Owen can always come and stay. It would be a new start. I think it would be very good for you.'

'Mark wouldn't agree. I don't think he'd ever want to sell.'

'Fuck him, Francesca. This is not about what he wants, it's about what you want. And I can tell you one thing here and now: if you want to sabotage that relationship of his the one way to do it is to tell Mark that you want a divorce.

'If you divorce him, he's no excuse not to marry your one. If he wanted to marry her he'd have asked for a divorce long ago. He's only using you as an excuse to keep her at bay,' Millie said sagely. 'She's desperate. Otherwise she would never have come calling on you that day. You divorce him and they'll be split up in six months.'

'You think so?'

'I know so,' Millie said confidently. 'And then he'll come running back to you and you'll be holding the trump cards.'

'Could you imagine what Ma would say if I told her I was getting a divorce?' Francesca groaned.

'Tough, Francesca. She'll just have to get over it. You only have one life, you can't live it to suit Ma's sensibilities. It was bad enough when she heard that I was going away for a week and leaving the kids with Aidan. Boy did I get flared nostrils and disapproving sniffs. You work out what's best for you, not what's best for Mark or Ma or anyone else.'

'Oh, let's not think about things like that just now,' Francesca murmured. 'Let's just enjoy the sun.'

'Sorry for lecturing,' Millie apologized. 'I didn't mean to get up on my high horse.'

'I know,' Francesca said fondly. 'You'd think it would be the other way around, me being the eldest and all.'

'You couldn't lecture if your life depended on it. I got all the bossy genes.' Millie yawned. 'Wake me up for a cocktail at four.'

'Yes, boss,' Francesca drawled. She closed her eyes and felt the tiredness of the past months drain away as a delicious lethargy suffused her body and she drowsed under the hot sun.

It was a delightful snooze and she felt refreshed an hour later when she woke up. Millie was snoring gently beside her. Francesca gazed in envy at her younger sister's long golden limbs. Naturally athletic, her work as a gym teacher kept her fit and toned and beside her Francesca felt flabby and matronly. On the lounger next to her, a young blonde German girl sunbathed gracefully. Wearing only the skimpiest thong, she looked like a supermodel. It was depressing to say the least so Francesca averted her envious gaze and decided to go for a swim. Some brisk laps of the pool might help to stop everything from going south. She'd start her fitness regime in Portugal with swimming and walking and keep it up when she got home, she decided.

The water was cool and soothing to her warm limbs and Francesca swam contentedly, emptying her mind of thoughts and just concentrating on her stroke.

Millie had just woken up when she emerged twenty minutes later, invigorated. 'It was fabulous. I really enjoyed it. You should get in,' she told her sister.

'Maybe later,' Millie said lazily. 'I'm thirsty. Is it cocktail time?'

'Any time is cocktail time.' Francesca grinned. 'What do you want?'

'I think a dressed Pimm's might hit the spot.'

'Hmmm, sounds good to me. I'll go and get them.'

'Thank you, wee slavie.' Millie stretched languorously and turned on her side to ensure an all-round tan. She watched her sister weave her way between the loungers. She was so glad that she'd acted on impulse and booked the holiday for them, and for all her giving out, Aidan hadn't minded a bit about taking a week off to mind the kids. She'd buy him something really nice; she was looking forward to a good dollop of child-free shopping.

She heard a faint melodic tone coming from the depths of Francesca's beach bag. It was hardly Aidan, she'd spoken to him earlier in the day on Francesca's phone. Her own mobile wasn't able to receive calls outside of Ireland.

She rooted frantically and found the ringing phone. 'Hello?'

'Who's that?'

Millie's jaw dropped. It was Mark. She hadn't spoken to him since Francesca had kicked him out.

'It's Millie,' she said shortly.

'Oh. Oh, Millie. How's it going? Could I speak to Francesca please?' He sounded uncomfortable.

'Aaah, she's . . . she's in the Ladies at the moment,' Millie fibbed. She wasn't sure if Francesca had said anything to Mark about her holiday. She had the feeling that she hadn't.

'Where are you?' Mark asked casually.

'Out,' she said tersely. 'I'll get Francesca to call you back. Bye.'

She sat chewing her lip. Should she tell Francesca that Mark had called? Maybe it was something urgent. Although he hadn't sounded as though anything was amiss. It was obvious he didn't know that she and Francesca were on holiday. Otherwise he surely wouldn't have asked where were they. What a nuisance. And so early into their holiday too. She saw Francesca heading back towards her carrying a tray.

'Got us some peanuts and crisps to keep us going,' she said cheerfully as she handed Millie a tall, ice-cold glass with a cocktail umbrella stuck in a red cherry.

'Thanks,' murmured Millie, taking a sip. It was delicious. 'What did you get?'

'A daiquiri.' Francesca settled on her lounger and took a slug.

'Er . . . there was a phone call for you when you were gone.'

'Oh? Who was it?' Francesca popped a couple of

300

peanuts into her mouth and proffered the dish to Millie.

'Ah . . . um . . . it was Mark.'

'Bloody hell!' Francesca fumed. 'Oh shit! That's all I need. What on earth does he want?'

Chapter Thirty

'What did he say? What did you say to him? I bet he got a surprise to hear you at the other end of the phone,' Francesca said grimly.

'He didn't know who I was at first. I had to tell him,' Millie replied. 'He asked where we were.'

'And what did you say?'

'I just said we were out and that I'd tell you to call him back. Then I hung up. I wasn't too anxious to get into a conversation with brother-in-law dearest. He obviously doesn't know that we're away on holiday,' she remarked casually.

'I didn't tell him.'

'Well, why should you? It's none of his business what you do any more.'

'I haven't told him that I've got a job either,' Francesca said defiantly as she downed her drink.

'That's none of his business either,' Millie retorted.

'Well, I was going to tell him after a while. It's only fair so that he can adjust my allowance,' Francesca said slowly. 'I just wanted to make sure that I liked the work and see that I could handle the job first.'

Millie's face darkened. 'Don't call it an allowance, Francesca. It's money you're damn well entitled to.'

'Ach, Millie, I hate taking his money. I feel I'm a dependant. I want to have my own money. That's why I took the job. I want to stand on my own two feet and not be under an obligation to him. It's horrible to feel beholden.'

'But you're *not* beholden to him, Francesca. You're entitled to half of everything up until the time you separated anyway. And he knows that.'

'He's not too bad. He's not tight with the money,' Francesca defended her ex.

'He's keeping you sweet, that's why. Francesca, he knows you could cause him plenty of hassle. Do you want to stay living in the house on your own? Would you not like a fresh start in a place that's yours?' Millie persisted.

'It would be nice, I suppose,' Francesca admitted.

'Well, divorce the bastard and get what you're entitled to from the sale of the house. It's worth a mint and at least you'll have security at your back and a place of your own. And he'll weep into his coffee every morning, I can guarantee that. I'm telling you, Francesca, half the separated men in Ireland who are with other women nearly had a mickey-fit when divorce was introduced there, because they were perfectly happy the way they were. And Mark's one of them.'

'I suppose I'd better call him back and see what's up.'

'Don't be in a rush.' Millie sniffed. 'I'd let him cool his heels. In fact I wouldn't even bother to return his call until you get back.'

'Well, I'd prefer to call him now and get it over and done with. Otherwise I'll be lying here on edge wondering what's up,' Francesca said mildly.

'You're too soft with him, Francesca. You let him away with murder,' Millie said crossly.

She laughed at her sister's indignation. 'He's not the devil incarnate, Millie.'

'Listen to you defending him. Can't you see he's controlling you? I just don't like to see him pulling your strings. Take a bit of control back,' her sister advised bluntly.

'He's not controlling me,' Francesca said hotly.

'Well, we're looking at it from different sides of the fence,' Millie retorted.

Francesca scowled. She hadn't come on holiday to be lectured by Millie. And blast Mark for calling her and ruining the lovely relaxing tenor of their afternoon. She picked up her phone and dialled his number.

'Hi. Millie gave you the message,' he said silkily.

'Yes! What's the problem?' Her frosty tone let him know that she was not interested in polite chit-chat.

'Viv Cassidy phoned me. She was looking for you to play a game of mixed doubles. Said she hadn't seen you around at home and couldn't get you on the phone. So she rang me hoping I could give you the message,' Mark explained patiently.

'Did she now? Well she won't get me at home

because I'm not at home. I'm in Portugal,' Francesca snapped.

'Oh! You never told me you were going away.' He sounded miffed.

'Why should I? It's none of your business,' Francesca said coldly. Millie gave her the thumbs up.

'Don't be such an ungracious cow, Francesca,' Mark exploded. 'If you'd have told me you were going I could have given you something extra in this month's cheque, that's all. I was only trying to be nice. I'm sure a few extra bob would have come in handy.'

'Mark, I don't need your charity and please don't ring me again unless it's absolutely necessary,' Francesca raged, furious at being made to feel like a pauper yet again.

'Francesca Kirwan, you're a childish, ungrateful, self-centred—'

Francesca didn't wait to hear the rest of his diatribe. She hung up and flung her phone into the bag. 'Patronizing bastard!' she hissed wrathfully.

Millie raised an eyebrow.

'He said I should have told him that I was going on holiday so that he could have given me a bit extra in this month's cheque. He thinks a few extra bob might have come in handy.'

'Magnanimous of him,' drawled Millie, biting into a cherry.

'Then when I told him I didn't want his charity—'

'I enjoyed that bit,' Millie interjected, eyes twinkling.

'He launched into a tirade of abuse and said I was

selfish, ungrateful and childish. The bloody nerve of him. That's when I hung up.' Francesca glowered at her sister.

'Francesca, do yourself a favour. Get out of it,' Millie advised.

'Oh, let's forget it for the time being,' Francesca said wearily. 'I came on holiday to relax, not to be thinking about the mess I'm in.'

'You're not in a mess. You're doing fine,' Millie soothed. 'And now I'm going to get us another drink, and after that we're going to go up and open a bottle of wine and sit on our fabulous balcony and get the last rays and then we're going to find somewhere nice to eat and then we're going on the piss. How about that?'

Francesca managed a weak smile. 'I'm exhausted already, listening to you.'

'Oh, come on. Cheer up. I think I'd like a margarita. I'll get us a pitcher and we'll take it from there.' Millie leaped up from her lounger with a gleam in her eye. 'I haven't been on the tear in yonks. It's just what we need.'

'You'll get no arguments from me.' Francesca drained her glass and handed it back to Millie.

'That's my girl. You've led too sheltered a life, that's your problem. Fortunately I'm here to rectify that. One pitcher of margaritas coming up. Oh men of Portugal, watch out. Women on the loose.'

A pair of gangly, spotty teenage boys walked past their loungers on their way to the pool. 'Want to grow up quick, boys?' Millie murmured giddily.

Francesca burst out laughing as Millie sashayed up to the bar. She was irrepressible. Just the tonic

Francesca needed. Mark's impertinence had really got to her, but this wasn't the time to dwell on it. She was damned if she was going to let him ruin her holiday.

Mark capped and uncapped the fountain pen in his hand. He was raging. It was time Francesca was given a good talking to. She was living on the pig's back thanks to him and she wasn't one bit grateful. It was nice for her to be able to swan off to Portugal on his hard-earned cash, he fumed. Didn't she realize that she wouldn't have the cushy lifestyle she had if it wasn't for his damn hard work?

When she came back off her holiday he was going to have it out with her. She could start being civil and treating him with a modicum of respect. It was the least he deserved, he thought self-righteously. That was one thing about Nikki, she paid her way and expected nothing from him financially. And he really admired her for it, Mark thought angrily. Francesca was a bloody parasite with no manners and she could get lost. She might change her tune if the monthly cheque wasn't lodged in her account once or twice. She might show a bit of politeness then. He day-dreamed of Francesca ringing to ask for her money and he being gracious and suave, the way he was with clients, telling her that he'd see to it eventually as he was up to his eyes. It would be good for her to know that she wasn't the centre of the universe.

Not that he could really go down that road, he thought regretfully. She might start making waves and he needed that like he needed a hole in the head. Mark flung his pen onto his desk and got up and walked over to the window, his face set and hard. He was totally pissed off with Francesca and her damned rudeness. He was going to give her a good talking to, nevertheless.

Enough was enough.

Chapter Thirty-one

'Isn't this lovely?' Francesca inhaled the fragrant night air, scented with jasmine and honeysuckle. It was the last night of their holiday. They were sitting in the courtyard of a small, family-owned restaurant and the smell and sound of sizzling steak, lamb and pork drifted from the huge barbecue pit as the chef seared the meat and the smoke rose to waft under the noses of the hungry diners.

Francesca speared a chunk of fresh tuna from her tuna salad starter and ate it appreciatively. 'It's so tasty. God! I've put on a stone since we discovered this place,' she moaned. The Casa Velha restaurant was just across the road from their apartment block and they had discovered it on the third night of their holiday. They'd eaten there ever since, the food was so delicious.

Millie pronged a luscious fat prawn, smothered in the most divine sauce she had ever tasted and drooled over it. 'Do I have to go home? Do I have to get in front of a cooker again and *cook*? Francesca, this week has been paradise.'

'Yeah, it's been great, hasn't it? Millie, thanks so much for booking it. I've really enjoyed myself.'

'Oh, don't thank me.' Millie laughed. 'I was just using you as an excuse to get away. It's been absolute bliss.'

'It has been fun,' her sister agreed. 'It's the first time I've laughed and really enjoyed myself since . . . well, you know.' Francesca made a face.

'I know.' Millie reached over and squeezed her hand. 'And it's only the beginning. You stick with me, babe . . . fun's my middle name.'

'Mad is your middle name,' Francesca teased.

'Why don't you come to France with us for a week in August when we take the gîte?' Millie suggested as the waiter cleared away the first course.

'I don't think I could, really. It wouldn't be fair on Ken. I'm not in the job a wet week. Maybe I might get over for a long weekend. We'll see.'

'Tsk. I forgot you're working now. Dang!' Millie took a sip of wine.

'That's me: Francesca Kirwan, Career Woman,' Francesca said cheerfully as the waiter placed a platter of medallions of pork and sauté potatoes and mixed vegetables in front of her.

'I'll drink to that,' giggled Millie, taking another slug of wine. 'You know something? I'm tipsy. It's dreadful. I'm turning into a lush!'

'Now, we're not drinking as much as we did the first night we went out,' Francesca warned.

'Oh, don't remind me!' groaned Millie as she tucked into her swordfish. 'That was the mother and father of a hangover the next day, wasn't it? I never saw you green in the face before. But we *did* have extenuating circumstances,' she pointed out, topping up Francesca's glass.

'True,' Francesca conceded as she ate a mouthful of succulent pork. 'Mark is definitely an extenuating circumstance. Oooh, this is mouth-watering, Millie, have a taste,' she offered.

'I don't mind if I do.' Millie took a forkful of meat and savoured it. 'It's scrumptious. I wish I could kidnap the chef and bring him home with me. Maybe I could seduce him. Lord above, Francesca, how are we going to get back to real life?'

'With great difficulty,' Francesca assured her solemnly as the wine began to kick in and she could feel giddiness bubble up. She gave a little giggle.

'What are you laughing at?' demanded Millie, starting to titter herself.

'I was just thinking: if Ma could see us now, pissed as newts, me on the verge of divorce and you considering seduction and asking young boys if they want to grow up quick – what a disappointment we must be to her.'

'Ha ha ha,' guffawed Millie.

'Ha ha ha,' echoed Francesca, much to the amusement of the other diners. They chuckled heartily for five minutes before composing themselves enough to resume eating their meal and order another bottle of wine. It was that sort of night.

Nikki studied Mark surreptitiously over the top of her *Business and Finance*. He'd been like a bull this past week and she was mystified. 'See the Euro's not doing great,' she remarked casually.

'Umm,' he muttered.

Nikki closed the magazine. 'What's up, Mark? You're in very bad form,' she asked bluntly.

He scowled. 'Oh, nothing.'

'Come on. Tell me.' She went over and joined him on the couch and put an arm around him. 'It's not like you, darling. Usually you're fairly up. I'm worried about you,' she said tenderly.

Mark smiled at her and kissed her on the nose. 'It's nice to know that someone's worried about me,' he said dejectedly.

'Who's been getting at you? Tell Nikki,' she wheedled, stroking his cheek.

Mark gave a sigh that came from his toes.

'Come on . . . share,' she urged.

'No-one's been getting at me exactly,' he hedged. 'It's just, well, Viv Cassidy – a friend, or rather I should say an acquaintance of Francesca's – phoned me last Monday looking for her. She couldn't get her at the house and she didn't have her mobile number. She's a nosy old cow anyway, she likes sticking her nose in people's business,' Mark said crossly.

'And?' prompted Nikki. This wasn't all about some nosy old biddy.

'Anyway I wouldn't give her Francesca's mobile number. I bloody should have,' he growled.

Nikki listened with growing interest. Francesca was in the doghouse, she inferred . . . with great pleasure. What was rare was wonderful.

'I rang Francesca to give her the message and her sister answered. And she was pretty damn rude too.'

Better and better, thought Nikki happily but she stayed silent. Let him get it all off his chest. If she butted in with a comment he might clam up.

'She said they were out and that Francesca was in the Ladies,' Mark continued. 'Anyway, I left a message with Millie asking Francesca to call me back.'

'And did she?' Nikki murmured.

'She did and it transpired that they were in Portugal. Imagine! She never even had the manners to tell me that she was going.' His indignation was a joy to behold. This was *wonderful*, Nikki rejoiced.

'And when I mentioned to her that if she'd told me that she was going I'd have put a couple of extra bob into the account, she had the fucking cheek to insult me and tell me that she didn't want my *charity*.' Mark was still steaming about it. 'I ask you, Nikki, there she is swanning around Portugal thanks to my generosity, and she can't even show a bit of common civility. I've just had it up to here.' He waved a hand under his neck, his eyes hard and angry.

'That was extremely rude of her, darling. You've been so good to her financially. No-one could accuse you of being at all selfish. It really upsets me that she takes it all for granted and doesn't treat you very nicely,' Nikki exclaimed indignantly.

'Well, I've had enough of her nonsense and bad behaviour. I'm going to have it out with her once and for all and tell her to show a bit of respect. I'm not mean, you know that, Nikki, but I can tell you I was damn nearly thinking of not lodging her allowance this month. Well, delaying it for a while even,' he amended.

Yes! Yes! Yes! exulted Nikki silently. This was music to her ears. The worm was turning at long long last. Her patience was paying off.

'You'd be well within your rights to. It might make her realize just how lucky she is that you're decent,' comforted Nikki, stroking his cheek.

'Well, we'll see,' Mark said wearily. 'I'm going to give her a good talking to in any case.'

'You do what you think is best, Mark. Maybe it would be good to clear the air.' She didn't want to jump in and say that a good talk was a terrific idea. She didn't want to sound too gung ho about it so she kept her tone light and casual, but the idea of Mark giving that lazy, selfish slob an ear-bashing was orgasmic. Maybe if they were at each other's throats the idea of divorcing his precious Francesca might be more appealing, although she didn't seem at all precious to him at the moment, Nikki thought smugly as she nibbled his ear.

'Darling, it's been a long week and you've had a lot on your mind. Why don't we go to bed and I'll light some scented candles and play some soft music and I'll give you a nice relaxing massage?' Nikki offered.

'I think it's just what I need, darling. The muscles in the back of my neck are giving me hell,' Mark complained.

'I'll look after them,' Nikki soothed.

'You're very good at looking after me,' he said gratefully, drawing her close.

'That's because I love you,' Nikki replied firmly.

'And I love you too,' Mark murmured, resting his head on her shoulder.

Nikki stroked his forehead. 'You shouldn't let it get to you so much,' she murmured.

'I know.'

'Maybe you should disengage a bit and let Francesca get on with it.'

'Maybe you're right,' Mark agreed.

'Come on,' she ordered. 'Let's forget it for now.' She didn't want to overplay her hand. Arm in arm they went into the bedroom and she undid his shirt buttons and unbuckled his belt. 'Into bed with you now and I'll get the oils and light the candles,' she instructed. She undressed and slipped into a silk dressing gown and quietly lit the candles and put a CD on the player as Mark lay face down in the middle of the bed, his face resting on his forearms.

When she was ready, she knelt astride him and poured some oil into her palms. Slowly she began to massage his tense muscles and gradually he began to relax under her light touch. Although her movements were slow and rhythmic her mind was racing. She was exuberant. The cracks were getting wider and wider in the Kirwan relationship and that suited her just fine. Never before had Mark shown such naked hostility towards his estranged wife.

Madame Francesca might soon be getting her comeuppance and it wasn't before time. Nikki smiled as she massaged a particularly tense spot, causing Mark to sigh with pleasure.

Francesca sat at the departure gate in Faro Airport waiting for their flight to be called. Millie was doing some last-minute shopping in the chocolate shop, to use up her escudos. She'd invited Francesca to spend the night with them so that she wouldn't be on her own the first night home. Francesca had been tempted. It had been great having Millie's company for the week and she was dreading the thought of opening the front door to an empty house. But it had to be faced and the sooner she got it over and done with the better. Besides, she needed to get her clothes sorted for work the following week.

It was hard to believe that the holiday was over. It had flown by so quickly. She'd enjoyed it though. For the first time in years she'd had no-one to fuss over or compromise with. Mark wasn't a sun-worshipper like she was. He liked visiting art galleries and museums and touring around whatever country they were in. Often on holiday with Mark she'd ended up wandering around an art gallery, going bananas because the sun was shining outside and she longed to be relaxing in it. Not so with Millie. It had been glorious just to plonk herself on her lounger and read her books, knowing that her sister was perfectly happy to do the same. Now the idyllic few days were over and it was back to reality.

At least she had her job to go to, she thought gratefully. It was better than sitting home alone feeling sorry for herself. 'Sure you won't stay the night?' Millie sat down alongside her, laden down with bags.

'No, Millie, I won't, but thanks for asking,' Francesca smiled.

'Well, let's have one last drink, to send us on our way even though the sun isn't over the yardarm yet,' Millie suggested, 'loose lushes that we are.'

'I'll drink to that,' laughed Francesca.

It was after four by the time she slid the key into her front door. She'd had coffee at Millie's and enjoyed the excitement as her nieces had opened their presents. Trixie had greeted her joyfully, licking her all over and gazing up at her with her big brown eyes, her tail wagging furiously. She'd been very well fed during her sojourn with Aidan and the girls. She'd need some brisk exercise just like her mistress, Francesca thought wryly as she patted her silky coat. Aidan dropped her home and carried her case into the house and when she closed the door behind him, the silence dropped around her like a cloak and her heart ached with loneliness.

She walked through the rooms feeling the emptiness. Once this house had been her castle. She'd reigned happily as its queen. Now it was her prison. Maybe Millie was right. She should sell up and get a smaller place of her own. Close that chapter of her life and start a new one. It was much easier said than done, though. Selling the house would be an admission that her marriage was well and truly over and part of her wasn't ready to admit that yet.

She unpacked her suitcase and filled the washing machine. The silence was driving her nuts. 'Come on, Trixie, let's get out of here,' she muttered. She changed into a pair of jeans and a sweatshirt. It was cold after the heat of Portugal. The sky was grey and the breeze fresh and cool as she walked out to the garage to get the car. She'd only had one G and T at the airport, and that was hours ago, like another lifetime ago, she thought, half shocked at coming back to earth and reality with such a bang.

She drove down to Howth Pier, parked and set off on a brisk walk with Trixie tugging on the leash excitedly. Gulls circled and screamed overhead as the trawlers sailed into harbour with their catch. The wind on the top of the pier was fresh and salt laden and she inhaled deeply as she walked along. This time yesterday she'd been sitting on her balcony in Oura Praia sipping a beer while Millie had her shower.

'Deal with it,' she muttered, head down as she hurried along pushing against the wind. On a whim, on the way home she drove into Corr Castle, an exclusive new development that still had apartments for sale. She drove around the well-laid-out complex and felt a stirring of interest. There'd be no harm in having a look at the show apartment, she decided. In fact she should start looking at the property pages just to see what was on the market. She wasn't sure if apartment living appealed to her. She'd miss her garden. A dormer bungalow might be nice, she mused. It would be fun to decorate and furnish from scratch. She'd go for a completely different look to the plush elegance of home. Lots of wood and glass and light. That would be nice, she reflected as she drove back out onto the main road. She'd start viewing property and show houses at the weekends. It would give her something to do. There was no harm in keeping a weather eye open.

By Tuesday of the following week Francesca felt as though she'd never been away. There was a large backlog of filing to get through and 200 invitations to be enveloped and addressed when she arrived in the office on Monday morning and the phone never stopped ringing. She'd gone home that evening exhausted and fallen asleep in the armchair.

At four-thirty the following afternoon she headed across town to Smithfield to link up with Ken at Chief O'Neill's for the launch of an art exhibition.

Several artists were exhibiting and nerves were fraught as they argued over the right and wrong way to hang the paintings.

'Look, why should Darina get prime position? I'm a far better artist than she is. At least I'm original. Picasso could sue her for plagiarism,' a wild-haired, bespectacled young man ranted.

'You obviously don't understand the meaning of plagiarism, you illiterate little shit. Nor do you know anything about hanging paintings. Go back to your crèche and practise colouring in, it's all you're good for,' Darina, a tall anorexic-looking girl, sneered.

'Skinny bitch! Grow your hair a bit longer and they could use you for a paintbrush,' the bespectacled one insulted her back, magnificently in Francesca's opinion. Darina's eyes glittered dangerously.

'Listen here, you pathetic little nerd, the cavemen could paint better than you. We'll see who sells the most paintings tonight and I can tell you right now it won't be you.'

'Do you want to put your money where your smartass mouth is?'

Francesca slipped away to find Ken, leaving them to trade insults. Her boss was on his mobile, left hand gesticulating wildly. Something was up. Ken only gesticulated when he was agitated. He saw her and waved frantically in her direction as he ended his conversation. 'The guest of honour just phoned to say he's got the trots and he's waiting for his doctor to give him a shot. That's all I need. Have you heard that lot?' He indicated the arguing artists.

'I have,' said Francesca.

'It's going to be one of those nights. I hope the art critics savage them,' Ken said nastily. 'They're worse than children. Oh hell, here's the TV crew, they're doing a spot for an arts programme. They'll be wanting to set up lights and cameras. Francesca, would you make sure the bar is organized and sort out the caterers?'

'Sure,' Francesca agreed, looking around to find out where the drinks were to be served. She saw a long trestle table covered in white tablecloths and set off to do her duty.

By the time the unfortunate guest of honour had arrived and been introduced, the artists were well lubricated and all animosities were forgotten as they hugged and congratulated each other. Despite his affliction, the guest, an artist and gallery owner Francesca had never heard of, made a short, witty speech that was well received, and once the rest of the speeches were over and the photos had been taken, Ken pushed his way through the crammed, stuffy room towards her.

'All's well that ends well. They can do what they like from now on, our bit's done and dusted.' He rubbed his hands together happily and surveyed the vibrant throng. 'Three newspaper critics, one art magazine writer, TV spot and radio interview, two social diarists. A good haul, Frannie.'

'Stop it,' she warned.

'Spoilsport!' he grinned. 'Why don't you head on home if you like? I can take it from here.'

'Are you sure?'

'Do you really want to be here with this lot? Go

on, it's been a long day and you're only back from your holliers.'

'Are you insisting?'

'I'm insisting,' he assured her.

'Thanks, Ken,' she said gratefully. 'I'll see you bright and early in the morning.'

She eased her way through the crowd. Her feet were killing her. She'd worn sandals for the entire week of her holiday and her high heels were murder. It was starting to rain as she left the building and she hurried to her car hoping to avoid the downpour.

It had been clamped. She couldn't believe her eyes. But there it was, the bright yellow wheel clamp like a limpet on her tyre.

'You wanky, fucking bastards,' she yelled as the heavens opened and she was drenched. She dialled the number on the notice and gave details of her whereabouts to the clamping firm. She'd been so busy sorting things out inside she'd forgotten to come out and feed her meter.

'I hope you get the pox,' Francesca cursed the unknown clamper as she sat fuming in her car waiting to be freed. She couldn't bring herself to speak to the middle-aged man who unclamped her half an hour later and she wrote out her cheque in a fury before driving off like a bat out of hell.

She had just stepped out of the shower in her en suite and was towelling her hair dry when the doorbell rang. Puzzled, she glanced at her watch. It was just after nine, she wasn't expecting anyone. Maybe it was Millie. She hoped it was, she needed someone to unload to.

She slipped into her towelling robe and shoved her

feet into a pair of mules and hurried downstairs. Trixie came galloping out of the kitchen, nearly tripping her up. She was barking excitedly.

'Shush! Be quiet,' Francesca said as she pulled her belt tighter around her and opened the door. Her heart sank when she saw Mark standing on the doorstep.

'Well, this is a perfect end to a perfect day,' she said sarcastically as she stood glaring at him.

Chapter Thirty-two

'As civil as ever, I see,' Mark observed drily as he stooped to pat Trixie who was licking him ecstatically. *Traitor*, Francesca thought churlishly.

'What do you want?' she demanded.

'I'd like to come in, if you don't mind,' he said coolly. 'I don't want Viv Cassidy out with her binoculars.'

Francesca stood back to let him in. He looked tired, she noted. He was wearing a beautifully cut grey mohair suit. New since he'd been with her. She wondered if Nikki went shopping for his clothes with him.

He walked into the kitchen and stood looking out at the back garden. 'It looks really nice. And it's so private. You never get gardens like that now. The roses are flying, aren't they?' he said wistfully.

No thanks to you, she wanted to say, but she kept silent. 'I must organize to get the deck treated. It could do with a coat of something,' he remarked casually.

Francesca felt resentment bubble. He was going on as if he still lived here. Why didn't he just butt out of her life? If she wanted the deck treated she could get someone and bill him for half of it. He was being far too familiar.

'It looks fine to me,' she said.

'There's no point in letting it go, Francesca. It needs doing at some stage.' He was speaking to her as though she were a ten-year-old.

'Fine,' she snapped. Maybe he was right. It would be worse if he refused to spend the money on it, she supposed.

'Did you have a good holiday? You look very well,' he said politely, turning to face her.

'It was a lovely holiday, thank you, Mark, but I've had a long and tiring day. What was it you wanted to see me about?' she said pointedly as she began to dry her hair with the towel it was wrapped in.

'Would you mind if I put the kettle on for a cup of tea? I'm on my way ho— . . . er, from the airport and I'd love a cup,' he ventured.

She shrugged. She hadn't missed the way he'd been about to say he was on his way 'home' but changed it. Did he think he was saving her feelings? she thought bitterly. So the posh apartment was 'home' now. It hurt.

'What were you doing that made the day so long and tiring?' he asked diffidently as he busied himself filling the kettle and getting two mugs down from the press. It was like old times, she thought with a funny little heartache as she bent her head forward and dried the back of her hair.

'Well, I got clamped for one thing,' she sighed as

she rubbed hard, the towel hanging down the sides of her face.

'Oh Lord! Bastards! Where did that happen?' He was genuinely sympathetic.

'Outside Chief O'Neill's.'

'Who's Chief O'Neill when he's out and about?' Mark rooted in the fridge for the milk.

'It's a hotel in Smithfield.'

'What were you doing in Smithfield, in the name of God?'

'I was working,' she explained, off guard, annoyed at his disparaging tone.

'*Working!*'

Francesca's heart lurched. *Oh damn!* she thought, cursing her stupidity. Now it looked as though she hadn't planned to tell him, as though she was doing something sneaky. She kept her head under the towel.

'Yes. I was working. I've just started a new job.' She was mega impressed with how casual she sounded.

'And when were you going to tell me about this new job, Francesca? This has tax implications for me, you know. That's unless you're being paid under the counter.' His censorious attitude was like a red rag to a bull, especially when he added irritably, 'What do you need a job for? I pay you more than enough to keep you in comfort.'

She flung back her head, spraying him with little droplets of water. 'Look, I started the week before I went on holiday. I'm just back. I was going to get in touch about it when I had a minute. And the reasons I got a job are *my* business,' she said heatedly.

'And what are you working at?' he drawled, unimpressed.

'I'm working for a PR company as it happens.'

'Which one?' He dumped two teabags into the teapot.

'Ken Kennedy PR.'

'Never heard of them,' he said dismissively. 'Is it legit or under the counter?'

'It's legit,' Francesca retorted.

'That's going to affect my tax-free allowance and that's going to be a real pain in the ass. How much are you earning?'

'Fifteen thousand plus bonuses,' she answered sullenly.

'Oh, for God's sake, Francesca, it's a pittance.'

His condescending tone made her want to slap him hard across the face but she curled her hands in the pockets of her robe and said tightly, 'Well, it might be a pittance to you, but it's *my* pittance and you can deduct my salary from your monthly allowance. You can buy little trinkets for your mistress with it,' she said icily.

'Francesca, you shut your damn smart mouth.' Mark flung his mug angrily down on the worktop causing the tea to slop out of it. His face was puce with fury. 'I came here to tell you that I've had enough of your crap. You're rude, ignorant and totally ungrateful for all I've given you. I've looked after you better than a lot of men in my position. You have the house. I pay for the upkeep, I give you a more than generous allowance and all I want is for you to keep a civil fucking tongue in your head. Surely that couldn't be too difficult . . . even for you,' he exploded.

'Listen to who's talking about keeping a civil tongue in their head,' Francesca retorted witheringly. 'Let me tell you something, Mark Kirwan. I don't care how damn "generous" you are. I am not beholden to you. This is as much my house as it is yours. And forgive me for not being all sweetness and light when we talk, but I just don't feel like being "civil", believe it or not. I have no respect for you. I despise you. And right now I don't even like you. So don't expect me to put on a façade and pretend a civility I don't feel. If you can't handle it stop ringing me and don't set foot on my doorstep again.' She was seething.

'*Our* doorstep, Francesca! *Our* doorstep!' Mark snarled.

'Oh, get out,' Francesca shouted. 'Go "*home*" where you belong.' She turned on her heel and marched out of the kitchen, afraid that if she stayed another minute she'd pick up a knife and stab him. She was overwhelmed with anger and was holding on to control by the skin of her teeth. The urge to violence was so strong it shocked her. She wanted to batter and bruise him and throw things at him and smash up the house. *His* fucking goddamn house. How dare he look down his nose at her job? Just because the bitch he was living with was a high-flying banker earning a fortune. How *dare* he? She'd never felt so humiliated in her life. Tears smarted in her eyes. She stood at her bedroom door waiting for him to leave and when he did slam the front door behind him she yelled, 'Good riddance to bad rubbish, you patronizing fucking bollocks!' at the top of her voice before collapsing in a heap on her bed, howling with rage and grief and helplessness into her pillow.

Mark got into the car and felt like ramming his foot on the accelerator and driving the car in through the front door. God, that woman would drive a pioneer to drink. What a waste of a bloody journey. He was never going to get anywhere with her. And now he had this shagging job of hers to contend with. A fine mess of his taxes that was going to make! He'd have to get on to his accountant first thing to get it sorted. As if he didn't have enough on his plate.

He gunned the engine and roared out of the drive. It would be a long time before he'd bother his ass to come and see that vindictive bitch again, he swore as he braked to avoid another car. And because she was being so obnoxious and ungracious he *was* bloody well going to deduct her salary from her allowance.

The apartment was dark and empty when he got home. Nikki was in London and he missed her. He could have done with her company tonight, he thought, depressed. He flung his jacket on a chair, loosened his tie and took a can of Bud out of the fridge. After all these months his relationship with Francesca was getting worse instead of better. He was going to leave her to her own devices. To hell with treating the deck and all the rest of it. If she ever wanted his help she could come crawling for it from now on.

The phone rang. He picked it up and gave a small smile as Nikki's greeting came down the line.

'Hello, love. I miss you.' He sighed.

'And I miss you, darling. How did it go?'

'Don't ask,' groaned Mark as he took a long

draught of beer. 'Francesca was her usual charming self. That's to say, she was a total bitch and I got nowhere. And the icing on the cake is the news that she's got some job or other and that's going to muck up my tax allowance big time. What the bloody hell she has to go off at half cock and get a job for is beyond me.'

'What kind of a job?' Nikki asked, intrigued.

'Oh, some sort of PR thing. It can't be much, the salary's crap.'

'How much?'

Mark yawned. 'Fifteen K.'

'Oh!' Nikki sounded disappointed.

'It was such a bummer of a day,' Mark rubbed his jaw wearily. 'Maurice St Deville walked out of the meeting in a huff and Anton had to spend half an hour pacifying him. I got delayed at Charles de Gaulle for two hours, then I was sitting beside a chatterbox on the flight home, and then I had Francesca to contend with. I truly don't know which was the worst, her or Maurice.'

'Poor darling,' Nikki said sympathetically.

'I think I'll hit the sack, Nikki. Talk tomorrow.' Mark yawned again.

'OK, 'night, Mark.'

'Goodnight, Nikki.' Mark hung up, finished his beer, switched off the light and, twenty minutes later, was sprawled out in Nikki's bed snoring.

Nikki hung up the phone and lay back against the pillows. She should be on top of the world to know that Mark and Francesca had had what appeared to have been a massive row. It was good news, of course it was, she assured herself. So why wasn't she on a high? It was the phone call that was causing her to feel so agitated. Mark had told her all about *his* bummer of a day, and *his* fraught meeting, and *his* delayed flight home, and never once asked how she'd got on.

As it happened, she'd had a bummer of a day herself. She'd been stuck on the Underground for over two hours due to a breakdown and had missed a very important meeting. The hotel her secretary had booked her into had been overbooked and she'd ended up in a grotty little garret of a room and when she'd gone to have a bath, the water had trickled out of the taps and to describe it as lukewarm would have been a gross exaggeration. But did Mark know any of this, or did he even care? Nikki chewed her lip unhappily.

What was it about men that made them so selfish? Why was it that they truly felt they were the centre of the universe? She had even gone to the trouble of buying that Mars/Venus book early on in their relationship in an effort to understand Mark. She should have known better, she thought irritably. It was written by a man. All that nonsense about men going into their caves and comparing them to rubber bands that pull away and then spring back when they need intimacy again. Talk about feeling sorry for themselves. Men just had it *every* way. Nikki scowled.

So his lazy lump of a wife had got a job in PR. Her home truths about being a parasite must have stung, Nikki thought with satisfaction. It was a pity the pay was buttons, she'd still be hanging on to Mark's financial apron strings.

Thank God she was a financially independent woman and hoped she always would be. Mark would never have to worry about keeping her, she vowed. And he knew that too, so why couldn't he commit emotionally? Theirs was a relationship of equals. He needn't worry that she'd sponge off him, she fretted. Didn't he see their relationship as a long-term one? He hardly entertained notions of ever going back to Francesca. That was ludicrous, she assured herself. If only he would realize that in spite of her independent nature she needed emotional security as much as the next woman. Was it so much to ask of him? Why did he withhold it from her? Would these bloody unanswered questions ever stop rampaging around her head?

She felt like a drink but the shack she was holed up in didn't do room service and she couldn't face the crappy little bar. She slid off the bed and started to undress. She was wrecked and tonight she was totally fed up. She loved Mark but she wanted his love in equal measure and lately it wasn't even coming close to that. She was doing all the giving and he was doing all the taking. Was this the way she wanted to live her life? In her heart of hearts she knew she couldn't lay all the blame on Francesca. Mark was responsible for his own behaviour. And tonight had been all about him. She hadn't even rated a 'how are you?'

It was time she told him a few home truths, Nikki decided irately as she got into bed and switched out the light.

Chapter Thirty-three

'Hi, Janet, it's me, sorry I haven't been in touch in ages. Things have been a bit mad lately,' Francesca said apologetically. She was on her coffee break, and knowing that her friend Janet was interested in things spiritual, she wanted to tell her about the author she was taking out to TV3 and Gerry Ryan.

'Francesca, hi, how are you? Would you believe I was planning on calling you today, talk about synchronicity,' exclaimed Janet.

'If you say so,' laughed Francesca. 'Listen, Janet, I'm working in a PR firm. I got myself a job, finally, and I thought you might like to know that I'm bringing a Mind Body Spirit author out to TV3 in the morning and later on she's going to Gerry Ryan. She's some sort of a healer. She sees energy and auras and all of that. And I thought of you.'

'Francesca, you're working, that's wonderful. When did you start?'

'Just a couple of weeks ago. I'm enjoying it. I'm

working for Monica's nephew, Ken. He's a dote,' Francesca said.

'Excellent. That's terrific news. And how are things otherwise?' Janet asked kindly.

'Not great,' Francesca admitted. 'Had a row with Mark last night. He doesn't think much of my job or my salary and he's whingeing about his tax-free allowance.'

'Of course he is,' chuckled Janet. 'And don't let him fool you about the tax issue. That's part of it, of course. But he's just finding it hard to cope with the fact that his passive little Francesca is taking her own power back and he doesn't like it one bit. I've been there, Francesca, don't forget. I know all about it,' Janet said lightly. 'He can feel you closing the door in his face and he can't handle it.'

'Is that what I'm doing?' Francesca gave a wry smile. 'I feel like I'm on a rollercoaster. One minute I'm flying high and full of optimism, then after an episode like last night I'm at rock bottom and haven't a clue where I'm heading.'

'You're heading in the right direction, don't you worry,' Janet comforted.

'I'm full of anger and full of hate,' Francesca whispered and felt that hard horrible knot of grief lodge in her throat.

'It will pass, Francesca. Honestly. If your intention is to let it go then it will go. If your intention is to hold on to it, well, lovie, you'll only do yourself harm,' Janet said quietly.

'I *do* want to let it go but it's what keeps me going. I want to prove things to the bastard. I want to prove that I can get on without him.'

'Well, do that, Francesca. That's fine. But you don't need the anger to do it. Your own resources are perfectly adequate. When the anger comes up, ask for it to be released and let go.'

'Who do I ask?' Francesca asked, bewildered.

'The Divine, your Creator, Jesus, Mary, the Angels, your Higher Power, Buddha, Mohammed, a saint you pray to, St Michael, St Anthony, you know them all. Whatever or whoever is authentic for you.' Janet spoke with absolute authority.

Francesca sighed. 'Oh, you have such faith in all of that. I don't.'

'My faith was hard got, Francesca, I came from a tough, unforgiving place of hatred and bitterness. I learned my lessons of forgiveness and letting go a hard way and it doesn't have to be like that. Learn from me, my dear, learn from me,' Janet said cheerfully. 'Why don't we go for a drink or a meal some evening after work? I promise I won't preach.'

'I'd like that. And I don't mind you preaching. You're my inspiration. You did it. You got back on track and made a life for yourself. And you're not embittered.'

'And that's *exactly* what you're doing now. Stop being so hard on yourself. You're human, Francesca. Your heart is crushed but it will mend and so will you as long as you keep going forward. Listen to what that woman has to say tomorrow. She might say something that will resonate with you. Sometimes it can be the simplest things that make the difference.'

'OK, I will,' Francesca promised. 'And we'll fix up an evening soon.'

'I'll be looking forward to it,' Janet assured her.

Francesca put the phone down, smiling. Even though she found it hard to accept the truths Janet was explaining to her, she always felt better after talking to her. Her optimism began to reassert itself. An evening out with her friend would be delightful. Mark had never bothered much with her book-club friends. In fact, most of their mutual friends had started out as his friends. Her friends from her youth had gradually dropped out of the picture. The old familiar anger reminded her of its presence when she thought of Mark. 'I want to let it go,' she whispered. 'Whoever is out there, I want to let it go.'

Nikki popped her head around the door of Mark's office. 'Let's have lunch, Mark, I need to talk to you.'

'Don't I even get a kiss?' he demanded. 'When did you get back?'

'Five minutes ago. Have to dash. See you at one.' Nikki gave a brisk wave and closed the door. No more Miss Nice Girl, she smiled grimly. Today was going to be *all* about her.

She hurried down to the lift. She had a report to write up and she wanted to get started. The seven a.m. breakfast meeting had gone very well, much better than she'd hoped for, and she was buzzing. Work, there was nothing like it to get the adrenalin going.

'Elaine, coffee,' she ordered peremptorily as she strode into her office.

' "Please" would be nice,' Elaine muttered as she got up from behind her desk. Sometimes Nikki could be extremely hard to take. She was obviously in one of her hyper moods today. It would be best to keep her head down.

Nikki was busy writing when Mark knocked on her door and strode in. 'It's ten past one. I was waiting for you,' he announced.

'Where?' she asked without raising her head.

'In my office,' he said in surprise.

Nikki raised her head and smiled at him. 'Well, I was waiting for you in mine and here you are. Let's go.'

He frowned as he held her coat for her. 'You're in a funny humour.'

'Funny? What do you mean?' Nikki asked lightly as they closed the door behind them.

'I don't know. Abrasive. Brittle,' he grumbled.

'Really? I don't know what you're talking about.' Nikki jabbed her finger on the lift button. There were several people in it when the doors swished open and she and Mark stood in silence.

'I thought Mamma Mia's would be nice,' she said as they hurried through the foyer and down the marble steps.

He made a face. 'It's very quiet and I don't want a big banquet.'

'No starters, just a main course then. I want to go somewhere quiet. I want to talk to you.'

'About what?'

'About us,' Nikki said firmly.

'About us!' Mark looked startled. 'I hope you're not going to give me grief, Nikki. I'm having a tough day. We're going to have to pay a fortune in tax thanks to these bloody tribunals. It's going to make a hell of a dent in our profits.'

Nikki's lips tightened. He was doing it again. She said nothing as they crossed Stephen's Green in the direction of Baggot Street.

Ten minutes later, they were seated at a quiet table in Mamma Mia's and had ordered a Caesar salad each.

'What's wrong with you, Nikki? What's this all about?' Mark said grumpily as he took a gulp of beer.

'It's about you doing all the taking and giving nothing back, Mark,' Nikki said quietly. 'And I'm getting sick of it.'

'Oh, for God's sake!' He raised his eyes to heaven in exasperation. 'Do we have to have this discussion *today*? Your timing, like all women's, is lousy.'

'There! You're doing it again, Mark. This is not about you, this is about me,' Nikki hissed. 'Just like last night. You told me all about your bummer of a day. You never once asked me how I'd got on or what my day was like. Aren't you interested, Mark?' she demanded.

'Don't be ridiculous, of course I'm interested,' he snapped.

'Well, why didn't you ask, then?'

'Nikki, I was *tired*,' he explained with feigned patience.

'So was *I*,' she retorted. 'I'd had just as bad a day as you had, but you didn't even have the courtesy to ask.'

'Well, I'm sorry,' he growled. 'I'll ask about your day in future.'

'Mark, why are you with me?' she asked quietly.

'For crying out loud, Nikki, do we have to have this conversation *here*?' Mark rasped.

'Here's as good as anywhere, Mark. Why are you with me?'

'Because I want to be with you,' he retorted.

'Well, I think that if Francesca hadn't found out about us we would still be having an affair and you'd still be living with her,' Nikki pointed out calmly. 'And sometimes I feel that you're with me out of convenience.'

'Nikki, that's not fair!' expostulated Mark.

'That's the way I feel,' she repeated.

He bristled. 'Well, don't feel like that, because it's not true.'

'Then try and make an effort to acknowledge my feelings and give me some emotional support because right now I'm not happy with the way our relationship is going,' she said coldly. She sat back to allow the waiter to place her meal in front of her.

They ate in silence.

'Do you want coffee?' Mark asked when she pushed her plate away.

She shook her head. 'No. I have to get back, I'm up to my eyes.'

'You go on then. I'll have a coffee and pay the bill. I'll see you tonight,' he said offhandedly, not looking her in the eye.

'Fine,' she said tightly and walked out of the restaurant with her head held high.

Bastard! she swore silently as she strode down Baggot Street. He could go and sit in his damn cave and stay there for all she cared.

Mark sat frowning, drinking a mug of strong coffee. Was it something in the air? Was it a full moon?

Were they suffering from dire PMT? He couldn't figure it out. Both of them, Francesca *and* Nikki, like two viragos. And he was the one bearing the brunt of it.

What was wrong with Nikki? He was living with her, wasn't he? It was unfair of her to say that he wasn't interested. Generally – with a few exceptions such as last night – he always enquired about her work and he was genuinely interested because she was an interesting woman to talk to. He enjoyed talking to her. Surely she knew that. He was disappointed in her attitude. She seemed like a different Nikki to the woman he'd been enchanted with and fallen in love with. He'd very much liked her independent spirit and assured woman-of-the-world air. Mark sighed deeply as he pondered the change in her. If he was honest, one of the attractions had been that he'd felt she wouldn't demand a lot of him because she seemed so self-sufficient. Big mistake, he thought ruefully.

What was it with women that they always needed to be told that they were loved? He could say it a dozen times a month and still it wouldn't be enough. Why did they need this constant reassurance? They were a mystery to him. Sometimes he felt he'd be better off living on his own.

Would he have left Francesca for Nikki? Who knows? he thought dispiritedly. The decision had been made for him so there was no point in speculating about it. Why couldn't Nikki be content with what they had? Why did she keep pushing for more?

Heavy-hearted, Mark finished his coffee and paid the bill. It had started to rain and he didn't have his coat with him. That was all he needed, he thought self-pityingly as he trudged along Baggot Street towards Stephen's Green. If yesterday had been a bummer of a day, today was just as bad and work was the last place he wanted to be. He might try and fit in a quick round of golf later, he needed a bit of relaxation badly with all the stress he was enduring lately.

The alarm shrilled, jolting Francesca to unwelcome wakefulness. She gazed at the clock askance. Five-forty-five a.m. What had she been thinking of to set her clock at that unearthly hour? And then she remembered she was taking that aura woman to TV3 for the breakfast show. She dragged herself out of bed yawning and blearily rubbing her eyes. Katherine Kronskey, her author, was overnighting at the Great Southern Hotel at the airport. She had to pick her up, take her to the TV studios and then on to RTE. She'd want to get a move on.

She made good time to the airport and at six-thirty-five was standing in the foyer of the hotel, curious to meet her new assignment. She wasn't sure what to expect. Reading energies and auras seemed very way out. Maybe she was one of these earth mothery types in long flowing skirts wafting incense sticks around. She'd sounded fairly normal when Francesca had phoned her room to let her know that she was in the foyer. The reception was busy with guests on early-morning flights checking out, so Francesca moved over to the lifts to watch out for her charge.

The lift doors opened and two men and two

women emerged. Couples, assumed Francesca, but the tall, elegant woman with the magnificent bone structure and the chic ash-blond bob moved away from the others and looked around her.

'Katherine?' Francesca asked hesitantly, thinking she couldn't possibly be the aura woman.

She turned and smiled broadly and held out her hand. 'Yes, I'm Katherine. And you must be Francesca?' she said with a Bostonian twang. Her handshake was firm, her hazel eyes wide and friendly and Francesca felt a wave of relief. Memories of Magda were still relatively fresh in her mind. 'I'm so sorry to get you up at this unearthly hour, but mind you, it's much more civilized than the States. I've been out in studios at five a.m.,' Katherine laughed.

'Did you have breakfast?' Francesca asked as she led the way to the car.

'God no.' Katherine shuddered. 'Coffee was all I could manage at that hour.'

'Oh!' Francesca was surprised. She hadn't imagined someone into healing and energy and all of that sort of stuff would drink coffee. Carrot juice, yes.

'I do allow myself a cup of coffee in the morning. It's one of my many weaknesses.' Katherine's eyes twinkled.

Francesca had the grace to blush. 'Sorry. I just wasn't sure what to expect. And I want to make sure that you're comfortable and well looked after,' she explained. 'You're only my second author and my first was a nightmare.'

'Really? Tell me about them so I see how far I can go,' Katherine said good-humouredly as she got into the car. Francesca gave her a witty account of Magda's shenanigans as she took the M50 and accelerated up to seventy. Katherine laughed heartily. 'I've a lot of leeway it seems,' she joked and Francesca relaxed. Katherine Kronskey was nice, and normal.

Katherine studied her curiously. 'So how come I'm only your second author?'

'I've just started working with Ken Kennedy PR,' Francesca explained as she overtook a juggernaut.

'And what were you working at before this?'

'I was a housewife,' Francesca said drily.

'In the States I've heard housewives described as CEOs of the home.' Katherine smiled. 'I was a housewife for twenty years before I started my present work.'

'Really?' Francesca was surprised. 'How did you start?'

'I got dumped by my husband, then got cancer, then tried to commit suicide and then had my road to Damascus experience and here I am!' Katherine said cheerfully.

'My God! And I thought I was bad,' Francesca exclaimed, shocked and astonished that the other woman could talk about trying to commit suicide so lightly.

'What happened to you?'

'Oh, I got dumped by my husband too. Well, not exactly, I caught him with another woman and I dumped him,' Francesca clarified.

'And you're still shattered,' Katherine said sympathetically. 'It's tough.'

'Yes, it is,' Francesca agreed, waiting for the kindly

meant advice on releasing anger and feeling the fear but doing it anyway and possibly the embracing-her-inner-child tip.

But Katherine made no reference to their conversation; instead she looked out of the car window and said, 'Your beautiful countryside is balm to the spirit, I wish I could stay longer.'

'You've a very tight schedule, I was reading it earlier on. Two interviews in London later this afternoon. How do you do it?'

Katherine laughed. 'Francesca, at this stage in my career as a healer if I didn't know how to conserve my energy I'd be pretty poor at my job. I meditate every morning and evening and I do self-healing. And I get the Graces I need,' she said simply.

It was hard to believe that as radiant a woman as Katherine had suffered cancer and attempted suicide, Francesca reflected as she pulled into the TV studios. Later, as she watched her on the monitor, coiffed and made up, waiting for her interview to begin, Francesca could not but be impressed by her poise and serenity. The woman hadn't one ounce of self-pity, Francesca thought, a little ashamed of herself for feeling such a 'poor me'.

Remembering Janet's advice to pay attention, in case something resonated with her, Francesca listened carefully. The interview was fascinating.

'Our wounds don't hurt the people who hurt us, they only hurt *ourselves*. If we hold on to negative energies instead of moving through the pain, griefs, rage and resentments within us, for whatever reasons, our bodies become toxic and we suffer disease. In other words, if our spirits are not harmonious our bodies will reflect that,' Katherine said matter-of-factly and Francesca had the strangest sensation of a penny dropping.

She would have liked to get into a further discussion about the matter on the way to RTE, but felt too shy to bring up the subject, and besides the traffic was heavy – they were right in the middle of the morning rush hour – and the journey across the city took all her concentration.

Once they got to RTE, Katherine was whisked off to the studio as the PA announced airily that the programme's running order had been changed and Katherine was on earlier than scheduled. In one way it was a relief. It meant Katherine wouldn't be hanging around waiting to go on and she'd have time for a snack before Francesca took her back to the airport.

'I enjoyed that interview,' her author announced three-quarters of an hour later as they walked out to the car park. 'He's quirky and very intelligent.'

'I like listening to Gerry Ryan, he's very blunt but he empathizes,' Francesca said, delighted with herself that her two interviews had gone smoothly this time. 'Are you hungry, Katherine? Would you like to go for a quick bite to eat?'

'I'm starving!' the other woman admitted. 'I could eat a horse.'

Not wishing to go through town as she wanted to take the East Link, Francesca decided on the Herbert Park Hotel, where they had a tasty snack before the journey to the airport. She really was enjoying this aspect of her job, she thought as she paid the bill and tucked the receipt into her wallet to go on her expense account.

Dealing with Katherine Kronskey had been a delight compared to poor Magda she reflected as she waited for the author to check in.

Katherine turned to her as they walked away from the check-in desk. 'Thank you so much for taking such good care of me.'

'It was a real pleasure,' Francesca said warmly. Instinctively the two women embraced.

'You know, you have to close the door yourself before the next one opens fully.' Katherine smiled. 'The old sayings are so true. The only thing to fear is fear itself. Conquer that and you've conquered the world. Goodbye, Francesca. If you were one of my patients I'd say to you: release, relax and let go and all will be well.'

'I'll try,' Francesca promised.

'I know you will,' Katherine said encouragingly and with a wave and smile was striding towards her departure gate, a woman completely at ease with herself and the world.

Release, relax and let go. Release, relax and let go. The mantra played in her head the whole way back to Clontarf. She intended to take the train back to the office. She parked in the Dart station and waited for the next train, reflecting on her morning. It had been eye-opening for sure, she acknowledged as she finally stepped into the carriage.

Let go, let go. The wheels of the train clickety-clacking along the tracks seemed to urge her. *Let go, let go, let go.*

Was it that easy? Once Janet had made her decision doors had opened for her. Listening to Katherine had been positively inspiring. The author seemed to have it all now. She had a new partner, her work, health and vitality and true peace of mind.

What about the boys? They had to be considered.

Francesca gave a wry smile. Owen certainly wouldn't thank her for using him as an excuse not to make a decision and neither would Jonathan. She'd be surprised if Jonathan ever came back to Ireland to live. He'd made a very good life for himself in America and he liked it there. It was too early to say what Owen would do. But he had no time for Mark now and she could only hope that that would change in the future.

Nix that, Francesca, you can't use the boys as an excuse, she chided herself. *Release, relax, let go.* She stared unseeingly out of the carriage window, lost in thought. She'd like to follow the advice, it seemed so simple, but had she the nerve? *The only thing to fear is fear itself.* How did you stop being afraid?

Did she want to live in fear for the rest of her life?
No.
Did she want her independence?
Yes.
Did she want to make life difficult for Mark?
Not very nice, in fact vindictive would be an apt description of her reasoning there; it was most definitely not the way Katherine meant for her to be thinking but she wasn't perfect and the answer to the question was very definitely a massive big YES!

Hadn't she proved herself capable of doing her job?
Yes.

So went the internal dialogue as the train whooshed into Landsdown Road and a minute later sped off again.

Only a couple more stops, clickety-clack, clickety-clack, release, relax, let go. It's time to close the door so the next one can open fully. Clickety-clack, clickety-clack. Release, relax, let go.

'OK then, go for it,' she murmured aloud – to her own surprise and that of the woman opposite her.

'Sorry,' Francesca excused herself.

'Not at all,' smiled the woman. 'Go for it.'

'Thank you,' said Francesca. 'I think I will.'

Chapter Thirty-four

'So it's best of all, Mrs Kirwan, to have a chat with your husband and see how the land lies. Then let me know the outcome and we'll take it from there,' Jessica O'Farrell said briskly as she held out her hand and gripped Francesca's in a no-nonsense handshake.

'OK, I'll do that,' Francesca agreed. She picked up her bag and walked out of the solicitor's office. Her heart was thumping. She couldn't believe that she'd actually made the appointment and gone through with the meeting.

She'd asked Ken for a couple of hours off work, time she was owed, and he'd obligingly told her to take as much time as she needed. They got on extremely well, she enjoyed his wit and he'd told her more than once that he couldn't thank his aunt enough for suggesting her for the job. Even though she'd only been working for a very short length of time the self-assurance the job had given her was a revelation to her. Thrown in at the deep end, she'd handled herself and the job with a confidence that had surprised her. Monica had been right, all her years of entertaining Mark's clients had paid off. How ironic that she could now thank him for that. His disparagement of her work had been a real slap in the face but maybe it was the best thing to have happened to her, she brooded. It had motivated her to move on in a way nothing else had. But whether it had motivated her or not he still had an awful cheek. Patronizing bastard. She scowled, mad with him again.

Don't shilly-shally, she told herself sternly, and on a swift and sudden impulse she hailed a passing taxi and gave the address of Mark's bank. It had to be done and the sooner she got it over with the better, she decided. Otherwise she'd go home and think about it and lose her nerve and it would all come to nothing.

Perhaps he was in Brussels, she thought suddenly. Damn! It would be a bit daft waltzing into the bank to confront her husband and then to find out that he was abroad. She took her diary out of her bag and found the bank's main number. She swiftly tapped it in on her mobile. The girl on the switchboard was crisp and efficient: Yes, Mr Mark Kirwan was in his office today and yes, Ms Nikki Langan likewise, she informed Francesca.

If I wasn't meant to do this they wouldn't be there, Francesca comforted herself as her nerves began to get the better of her. She took out her make-up bag and studied herself in the mirror. She looked well enough. She still had her tan and it made such a difference. She was no longer wishy-washy and pasty-faced. Her eyes were bright and clear; a little bit of eye liner and a touch of mascara to emphasize them would work wonders. Her eye shadow was fine. She dusted some bronzing powder over her cheeks, attended to her eyes, retouched her lipstick, ran her comb through her hair and was satisfied. A quick spray of perfume on her neck and wrists and she knew she was as ready as she'd ever be. She was wearing a tailored check jacket and black cami with a black pencil skirt and she knew she looked smart and sophisticated. She was so glad she'd worn that particular outfit, it was very slimming and it made her feel good.

The taxi drew to a halt outside the headquarters of EuroBank Irl. and as she gazed up at the familiar building, her stomach tightened. How often she'd run up those marble steps to meet Mark for lunch. Who would ever have thought that they would end up like this? She paid the taxi man, took a deep breath and climbed out of the taxi. It wasn't too late to reverse her decision. She could get right back in, give the taxi man her office address and forget the whole thing, but instinctively Francesca knew that if she didn't follow through with what she'd started, she'd be unhappy for the rest of her life.

She hurried up the steps and the automatic doors slid open to allow her to enter. She knew where Mark's office was, of course, unless he'd changed offices since they'd split up, but she didn't know where Nikki's was. She walked calmly over to reception and said to the receptionist, whom thankfully she didn't recognize and who didn't recognize her, 'Just checking, Mark Kirwan's office, third floor first on the left?'

'That's right,' the young woman said politely.

'And Nikki Langan's?' Francesca said nonchalantly.

'First floor, fourth on the right.'

'Thanks a million.' Francesca moved away calmly to allow someone else make a query.

The lift doors were open and she didn't have to wait, otherwise she might have taken to her heels, she thought, half shocked, half amused at her totally uncharacteristic behaviour. It was strange, her earlier nerves were gone. She felt calm and cool and in control, almost as if she were observing the whole thing at a distance.

The lift doors parted and she hurried down the carpeted corridor. Fourth on the right. There it was, that woman's name plate, polished and gleaming. Francesca felt like spitting on it.

Before even thinking what she was going to do or say, Francesca knocked and marched in. A secretary working at a computer looked up, startled. Francesca held up her hand. 'Just have to pop in to Nikki, she's not in a meeting, is she?'

The secretary took her Dictaphone out of her ears. 'No, whom should I say is here for her?'

'This won't take a sec, don't worry. We know each other,' Francesca said breezily as she kept moving towards the inner door.

'Oh! OK,' the secretary said doubtfully as Francesca knocked very lightly on the door and let herself into Nikki's office.

The other woman was sitting in a cream leather swivel chair with her back to her. She was on the phone.

Francesca marched over to the desk just as Nikki

pivoted around. Her jaw dropped and her eyes opened wide. She put her hand over the mouthpiece. 'How did you get in here? Can't you see I'm on the phone?'

'I walked in here and not now you're not,' Francesca retorted coldly, whisking the phone out of the astonished younger woman's hand and replacing it on the cradle.

Nikki jumped up furiously. 'Just what the hell do you think you're doing?' she demanded, stupefied.

'I'm here to have a little chat, just like you came to have one with me,' Francesca snapped. 'So shut up and sit down.'

'How dare you speak to me like that?' Nikki flared.

'Oh, pipe down, Nikki, and let's get this over, I'm a busy woman,' Francesca drawled. 'I came to tell you that I intend divorcing Mark. He's all yours. You can have him. You're welcome to him. I'm sure you'll both live very happily together for many years to come. Don't bother inviting me to the wedding, it wouldn't be one I'd care to attend,' she added bitchily. 'Watching Mark make another set of vows would be just a little hard to swallow, but I'm sure it won't bother you. Have fun,' she said airily and almost laughed at the dumbfounded expression on Nikki's face. She was utterly speechless and had not regained her composure as Francesca strode out of the office, exhilarated. *One down. One to go.*

She walked down the corridor smiling at one or two people she recognized. A young woman carrying a bundle of files stopped and did a double take and Francesca nodded politely. She recognized the girl from various bank events. News of her visit was going to spread around the building like wildfire, she thought with satisfaction. Good. The gossip would annoy Mark. She couldn't care less.

She pressed the lift button and waited patiently for it to arrive. She was utterly calm now, almost detached. It was as though once she had made her decision and verbalized it, the whole thing had taken on a life of its own. No doubt Nikki would have phoned her husband to alert him of her arrival. Pity about that. She would have liked to surprise him. But her main target had been Nikki. Francesca wanted her to know that she was divorcing Mark.

It had felt good to give him away, she thought viciously. It had been a very powerful moment. Her husband had been reduced to nothing more than a commodity. She remembered the expression on Nikki's face when she'd said 'you can have him'. Shock and a flicker of fear.

Millie had been so right in her assessment of the situation, Francesca thought triumphantly as she rapped on the door of her husband's office. Nikki, for all her sophisticated, career-woman image, was desperately unsure of Mark. That suited Francesca's agenda just fine. Not only was she causing Mark grief, she was causing that bitch mega grief. Sauce for the goose was sauce for the gander, she concluded with immense satisfaction.

As Francesca let herself into the plush outer office she saw her husband standing at the door that led to his office. His secretary was not at her desk. Mark was grim-faced with anger as he silently held the door open for her and motioned her inside.

'What the hell are you playing at?' he said through gritted teeth as he closed the door behind her.

'I'm not playing at anything, Mark,' Francesca replied coldly as she sat gracefully in a chair and crossed her legs. 'I'm simply here to tell you that I spoke to my solicitor this morning and I intend divorcing you, with or without your consent.'

Chapter Thirty-five

'Don't be ridiculous,' Mark derided. 'That really is going over the top, even for you, Francesca.'

'Excuse me,' she said icily. 'I'm deadly serious, Mark. I want a divorce.'

'For what?' he asked, nonplussed.

'That should be obvious. I don't want to be married to you any more.'

'But what's wrong with leaving things as they are? You have the house and a generous allowance, what more do you want?' Mark demanded angrily.

'I've just told you, Mark. I don't want to be married to you any more,' Francesca reiterated. 'Nikki can have you. She can be the second Mrs Kirwan if that's what she so badly wants. A dubious honour, I can assure you,' she drawled, sticking the knife in good and hard. She was actually enjoying herself, she thought, half shocked. Mark didn't know what had hit him.

'I don't want a divorce,' her husband exploded.

'Tough. You should have thought of that before

355

you climbed into Nikki Langan's bed,' Francesca said nastily. 'In case you're in any doubt this is not about what *you* want, it's about what *I* want. I certainly have grounds for divorce. The solicitor told me it's pretty straightforward, so I want first of all to put the house on the market—'

'No way, Francesca! No way. I'm not selling the house,' Mark ranted. 'It's the family home.'

'Now *you're* being ridiculous,' Francesca taunted. 'What family? You're gone. Jonathan's in America for good and it wouldn't surprise me if Owen stays too. So all that's left of the *family* is me and I don't want to stay in that big house all on my own. I want a fresh start.' Francesca shrugged. 'You can buy out my share if you don't want to sell it. At market value, of course.'

'I'm damned if I'm going to pay a fucking fortune for my own home. The home I paid the mortgage off on years ago because of my bloody hard work.' Mark was getting more agitated by the second.

'Oh, and of course I did nothing, just sat back like a lady and didn't make any contribution. Get lost, Mark. I'm entitled to a half-share of the house and I want it. I'm entitled to a half-share of everything actually, but I'm not greedy. Sell the house and give me my share and you can keep the rest of the stocks and shares and the pension fund and the other investments that you've worked so *bloody* hard for,' Francesca said in disgust.

'I'm not giving you a divorce,' Mark blustered.

'I'm not *asking* you for a divorce. I'm here to tell you that I'm getting one whether you like it or not.'

'I'll contest it,' Mark threatened.

Francesca gave him a look of such utter contempt he dropped his gaze.

'You can do what you like, Mark. If you contest it – and let me remind you that you don't have a leg to stand on since you're the one who had the affair – it will only cost a lot more money so your pettiness will get you nowhere in the long run. And if you do contest it I'll take everything I'm entitled to. The choice is yours,' she said scathingly.

'It seems I don't have a fucking choice then, do I?' he said bitterly.

'Not really, no,' Francesca agreed as she stood up to go. 'You made your choice when you started seeing that woman. But she can have you now. You can marry *her* and make an honest woman of her.' Her tone was acerbic and for Mark the last straw.

'Listen, you, one marriage was more than enough, believe me. You've turned into such a bitch, Francesca, I wouldn't wish you on my worst enemy,' he burst out.

'Oh dear,' murmured Francesca. 'Poor Nikki, she seems to have her heart set on becoming the next Mrs Kirwan. Still, it's no skin off my nose and it's none of my business. You sort out your affairs, Mark, and I'll sort out mine.' She dropped a business card on the table. 'My solicitor's name and address. She's very good at family law, I gather. She'll be writing to you.'

Mark picked up the card and threw it in the bin.

'Don't be childish, Mark, it doesn't suit the image,' Francesca advised as she walked out of the door. She was on an absolute high. Now Mark was the helpless one, she gloated, remembering her own fear and terror when she'd discovered him kissing that woman at Dublin Airport. Now he was the one who would suffer the torment of sleepless nights just as she had. She'd really hurt him where it hurt most. His purse strings. And best of all she'd heard him declare with his own lips that he wasn't going to marry again. Nikki Langan was on a hiding to nothing and, what was more, she knew it, Francesca thought with immense satisfaction. Soon she'd know what it was like to be rejected. Soon she'd know hurt and pain and grief and rage and sorrow when she finally realized that Mark had only been using her. See how strong the relationship was now, Francesca laughed to herself. Having a lot in common would not be enough to keep a woman whose heart was set on marriage happy. She'd like to be a fly on the wall in the apartment tonight, she mused happily as she took the lift to the foyer and strolled out of the door, astonished at what she'd achieved.

Bubbling with adrenalin, she dialled Millie's number. 'Hi, it's me,' she said gaily when she heard her sister answer. 'Guess what? I've just told Nikki Langan she can have Mark, I'm divorcing him. And I know I've just given my cheating husband the biggest squit attack he's ever going to have. When I told him I was putting the house on the market and wanted half the proceeds he got such a shock I thought he was going to make me a widow there and then,' Francesca gabbled.

'What?' shrieked Millie agog. 'I don't *believe* it. We have to meet. I want to hear every single syllable. My God, girl, but you don't waste time. I can't let you out of my sight for ten seconds and there you are, practically divorced. I take my hat off to you. What brought this on? What did Nikki say when you told her? Where did you meet her or did you meet the two of them together? This is so *frustrating*. I want to hear all about it right this second!'

'Can you come into town on the Dart now? I could meet you for lunch in the Harbour Master in the IFSC,' Francesca suggested.

'You're on. The kids are gone on a day trip to Butlin's for their summer project. I'll be there lickety split,' said Millie. 'Way to go, babe. Way to go. I'm dang proud of ya.'

'Oh, Millie, I'm dang proud of myself. I feel scared and excited at the same time. I'm on a high now, I hope I won't change my mind when I come back down to earth.'

'And let Mark off the hook? Don't talk rot,' scoffed her sister. 'See you soon.'

Mark sat at his desk with his head in his hands. His stomach was churning. He felt nauseous. Was he having the worst nightmare of his life? Would he wake up in a minute bathed in sweat but feeling utterly relieved? The phone rang, its discreet but persistent burr letting him know in no uncertain terms that he was wide awake and enduring a catastrophe.

'Hello? . . . Oh, hi, Nikki,' he said slowly.

'Is Francesca gone?' Nikki asked.

'Yeah,' he said wearily.

'Does she really want a divorce?'

'It seems so,' Mark answered guardedly.

'I see. You'd better get a good lawyer,' Nikki

advised coolly. 'Oh, and by the way, it's all around the building that Francesca was in, and it's getting more lurid by the minute, seemingly. She could have had the decency to meet us outside of work.'

'Well, she didn't,' snapped Mark. 'Look, I have to go. I'll see you at home tonight.'

'What about lunch?'

'I can't,' Mark responded. 'See you later.' He put the phone down and rubbed his eyes tiredly. He could have met Nikki for lunch but right now he just wanted to go into some crowded anonymous pub and nurse his sorrows over a pint. Not only was he going to have to deal with Francesca and this divorce whim, he was going to have to tread very carefully with Nikki. He could see signs of a major battle about 'commitment' coming up, especially after her tirade in Mamma Mia's the other day. Mark groaned at the idea.

He truly didn't want a divorce. It would make his life extremely complicated and life was bad enough as it was at the moment. He desperately didn't want to sell his beloved house. How could Francesca want to leave it? He'd hated leaving it. He held it very dear. All the memories of their children were entwined with that house. He'd banked on sentiment keeping her there. He'd have to cash in a hell of a lot of his investments to pay Francesca her share of the market value of the house. Or else borrow. What a pain in the ass at his age.

And even if he did buy her out, he wasn't sure if he wanted to live there with Nikki. That would seem strange, out of kilter in some way. It wasn't a Nikki sort of a house. Besides, she'd want to refurbish and redecorate and that would cost another arm and a leg and it certainly wasn't a house for the modern, minimalist-style décor she liked.

Mark shook his head, almost dazed. There had to be some way around this. Surely he could talk Francesca out of it. She wasn't thinking straight, she couldn't be. She wasn't herself, he thought agitatedly.

But she didn't look like a woman in disarray. She'd looked extremely well, better than he'd seen her look in ages, especially with the tan. But it was more than the tan that made the difference. There was a spark there that he hadn't seen in a long time. Some of her old vibrancy was back. And there was a hint of steel that he'd seen rarely in their marriage. Now she was so cold and vengeful. Not the Francesca he knew at all. It was true what they said about a woman scorned. Mark leaned forward in his chair and picked the business card he'd discarded earlier out of the bin. Jessica O'Farrell. He'd never heard of her. According to Francesca she knew her stuff on family law. Mark knew enough himself to know that he was on very shaky grounds contesting the divorce if Francesca truly wanted one. He also knew that unless they were in agreement on all points it could be an extremely costly business. If they were going to divorce it was in both their best interests to be in accord. But surely she really couldn't be serious about it. Starting afresh at this stage of her life must be a daunting prospect. Buying a house, taking a new job that paid buttons – why was she putting herself to such trouble and upheaval when he had provided her with an extremely comfortable lifestyle and made no fuss about it either? He just couldn't understand her reasoning. He'd have to think of some way around it. But what?

And Nikki? Did she really want marriage? She had it all as it was. Why on earth would she want to change the status quo? He didn't want to marry her. It was nothing to do with his feelings for her. After his experiences with Francesca he simply wasn't anxious to go down that path again. Maybe he could plead religion and pretend that he didn't believe in divorce, he thought gloomily. He could say it was a deep-rooted conviction despite the fact that he didn't observe any religious practices. He couldn't remember the last time he'd been at Mass. Nikki would never believe him. It *was* a pathetic cop-out, he conceded. He could hardly insult the woman's intelligence with it.

His life was in total crisis, Mark thought morosely as he pulled on his trench coat. Maybe he'd be inspired over a pint. Because if ever he needed help and inspiration it was now.

Nikki chewed the end of her silver Sheaffer fountain pen, a gift from Mark. This should be one of the happiest days of her life. Francesca was doing exactly what Nikki had wanted her to do all along. She was divorcing Mark. He was going to be a free man. So why was she miserable? Why did she have this feeling of dread and what felt like a block of cement lodged in the pit of her stomach? Why was she so afraid that even though things seemed to be going just the way she wanted them to, it was all going very badly wrong?

It was the way Francesca had swanned in, looking

not the slightest bit slobby but tanned, vibrant and very elegant – and, even worse, completely in control. Nikki had hardly recognized her as the same woman who'd opened the door to her in her dressing gown. The patronizing way she'd told Nikki that she could have Mark as though she were handing him over on a plate grated. Nikki grimaced. There was something almost spiteful in the way Mark's wife had behaved. There'd been a look of triumph in her eyes that worried Nikki.

What had made the other woman change her mind about the divorce? She'd been so adamant that she wasn't divorcing Mark, the day Nikki had confronted her. Why this sudden sea change?

And Mark? What about him? Nikki thought uneasily. He'd sounded shattered on the phone and he wouldn't have lunch with her. Surely he'd be glad to have things sorted. They couldn't keep going on in this limbo for ever, neither one thing nor another. Divorce was the only logical step, couldn't he see that? She knew he didn't want to sell the house. But it was only bricks and mortar and besides it was worth a fortune. Liquidating an asset like that would be a smart move, especially as he'd make an enormous profit from it. So what if he had to give half to Francesca? He'd still have plenty left over to buy a big new house for himself . . . and her.

But that was the problem. She knew that he'd feel trapped. And that wasn't the way she wanted things to happen. Why couldn't it have been him that pressed for the divorce? Why hadn't he wanted her enough to make the moves? Why had he been so passive about it all? He'd have left things the way they were for ever and a day, Nikki thought angrily. He made no concession to her feelings at all. Would this new development change things? He'd been pretty cool with her since her outburst in the restaurant.

Her private Christmas deadline was looming and if things hadn't changed radically by then he was out on his ear. There was no point in hanging on if the writing was on the wall. She wasn't that much of a wimp. She'd play things cool for a while. She wouldn't even mention the divorce unless he brought it up. In fact she'd phone one of her friends and arrange to go out clubbing tonight. That would show him just how blasé she seemed about the whole thing, Nikki decided as she scrolled through her palm-top diary looking for her friend's work number.

Elaine knocked and came into the office. She seemed to have a knowing smirk on her plain face. It was a mega pain in the ass working in the same building as Mark. Everybody seemed to know their damn business. No doubt Elaine and her silly friends had been down gossiping at the photocopier.

'Yes?' she said curtly.

'Here's the Richmond Bank file you were looking for,' Elaine said sweetly. 'Can I get you coffee or anything?'

'No, thank you. Oh, and Elaine' – she handed her secretary two typed letters – 'there were several errors in these letters you typed out for me this morning. You obviously didn't have your mind on the job and it's simply not good enough. Kindly do them again, immediately,' she instructed coldly. 'I want them to catch today's post.'

'Sorry,' muttered Elaine, taking the letters which were held out to her so disdainfully between finger and thumb. Sarky bitch, she swore silently as she closed the door behind her.

That wiped the knowing smirk off your smug little face, Nikki thought with some small degree of satisfaction. Maybe she should go and look for a job with another organization. She'd have no problem getting a position elsewhere, but she liked her work at EuroBank Irl., the remunerations were excellent and it was far too high a price to pay to leave her job because of a relationship that was possibly going nowhere. She could change her secretary though, she thought nastily. She was going to start a little file on Madame Elaine. Shoddy work was not acceptable. From now on, Elaine was on borrowed time.

Nikki stood up and stretched wearily. Elaine wasn't her problem really, she was just an irritation. Mark was her problem. Or rather her needs in relation to Mark were her problem. One way or another she was going to have to deal with it. Putting time frames on it was only putting it off. Christmas seemed like a long way away, she thought despondently as she waited for her friend to answer her phone.

Chapter Thirty-six

'I'd love to have seen her face.' Millie laughed as she sipped her cappuccino. 'But are you really sure it's what you want? You've thought it all out?' she asked.

Francesca shook her head. 'I haven't thought it out at all, beyond knowing that I want a house that's mine. And I want to keep working and I suppose really I want some sort of closure – isn't that what the Americans call it? If Mark hadn't been such a condescending shit about my job I'm not sure I'd have made the decision so fast. It was the last straw, Millie. He made me as mad as hell and then when he kept going on about the house being *our* house I felt a total lack of control over my life. So I'm taking my control back.' She gave a wry smile. 'Ma will be horrified.'

'Poor Ma,' her sister said fondly. 'We're a grave disappointment to her. Do you think Mark will ever marry Nikki? Would you mind if he did?' she asked, in her usual forthright way.

'I suppose I would get a bit of a shock,' Francesca

admitted. 'Especially when part of the reason I'm asking him for the divorce is to make him run a mile from such an eventuality. He really was horrified. He certainly never thought that *I'd* be the one asking for a divorce. It's awful. All the affection I ever had for him is gone and I just want to hurt him the way he's hurting me. It was a great feeling to know that I was getting to him. Doesn't say much about me, does it, I suppose.' Francesca made a face.

'For what it's worth I do think that you're doing the right thing, whatever the reasons. And making Mark feel bad is only part of it. At another level you're picking up the pieces, putting them together again and getting on with things. That's very positive. Lots of women in your position wallow in their misery for the rest of their lives. You've done really well, Francesca. I think you're great,' Millie said warmly.

'Thanks, Millie. I'd have been lost without you.'

'That's what sisters are for. You'd do the same for me. Will you feel bad leaving the house?'

Francesca sighed. 'It was weird. When I came back from my holidays it was so quiet and so lonely I got this feeling that I didn't want to live there any more. There are too many ghosts. Anyway, it's far too big to live in on my own. And it's a house that needs life in it. It needs children. I hope a family buys it. I'll have an absolute fit if Mark buys me out and installs her nibs in it. I'll really be hoist by my own petard then.'

'You're getting it valued by an auctioneer, aren't you?' Millie said sharply.

'Of course I am. I told Mark if he was buying me

out it would have to be at market value. He nearly passed out peacefully.' Francesca popped a mint into her mouth. 'Honestly, Millie, he thought that I was going to spend the rest of my life there on my own, being kept by him. What sort of woman does he think I am? He can't understand how I'm throwing it all back in his face. He thinks I'm ungrateful. No wonder he found me boring,' she said dolefully. 'He thinks I have no passion. That I'm flat and two-dimensional. He just stopped seeing me, you know. I was part of the furniture.'

'Well, he's seeing you now, babe, in a whole new light. And I must say it suits you. I haven't seen you looking as well for ages either. Have you any idea where you'd like to live?'

'I haven't really thought about it or started looking yet. Honestly, Millie, when I got up this morning I had no idea that I was going to march into that bank and say what I said to Mark and Nikki,' Francesca confessed. 'I like Monkstown. It would be very handy for the job. It's on the Dart. It's beside the sea. It wouldn't hold sad memories for me. I think I'd like to move out of Howth.'

'But all your friends are there,' Millie pointed out.

'A lot of them were my friends when we were a couple. It's amazing how many people drop you like a hot potato when you split up. Single unattached females of my age are not the ideal guests for dinner parties,' Francesca said wryly. 'Janet Dalton and Bart and Monica are the friends who really stood by me and I can Dart over to see them any time I want to. I can Dart over to you. We'll see. I'm not going to get into a panic about it.'

'I know, but once you put the house on the market it's going to sell in no time. Properties in Howth are very sought after, especially big houses in their own grounds.'

'I know,' sighed Francesca. 'I suppose now that I've set events in motion I should get my ass in gear and start looking. What are you doing at the weekend?'

'Let me guess, house-hunting?' grinned Millie.

'Correct,' said Francesca as she waved her credit card at a waiter. 'But before I do anything I want to ring the boys and tell them. I hope they don't mind.'

'They won't. They'll only want what's best for you,' Millie said supportively.

'I hope so,' Francesca murmured as she signed the docket.

They walked briskly back towards Connolly Station. A light drizzle had started and they took out umbrellas. 'Some summer we're having,' moaned Millie. 'Just as well we had the week in Portugal.'

'At least you've got France to look forward to,' Francesca reminded her.

'Please try and come, won't you, Francesca?' Millie urged. 'We're there for a month.'

'If the house is sold by then I'll try,' Francesca promised. 'I won't have Mark saying I'm swanning around Europe on his hard-earned money.'

'You're on,' Millie agreed as they clattered up the steps to the station. 'So get out there and start looking for houses.'

'I will then.' Francesca smiled as they parted to take trains in the opposite direction, Millie to home and Francesca back to the office.

'Everything OK?' Ken enquired cheerfully as she arrived back at work twenty minutes later.

'I think so.' Francesca made a face as she shrugged out of her damp coat. 'I told Mark, my husband, that I wanted a divorce,' she blurted out.

'Oh dear. Should I say congratulations? I didn't mean to pry. I thought you were gone to the dentist or something,' Ken said hastily.

'Don't be silly, you're not prying. Anyway I think I'm glad I did it. But I need to go and look for a house to live in. I was half thinking of Monkstown,' she confided.

'It's nice here. Some lovely houses. But pricy,' Ken warned.

'I think I should be able to afford it by the time we sell the house in Howth,' Francesca murmured.

'Of course, I forgot about that. You'll get a nice house here or in Sandycove or Glasthule, no problem. Why don't you pop into the estate agent's down the road?' he suggested.

'Good idea, my young genius,' Francesca teased.

Ken looked at her. 'Well, go on, what are you waiting for?'

'Now?'

'Why not? Is the phone ringing? Is there a queue outside looking for us? Go, Frannie, go, Frannie, go, Frannie, go.'

'I'll box your ears, Kenneth, if you don't desist from calling me Frannie,' Francesca said sternly.

'Assaulted by an older woman, mmmm,' said her irrepressible boss as he held her coat for her.

'Little brat,' rebuked Francesca fondly. 'I'll get you a gooey cake for afternoon tea.'

'Better than sex.' Ken licked his lips. 'You do look after me so well. My girlfriend's *quite* jealous.'

Francesca laughed. 'I'd say now that Carla's the jealous type all right.'

'Well, maybe not exactly jealous, then,' Ken agreed. Carla was an attractive, no-nonsense sort, a nurse, and Ken was mad about her. 'Go buy a house. It will be a great excuse for a party. I'll bring Carla and when she sees how devoted you are to me, it might make her look at me in a different light. Yup, Francesca's Party will be a turning point in all our lives,' he declared dramatically.

'You're mad, you know that?' Francesca retorted. Ken rolled his eyes wildly and she had to laugh. Thinking of how alike he and Owen were gave her a pang of longing to see her son. She missed his exuberance and *joie de vivre*. The empty house was a constant reminder that both her sons had their own lives to lead, just as she now had to move on and live hers. It would be difficult phoning them to tell them that she was divorcing their father.

It had stopped raining. She hurried towards the main street wondering whether there would be anything that appealed to her. Several properties caught her eye that would be well within her price range. One, a three-bedroom, architect-designed mews, looked very inviting. Viewings were scheduled for the following Saturday. She took the property descriptions to show them to Millie later on, then headed back to work.

'Anything interesting?' Ken asked.

She showed him what she had and he studied

371

them intently. 'I like that one,' he said, pointing to the mews. 'It's got character.'

'I like it myself,' she admitted.

'You'd probably want to move fast on it. Places like that are snapped up,' Ken advised.

'I suppose so. I'm viewing it on Saturday.'

'The best of luck with it, Francesca,' Ken said as both phones rang simultaneously and it was back to work with a vengeance.

That evening Francesca phoned both her sons. She connected first with Owen. 'Hi, love, it's me. How are you?' she asked cheerfully.

'Mam, howya? How's things? How's the job going?' Owen was delighted to hear her.

'It's great, Owen. I'm really enjoying it. I've booked to do a computer course next week, so I'll probably be a dab hand at e-mails before you know it, although I much prefer to talk to you on the phone.'

'That's great news, Mam. I'm glad things are going well for you.'

'Listen, Owen, I've phoned you to tell you that I've asked your father for a divorce,' she said hesitantly. There was a stunned silence. 'Owen, are you there?'

'I'm here, Mam,' he said gruffly, 'and I think that it's a good thing for you to do.'

'Do you, Owen?' Francesca suddenly didn't feel quite so sure.

'Yeah, Mam. It's a very positive step. It means you're getting on with things. At least you're not pottering.'

Francesca laughed. 'It will mean selling the house and buying a place of my own.'

'I bet Dad's going mad about that,' Owen said astutely.

'You can say that again,' Francesca agreed.

'Good enough for him.'

'Owen, don't be like that,' chided his mother.

'Sorry,' he apologized. 'Mam, would you mind if I stay out here for a couple of months longer? I really like it and I've met a very nice girl. She's Scottish, she's studying law here. You'd like her. Her name's Morag.'

'Of course I don't mind, love. I'm delighted that you like it there. And I'll be looking forward to meeting Morag,' Francesca assured him.

'Do you think that you'll be selling the house soon?' he asked.

'Well, I'm going to look at a place in Monkstown on Saturday.'

'Monkstown?' he sounded surprised.

'It's near work and it's on the Dart and I want to get out of Howth. Too many memories,' she explained.

'Good idea. Mam, don't throw out my footie gear, sure you won't?'

'I'll pack all your stuff and put it in your new bedroom,' she promised.

'Thanks, Ma. I hope it all goes well for you. Will Millie and Aidan help you with the move?'

'Of course they will. And don't worry about your stuff. OK?'

'OK, Ma, I love you.'

'I love you too, talk to you soon. I'll phone on Sunday and let you know if I'm buying.'

'OK, see ya, Mam.'

She had tears in her eyes when she hung up and had to compose herself before ringing her eldest son.

Her conversation with Jonathan was very similar to the one she'd had with Owen.

'Mam, if you feel divorce is the way for you to go, then do it. Dad's with that other woman, he's made a new life for himself. You go and do what you have to do for yourself. Owen and I support you all the way,' he assured her. 'If you like I'll try and get a week off to come and help you move.'

'Well, it's a bit soon for that yet, but I'd love to see you, darling, and thank you for the offer. I really appreciate it, pet.'

'I'd like to do something to help. You've had a crap time,' Jonathan said.

'It's been hard, I won't deny that,' Francesca acknowledged. 'But I love my job. And it's not as difficult as it was, emotionally. I'm not bawling my eyes out all the time any more.'

'Well, Mam, you just let me know when you're moving and I'll come home and help out,' Jonathan said firmly. 'It's the least I can do.'

'All right, love, I will,' Francesca promised. The knowledge that her eldest son would be home to help her take the biggest step of her life made it seem less daunting. She was half excited now at the idea of moving. She was looking forward to viewing the houses for sale. If all went well one of them might end up as her new home.

Chapter Thirty-seven

'I wouldn't be mad about this place, in all honesty,' Millie murmured as they followed the estate agent around the musty-smelling bungalow. 'It's very linear and those dreadful brown wooden doors. It's like a corridor of cells.'

'I know. The gardens are nice, though, and I could gut it and start from scratch,' Francesca said doubtfully.

'No, Francesca, I don't think so. Not here. I'd be in dereliction of my sisterly duty if I let you buy this. Besides, it's only the second place you've looked at. Although I wasn't crazy about the first place either. There's no mad rush to buy, so stay calm,' Millie instructed.

'Yes, Millie. Whatever you say, Millie,' Francesca said meekly. 'Sorry for living and all of that.'

'Sorry.' Millie had the grace to apologize. 'I was being bossy again.'

'A tad,' Francesca agreed. 'Come on, let's go look at the mews, I'm dying to see it.'

So were a host of other interested viewers. There were little knots of people gathered outside the property and Francesca's heart sank. It was a seller's market these days, which would be good for the sale of her own house, but if she saw a place that she really liked she'd have to go after it quite aggressively, she realized. If only she had some money behind her, she'd feel much more confident about making an offer.

The mews lived up to the auctioneer's description. Its outside appearance was deceptive. She'd thought it looked quite small but when she stepped into the airy hall she was pleasantly surprised. A spacious lounge ran the width of the house. Wooden maple floors and floor to ceiling French windows that led to a landscaped courtyard gave a sense of light and spaciousness that appealed to Francesca. The walls were painted a warm buttercup that lent a cosy air of warmth and Francesca decided that if she bought the mews she'd keep the colour scheme. The small but well-equipped kitchen with its Shaker-style presses led to a small dining room that opened out onto the courtyard.

Upstairs the master bedroom, with a delightful window seat, had an en suite and a well-designed, roomy, fitted wardrobe. The other two bedrooms were small but tastefully decorated but far less commodious than those Owen and Jonathan were used to at home.

'They're a bit on the small side,' she said doubtfully to Millie who was oohing and aahing in delight.

'Would you get a grip, Francesca? Jonathan and Owen have cut the apron strings. They're not children any more. They're adults and they're making lives of their own now and eventually that will include homes of their own. What's the point in having huge big bedrooms empty for months at a time? If that's the case you might as well stay where you are,' Millie pointed out reasonably. 'Francesca, this place is gorgeous. It's ideal for you. You'd be mad not to put in an offer.'

'Do you think?' Francesca poked her head around the bathroom door. 'It's so modern. Look at the shower.'

'Look at the tiles,' Millie enthused, running her hand over the hand-painted floral design. 'I'd *love* to live in a house like this. My semi-d. is so *boring* in comparison.'

A couple edged past them into the bathroom. 'I want it,' they heard the woman say.

'Tough,' muttered Millie, 'so does my sister.'

'Stop it, Millie.' Francesca giggled.

'Get down there to that estate agent right this minute and tell him that you'll give him the asking price and under no circumstances is he to sell it to anyone else,' Millie ordered. 'And this time I'm being bossy for all the right reasons.'

'I know. You're right. Let's go,' Francesca said decisively.

'Atta, girl. Go, girl, go!' Millie practically pushed her down the stairs so eager was she for Francesca to secure the mews.

Stephen Boyle, the estate agent, was brisk and professional when Francesca told him that she'd pay the asking price, subject to contract and loan approval and asked that he wouldn't let the property go to anyone else.

'The vendors are looking for a quick sale, Mrs Kirwan. If we have a cash buyer immediately, I'm afraid I'll have to let it go.'

'Look, hang on to it for a day or two until I sort something out,' Francesca said firmly.

'I'll keep you abreast of all developments,' he promised.

'What are you going to do?' Millie asked. 'It's a pity your place isn't sold. You could have given him cash then.'

'I'll have a chat with Mark. Maybe he could organize something with the bank until we've sold our own place,' Francesca said.

'Being a bit optimistic, aren't you?' Millie remarked as they walked back to the car.

'Maybe. What else can I do? I don't have that kind of cash.'

'You could get a loan,' Millie suggested.

'I know enough about banking to know that I wouldn't get next or near that kind of money with the collateral I have to offer,' Francesca said drily. 'Mark's my only hope.'

'That's bloody ironic, isn't it?' Millie said in disgust as she sat in the car.

'I suppose I better get it over and done with. At least it will show him that I'm serious,' Francesca said glumly as she started the ignition. It was infuriating to know that this momentous decision about her future would be influenced by her husband and whether or not he was prepared to be helpful. The sooner she had cut all financial ties with him the better, she thought grimly as she drove along the seafront and watched the sun glittering on the grey-green sea. She liked the area, she wanted to live here, she'd seen the house she wanted to buy and it bloody well depended on Mark. Life was damn unfair, she was getting the short straw all the time, and she was heartily sick of it. If Mark got stroppy she was going to lose the house and there was nothing she could do about it. And if she lost it because of him she'd never speak to him again and she'd take him to the bloody cleaners in the divorce case, she vowed as she turned right for Blackrock.

'I wonder would he be in the apartment? It's somewhere off Mount Merrion Avenue.' She spoke her thoughts aloud.

'Would you go and knock on the door?' Millie was taken aback.

Francesca made a face. 'I wouldn't fancy running into that Nikki one. I'd like to sort something out with him as soon as possible though.'

'Why don't you ring him and ask him to meet you? You can drop me off at a Dart station,' Millie suggested.

'That's not very fair,' protested Francesca. 'I asked you to come looking at houses with me, I don't want to be doing the hot-potato act on you.'

'Don't be daft. I'm only five minutes from Sutton Dart station and this is important. Go and ring him,' Millie ordered.

'Yes, boss,' Francesca said drily.

'Sorry,' Millie held up her hands in mock surrender. 'Won't do it again.'

Francesca dialled Mark's mobile and felt suddenly nervous as she heard the ringing tone. It was galling to have to be civil when she'd walked out so snootily after their last encounter.

'It's me,' she said peremptorily when he answered the phone.

'I recognized your number,' Mark said coolly.

'I need to talk to you and I happen to be in Blackrock. I was wondering if you could meet me? I know it's short notice but something's come up.'

'Are the boys OK?' he said sharply.

'They're fine. It's nothing to do with them. It's about what we were discussing the other day,' Francesca said hastily.

'Oh!' Mark sounded wary.

'Look, can you meet me or not?' Francesca was losing patience.

'Excuse me. I need to have a word with Nikki.' He pressed the mute button and Francesca felt a surge of rage. How dare he press the mute button on her? How dare he make her feel so excluded? she thought irrationally.

'I hope that bastard gets his come-uppance some day,' she fumed. Millie's eyebrows rose. 'He's having a word with Nikki. I've been put on hold,' Francesca informed her in fury.

'Stay calm. Breathe deep. Think of that lovely mews,' Millie soothed.

Mark came back on the line. 'Where do you want to meet?'

'Er ... er ... mmm.' Francesca was caught off guard. 'I could meet you outside your apartment complex, save you taking out the car,' she suggested.

'Fine. Ring me when you're there. It's halfway

down on your right as you're coming from Blackrock,' her husband said curtly.

'OK.' Francesca hung up. 'Oh God, Millie, I'm dreading this,' she groaned.

'Well, I'll stay if you'd like me to, Francesca, but I don't think it would help your case very much,' Millie offered. 'And I can't guarantee that I wouldn't clock him one.'

Francesca laughed. 'Thanks, Millie, but my nerves are fragile enough as it is. Much as I'd enjoy watching you give Mark a sock in the chops, this isn't quite the appropriate time for aggro.'

'Unfortunately,' Millie said regretfully. 'Drop me off outside the shopping centre, you can turn left into Mount Merrion Avenue and I can cross through the park for the Dart. And ring me as soon as it's over.'

'I will,' promised Francesca.

Five minutes later she was stopped outside the impressive black gates that led into the apartment complex. She wondered which one was Nikki's as she dialled Mark's mobile.

'That was quick, I'm on my way,' he said crisply.

Francesca sat waiting for him, myriad emotions churning inside. Did she ever think that she'd be waiting on her husband to come to her from another woman's apartment? An apartment that he now called home. How had this nightmare happened? She felt overwhelmed with sadness as she saw him stroll along the footpath towards the car, dressed in a pair of chinos and a pale cream Lacoste short-sleeved shirt. He always wore his clothes well, she thought with a pang of loneliness.

'Hi,' she murmured, subdued, as he opened the door and got into the car.

'Hello,' he said cautiously. 'What's up?'

'I've seen a place that I want to buy. But I need the cash quickly,' she blurted.

'What!' he said, aghast. 'Francesca, what's the big rush with you? I don't think you've thought out the implications of all of this. You can't really want to sell the house.'

'I do,' she said emphatically, her heart sinking. What kind of a fool was she? Had she really thought that he was going to say *OK, Francesca, here's the cash*, or *I'll sort out a short-term loan for you*?

'Do you want to buy out my share?' she demanded truculently.

'Are you mad, Francesca? It's crazy to expect me to shell out a fortune for my own home when I paid off the mortgage years ago,' Mark said angrily. 'It's more than trebled in value since we bought it. It would be ludicrous to spend money like that.'

'Look, Mark, it's not your home any more. That was a choice you made when you had an affair with that woman. I had no choice in the matter, you did.'

'You kicked me out, I'd no choice in that,' he muttered.

'What did you think I was going to do, let you stay and conduct your sordid little affair under my nose?' Francesca snapped.

'You never gave me a chance to try and work it out,' Mark accused.

'Why would I want to work it out, you stupid bastard? You told me I was boring, remember, and that you'd felt trapped into marrying me,' Francesca shouted, losing her temper.

Mark threw his eyes up to heaven. 'Oh, let's not go through all that again.'

'Look, Mark. Are you going to help me out here or not? I really like this place, and I want to make a fresh start for myself,' Francesca demanded.

Mark played his trump card. 'Don't you mind selling off the boys' inheritance?'

'That's really low, Mark. The ultimate in emotional blackmail.' Francesca was disgusted.

'Well, it's true,' he blustered.

'I spoke to the boys and they were more than supportive of my decision to divorce you and sell the house. Jonathan even offered to come home and help me move. Get out of my car, Mark. My solicitor will be in touch. I'll buy a place when I get my share of the sale,' she said contemptuously.

'What else did you think they were going to say? I'm the big baddie here. Of course they're going to take your side,' he said bitterly.

'That's unfair, Mark,' Francesca protested heatedly. 'I never wanted anyone to take sides. This is between you and me and let me tell you, I did my level best to get Owen to sort things out between you before he went away.'

'And I suppose you expect me to believe that?' he sneered.

Francesca stared at her husband in dismay. 'You've turned into a horrible person, Mark.'

'You've turned into an embittered, manipulative, selfish bitch,' Mark swore as he opened the car door and got out.

'And you're a petty, controlling, arrogant shit,' she shot back as she turned on the ignition and leaned over and slammed the door shut.

With tears of anger and humiliation streaming down her face, she drove back the way she'd come, knowing that the mews wouldn't be hers and that she had a battle on her hands to get what was rightfully hers.

Chapter Thirty-eight

Nikki opened the balcony doors and placed her cup of coffee and a sheaf of papers on the white wrought-iron table. She'd watched Mark's progress as far as she could, but unfortunately the apartments at the front of the complex blocked her view of the gates so she couldn't see whether he and Francesca had driven off or were chatting in the car.

She was determined that she wasn't going to ask what Francesca wanted to see him for. Play it cool was her motto. Mark had been more than surprised when he'd come home from work in a foul humour the day Francesca had demanded a divorce to find Nikki preparing for a night on the tiles. She hadn't mentioned a word about the day's events and she knew it was bugging him. He wanted to get it off his chest but his pride wouldn't let him bring up the subject first. She was damned if she was going to appear at all interested.

The trouble was, she was gagging with curiosity.

Why was Francesca in Blackrock and what did she want to see Mark about? Maybe she'd changed her mind about getting the divorce. Nikki's heart sank. That would suit Mark down to the ground. He'd agree to that like a shot. It was all so bloody nerve-racking. She took a sip of coffee and picked up a draft of the report she was working on but the words meant nothing as she read the same line three times. Her concentration was zilch these days, she reflected, raising her face to the sun.

It was warm and peaceful on the balcony. A slight breeze rustled the leaves of the poplar trees and only the sound of birdsong disturbed the silence. Nikki yawned. She was tired. She could do with a break, she felt. It had been a tough couple of months emotionally. A few days in the south of France would be good. A friend of hers had an apartment there, but it was the high season and she had probably let it for the summer.

Where could she go? Somewhere nice and peaceful, on her own. It would have to be somewhere at home. Getting flights abroad at this late stage would be a nightmare and she didn't want hassle. Friends of hers had a small house practically on the beach a few miles south of Brittas Bay on the Wicklow–Wexford border. Not as exotic as the south of France but it would do for a mini-break midweek.

She had one important meeting on Monday afternoon, she could easily get off work early on Tuesday and stay until Friday. Her friends used the house every weekend in summer, she wouldn't like to put them out. She could come back home on Friday. It might give Mark something to think about and it would give her a break from his foul humour.

She dialled her friend Jacquie's mobile and made her request.

'Of course, come down. It's turned nice at the moment, although we had rain all last week until yesterday. But the good weather's supposed to last. I'll put clean sheets on the bed for you and leave the key under the flowerpot by the back door.' Jacquie was very hospitable. 'Is Mark coming with you?'

'No, I'm going to have a few days' peace and quiet on my own. He's having a spot of bother with his ex-wife and he's like a bull,' Nikki confided. 'We need a bit of space right now.'

'Good thinking,' Jacquie approved. 'Why don't you come down this evening? We're having a barbie.'

'I can't unfortunately, Jacquie. I've got a meeting that I can't miss next Monday so I'm stuck until then. But I'll take a half-day on Tuesday and go directly from work.'

'Well, enjoy it. Stay for the weekend if you like. We'll be down on Friday evening.'

'We'll see.' Nikki could see Mark marching around the corner with a face like a thundercloud. 'Jacquie, thanks a million. I have to go. I'll be in touch,' she said smoothly as she pretended to study the page in front of her intently. Out of the corner of her eye she could see Mark looking up but she didn't let on that she'd noticed. A couple of minutes later she heard his key in the front door and kept her head bent as she heard his deep sighs as he flung himself onto the sofa.

The meeting hadn't gone well, obviously, she deduced as the sighs got even deeper. 'There's coffee in the percolator,' she called through the open doors.

'Don't want it, thanks,' he growled. Nikki kept silent. Eventually it got too much for Mark. He came and stood at the doorway.

'Come and sit down,' she invited.

'What are you doing?' he asked.

'I'm working on my report. Will you read over it and give me your opinion when I'm finished?'

'OK,' he said unenthusiastically. Nikki felt irritation rise.

'What's up?' she asked, since it was clear that he wanted her to ask.

'Nothing,' he muttered grumpily.

'Doesn't look like that from where I'm sitting,' she said flatly.

'Oh, Francesca is such a selfish bitch,' he raged. 'She actually had the nerve to ask me for money to buy a place until our house is sold. I told her she was selling the boys' inheritance and that didn't make one iota of difference to her. She's being most unreasonable. It's the family home after all.'

'Mark, how can you say that?' Nikki retorted. 'She's not being unreasonable at all. *You're* the one who's being unreasonable. Grow up and get over it. Take responsibility for ending your marriage and stop acting like a sulky little boy who can't have his cake and eat it.'

'Well, thank you, Nikki. Whose side are you on?' Mark was furious at her disloyalty.

'It's not a question of sides,' she said reasonably. 'You've got to face facts, Mark. It's time to move on. She obviously wants to sort herself out and get a place of her own and she's entitled to a half-share of the house. You're just being a dog in the manger.'

Mark jumped to his feet. 'I don't need you to tell me how to conduct my affairs, Nikki. If it wasn't for you interfering where you weren't wanted and putting the notion of divorce in her bloody head none of this would have happened. I'll thank you to keep your nose out of my business, you've done enough harm as it is.' He marched into the lounge, grabbed his car keys and slammed the door after him.

'Go fuck yourself, Mark,' Nikki swore, humiliated by his stinging rebuke. If he wasn't damn careful he'd find his cases filled with all his belongings down in the foyer when he came back and then where would he go? He could hardly go running back to Francesca, he'd obviously burnt his bridges there.

Nikki went into the kitchen and poured herself more coffee. Her patience was running thin. Just as well she'd arranged to take the few days' break because, as far as she was concerned, Mark Kirwan was treading on very thin ice and had pushed his luck just as far as it would go with her.

'I did tell you not to get your hopes up,' Millie said gently.

'I know.' Francesca wiped her eyes. She'd just indulged in a therapeutic bawl. 'It's just that I'd hoped he'd agree not only because of the mews but because I wanted to know that his sense of decency was still intact. His sense of fair play. I wanted to respect him. To lose respect for someone you once loved is the most horrible thing of all. I *can't* believe he accused me of selling off the boys' inheritance. That *really* hurt.'

Millie's eyes hardened. 'That was the lowest of the low, Francesca. Take no notice and just let your solicitor deal with him from now on.'

'OK,' Francesca said wearily. She was tired. The day that had started so well had ended up a disaster. She felt she was almost back to square one. She took another sip of wine and nibbled at a Ritz cracker smeared with some of Millie's to-die-for home-made chicken liver pâté.

'Thanks for coming over,' she said gratefully.

'Don't be silly. I'll stay if you like,' Millie offered.

'No, not at all. Aidan will be sick of me monopolizing you,' Francesca protested.

'Look, he's having a wonderful evening plonked in front of the TV watching sport and drinking beer without having to listen to me giving out. I do loathe sports on TV.' Millie demolished a cracker in one bite.

'I'll be fine. I'm just a bit disappointed about the mews. I liked it. I could see myself living in it. It was a real Millennium-woman-style house, wasn't it?'

'Francesca, today was the first day you've gone viewing. Give yourself a chance. There's lots of other nice places to see. Stay calm, girl.'

'Whatever you say, Millie.' Francesca managed a smile before giving a huge yawn.

'I say that you should get your ass up to bed lickety split and have a good night's sleep and maybe you should postpone viewing places until the house is up for sale so you won't be disappointed,' her sister advised as she carried the supper dishes out to the kitchen.

It was good advice, Francesca reflected as she lay

in bed half an hour later. There was no point in setting herself up for disappointments. When she had cash in hand was the time to make offers for houses. And that looked like it wasn't going to be in the foreseeable future. The thought depressed her. Now that she had made her decision she was anxious to get on with things. She felt restless and unsettled in the house. She felt it was no longer hers.

So much for releasing, relaxing and letting go, she thought wryly as she tweaked her pillow into a more comfortable position. Today had been one of the angriest, most upsetting days of her life. She'd felt hatred for Mark. And huge resentment that he still had the power to interfere in her life to such an extent.

How was it possible to release such anger when she felt so resentful and helpless? What would Katherine Kronskey have advised if she'd witnessed today's unedifying episode? She cast her mind back over the author's interviews. She'd spoken a lot about trying to break from negative thinking and substituting positive thoughts instead. The trouble was, right now she couldn't think of anything positive concerning Mark.

She would put the whole episode out of her head, Francesca decided firmly. She would not replay it over and over as she had done with their rows in the past. She would allow herself to think of it for no more than ten minutes every day so that it would not have space in her head. Then her mind would be free to come up with new ideas or new inspirations. Maybe that was what Katherine had meant when she spoke of release and letting go.

She'd get the hang of that advice some day but there had to be a start and right this very minute was *her* start, Francesca decided. She wouldn't let Mark control her thoughts and feelings any longer. He might hold the purse strings now but that would change; until it did it was up to *her* to control her thoughts and emotions and she was damned if she was going to spend the night tossing and turning in turmoil because of him. Maybe today wasn't a total disaster then, she decided as she settled herself more comfortably and picked up Katherine's book on healing the body by healing the spirit.

Reading the first chapter, as Katherine described how her husband had walked out on her, Francesca could almost hear the tall, elegant woman's voice in her head. She read for an hour, completely absorbed, and then curled up in a ball and put out the light. She was asleep before she knew it.

'Oh Aidan, I felt so sorry for her,' Millie said to her husband as she lay snuggled up beside him in bed.

'He's just lashing out because he's panicking. You know, I bet you Mark never thought his life would turn out like this—'

'Don't you stick up for the bastard!' Millie exclaimed indignantly.

'I'm not sticking up for him, Millie, I'm just trying to explain where I think he's coming from,' Aidan said mildly.

'He's being a bollocks,' Millie snorted.

'I know that, but he's a scared bollocks neverthe-less,' her husband maintained.

'Would you treat me like that if we were in the same position?' Millie asked.

'Are you kidding me?' Aidan grinned. 'I value my life *and* my goolies.'

'Idiot,' giggled Millie as she snuggled closer.

'Any chance of a ride, woman?' Her husband's hands slid down to the curve of waist and hips and pulled her close.

'Every chance, man,' she murmured, smiling, before kissing him hotly and tracing her fingers down the lean flat plane of his belly until he groaned with pleasure at her touch.

Later, wrapped in each other's arms, Millie sent a prayer of thanks heavenward for the gift of her husband. She was so lucky, she thought gratefully, remembering her sister's tearstained face.

'We could remortgage or put up the house as collateral for Francesca,' Aidan suggested sleepily, his face buried in the curve of her shoulder.

'Oh Aidan, do you mean it?' Millie shot upright and looked down at her bleary-eyed husband.

'It's an option worth considering. Come back here, woman, I was lovely and cosy.' He pulled her back down to him.

'God, wouldn't that be great? I'd love to see the look on that bastard's face if Francesca got that mews in spite of him. You're a genius, Aidan. You know you'll get the money back as soon as the house is sold,' Millie said excitedly. 'Oh, I can't wait to tell her. And for being so magnificent and kind and the best husband in the world and wild in bed, you can have another ride first thing in the morning.'

'There's method in my madness, woman,' her

husband murmured sleepily as his arms tightened around her.

Millie held him close and tried not to feel guilty as happiness filled her being and she wondered how her life could be so good and her sister's so awful.

Well, perhaps if all went to plan Francesca might get her mews after all and Mark Kirwan could go to hell.

Chapter Thirty-nine

'Millie, I couldn't let you and Aidan do that. But thanks all the same. It's very, very kind of you.' Francesca was deeply touched at her sister and brother-in-law's more than generous offer.

'Look, let's see what the bank manager has to say at least. Aidan's popping up to see him at lunchtime. Wouldn't it be great to have your own place despite Mark? He'll have to sell up sooner rather than later. Your only problem at the moment is cash flow. That will be sorted once the sale goes through. Just let's see what happens,' said Millie. 'I'll talk to you later.'

'OK then, and, Millie, thanks *very* much.' Francesca hung up and felt a little flicker of excitement. Wouldn't it be wonderful if somehow she was able to get her hands on the money? Even if she was skint paying off the loan it wouldn't matter. Money would come to her eventually. She sighed. She had to be realistic. It could take four years for the divorce to come through. And if Mark continued to be obnoxious and opposed the sale of the house there could be long delays ahead. She'd planned to phone the estate agent to tell him that she was no longer interested in buying the mews but after Millie's phone call she decided to hold off. Just in case a miracle happened.

'I'll see you on Tuesday night,' Mark said, snapping shut the locks on his travel bag.

'No, you won't,' Nikki informed him. 'I'm going away for a few days. I'm going straight from work on Tuesday.'

'Oh!' Mark was taken aback. 'You never said anything to me about going away.'

'We weren't speaking,' Nikki drawled sarcastically.

'Where are you going?'

Nikki sat up in bed. 'It doesn't matter where I'm going. It's why I'm going you should be interested in.'

'And why are you going to this place you won't tell me about?' he said acidly.

'I'm going away to be on my own, to get a break from you and your moods. Basically I'm going away to think whether I want to stay in a relationship with you or not.'

'I see,' he said coldly as he shrugged into his jacket. 'Make sure to let me know when you've made your decision.'

'Don't worry, you'll be the first to know,' Nikki retorted. She lay down, pulled the duvet up under her chin, turned on her side and closed her eyes. She lay like that, seething, until she heard the hall door close.

'That's it,' she muttered. 'I've had enough. He's out on his ear.'

* * *

Mark sat angrily in the back of the taxi. He was totally pissed off. Nikki, who should be supporting him at this time of crisis, was being as bitchy as Francesca. Did she think that he was going to beg her to stay with him? For two pins he'd walk out on her and get a place of his own. But that would suit Francesca down to the ground. Women! They were the bane of his life. It was a relief to be going to Paris. Pity it wasn't for six months, he thought grimly.

Work was a welcome relief and he threw himself into a round of meetings, banishing his personal worries to the back of his mind. That night he joined French colleagues for a meal and crawled into his bed in the early hours after a night of clubbing and drinking.

I'm getting too old for this, he groaned the following morning as the phone shrilled with his wake-up call. His head was pounding; his eyes were having difficulty in focusing. He'd pulled a bird though, he reminded himself. They'd had a drunken snog but he hadn't invited her back to his hotel. He'd never behaved like that before. He'd want to cop himself on, he thought wearily as he staggered into the shower and tried to get his head back together.

He was mad to have gone on the piss last night. He had a meeting later in the morning with his French counterpart, Louis Vevasse, and he needed to be on his toes. Vevasse was a thirty-year-old whizz kid who had shot up the career ladder like a rocket. He was destined for big things. They might be on the same level career-wise right now, but that wouldn't be for much longer. Rumour had it that changes were on the agenda and Vevasse was earmarked for several jumps in promotion. He often worked seventy-hour weeks, coming in at weekends because it was expected, just like some of the young whipper-snappers at home. Vevasse was hungry, like Mark had been once. Being with him always made Mark feel old and on the slippery slope down, heading for sidelining and oblivion. Lately he was reluctantly admitting that he'd lost the drive and ambition that had fuelled his career. Nikki would understand exactly what he meant if he confided in her. They'd discussed burn-out generally on a few occasions. But he couldn't open up to her about it. Part of his attraction for her was his power and position. *Had been*, he corrected himself as he raised his face to the steaming spray and soaped his body. She hadn't given the appearance of a woman who was one bit attracted to him yesterday morning, he thought rue-fully, and he could hardly blame her.

She was right to be browned-off with him. He was venting all his anger about Francesca onto her. Which wasn't fair, he admitted. He was behaving like an ostrich with its head in the sand but it had hurt that Nikki had accused him of behaving like a sulky little boy and being a dog in the manger. He felt he'd been more than fair to Francesca but she obviously didn't see it like that. It hurt that she wanted to go it alone. Providing for her helped assuage his guilt for having the affair with Nikki. His house was visible, tangible evidence of his hard-won achievements. Selling it was like watching his carefully constructed kingdom erode and crumble away. He felt like he was standing on shifting sands and it was most unnerving. Couldn't Francesca or Nikki understand how *he* felt? If push came to shove he could release capital from his offshore accounts, but it was risky to say the least with all the furore surrounding unpaid DIRT tax at the moment. He'd prefer to keep a low profile in that area. But to have to hand over three times what he'd paid for his home fifteen years ago and watch Francesca swanning off with a fortune would be too much to bear.

He'd have a chat with his solicitor, he decided, maybe he might be able to come up with something. And he'd better arrange to have some flowers sent to Nikki before she left for her unknown destination. He'd have them sent to the bank; she'd be sure to get them there.

When he arrived at the EuroBank's French HQ, a confrontation of some sort was taking place in the foyer. He recognized Jean Boudet, one of the investment fund managers, arguing furiously with security men.

'What was all that about downstairs with Boudet?' he asked Louis Vevasse as he took the mug of coffee proffered by the younger man.

'Didn't you hear? Boudet's leaving. He's been headhunted by the Germans for VWB Investment. Security won't let him up to his office to collect his personal belongings.' Louis gave an eloquent Gallic shrug. 'Standard procedure, of course. They'll be posted out to him. He knows that. Why does he think it should be different for him? Boudet always likes to cause a scene. He's always the prima donna, no?'

'VWB, big money there,' Mark said enviously. 'Wish they'd head-hunt me.'

Louis laughed. 'Fund managers live short lives. You, my friend, would truly not want his job. And did you hear George Dupont had a nervous breakdown? He's been given early retirement whether he likes it or not. *Mon Dieu*, he's only forty. We must be *crazeee*, Mark, to work in this business. But I love it.'

You're riding high now. But talk to me in ten years' time, Mark thought as he opened his briefcase and took out the files he needed. His head had eased off a little. The coffee was helping. Vevasse was a gossipy, sly little operator. Mark didn't want him making any comments to interested ears that he'd been hungover or below par. He took a deep breath, focused his mind and said briskly, 'Let's get down to business, Louis, we have a lot to cover.'

'*Oui, oui*,' the Frenchman agreed. Minutes later the two bankers were in deep discussion and all of Mark's other worries were well and truly relegated. Work, as always, took top priority.

Nikki checked the sheaf of letters Elaine had given her to sign. No mistakes. Was that good or bad? she pondered. Given that she was trying to get rid of the little madam a mistake here or there would have suited her purpose, but Elaine was obviously on the ball today and they were all perfect. She signed them in her stylish script and was about to press the intercom to call her secretary when Elaine knocked on the door.

'Come in,' Nikki called. She couldn't contain her surprise when she saw her secretary standing at the door with a large bouquet of yellow roses and a smaller one of freesias.

Elaine smirked. 'These came for you.'

'Thank you, Elaine.' Nikki smiled sweetly. 'And these are for you.' She handed her the sheaf of signed letters. 'And this' – she picked up another document – 'is a list of work I want you to do while I'm away. Thank you.' She nodded her dismissal.

'I'll get a vase, shall I?' the younger woman said sulkily.

'No, I'll take them with me.' Nikki lowered her head and began to write, much to Elaine's disappointment. She was dying to know whom the flowers were from. The card accompanying them had been sealed, otherwise she would have had a quick peek. Mark would hardly have sent them to her at the bank. He wasn't at all flashy. He rarely came to her office even. And when they were together they were always extremely businesslike and not at all lovey-dovey, much to Elaine's chagrin. A romantic at heart, she was always eagle-eyed, hoping to catch some little interaction. What he saw in that hard bitch was a mystery to Elaine. Francesca was much nicer. Maybe Nikki had a new admirer and the great romance was heading for the skids. Hmmm, interesting, thought Elaine as she folded the letters neatly and slid them into the typed envelopes. She paused at her task and went off into a little daydream. If the love story was ended maybe she could offer succour to the rather yummy Mark who, despite his somewhat reserved ways, was a popular boss and well liked. The quiet ones were always the most interesting and Mark, even though he was older than a lot of the hot shots in the office, could give them all a run for their money in the 'intriguing' stakes. Nikki Langan didn't deserve him!

Nikki ripped open the sealed envelope that accompanied the flowers, and read the enclosed message with a mixture of emotions.

Sorry, darling. I love you. I sent the flowers to work to make sure you got them before you went away, hope you don't mind. Have a nice break, ring me if you feel like it.

Love, Mark.

Not only had he sent yellow roses, he'd also sent her beautiful sweet-scented freesias, her favourite flower. *That* was thoughtful, she conceded. But it didn't solve any of their problems. And it gave her another more immediate one. She'd taken his cases out of the storage press and left them on the bed with a curt note asking him to be out of the apartment by the time she got back on Friday. After this gesture of reconciliation, did she still want him to move out or would she give it one more try and wait until Christmas, which was her original plan? Nikki drummed her fingers on her desk. If he'd just sent the roses, she might not have bothered. Anyone could send roses. But the freesias were a thoughtful and loving gesture and maybe if left on his own for the few days he might suddenly realize that he was putting their relationship in jeopardy by his behaviour. Her heart softened. He'd obviously been thinking about her and how he'd treated her and guilt had set in. That was a positive step.

She'd go home en route to Wicklow and put the cases back in the storage press and tear up the note.

She might let him cool his heels for a day or two before she phoned. She'd see. Nikki slipped the note back into the envelope and put it in her bag. She was always extremely careful about what she left lying around the office. She certainly wouldn't put it past Elaine to go snooping in the bin. Well, little madam wouldn't find much there, she thought in satisfaction as she buried her nose among the freesias. Mark had written that he loved her but it would take more than a bouquet or two of flowers to convince her that he was serious.

'Simon, I need to talk to you sooner rather than later. Francesca wants a divorce. I don't. She wants to sell the house and split the proceeds, I don't—'

'Is it in joint names?' Simon Carter's calm voice crackled across the airwaves. It was a very bad line to Dublin. Mark was in his hotel room preparing to leave.

'Yes, it is.'

'Hmmm. Who's acting for her?'

'Someone called O'Farrell, Monica I think is the name.'

'Jessica O'Farrell, she's excellent. She specializes in family law. Hmmm. Look, we'll talk when you get back from Paris. How about tomorrow morning, nine a.m? I'll reschedule that appointment.'

'Appreciate it, Simon,' Mark said. 'See you then.' He put the phone down and went and stood at the window. It was a hot muggy day and a low rumble of thunder echoed in the distance.

There had been no reassuring words from Simon. Even though he had to be realistic he'd been hoping against hope that Simon would say something comforting like: *Don't worry, we'll sort it out*. His 'hmmms' hadn't sounded at all reassuring.

He glanced at his watch. Two-fifteen. Nikki should surely have got her flowers by now. He'd had his phone turned off for his meeting with Vevasse but there were no messages, not even a text message to say thanks. She must still be pretty mad with him. He sighed. He didn't feel like going to work straight from the airport, he felt like going to bed and sleeping his brains out. Maybe he'd do just that. To hell with the whizz kids hot on his heels. He was tired, still hungover, and his life was about to be turned upside down. What was the point in killing himself before he'd endured all the hassle? he thought wryly. What he'd really like to do was sit out in his back garden in Howth with a chilled beer from the fridge and the *Irish Times* crossword but it looked like he might never do that again. A wave of grief and sadness enveloped him and Mark sat on the side of the bed and buried his face in his hands as hot tears spurted between his fingers and sobs racked his body.

Chapter Forty

'Francesca, I'm terribly sorry. My bank manager wouldn't sanction the loan because the mortgage we have is still too big, and he wouldn't let me remortgage because he didn't have cast-iron guarantees that you'd be able to come up with the money. I did my best,' Aidan assured her as they sat in her kitchen having a quick cup of coffee before going to work.

'Don't worry about it, Aidan. Thinking about it afterwards, I realized I wouldn't have been happy about it anyway. Not until I see what way the divorce goes. I basically shouldn't have gone looking at houses until I had cash.' Francesca gave her brother-in-law a hug and received a warm one back in return.

'Would you like me to speak to Mark?' he offered.

'Aidan, I wouldn't let you waste your breath, but thanks a million for offering. It's nice to get the support and I can never thank you and Millie enough for the way you've stood by me,' Francesca said gratefully. 'I'm going back to my solicitor next week and we'll take it from there. If Mark wants to get nasty, it's up to him, but he'll find I'm no pushover.'

'Well, any time you need us, you know we're there, and I hope it won't turn nasty and that Mark sees sense. I think he's probably being stubborn because you've asked for a divorce. I would imagine he wasn't expecting that,' her brother-in-law said easily. 'He might see it differently when he's had time to think.'

'It will be too late for me then, unfortunately, that mews will be snapped up,' Francesca said regretfully.

'There'll be other places. The property market is so buoyant at the moment and perhaps Mark will be singing a different tune in time.' Aidan placed his coffee mug on the kitchen table and stood up to go.

'I won't be holding my breath,' Francesca said, following him into the hall. 'Thanks for coming over. I hope it won't make you late for work.'

'Naw, I'm fine. The traffic's not too bad now with the kids off school for the summer.'

'Tell Millie thanks and I'll be in touch. I'm off to Cork with Ken tomorrow, we're doing publicity for an arts festival.'

'Have fun,' Aidan said.

'I enjoy it very much. I'm delighted I got that job.' Francesca's eyes sparkled. 'It's a whole change of lifestyle for me.'

'Good. Liking your work is the important thing. It's a pain in the butt otherwise.' Aidan raised a hand in salute and as she closed the door behind him, Francesca reflected that her sister had married a very stalwart man. A quality she had once thought Mark possessed.

Maybe he still did possess it but it wasn't there for

her any more. Nikki was the recipient of all her husband's redeeming attributes now, she thought sadly, and felt an urge to cry.

'Oh, for God's sake,' she muttered in exasperation as her heart stung and tears ran down her cheeks yet again. When did the pain and grief of it go? When did the jealousy and bitterness lessen? Why had God picked on her? She sat at the bottom of the stairs and cried her eyes out.

'It's like this, Mark, and I speak as a friend as well as your solicitor, my advice to you would be to have your divorce and settlement as amicable as you can both make it. In the long run you'll spend far less money and the wounds won't take as long to heal. You can dig your heels in and I can fight tooth and nail over every penny, but I warn you, Mark, when things get dirty you could end up losing a lot more than you would if things were amicable. Hell hath no fury and all of that. I've seen some bitterly fought divorce cases and the husband has ended up ruined. Finances can be gone over with a fine-tooth comb. In some cases this has resulted in ... er ... embarrassing discoveries, shall we say,' Simon said smoothly.

'It's all right, Simon, I know what you're getting at,' Mark said wearily. 'In other words, you think I should agree to the divorce and sell up.'

'Unfortunately, under the circumstances, it's the option that is most suited to your situation. You can fight, as I say, but at the end of the day, Francesca will be seen as the injured party because of your infidelity and perceived intransigence. The house is in joint names and you did say that she said she would settle for half the proceeds and not come after savings and investments. She could look for a lot more if you make things difficult for her.' Simon sat back in his chair and lit his pipe. 'I'm sorry, old man, but there it is. Better to lay the cards on the table straight away and not lead you up the garden path with false hope.'

'Thanks, Simon, I appreciate your honesty. I suppose I knew all this myself. I just had to hear it said,' Mark said heavily.

'You'll still make a tidy profit on the sale,' Simon said heartily. 'It's not the financial disaster it could be.'

'It's my safety net gone,' Mark murmured, almost to himself.

'Oh, come now, old chap, you haven't let the grass grow under your feet. You're a wealthy man and you're working in the best possible place to take advantage of sound investment advice and opportunities. This is just a temporary little setback, you'll bounce back,' Simon encouraged.

'I don't have any other choice, I suppose.' Mark sighed. 'You'll look after the sale for me?'

'Of course,' Simon said suavely, 'and I'll get on to Francesca's solicitor and see what we can come up with that will be most beneficial to you. Oh! Just a thought, perhaps you could speak to Francesca about the estate agent and select one that is mutually acceptable. Better all round not to have her feeling excluded from the decision. It makes things easier in the long run.'

'Fair enough, Simon. Good point.' Mark stood up and held out his hand. 'Thanks for the advice. I'll keep in touch.'

'Don't worry, Mark. We'll keep your losses to a minimum, but as I say, consensus is the best strategy all round.'

You mean surrender, Mark thought to himself as he walked out of his solicitor's office. He switched on his mobile phone and checked his messages. Two from the office, one from Paris, none from Nikki. She hadn't even bothered to acknowledge his flowers. He'd checked with Interflora and they'd been delivered. Heavy-hearted, he strode along Wicklow Street. The sun was shining and tourists abounded. The sound of foreign accents lent an exotic air of liveliness to the coffee shops and cafés. On impulse Mark headed for Café Rio and ordered a cappuccino. He'd just done the first clue of his crossword when the phone rang. Thank God, he thought in relief as he saw Nikki's number come up.

'Hi,' he said gingerly, unsure of his reception.

'Hi, Mark. Thanks for the flowers.'

'I was worried that they hadn't arrived.' He couldn't resist a little dig at her tardiness in responding.

'They arrived yesterday. They're beautiful.'

'Where are you?' Mark asked.

'I'm walking on a deserted, secluded little beach right this minute. I'm staying in Jacquie's place for a few days.' Nikki sounded remarkably cheerful.

'It sounds lovely,' he said wistfully, half hoping she might invite him to join her.

'It is. It's just what I needed. Where are you?'

'I'm sitting in Café Rio on Wicklow Street having a cappuccino.'

'At this hour of the morning!' Nikki exclaimed. Mark smiled, now her interest was up.

'I was at my solicitor's,' he said.

'Oh! Is everything all right?'

'I'm putting the house on the market. I hate doing it.'

'And you wouldn't consider buying Francesca out?' Nikki queried.

'No! It's not an option.'

'Well, you know what's best for you, darling. The line is very crackly so I'll let you go. Talk to you tomorrow.' Nikki's voice came faintly down the line and then he heard the click and she was gone. Mark frowned. She hadn't shown much reaction at the news that he was selling up. Maybe he'd misjudged their situation but he'd expected more of a response from her, particularly as she had jumped so vehemently to Francesca's defence when he'd told her that she wanted to divorce him and sell the house. Today she'd seemed almost offhand about the whole thing. Mark felt a little chill of unease. Maybe Nikki, after reviewing her options, was deciding that life with him wasn't one that she cared to pursue. He didn't want to be alone right now. But on the other hand he certainly didn't want to venture into marriage again. Once was enough to lose his shirt. If Nikki couldn't deal with that, there was no hope for them.

Nikki stood at the water's edge and let the frothy sea wash over her bare feet. She inhaled, drawing the tangy sea air deep into her lungs. She didn't know what to think. What on earth had changed Mark's mind about selling the house? He'd been utterly against the idea. The solicitor must have talked sense into him, Nikki surmised. Maybe once it was sold and the financial ties were cut with Francesca things would change between him and herself. He obviously didn't want to end their relationship. Their rows had given him any number of opportunities to walk out but so far he hadn't.

Nikki walked along the beach towards the house. He'd wanted her to invite him down to be with her. She knew he'd been angling. It would have been nice to spend a quiet day with him because right now she was agitated and tense. She was finding it extremely difficult to wind down even in the peace and quiet of her rural backwater retreat. She'd forgotten how isolated the house was, stuck at the end of a winding country lane. The nearest shop was two miles away. She sat on the rocking chair on the veranda and picked up her book, a thriller that required more concentration than she was prepared to give it. So she just rocked, staring out at the sparkling flat-calm sea. After a while the book dropped from her hand and her head drooped. She curled up on the soft cushions as the rhythmic sounds of the sea began to work their magic. Her breathing deepened; her body relaxed. Nikki slept.

'Haven't seen you around before! Ralph Casson, arts journo with the *Daily Press* and *Contemporary Arts*.' A tall, black-haired man, with impossibly long black lashes and heavy-lidded brown eyes held out a hand and gripped Francesca's firmly.

'Hello. I'm Francesca Kirwan. I work with Ken Kennedy PR. Nice to meet you, I think we spoke on the phone once.'

'Lucky old Ken Kennedy.' Ralph eyed her up and down so blatantly that Francesca blushed. 'A woman who blushes, what a find,' he teased. 'What's a very attractive woman like you working for a scoundrel like Kennedy for?'

'That's a long story,' Francesca said crisply, raging with herself for blushing. She hadn't done that since she was a teenager.

'It's one I'd like to hear. How about we go for a drink and you can tell me your long story?'

Francesca smiled sweetly. 'Thanks but I'm working.'

'So am I, but that never stopped me having a drink.' Ralph laughed. 'How about if I do a feature on "Women in PR"? I can interview you and discover all your trade secrets, while hearing the long story.'

'I thought you covered the Arts,' Francesca said caustically.

'Oh, I do,' he assured her. 'But I write under a variety of names. You might have read articles under the byline Brenda Carroll?'

He raised an eyebrow in enquiry.

'Hmm. She's always writing about what women want in a man and how career women are losing their libido – that sort of thing. *Cosmo* stuff that hasn't changed in the past twenty years.' Francesca was unimpressed. 'Are you saying that you're Brenda Carroll?'

'Guilty as charged,' Ralph bowed. 'I've even got the frocks to prove it.'

'Brenda's a bit old hat, she needs a bit of updating if you ask me.'

Ralph grimaced. 'You don't pull your punches, do you?'

'You wouldn't like me to tell you fibs just to flatter your ego, now would you?' Francesca said lightly as she handed him a press release. 'You being a journalist and seeker of the truth and all that?'

'Maybe you could give me pointers on updating Brenda's image,' he said slyly, his eyes twinkling.

He's got dead sexy eyes, Francesca noted with a little shock. She hadn't noticed that in a man in years.

'Well?' Ralph encouraged.

'Well what?' Francesca asked.

'Are you coming for a drink with me?'

'Thanks for asking, Ralph, but really I *do* have to work and so do you. And if your schedule is the same as mine you're due to interview Kris Synott in five minutes.'

'That boring old fart,' Ralph snorted. 'Who wants to listen to him pontificating? He adores the sound of his own voice. I'd far prefer to go for a drink with you. You're a gorgeous, sexy woman, you know.'

Francesca's jaw dropped.

He studied her in amusement. 'You must have been told that a thousand times. Why do you look so surprised? Doesn't your lucky sod of a husband tell you?' He indicated her wedding ring. 'If you were my wife I'd tell you every day.'

'I'm separated,' she said faintly.

'Oh! Me too. How long?'

'Since before last Christmas.'

'A mere novice,' Ralph scoffed. 'I'm single and available these past two years. Maybe we were fated to meet. I believe in fate. Do you? I think you could be my soulmate, the one I've been searching for. I feel I know you already. We could have had a past life or two, who knows. I think you're the woman I've been seeking endlessly for. And now I've found you.' He was teasing her, smiling into her eyes, his lean face creased in a most attractive smile.

Francesca gathered her wits about her. 'You'll be seeking another job if you don't interview Kris Synott. It was nice meeting you but I really have to go, I've to liaise with Ken. Please don't keep Kris waiting, he gives us a very hard time as it is. I'll look forward to reading the interview. See you.' She turned and walked across the foyer of the hotel, conscious of his stare.

'I don't give up easily,' Ralph called and she smiled.

'I don't give in easily,' she murmured as she hastened to her rendezvous with Ken.

Chapter Forty-one

Francesca opened her eyes, yawned, blinked and remembered where she was. 'Sorry, Ken,' she apologized. 'I fell asleep, hope I didn't snore.'

Ken glanced over at her. 'Snore! I thought I was driving through a thunderstorm.'

'Oh, stop! Was I bad?' She was mortified.

'I'm joking, Francesca. You were like the Sleeping Beauty, not a peep out of you.'

'Where are we?' She stretched as much as the constraints of the seatbelt would allow.

'Just coming off the Naas roundabout onto the M50. I'm going to cut across through Tallaght.'

'My God! You must have driven like Mika Hakkinen. We're in Dublin already!' Francesca rubbed her eyes and stared out at the rolling fields and the Dublin Mountains ahead of them as they headed south on the motorway.

'Francesca, you were asleep before we left Mallow and that was at half six. It's now ten a.m.'

'You must be knackered.'

'I am a bit,' he admitted. 'I wouldn't have minded a lie-in. I didn't get to bed until after two.'

'Look, when we get to the office, why don't you nip home for a couple of hours' kip? I'll sort out the invites to the Carey Awards and get them mailed out and when you come back in the afternoon we can confirm the schedule for that author tour and have it faxed to London by five,' Francesca suggested.

'There's an awful lot of invites to be sent out. Over three hundred. The Carey Awards is a big event. They need to be in the post today.' Ken yawned.

'They will be, trust me,' Francesca assured him.

Ken changed down to take the exit off the motorway. 'You're really good at this, you know. When Monica first suggested you, I thought it wasn't going to work out but I was desperate—'

'So was I,' interjected Francesca.

Ken laughed. 'No, I mean I didn't have great expectations, to be honest. I certainly didn't think you'd be taking over and organizing events on your own and making big impressions on journalists,' he added wickedly.

'What do you mean by that?' she demanded.

'Oh, a certain Ralph Casson cornered me in the bar and wanted to know all about you. He thought you were intriguing!' Ken informed her.

'And what did you tell him?' Francesca asked curiously.

'I told him that you were brilliant at your job, that you'd saved my bacon, that we got on like a house on fire and that you weren't interested in men right now. I told him your career was your priority.'

Francesca eyed him in disbelief. 'You didn't say that.'

'I did. He's a bit of a charmer, Francesca, believe me. But you probably sussed that already.' Ken overtook a Volvo and put the boot down.

'He had the gift of the gab, all right. Where does he live?'

'He has an apartment on the canal somewhere, I think. His wife and two daughters live in Ranelagh.'

'Oh!' Francesca digested this piece of information.

'Traffic's not bad, sure it's not?' Ken remarked as they cruised through several sets of green lights. 'We missed the worst of the rush hour and we're going contra flow which helps.'

'Hmm,' murmured Francesca. She wasn't at all interested in discussing traffic. She wanted to get back to the subject of Ralph.

'Is he a good journalist?' she asked a while later.

'Who? Oh, Ralph.' Ken was obviously miles away. 'He knows his stuff, but he's a nightmare to pin down and often turns up half an hour late and more for interviews. It's a pity because he's a good writer.'

'I must keep an eye out for his articles. He told me that one of his pseudonyms is Brenda Carroll.'

'I know. It's a hoot. Lots of journalists write features under different names. I was often tempted to try and write myself.'

'Now that *would* be something I'd like to see,' jeered Francesca.

'You may mock. One day I'll surprise you,' Ken retorted as he pulled up outside the office.

'Go home and have a couple of hours' sleep. I'll phone you at half one,' Francesca ordered.

'Are you sure, Frannie?'

'Perfectly, Kenneth.'

'Right so. I don't need to be told twice. You're a little pet,' Ken said.

'Little!' drawled Francesca as she got out of the car. 'You certainly have the imagination for a writer. I'll see you.' She waved him off and let herself into the office. While she was waiting for the kettle to boil she played the answering machine and took down names and numbers to call people back. She checked the e-mails. Ken had given her a guided tour of e-mail and she was quite confident about it now. She then turned her attention to the post. She was throwing junk mail in the waste-paper basket when her mobile rang. She didn't recognize the number that flashed up.

'Hello?'

'Hello, this is Stephen Boyle—'

'Oh, the estate agent,' she cut in, her heart sinking. 'I've been meaning to call. I was in Cork on business,' she apologized.

'Ah, Mrs Kirwan. I need to know if you're still interested in the mews? I have a firm offer. But I did say I'd let you know what was happening.'

'That's very kind of you, Mr Boyle. I was going to call you this afternoon. I'm afraid there's been some complications with my own house and I have to withdraw. I'm very sorry,' she said regretfully.

'Don't worry,' the estate agent said kindly. 'These things happen. I have your number and if anything comes up that I think might be of interest to you, I'll give you a shout.'

'Would you? That would be great. I possibly won't

418

be in a position to buy for a while,' Francesca explained.

'Whenever. We'll keep in touch,' the estate agent promised.

'Great. Thanks a lot.' Francesca sighed as she hung up the phone. One lost opportunity, thanks to Mark. She wouldn't give him the chance to put her in that position again.

She'd just made herself a cup of strong coffee when the phone rang. 'Good morning, Ken Kennedy PR,' she answered crisply.

'Is that the wildly sexy gorgeous Francesca by any chance?' a husky male voice said in her ear.

Francesca couldn't help smiling. 'Who wants to know?'

'You deserted me. I'm here in Cork trying to make Kris Synott seem interesting because you told me you were going to read the interview and now I've got writer's block. Beautiful Francesca, how could you do this to me?' Ralph Casson asked plaintively.

'You must still be pissed after last night,' Francesca said, stirring her coffee.

'Francesca! You wound me. If I was pissed would I have remembered where you worked? Would I have been together enough to track down your number—'

'Directory Enquiries would get it for you very quickly,' Francesca pointed out swiftly.

'Sexy, voluptuous, intelligent, but very *very* suspicious. Dear oh dear. But I'll persevere.' She could tell he was smiling too.

'What can I do for you, Ralph?' she asked in a businesslike tone.

'Oh Francesca.' Ralph gave a deep sigh. 'Don't ask leading questions like that. I'd like to see you. Talk to you. Do soulmatey things with you.'

Francesca couldn't help herself, she burst out laughing. 'Ralph, I'm up to my eyes, I really have to go.'

'Don't give me the bum's rush. I'll be back up in Dublin tonight, tell me that you'll at least come for a drink with me.'

'Ralph. Thanks for the invite, another time maybe. I've a million and one things to do. Now I absolutely must go. Thanks for phoning,' Francesca said briskly. 'Good luck with the writing,' she added before hanging up. She smiled, amused. Wait until she told Millie that she had an admirer. Didn't someone say that life began at forty! Just as well for her that she didn't take him too seriously. Ralph Casson was a complication she could do without.

Ralph hung up the phone with a deep sigh. His head throbbed. He wouldn't mind a couple of shots of whiskey. He leaned back against the pillows and closed his eyes and tried to remember her. The lovely wide grey eyes. The cheekbones he'd like to run his finger along. The lips that were made for kissing. The full firm ripe breasts. The waist that curved in so voluptuously, inviting hands to encircle it. And those womanly rounded hips that would fit so perfectly against him. Francesca was the kind of woman he liked. Ripe as a peach, soft in the right places and sweet, sweet, sweet. Far more sensual than some of the young scarecrows teetering around in their skimpy little dresses.

He wasn't used to women resisting his charm at the beginning. And she wasn't playing hard to get, either. He'd been around women long enough to know the difference. That guy Ken that she worked for had said she wasn't interested in men. Nonsense. A woman like Francesca was made to be with a man. The right man. He wondered if she'd been with anyone since her split. He hoped not. He'd like to be the one to pop her cork again. He *would* be the one to pop her cork again, Ralph decided. He flicked through his dog-eared diary and found the entry for Ken Kennedy PR. Monkstown, he noted. Fine. He'd pop into the Cork office, file his piece, drive home, have a shower and be waiting for this magnificent new woman who'd entered his world, and this time he wouldn't take no for an answer.

Chapter Forty-two

Mark finished reading the report on his desk, made a few notes, signed some letters that his secretary had left for his attention, then stood and stretched. It was just gone six. The trouble was, he wasn't in the humour for going home to an empty apartment.

He could call in and see his father, he supposed, he'd been neglecting him of late, but an hour in Gerald's company was the last thing he needed. He could drive over to Clontarf and play a few holes on the golf course. It would be nice to get some fresh air. Maybe while he was in the area he could call in on Francesca and tell her that he'd decided to agree to put the house up for sale. There was no point in procrastinating and making it harder on himself. If the deed had to be done, do it, he thought despondently. Agreeing to sell might put some manners on his estranged wife and make her feel bad for her rudeness. She might start treating him with a bit of respect for a change.

Nikki had phoned him earlier. She'd informed him that she'd slept like a log and hadn't woken up until after eleven. He was glad that she was relaxing. She'd been extremely irritable lately and he, better than anyone, knew the pressure she was under at work. Their personal circumstances hadn't helped. She'd been wise to nip her stress in the bud by taking time out. She'd made no reference at all to Francesca or the divorce or their own situation. That was a relief at least, if a tad unsettling. Maybe she was going to blow him out. He'd call her later and be nice to her and tell her how much he was missing her. She always liked it when he said things like that to her. Underneath that tough façade of hers she could be vulnerable sometimes. It had taken him a long time to see it. She was no different to any other woman in that respect . . . unfortunately.

He went into the small bathroom adjoining his office – one of his perks – undressed and stepped into the shower cubicle. He had a set of golfing clothes in his closet; the weather had picked up, it was a glorious summer's evening. He was going to enjoy it. It was time he relaxed and did what he wanted for a change. He soaped himself vigorously and felt the muscles around his neck and shoulders loosen a little under the hot spray. That was more like it, he thought with satisfaction, and felt his mood lighten. Maybe things weren't as bad as they seemed.

Nikki sat in the rocking chair munching on crackers and cheese between mouthfuls of coffee. There was still heat in the evening sun and she rocked gently backwards and forwards enjoying the balmy warmth. She'd had a delightful day, much to her own surprise. The sea air was better than any tranquillizer. She'd conked out in bed and shocked herself by sleeping until eleven, then she'd had a long leisurely brunch before walking across the dunes to the beach where she spent a totally relaxing afternoon flicking through magazines and listening to the hypnotic lullaby of the sea. She'd even fallen asleep again.

She was a far more relaxed woman than the jangle of nerves, stress and tension that had arrived the day before yesterday. Distance was what she'd needed, she decided. Mark had been quite solicitous when she'd phoned him earlier and she was missing him. Jacquie's big double brass bed was extremely comfortable and the view along the coast was stunning. A perfect place to make wild, passionate love and then snuggle up and listen to the song of the sea and watch the stars sparkle in an ebony sky. The thought of lying in Mark's arms, cherished and relaxed, was so appealing she was tempted to phone him there and then and invite him down.

She glanced at her watch. He'd probably be stuck in traffic now. She'd give him a couple of hours to go home, shower and eat and then phone to see what he had to say. It would only take him an hour or so to drive down. Her heart lifted. All the turbulence of the past weeks seemed to have faded and she felt she'd regained a good measure of equilibrium. In spite of her angry words and her ultimatums she missed Mark and she wanted to be with him. Maybe tonight she'd sleep in his arms and all her fears and uncertainties would miraculously be laid to rest.

Nikki gazed out at the sapphire sea. Little white-crested waves fringed the shore. The peace was such a contrast to her frenetic lifestyle. She knew that her friends thought she had it all. A high-powered career that was on the ascent, a plush apartment in a very up-market complex. A cool car, and a relationship with a very successful and attractive man. Eighteen months ago she'd have agreed with them. She'd have been utterly horrified to think that she would end up feeling so powerless and needy in her relationship with Mark. She'd been totally in control then. She'd held the power. Now the position was completely reversed. She'd become the kind of woman she'd previously despised. Nikki gave a wry smile. She'd never had any patience with girlfriends moaning and whingeing about unhappy love affairs. She'd never understood how they could hand over their power to a mere man. Men had their uses, sure, but put them back in their box, she'd counselled unfeelingly. Now they could have the last laugh. She was as bad as any of them, she'd just taken a lot longer to get there, she admitted. The knowledge disappointed her immeasurably. For the first time in her entire life she felt a complete and absolute failure.

Francesca rubbed the back of her neck. She was whacked. All she wanted to do was to go home and flop into bed. Five a.m. starts were for young ones with plenty of stamina. Still, the invites for the awards were in the post. London had been faxed with a confirmed author tour schedule, the filing was up to date, press cuttings sent out and the coffee mugs washed and put away. A very satisfying day's work, she thought as she switched on the answering machine.

Ken was working on the computer, clicking and scrolling, fingers flying on the keyboard. She watched him, fascinated. She hadn't got around to her computer course yet. But she wanted to do it. She wanted to be able to sit at that computer with confidence and not feel apprehension in case she wiped the whole damn thing clean.

'I'll see you tomorrow. Don't stay too long at that,' she warned.

'As if I'd get the chance. Carla's picking me up to lavish some TLC on me ... I hope. Thanks for letting me have a kip earlier. It was badly needed,' he said gratefully.

'You're welcome.' Francesca smiled as she touched up her lipstick and sprayed some perfume on her wrists. Just because she felt a wreck was no reason to look like one. She ran a brush through her hair for good measure. She was dying to have a shower and get out of her suit and high heels. The thought of getting the Dart made her heart sink and she was half tempted to take a taxi from Monkstown, but that would mean she'd be stuck in rush-hour traffic for at least an hour and a half. She'd be home in forty-five minutes if she took the train to Clontarf and took a taxi for the fifteen-minute journey home from the station.

She closed the door of the office behind her and inhaled the tangy sea breeze. It was a beautiful evening. She'd have her tea on the deck and then a nice snooze, she promised herself, looking forward to that delightful moment of pure relaxation, lying on her lounger, her body sinking into delicious lethargy and then sleep, with the sun warming her tanned limbs. It was her favourite part of the day and she'd missed it when the weather had been unseasonably wet and cold.

She was miles away, thinking she really ought to call in on her parents to see how they were, when a vaguely familiar voice said above the region of her left ear: 'Fancy meeting you here. It must be fate.' Francesca came to with a start as she recognized Ralph Casson.

'Good Lord! What are you doing here? I thought you were in Cork,' she exclaimed, relieved beyond measure that she'd retouched her lipstick and made herself look presentable.

'I was. But now I'm home and very much hoping that if you've nothing better planned, you might come and have dinner with me.' Ralph studied her with his deep-set brown eyes.

Francesca laughed. 'Ralph, I was up at the crack of dawn. I've put in a very busy day. The only thing I've got planned is bed.'

'Sounds good to me,' he murmured silkily.

'Alone,' she added drily.

'A drink, then,' he pressed.

'Ralph, honestly, I'm beat,' she said tiredly, marvelling at his persistence. Typical man, she thought in amusement. It obviously hadn't dawned on him that she'd be tired after her early start and full day's work, or that she might like to shower and change before having dinner.

'How are you getting home?' he asked, falling into step beside her. 'Here, let me carry that.' He held out his hand for her overnight bag. *Nice manners*, she thought, impressed.

'I'm taking the Dart to Clontarf. I usually park my car there but today I'm taking a taxi because Ken picked me up yesterday.'

'It's far too nice an evening to be squashed like a sardine on the Dart. I'll drive you home. Will I need my passport to cross the Liffey?' he teased.

'Ralph, there's no need. Really. I'll be home in forty-five minutes taking the train.'

'I came up specially to be outside the office when you left work,' he said quietly.

'Ralph, I'm in the middle of a marriage break-up, I'm not ready to get involved with someone new,' she said slowly.

'Dinner's not getting involved. It's just having a meal and a chat. And if that's all you want, that's fine,' he said.

'Well, look, maybe another night. I truly am tired,' she said.

'All the more reason that I give you a lift home. Please, Francesca.'

'OK then, if you really don't mind driving across town.'

'Don't mind it at all,' Ralph said cheerfully as he strode along carrying her bag.

His car, a ten-year-old black Saab, was parked down the street. He held the passenger door open for her. Mark had always held the car door open for her when they'd first married but had grown out of the habit. It was nice to be treated respectfully, Francesca thought as she slid into the passenger seat.

'Directions, madame?' Ralph smiled as he sat in beside her.

'Blackrock, Merrion Gates, Strand Road, East Link, right to Clontarf from Alfie Byrne Road and on straight.' Francesca smiled back at him.

'You have a beautiful smile, Francesca,' Ralph said as he indicated and moved out into the traffic.

'You've kissed the Blarney Stone,' she murmured. She wasn't used to such direct compliments. They unnerved her.

'I'm a journalist. I'm only telling the truth,' he declared. 'So what possessed your idiot husband to shack up with someone else?'

'How very inquisitive of you,' Francesca chided.

'I keep telling you, I'm a journalist. I have an enquiring nature. I like to get to the bottom of mysteries. And for a man to leave such a beautiful woman as you is surely a mystery.'

'There was no mystery, Ralph. He was bored with me,' Francesca said flatly.

'He's crazy.'

'Maybe he's right. How do you know that I'm not the most boring woman in the world? We've only met briefly. You don't know me at all.'

'True, I don't know you. But I know enough to know that I want to get to know you. And I can assure you – and you can trust me on this, as I've pointed out, I'm a journalist and I've a nose for such things – there is nothing, *nothing* boring about you.'

Francesca laughed. 'Ralph, did you ever think of writing fiction? You'd be good at it.'

'You don't take me seriously at all, do you?'

'Of course I do,' she said in mock earnestness. 'Now tell me how come you're separated?'

'My wife didn't like my lifestyle. Lots of travel, late nights, that kind of thing. The girls were young and I wasn't there as much as I should have been. I was trying to get as much work as I could. It led to a lot of friction.' His answer was honest and she respected him for it.

'Do you see much of them?' she asked, curious.

'Not as much as I'd like,' he said sadly. 'I was the baddie for a long time, because Jill was so angry with me.' His mouth tightened. 'I think it's important not to badmouth a parent to kids but my ex doesn't agree.'

'I'm lucky. My sons are grown up. They're in America. I didn't have to deal with that. I think it's an impossible situation.'

'You married young?'

'Yeah!' Francesca sighed. 'My husband saw that as part of the problem. He felt he hadn't had a chance to sow his wild oats, I suppose.'

Ralph glanced over at her. 'Do you miss being married?'

'Well, I'm still married, technically, but I know what you mean,' Francesca said slowly. 'I did very much at the beginning. I was lonely and scared and became quite reclusive. Then I copped on to myself.' She gave a little smile. 'I love this job. I'd never have done it if I'd still been with Mark. I feel reinvented somehow. And I like it. It's a whole new adventure, and it's *my* adventure. That probably sounds a bit silly,' she added, embarrassed.

'It's not silly at all. One door closes, another opens, one more step along the road,' Ralph remarked as he slowed to a halt at the Merrion Gates barrier. 'Isn't it the Chinese who use the same word for crisis and opportunity? It's not what happens to you in life that's important, it's the way that you deal with it.'

'I suppose that's one way of looking at it. Personally I could have done without the shock and the hurt and the grief.' Francesca yawned behind her hand. He was very easy to talk to and relaxing to be with. She felt comfortable with him.

'You've come through it,' he pointed out.

'And have you?' she asked.

'I suppose I have,' he said as the train thundered past. They chatted easily for the rest of the journey and Ralph whistled in admiration when he drove into the drive of her home. 'Nice place, Francesca. Worth a bob or two. You'll have no trouble selling it,' he said as he pulled up outside the front door.

'No,' she agreed.

'Well, the best of luck with it. And I hope you get the place of your dreams. I'm sure it's waiting for you.'

'Thanks, Ralph, I hope so too,' she said warmly.

'Sure you won't come to dinner?' he asked hopefully.

He had a boyish quality that was rather endearing and impulsively she found herself saying, 'I'm too tired to get dressed up to go out to dinner, but if you'd like to take pot luck when I see what's in the fridge, we could open a bottle of wine and have something outside on the deck.'

'You're on,' he said with alacrity, jumping out to open her door.

Twenty minutes later they sat on Francesca's deck,

431

sipping white wine and eating brown bread, smoked salmon and a selection of cheeses. The sun was still warm. It was a beautiful evening. She had changed out of her suit and high heels into a simple sundress and sandals.

'It's a pity you couldn't sell the house and take your garden with you, it's like being in the country here,' Ralph observed as he spread some Brie on a cracker and ate it appreciatively.

'I know. I'll really miss this. That's one of the reasons I liked the mews I told you about. The court-yard was a sun trap.' Francesca raised her face to the sun and lay back against her lounger.

Ralph stretched his long legs out in front of him. 'My apartment faces onto the canal. It's nice enough, but there's no privacy and the noise of the traffic is very intrusive although you blank it out eventually.'

The ding-dong of the doorbell startled Francesca. She wasn't expecting anyone to call. 'Excuse me,' she said politely. 'I'd better see who that is.'

'Tell them to go away. I want you all to myself,' Ralph instructed.

She slipped her feet back into her sandals and hurried out to the hall. Her heart gave a peculiar little lurch when she opened the door and saw Mark standing there frowning.

'You've guests I see, perhaps this is a bad time.'

What do I do? she thought in a fluster. *Do I ask him in or tell him to get lost?*

'Francesca?' Ralph appeared behind her and held out her mobile phone. 'You have a call.'

The two men stared at each other.

'Hello.' Ralph nodded politely. 'Take your call, Francesca,' he reminded her. 'I'll put your wine in the fridge so it won't get warm.' He sauntered back out to the kitchen.

'Who the bloody hell is that?' Mark demanded.

Chapter Forty-three

'Mark, don't be so rude,' she hissed, her hand covering the mouthpiece on the phone. She silenced him with a look. 'Hello?'

'Hi, who was Sexy Voice who answered your phone?' Millie demanded.

'Hi, Millie. Look, can I call you back? Mark's just arrived and I don't want to delay him.'

'And there's another man there with a sexy voice who answered your phone and Mark got ratty and asked who the bloody hell is he?' Millie queried.

'Exactly,' Francesca said succinctly.

'Wow! Never a dull moment in *your* life. Call me the very second you can,' her sister ordered.

'Will do,' Francesca assured her before hanging up. Mark had stalked down to the kitchen and was gazing thunderously out into the garden.

'Who's that joker?' He jerked his thumb in Ralph's direction. Ralph raised his glass and took a sip of wine.

'Don't be so derogatory, Mark. He's not a joker.

He's a friend of mine,' Francesca snapped, angered by his churlish attitude.

'And how long has this been going on? It all looks like a very cosy set-up to me. Is he the reason you want to sell the house?' Mark interrogated.

'Mark, Ralph is a friend. There is nothing going on. And if there were it would be none of your business. I'm as entitled as you to enter into another relationship, seeing as you were the one who ruined our marriage.' Francesca's eyes glinted dangerously. 'So don't you *dare* even attempt to go down that road. You should be ashamed of yourself. How dare you give me a hard time?'

'Sorry,' he muttered, taken aback at her vehemence.

'Now perhaps you'd be good enough to tell me why you called. I really would much prefer if you'd phone me and let me know that you're coming.'

'In case you're in bed with your . . . er . . . friend?' Mark retorted snidely. Her swift hard slap to his jaw caught him unawares. His eyes darkened with anger and he caught her roughly by the wrist.

'Don't you *ever* do that again,' he snarled.

'And don't you ever speak to me like that again, you lousy bastard.' Francesca's voice shook with anger and shock. She couldn't believe that she'd just slapped Mark in the face. But he'd deserved it for his low-down comment. 'Get out of here,' she raged.

'If I don't go will you invite pretty boy out the back to throw me out?' Mark drawled.

'You're pathetic, Mark. That woman is welcome to you, you truly deserve each other.' Francesca turned

435

away and walked towards the french windows, intending to join Ralph on the deck.

'Before you leave, I'm here to tell you that you can put the blasted house on the market. I wash my hands of it and you. It will be a pleasure to get you out of my life, because you're a walking bitch,' he swore, his face contorted with anger.

'That's rich, coming from a lying bastard,' Francesca riposted before walking out into the back garden.

Big deal, he was allowing her to put the house on the market. His solicitor had probably put the fear of God in him. And rightly so, she raged. Ralph stood up to greet her. 'Everything OK?' he asked in concern when he saw her face.

'Just a bit of a spat with my ex,' she said shakily.

'Things do get a little better with time,' he assured her kindly.

Her face crumpled and two big tears slid down her cheeks.

'Oh, don't cry, Francesca,' he said in concern, putting his arms around her.

'I can't help it,' she sobbed. 'He's turned into such a shit, Ralph, I really don't know him any more.'

'Anger turns us into different people for a while, we get back to ourselves eventually, don't worry,' he murmured into her hair. He glanced into the kitchen and saw Francesca's husband glowering out at them. Deliberately, Ralph drew Francesca closer and kissed the top of her head.

'Shush,' he murmured as if to a child. 'Shush.' When he looked up again, Mark had gone.

'I'm very sorry about this,' Francesca apologized with a sniffle as she drew away from him.

'Nothing to be sorry about. Don't forget I had a good head start on you. Been there, done that, worn the T-shirt. Now, why don't you sit down and I'll get the wine and we'll finish it and then I'll go on my way and you can go to bed and catch up on your beauty sleep,' he suggested kindly.

She sat down on her lounger. The sun was beginning to set. Even though the evening was warm, she shivered a little. She could still remember the sensation of her palm impacting against Mark's hard jaw. It made her feel a little sick. She hadn't thought herself capable of physical violence. This was her second time to have struck Mark. It was horrible.

Strangely she wasn't embarrassed to have cried in front of Ralph. He'd handled it all rather well, she thought admiringly as she watched him lope across the deck with the wine.

'Here's a clean glass. I took it from the press beside the wine rack.'

'Not a lot for me, Ralph,' she said tiredly. 'I need my wits about me tomorrow.'

'OK.' He half filled her glass and filled his own to the brim. 'Waste not want not,' he joked, taking a long slug. He poured the remainder of the bottle into his glass and sat down in the chair beside her. 'What did your ex want? Does he usually drop in unannounced?'

'I wish he wouldn't.' Francesca frowned. 'He told me that I could put the house on the market. I guess he had a talk with his solicitor and saw there was no other option. Well, I can tell you one thing, Ralph, I'm going to an estate agent's first thing. The sooner I sell up and get a place of my own the happier I'll be.'

'Don't go buying any old place just for the sake of it. Make sure it suits your requirements,' he warned, draining his glass. He stood up. 'I'll call you, if that's OK.'

'OK,' she agreed, standing up to show him out.

'Thank you for tea. It was very enjoyable, Francesca. I hope we can break bread together again soon. I don't have your home number.' He took a pen and small notepad out of his inside pocket and eyed her quizzically.

She called out the number. He had nice writing, she noted.

'And the mobile? I'm covering every option.'

Francesca smiled as she gave it to him. 'Thanks for the lift.'

'Any time.' He patted her on the shoulder. 'I'll let myself out. Stay where you are and relax. Goodnight, Francesca.'

'Goodnight, Ralph. Take care,' she murmured as he disappeared through the patio doors, turning once to wave.

She sat, numbly staring unseeingly into space. Mark had ruined her evening. An evening that had started off so promisingly. He had reacted surprisingly angrily to Ralph's presence. But why? she wondered. Surely he'd be glad to see her with someone new? It would help lessen his guilt. That was if he had any. Sometimes she doubted it. He was hardly jealous. That notion was too preposterous for words. Wearily, she tidied up and carried in the crockery and remains of their snack. After she'd washed up, she'd have a nice long soak in the bath and ring Millie and tell her the latest developments because the past two days had been nothing if not eventful.

Well, it hadn't taken her long to pick up a fancy man, Mark seethed as he drove past the entrance to the golf club and headed towards the city. He couldn't be bothered to go and play golf after what he'd witnessed. He should have gone straight to the golf club as he'd planned and then visited his wife. At least he'd have got a game in. It was pointless going for one now. He wouldn't be able to concentrate.

No wonder she wanted to sell the flaming house. She wanted to get a place of her own and set up a cosy love nest. How long had her little affair been going on? That bloke looked as though he was very comfortably installed. Rakish-looking bastard. Mark scowled as he drove like a maniac. The car was ancient. Obviously he wasn't wealthy. He was probably after Francesca for her money. Who else would have her? he thought nastily. His phone rang. It was Nikki.

'Hello?' he growled.

'Hi, darling,' she said cheerily. 'I'm terribly lonely without you. Do you want to come down for a night of unbridled passion? It wouldn't take you more than an hour. It's beautiful and peaceful down here.'

'Where is it?' he said heavily. He listened while she gave crisp, concise directions.

'OK,' he agreed. He didn't want to be on his own tonight. Seeing Francesca so relaxed in the company of another man had unsettled him. The way she'd gone into his arms had hit him like a physical blow. That bastard knew Mark had been looking when he kissed the top of her head. He might as well have said: *She's mine now*. He'd never thought of Francesca getting involved with another man. Stupid of him, he supposed. Why should she be on her own just because it didn't suit him? Why did he feel so bad about it?

That sundress was new, he hadn't seen it before. It made her look youthful. And it revealed far too much of her boobs, too. He scowled. And whatever she'd done to her hair suited her. That bloke fancied her like mad. He'd seen the way he looked at her. It was strange to think of someone fancying your wife. It made you look at her differently, he mused. He'd stopped paying attention years ago. Francesca was Francesca. She'd been part of his life for so long he'd taken her for granted. His attraction to and desire for Nikki had hit him like a thunderbolt and it had been mighty good. He'd felt alive. He still did when he was with her. He liked being with her, but seeing Francesca with that bloke brought a depth of feeling to the surface that baffled the hell out of him. What exactly – anger aside – were his feelings for her? The risk of losing her to someone else was not one he cared to think about. Why? How come he was reacting like this? Mark shook his head in frustration. Life was so damned complicated. And most of it was his own doing, which didn't help.

'So what does he look like? He sounds dead sexy.' Millie was agog with curiosity.

'He's very attractive. He's tall, which I like because it makes me feel less of an amazon—'

'Tsk! Don't be ridiculous, Francesca, you're not

that tall,' Millie interjected. 'And it suits you. Now tell me about Ravishing Ralph.'

'He's got lovely brown eyes, sort of sleepy looking if you know what I mean.'

'Come-to-bed eyes, you mean,' Millie corrected. 'And?'

'And he's got a craggy sort of lived-in face. He's been separated for two years, he has two young daughters. He lives in an apartment on the Grand Canal. He's a journalist and he keeps asking me out.'

'And why aren't you going?' Millie demanded.

'Well, maybe I will after this evening,' Francesca said.

'Oh, I'd love to have seen Mark's face when he saw him sitting out on the deck. What a kick in the ass *that* must have been,' Millie gloated.

'He was a real shit about it,' Francesca said sourly. 'Honest to God, I've never seen him act like this. I never thought he had it in him to be so obnoxious. He was horrible.'

'Of course he was. Why are you so surprised? He's jealous, you idiot.'

'Don't be ridiculous,' scoffed Francesca. 'He's just mad because he's got to sell the house and he thinks it's because I'm having an affair with Ralph.'

'I'm telling you, Francesca, he's emerald green,' Millie said firmly.

'But why? He's with the sexy high-flyer. Why on earth would he be jealous?'

'Well, part of it is because he's being a mean dog in the manger piss artist, but I'd say the shock of seeing you with another man made him realize what he's missing,' Millie said astutely.

441

'You're just biased, Millie,' Francesca said fondly.

'We'll see. Now, make a date with dishy Ralph. He sounds like he's just what you need right now.'

'I don't need complications,' Francesca retorted.

'Who's talking about complications, for God's sake! It's a date, that's all.'

'Dates are for teenagers. I'm forty, Millie, heading very rapidly for forty-one,' Francesca groaned.

'Oh, don't be such a wimp,' jeered Millie. 'I'll talk to you tomorrow. Bye.'

'Bye.' Francesca smiled as she hung up. Millie was such a tonic. And she was right. What harm could a dinner date do? It would be nice to have male company again. The next time Ralph called her, she'd accept his invitation to dinner. She wasn't interested in having a romantic interlude but the friendship could be nice. She meant what she said about complications. She'd seen friends whose marriages had broken down rush into disastrous relationships on the rebound and give themselves even more grief. She wasn't going to fall into that trap. Being single suited her just fine for now, she decided as she went to the *Golden Pages* and took down the numbers of several estate agents.

Ralph fumbled with his key and let himself into his apartment. He'd stopped off at the Barge and had a few snifters on top of the wine he'd polished off at Francesca's and he was a little under the weather, to say the least. He was feeling sorry for himself. He'd come all the way up from Cork to take the woman out to dinner and much good it had done him. He'd been hoping that right this very minute she'd be in his arms doing wild, dirty things to him. He gave a great sigh and belched. Alcohol fumes wreathed his head.

He might as well have another drink, he decided, lurching to his feet. He saw the red light on his answering machine flashing steadily. Sod it, he thought as he poured himself a generous tumbler of whiskey, some of it splashing onto the carpet as his hand shook.

He put the glass to his lips and took a swig, grimacing as the whiskey hit the back of his throat. He jabbed a finger at the *play* button and heard the whir of the tape.

'Ralph, you bastard. Where are you? You promised you'd be at Sally's summer project play. How can you do this to your own daughter? You do it to them all the time. How can you be so totally selfish? Have you no feelings for them at all? You're not fit to be a father,' his wife raged.

Ralph smote his forehead. He'd completely forgotten about Sally's play. Damn. Damn. Damn. He'd make it up to her. He'd take her to McDonald's and the pictures. She'd enjoy that. Jill had no business talking to him like that, he thought self-pityingly as he slumped into a chair clutching his precious tumbler of whiskey.

Chapter Forty-four

Nikki put the sheets into the washing machine, threw in some washing powder tablets and switched it on. She then turned her attention to the dishes in the sink. Her few days of peace and quiet had flown by. It was hard to believe it was time to go home. She stood at the sink, up to her wrists in hot, sudsy water, and stared unseeingly out of the kitchen window. She'd come to this place to sort things out in her head and she was going home as confused as ever, she thought dispiritedly.

She'd been on such a high looking forward to Mark's arrival but when he'd finally driven down the little lane and she'd hurried out to greet him, all she'd got was a distracted peck on the cheek. Eventually, after much prompting, the whole sorry saga had come erupting out of him, much to her dismay. He was hopping mad.

She just couldn't figure Mark out, she thought dejectedly as she washed the dishes and placed them in the drainer. *She'd* been over the moon to hear that the wicked witch of Howth was seeing a man. That was *precisely* the kind of news she'd been longing to hear for months. But Mark was like a demon.

'He drives a ten-year-old Saab, he's after her money, I'm telling you. No wonder she wanted to sell up,' he ranted. 'He knows that he's onto a good thing. And Francesca's such a softie she can't see it. But *I'm* not stupid. I know a chancer on the make when I see one.'

No matter what she'd said to try and allay his fears, he would not be placated. He'd made love to her perfunctorily, and then tossed and turned while she lay frustrated and disheartened beside him.

So what if that guy was after Francesca's money? It was her money and that was her lookout. She was big enough – in every way, Nikki thought viciously – to look after herself. What was it with Mark? Why did it matter to him? Why did he have to hang on to her? There really was only one answer that she could come up with, if she were being totally honest, and that was that he still had feelings for his wife. Otherwise he'd never react so strongly every time they had a tiff. Why couldn't he have phoned Francesca to tell her that he was agreeing to put the house up for sale? Why did he have to go traipsing over to Howth to tell her in person? she wondered unhappily. Was it just an excuse to see her? Did he still love Francesca?

Nikki rinsed her hands under the tap and dried them. She wandered out onto the veranda and sat down in the rocking chair. The sea breeze blew her hair into her eyes and impatiently she brushed it away. She felt she was fighting a losing battle.

Francesca seemed to have all the cards and she was playing a very skilful game. Maybe this Ralph guy was just a ploy to make Mark jealous enough to go back to her. That *would* be humiliating. She'd never be able to stay in EuroBank Irl. if that happened. But what could she do? She had to think of something, and fast, to bind Mark tightly to her.

There was one course of action she could take but it was rather drastic. And besides, the truth was she didn't want him to be bound to her. More than anything she wanted him to be with her because it was where he wanted to be. That was the only way that led to peace of mind. What a mess her life was. Deep down Nikki knew that hard as it was to live with Mark, it would be unbearable to have to live without him. On the other hand, if they stayed together it would always be on his terms. To think otherwise was only fooling herself.

'I'd be delighted to value the house for you, Mrs Kirwan, if you could give me a time and day that suits you,' William Lloyd of Lloyd & Flood, Estate Agents, Auctioneers, and Valuers, said briskly.

'How about tomorrow morning at eleven? I work during the week,' Francesca suggested.

'Fine. I'll be there. You'll certainly have no trouble selling the property, Mrs Kirwan, although it's mid-summer, a slow time in the property business. There's always a pick-up come the end of August, September.'

'That's fine, whenever,' Francesca replied. 'See you on Saturday.'

'Indeed I will. Goodbye, Mrs Kirwan.'

Francesca put down the phone slowly. This was it. She was committed now. The 'For Sale' sign would be up next week, she thought with a tinge of sadness.

Release, relax, let go. Her little mantra popped into her head. Selling the house would be a huge letting go, she acknowledged. There'd be no turning back then. She was reluctant to phone Mark to let him know that she'd engaged the services of an estate agent. She couldn't face another abusive tirade. A thought struck her. Of course. Why hadn't she thought of it before? She rooted in her bag for her wallet and withdrew a business card of Mark's. She'd never got around to throwing it out. Just as well, she thought, studying his business details. She sat at the computer and logged on to send an e-mail. It meant she wouldn't have to talk to the old crab but she could keep him up to date with developments.

She sent her husband a short note telling him of her choice of estate agents. She paused then, wondering if she should type: *if that's OK by you?* but decided that that would seem as if she were asking his permission, which certainly wasn't the case. She ended simply by saying that she would keep him updated. She reread it carefully before sending it off and wondered what his response would be.

It was a fraught day. She was up and down every ten minutes to see if he'd replied and every time the phone rang she jumped, half expecting it to be Mark ranting down the line. She was hoping, too, that Ralph would call to see how she was and perhaps suggest a dinner date over the weekend. As four o'clock came and neither of them had contacted her, she felt a mounting sense of disappointment.

Fortunately Ken was out of the office all day and wasn't there to observe her jumpy behaviour.

At ten to five she checked once more to see if Mark had responded. Her stomach clenched when she saw she had an e-mail. *Fine* was his terse reply and inexplicably it infuriated her. Was that the best he could do? He was so childish sometimes it was beyond belief.

She went home from work in a crabby humour and spent several hours cleaning the kitchen from top to bottom despite the fact that she had a cleaning lady who came once a week and who would have been mortally offended if she had known what Francesca was up to.

That night she went to bed with a vague sense of disappointment. Now that she'd finally decided to go out with Ralph the least he could have done was phone her, she thought irrationally as she lay in bed flicking desultorily through *Vanity Fair*. Maybe she'd put him off by her refusals. He was easily put off then, if that was the case, she thought glumly. Perhaps she should call him. That was the thing to do now. Women no longer had to sit by the phone waiting for a phone call from a man. They were allowed to be pro-active. It was an equal society, she assured herself. Far different from the one she'd grown up in.

If she hadn't heard from him over the weekend she'd call him on Monday, she decided, reading her horoscope at the back. It was all about Saturn being in her seventh house, she couldn't make head nor tail of it. It was no help to her, she decided as she switched off the bedside light and waited for sleep to come.

* * *

Mark yawned. Nikki had gone to bed ages ago. He should go himself but he wanted to be alone for a while. He went out onto the balcony and sat looking at the lights in the windows of the plush apartments. Small floodlights illuminated the grounds giving the shrubs and flowers strange shapes and shadows in the dark. The breeze whispered through the branches of the trees, carrying the scent of honeysuckle and stock. A sliver of new moon hung lopsidedly in the sky and stars twinkled faintly. It was hard to see them in the city. On the veranda of the beach house in the inky blackness of the countryside they had shone vividly, so near he'd felt he could reach out and pluck one from the dark velvet sky. It was a pity he'd been so agitated about Francesca's carry on. It had spoilt the night for him and Nikki.

Mark stretched his legs out in front of him. So the house was finally going up for sale. He'd received Francesca's e-mail with some surprise. When she'd been with him she hadn't known one end of a computer from another and here she was e-mailing. What next? he wondered drily.

He couldn't fault her choice of estate agents. Lloyd & Flood were top notch. There'd be no messing about there. She could deal with it, he thought stubbornly. She could do the Judas act. Soon enough he'd have no home of his own. He'd have to do something about that. He'd never envisaged living the rest of his life in Nikki's apartment. It was unthinkable. He liked to be his own man. Decisions were going to have to be made. His heart sank at the prospect.

A sense of loneliness enveloped him. All that he knew, all that was familiar had changed so completely. Once the future had held no fears for him, now he felt like a rudderless ship adrift on the edge of a whirlpool. The sale of his house would be the end of an era for him but where he would go from there he had no idea.

Ralph lay on the floor snoring, an empty whiskey bottle beside him. His phone rang, its piercing tone making no impression on his befuddled brain. On and on it rang, at regular intervals, to no avail. Dusk turned to darkness and slowly the night hours passed until a pale pink tinge in the eastern sky heralded the dawning of a new day. Oblivious to everything, Ralph slept in a drunken stupor, a little smile playing around his lips.

Chapter Forty-five

Francesca sat in the kitchen drinking coffee. Upstairs she could hear William Lloyd, the estate agent, going from room to room. She'd watched him making notes in his leatherbound notepad and wondered idly what his description of her home would be. She felt almost detached about the sale. The sooner it was over the better.

Once William Lloyd and his notebook were gone she was going to start the mother and father of a clearout. There was another thing she was going to have to do soon, and that was to tell her parents that she was getting a divorce. That wasn't going to go down well. Millie had told her that her mother had confided that she was praying to St Jude, the patron saint for hopeless causes, that she and Mark would have a reconciliation.

Fat chance, Francesca mused, given that they could hardly talk to each other without trading insults.

She heard William Lloyd stride into the bathroom.

He was extremely thorough. He'd been upstairs for so long he must be writing a novel, she thought moodily. No phone call from Ralph so far. She'd be dining alone, as usual, this weekend, it seemed.

Eventually the estate agent made his way downstairs to the kitchen. 'Excellent property, Mrs Kirwan,' he said, rubbing his hands. 'Couldn't ask for better. I'll have the photographer come out and take some shots whenever suits.'

'The sooner the better. I'm anxious for a quick sale,' Francesca informed him politely.

'Fine, fine, that's what I like to hear. I'll take a look at the grounds, if you don't mind.' Out came the black notebook as she opened the french doors for him and he strode out into the garden, pen poised. She saw him writing busily as he stood on the deck and couldn't help but smile. Definitely a novel, or at least a full page advertisement in the *Irish Times*.

The weekend passed slowly. Now that events were in motion she wanted to be gone. It was too painful to stay. A sense of failure enveloped her. This was never the way it should have been. She filled black rubbish sacks and charity bags, determined to be ruthless. But it was lonely work, as memory after memory surfaced and she cried for the recollection of what had once been a happy marriage.

'You're very down in the dumps, Frannie. What's wrong?' Ken asked as they had a quick cup of coffee the following Monday afternoon.

'I've put the house up for sale. I was throwing out stuff and giving things to charity. I felt terribly lonely,' she confessed.

'That's tough. It's bad enough moving when

there's only one of you. You have to make decisions what to throw out and what to keep for four people. Would your husband not give you a hand?'

'Are you kidding me? The last time we were together I gave him a sock on the jaw,' Francesca confessed.

'Oops!' Ken grimaced. 'That bad?'

'That bad.'

'Let him clear out his stuff when you're not there,' Ken suggested.

'That's what I'll have to do. Once the notice is in the paper, I'll e-mail him and tell him to get his ass in gear,' Francesca declared. 'And if he doesn't bloody well do it, I'll get a skip and dump the lot of it in it.'

'Ruthless, aren't you?' teased Ken as he rinsed her cup for her.

'Could I have an hour or two off some morning this week to let the photographer take some photos of the house for the paper?'

'I'd be afraid to say no,' Ken said. 'I don't want a sock in the jaw, thanks.'

'Don't tell anyone I told you that,' warned Francesca.

'*Moi?* I heard nuttin',' he assured her. 'Take whatever time you want.'

She was sending newspaper cuttings to clients the following Wednesday afternoon when the phone rang. 'Ken Kennedy PR, can I help you?' she said politely.

'Have dinner with me,' a deep familiar voice said.

'Hi,' she said, smiling. 'How are you?'

'I've been up to my eyes,' Ralph said. 'Brenda Carroll had a deadline. "Stress-busters for the

453

Stressed-out Career Woman". And I had a Fine Arts auction to cover. How are things with you?'

'Well, the estate agent came. The house will be in the paper next week—' The other line buzzed. 'Hold on a sec, my other phone's ringing.'

'Look, how about I pick you up tonight at home around seven-thirty and we go and have a bite to eat and catch up?' he suggested.

'OK then,' Francesca said impulsively. 'Have to go.'

She dealt with her caller, the organizer of a theatre festival, then sat back in her chair nibbling the top of her pen. What would she wear tonight? Would she have time to get a quick blow dry at lunchtime? She'd like to look her best. She picked up the phone to ring Millie to tell her the news. Her sister would be heading off to France soon, for a month. She'd miss her. They'd always been close but Millie had been a rock of strength through her marriage break-up. She was lucky to have a sister like her.

Ralph swirled a spoon in his glass of Alka-Seltzer and gulped it down. He felt lousy. He went back to his laptop and tried to concentrate on an article he was writing on antiques for a glossy magazine. He'd fed Francesca a hell of a spoof, he thought wryly. Today was the first day he'd even attempted to work after his bender. That was it, he vowed. He was swearing off the drink for good this time. He cursed as he closed the file by mistake. His fingers weren't too steady; he kept hitting the wrong keys. He needed to have the article in on time. He couldn't afford to lose the commission, he needed the money. He had maintenance to pay. If he was a second late with it, Jill was on his back screeching like a fishwife. She'd given him hell about missing Sally's play. He might go to collect his daughter from school and make a fuss of her tomorrow. But he'd need to clear it with Jill or she'd cause a rumpus.

He picked up the phone and dialled his wife's number. 'Hello, it's me.'

'What do you want?' Jill's icy tone boded ill.

'I was hoping to pick Sally up from school tomorrow and take her out for the afternoon.'

'I'm not going to say a word to the child. If you're there you're there and if you're not, she'll be none the wiser. I'll go to collect her just in case. I'm not going to take the risk of you not turning up.'

'There's no need—' he was in the middle of protesting when she hung up on him. Ralph groaned. A cranky woman was the last thing he needed right now. Jill never gave him a break. She'd always expected far too much from him. He was only human, for crying out loud.

Thank God for a lovely soft woman like Francesca. He was looking forward to seeing her again.

The doorbell's chimes surprised Francesca and she almost nicked her ankle with her Ladyshave. She glanced at the alarm clock on her bedside locker. It was only six-thirty. Ralph wasn't due to pick her up for another hour. It couldn't possibly be Mark again. She couldn't face another row. She slipped into Owen's room to peep out the front window to see if Mark's car was in the drive. It wasn't. Unfortunately she couldn't see the front door to see who was there. She wrapped the belt of her towelling robe around her and hurried downstairs. Her heart sank to her boots when she opened the door and saw Viv Cassidy smiling sweetly at her.

'Francesca, dear. I got such a shock when I saw the "For Sale" sign being erected. I'm *devastated* to think we're losing you as a neighbour.'

'Oh, Viv, hi. Come in. I can't offer you anything. I'm getting ready to go out,' she said politely.

'Anywhere nice?' Viv twinkled.

'I don't know yet.'

'Oh, a surprise. With someone special, I hope,' she probed.

'Just a colleague from work,' Francesca murmured.

'Dear, you were so lucky to get that job. It landed in your lap. Some women have such a difficult time when their marriages break up. You got along marvellously.' There was a hint of accusation in the saccharine observation. Francesca felt like saying, *Sorry for not collapsing in a heap, Viv, and ending up a basket case just to suit you*. She said nothing.

'And, dear, how much are you expecting for the house? It would be nice to have a guideline price should we ever consider moving.'

'It will all be in the property pages shortly, Viv. Now I really must go, but thanks for calling.' She ushered her nosy neighbour out the door.

'But where are you moving to?' Viv squeaked, discommoded.

'Haven't a clue. Bye, Viv,' Francesca said cheerfully.

'Are you sure you're doing the right thing, dear? People can make big mistakes under stress. *Very* big mistakes,' she added for emphasis.

'I'm perfectly sure I'm doing the right thing. Bye now.' Francesca waved, closing the door. 'Nosy old bat,' she muttered as she raced upstairs. Viv was one person she certainly wouldn't miss. She went and stood in front of her wardrobe. Ralph hadn't specified where they were eating. Should she dress up or dress down? Was it formal, informal or mega posh?

Five outfits later, she settled on a black sleeveless Dolce & Gabbana polo and a pair of cream linen trousers and a fitted black jacket. It was casually elegant. It would have to do. She slipped a slim gold bangle onto her wrist and inserted a pair of gold earrings in her ears. She didn't want to overdo the jewellery. She studied herself critically in the mirror. She certainly looked better than she had three months ago, she acknowledged. She'd managed to keep the weight down but she could certainly do with dropping another half-stone at least. She still had a tan. Her eyes were bright, her hair lustrous. Not bad for a forty-year-old broad. She traced coral lipstick onto her lips and sat down to paint her nails.

Viv was such a begrudging old bitch, she reflected. Yes, the job had landed in her lap, and she hadn't suffered any financial hardship, but that was due to luck and circumstances. It didn't lessen the emotional trauma. At least she'd hauled herself out of her shock and depression and got on with things. And if Viv or anyone else didn't like it, that was their problem. She was proud of herself, she decided. She blew on her nails to dry them. People were strange, for sure. Mark wanted her to stay in a rut, dependent on him for the rest of her life while he enjoyed a new relationship. Viv didn't seem to like the idea of things going right for her. Well, tough! She didn't have to answer to anybody now. She was her own woman, she thought with a grin. That sounded good. Her own woman!

She wondered if Ralph would be on time. She liked punctuality. Thought it showed respect. He had nice manners. Old-fashioned manners. He'd walked on the outside and held the car door open for her. That made her feel very feminine. Such a simple thing but she liked it, she thought with a little smile.

Ralph arrived at seven-twenty-nine. He carried a bunch of white lilies.

'For you.' He bowed gallantly.

'They're lovely, Ralph. Thank you.' She was touched.

'You look lovely.' His heavy-lidded gaze travelled lazily up and down.

She smiled. 'You look pretty snazzy yourself.' He was wearing a casual beige suit and black T-shirt. It suited his lanky figure. His eyes looked tired and faintly bloodshot. He must have been spending a lot of time on his computer, she thought sympathetically.

'Do you fancy the Trocadero? Or La Stampa? I haven't booked anywhere, I thought we'd just take pot luck?'

'We could always go out to Howth. The King Sitric does lovely seafood and we could go for a walk on the pier afterwards, if you'd like,' she suggested hesitantly. Now that he was here, all dressed up, she felt a little shy.

'Perfect! That would be very nice,' he agreed. 'I could do with a good blast of sea air.'

'Stuck at your computer for too long?'

'Yeah, you could say that, I suppose,' Ralph replied. 'Ready? I hope you're hungry.'

'I'm starving,' laughed Francesca. 'I have to confess I was a bit nervous about this evening so I didn't eat much today.'

'Nervous? You? Of going to dinner with me?'

'Don't forget you've had a year's head start,' she reminded him. 'This is my first dinner-date since Mark and I separated.'

'True. But I'm a pussy cat,' he assured her as she locked the door behind her.

Dinner was a pleasure. They talked and laughed as though they'd known each other for years and the food was mouth-watering. Francesca had lemon sole with almond butter; Ralph stuffed sea bass. As she sipped a glass of chilled white wine, Francesca began to relax. It was most enjoyable to be in a man's company again, she reflected. Ken was a pet, but he was younger than her as well as being her boss: it wasn't quite the same. Ralph was mature, sophisticated, her own age and a very entertaining companion. She hadn't laughed so much in months. It was only as they walked along the pier, much later, that she thought of Mark. This had been one of their haunts.

Ralph noticed her silence. 'What's wrong? Are you cold?' he asked solicitously.

'No, no, I'm fine. It's a lovely evening,' she murmured.

'But?' He eyed her enquiringly.

'Oh, it's silly really,' she said in embarrassment. 'It's just Mark and I used to walk here a lot. It's a little strange to be walking along the pier with another man.'

'Do you still love your husband?' he asked bluntly.

Francesca stopped walking and turned to face out to sea. The moon slanted silver rays on the indigo waters. How often had she stood here and watched the moon with Mark? Not so much in later years but during the good times of her marriage she'd spent many happy moments here with him. It had been daft of her to bring Ralph here. She hadn't been thinking straight. And the craziest thing was that she felt a little guilty. That was the thing that floored her most of all.

'Do you still love him?' Ralph persisted, his brown eyes staring into hers.

Francesca shook her head. 'I don't know, Ralph. I just don't know. I wanted to go out with you, but the crazy thing is I feel I'm betraying him. Would you bring me home?' she asked.

'If that's what you want, Francesca, I'll bring you home,' Ralph said, disappointed.

'Thanks,' she murmured.

She didn't ask him in. She couldn't bring herself to. She leaned over and pressed her lips lightly against his cheek.

'Sorry,' she whispered.

'It's OK. I'll call you,' Ralph said mildly.

'Will you?' she asked, surprised. She thought she'd blown it.

'Francesca, what you're going through is par for

the course. But you'll get over it. Believe me. It will probably be easier when you've got your new place and there are no memories. No past history. I had a lovely time with you and I hope we do it again.'

'I had a lovely time too, Ralph. It was fun. I'm sorry I got maudlin at the end.'

'Perfectly normal, I assure you. Or else I'm losing my touch,' he teased. 'Goodnight, Francesca.'

She watched him drive off and felt a tinge of regret. Why had she felt so uncomfortable? It was ridiculous. Ralph's question rang in her ears as she let herself into the empty house. Did she still love Mark?

Francesca locked the door behind her and set the alarm. Trixie came bounding out of the kitchen to meet her. Francesca buried her face in her soft pelt. Was the sadness she'd felt out on the pier because she still loved her husband or was it because she finally realized that her marriage was well and truly over? A bit of both, she thought sadly. In spite of all that had happened between them, Mark was the father of her sons and he'd been her husband for twenty-two years. How could there not be a love of sorts there? It was time to stop the fighting. Time to try and heal the wounds. Time to make a fresh start.

Chapter Forty-six

Do you think we could have lunch and not fight?

Mark studied Francesca's e-mail. He had to admit he'd been pleasantly surprised to receive it. It was such a change from her usual abusive tirades. It made sense to have lunch and discuss things, he supposed. They couldn't be at loggerheads for the rest of their lives and, besides, his solicitor's advice had been to conduct the divorce as amicably as possible.

He sat poised at his keyboard, then wrote decisively:

Tomorrow. 12-30 p.m. Dobbins? If you don't, I won't!

He waited impatiently for her response. Gratifyingly it wasn't long coming.

1 p.m. Marcello's? OK!

Mark smiled. Marcello's had been a favourite of theirs. A small intimate restaurant on the canal. A perfect choice for a civilized lunch for exes. He swivelled to the keyboard and typed in:

Marcello's fine. I'll book. See you there.

Mark buzzed his secretary. 'Book a lunch for two in Marcello's on the canal. One p.m. tomorrow, please,' he instructed. He felt a little frisson of anticipation. E-mailing Francesca had felt almost illicit. Nikki certainly wouldn't be too pleased if he told her that he was lunching with his estranged wife. He wouldn't mention their lunch date, he decided prudently. Life was complicated enough at the moment. It would be nice to have a lunch with his wife without warring. He'd make the effort, he promised himself. No snide remarks about lover boy. It would be hard, but if she was prepared to make the effort then so was he. He respected her maturity in sending the conciliatory e-mail. But then Francesca had never been one to hold a grudge. She'd always been the first to make up when they rowed.

Mark smiled. He was looking forward to lunch tomorrow. It was almost like going on a date, he thought in amusement. A date with his wife – who would ever have thought it?

Francesca studied her husband's e-mail with satisfaction. Marcello's was a restaurant that had many happy memories for them, and it was easier for her to get to than going into town. At least he was agreeable to her proposal. That was a start. He'd obviously calmed down since their last encounter. It was crazy to be fighting the way they were. It was too draining. Hopefully tomorrow they'd be able to solve their differences or at least be civil and discuss their financial situation. She wanted to look her best. Maybe she'd slip into town for an hour and buy something new for the occasion. She hadn't bought anything for ages and she wanted to wear something he'd never seen before. Pity she didn't have time to drop over to Diffusion in Clontarf. The boutique stocked clothes that were extremely stylish and classy, but unfortunately her time was limited.

She booked a cab. Time was of the essence, she didn't want to waste it looking for parking.

At one-fifteen precisely the taxi dropped her at the top of Grafton Street. At one-fifty she hailed a taxi for the return journey, the satisfied possessor of an extremely chic Jil Sander suit. It was perfect, Francesca thought happily as she settled her carrier bags in the seat beside her and gave the driver the office address. A charcoal-grey pencil skirt and three-quarter-length fitted jacket that had a superb cut. It exuded an elegant, don't-mess-with-me look. A silky black camisole, black high heels and her black Burberry briefcase and she'd look just as much the career woman as Miss Nikki Langan. If it was a career woman he wanted, it was a career woman he was going to get. She was going to get her hair blow-dried too, for good measure.

'You get the works done, girl, and let him see what he's missing. Personally I think you're extremely forgiving. It wouldn't be me,' Millie declared as Francesca gave her an update.

'I know. But it's crazy to be at each other's throats the way we are and I really did feel strange out in Howth walking along the pier with Ralph. I felt awfully sad that things turned out so bad between me and Mark,' Francesca explained.

'It wasn't your fault,' Millie pointed out.

'I know. But what's done is done. Ralph said something interesting the other day. He said it wasn't what happened to you that was important, it was the way you dealt with it. I haven't been dealing with it too good,' Francesca said.

'Francesca, you are not a saint yet. You are a mere mortal like the rest of us. Don't go soft on Mark and let him walk all over you!' warned Millie. 'Especially as I'll be gone next month and I won't be here to advise you and put the iron in your soul.'

'Millie, I'm just having lunch with him. I need to get the house sorted,' Francesca said patiently.

'Are you going to see Ralph again?'

'I hope so. He's terribly busy, you know. Deadlines coming out of his ears, he told me, but he said he'd give me a call.'

'Do you fancy him? Would you like to snog him?' Millie enquired in her usual forthright manner.

Francesca laughed. 'He has a certain *je ne sais quoi*, I suppose. I don't know, Millie, I'm not really looking for a romantic relationship. I kept thinking of Mark as we walked along the pier.'

'Well, don't go to places that you went to with Mark, you idiot,' her sister exclaimed.

'Right.'

'And don't, under any circumstances, kiss Mark. Remember he's a shit!' Millie ordered.

'Stop it, Millie!'

'Oh Lordy, Francesca! I worry about you,' Millie said in alarm. 'You're going soft on him. You stick to your guns and sell that house.'

'I have every intention of doing so, Millie,' Francesca said tartly.

'Good! Call me the minute lunch is over.'

'I might!' Francesca retorted.

'Ah, Francesca, don't leave me in suspense.'

'I won't, and stop worrying,' Francesca reassured her. She wished she had Millie's toughness. Sometimes her soft heart was her worst enemy.

She deliberately didn't arrive at the restaurant on time. She didn't want to look too eager and besides she wanted to see the look on her husband's face when she walked in in her new suit. Ken had whistled long and loudly when he had seen her that morning.

'You're not meeting that journo, are you?' he asked in alarm.

'No, why?' Francesca was surprised by his attitude.

'Just be careful, he's not very dependable,' Ken said.

'Well, that hasn't been my experience,' Francesca said evenly. 'But I'm not meeting "that journo", I'm meeting my husband for lunch.'

'Reconciliation time?' A thought struck him. 'Oh no, you'll leave me, and I can't do without you.'

'Selfish git.' Francesca laughed. 'I'm not leaving you, but for that little admission I'll expect a massive bonus. I'm merely having lunch with Mark to try and sort out the house. OK?'

'If you're leaving I want a year's notice.'

'No problem.' Francesca picked up her briefcase.

'Go grind him beneath your stilettos, Frannie.'

'Thank you, Kenneth. Don't be a sadist. Bye.'

In spite of herself, butterflies fluttered around her insides. What if they ended up having another row in the restaurant? That would be a disaster. She'd make a special effort not to make any reference to Nikki. She'd try and keep the conversation general. Or specifically about the sale of the house and what he was going to do about his possessions.

She parked in the small car park at the side of the restaurant, sprayed some Carolina Herrera 212 on her wrist, took a deep breath and got out of the car.

Mark was seated at a table for two by the window. He stood up to greet her and she couldn't help noticing the way his eyes widened in appreciation when he saw her.

Good, she thought with satisfaction. The suit had been worth every damn penny.

'Hello, Mark,' she said calmly. 'So here we are.'

Chapter Forty-seven

'Hello, Francesca,' he said slowly. 'You look very well.'

'Thanks.' They smiled uncertainly at each other. His eyes crinkled up in that attractive way she'd always liked. He looked tired. Her heart softened. Mark worked too hard. She'd always been at him to take life easier when they'd been together. 'This is a bit weird,' she remarked, forgetting that she was being cool and poised.

'I know.' He sat down opposite her. 'I'm glad we can talk things over.'

'Look, before we order, I just want to say I'm sorry I slapped you in the face the other day,' she said impulsively.

'That's OK, I deserved it,' Mark replied. 'I'm sorry I called you a walking bitch.'

'I suppose things have been a bit fraught between us,' Francesca admitted.

Mark fiddled with his soup spoon. 'I have to say I was surprised to get your e-mail.'

Francesca smiled. He was always a fidget. 'Well, the "For Sale" sign is up for the house. It will be in the papers next week. We're going to need to be in touch. And it's horrible fighting all the time. The past is the past. You've made your decisions and now I've made mine and we just have to get on with it.'

'I know.' Mark grimaced. 'I just wish the house didn't have to go.'

Exasperation engulfed Francesca, followed by a pang of hurt. He felt more for the damn house than he did for her. Great for the ego! She stayed silent.

'We should order,' Mark said. 'My treat.'

'Dutch,' Francesca said firmly. She was tempted to say *out of my pittance*, but she refrained. This was not the time nor the place. She was here in a spirit of reconciliation.

Mark laughed. 'You've changed, you know. I'm getting afraid of you, you're so assertive these days.'

'That's no harm,' Francesca said crisply. 'I don't want a starter. I'll have the lamb.'

'Me too. Haven't had lamb for ages. I miss your roast beef and mushy peas.'

Francesca raised an eyebrow. 'Doesn't Nikki cook them for you?'

'She's more into pasta and rice dishes,' Mark informed her. 'Healthy kind of food.'

'You look well on it.' Francesca couldn't help the edge in her voice. What was he implying? That she'd cooked stodgy, unhealthy food for him?

'Of course I'm working out at the gym too, that helps,' Mark added hastily, realizing what he'd said. Fortunately the waiter came to take their order.

'So.' Mark sat back when the waiter had gone. 'The sign's up.'

'Yeah. It's weird looking at it. Unreal, almost. Viv Cassidy nearly broke her neck to come over and interrogate me. I won't miss her in the slightest,' Francesca said caustically.

'I don't miss her at all.' Mark smiled. 'Are you going after the mews still?'

'It's too late. They had a cash buyer. I'll have to look elsewhere.' She took a sip of sparkling water.

'Oh!' He had the grace to look ashamed. 'I'm sorry I wasn't more helpful. I was shocked that you wanted to sell up. I got bull-headed.'

Francesca shrugged. 'There's plenty of properties out there. I'll get another one somewhere.'

Mark leaned across the table. 'Francesca, are you certain that you want to sell up?' he said earnestly. 'Have you thought it all through? Are you sure you're not making an impulsive decision that you'll regret later?'

Francesca shook her head. 'Mark, I've been on my own nearly eight months now, I've had plenty of time to think about it, believe me. Our marriage is over. What's the point in living in limbo? The house is too big for me and besides I want my own place. Psychologically it will be much better for me.'

'As long as you're sure.'

'I am,' she said firmly. 'That's why I wanted to have lunch with you. You need to come over and take what you want. You still have bits and pieces and all the books in your study. What about the china and the crystal? What about the paintings? We have to sort all this out. What do you want to do with them?'

'I suppose I'll have to put them in storage for the time being. There's no room in Nikki's place. She doesn't like clutter,' he said flatly.

'You could buy a new place with your share of the money,' Francesca said brightly. 'If Nikki sold her apartment you'd have a very substantial sum, surely.' She was fishing, curious to know if they were going to buy a place of their own, but unwilling to ask directly.

'We'll see,' Mark said noncommittally as the aromatic whiff of rosemary signalled the arrival of their lamb. They sat in silence as their meal was served. Francesca felt quite peckish, surprisingly.

'Have you told your parents yet?' Mark asked as he forked a portion of succulent lamb into his mouth.

'Nope. Have you told your dad?'

'God, no!' Mark exclaimed. 'What do you think I am? Brave?'

Francesca laughed and pronged a sliver of buttered carrot. 'I know *exactly* how you feel. Terrible, isn't it? We're in our forties, for God's sake. We've got grown-up children.'

Mark made a face. 'No matter how old you are there are times when you still feel like a child with your parents.'

'Once I mention divorce, I'm in for it,' Francesca groaned. 'But I suppose we should tell them. I wouldn't like them to read in the papers that the house is for sale. I'm sure they'd prefer to hear it from us. Unwelcome as it may be.'

'Are you sure about the divorce?' Mark ventured.

'There's no reason not to. It leaves you free to do

your thing and me free to do mine.' Francesca eyed him over the rim of her glass. He still obviously hadn't warmed to the idea of divorcing her. Millie had been so right.

'Well, it's entirely up to you,' Mark muttered.

'Don't you want to be free to make plans?' Francesca asked curiously.

'I'm happy enough the way I am.'

'I'm sure Nikki would prefer you to be divorced.'

'It really makes no difference to us,' Mark countered.

'I see,' Francesca murmured.

Hope ignited in her husband's eyes. 'So will we just sell the house and forget the divorce?'

'No, we might as well go the whole hog,' Francesca said, resolutely closing off that escape route.

Mark cleared his throat. 'I hope you don't mind me asking you, but does this have anything to do with that guy I saw you with?'

Francesca laid down her knife and fork. 'Mark, whether it has or not makes no difference. I still want a divorce. But as it happens it has nothing to do with Ralph or anyone else. It's what *I* want that counts for me from now on. Selfish of me, perhaps, but that's the way it is.'

'What does he do, this Ralph guy?'

'He's a journalist. I met him through work.' Francesca picked up her knife and fork and resumed eating.

'It's funny to think of you with someone else.' The remark slipped out unthinkingly.

'I felt the same about you and her,' Francesca retorted.

Mark leaned across and took her hand. 'I never meant to hurt you,' he said brusquely. 'None of it was planned.'

'I always loved your fingers,' she murmured distractedly, gazing at their entwined hands. Mark had long fingers, pianist's fingers. A wave of desire flooded her as she remembered how he used to turn her on with those fingers. She saw an answering desire in his eyes, and drew her hand away, confused. This was madness. 'I need to be heading off soon, I've to go out to RTE.' She caught the waiter's eye and called him over. 'Are you having dessert?'

'No, just coffee for me,' Mark said.

She smiled at the waiter. 'Two coffees, please.'

'What are you doing at RTE?' Mark sat back in his chair.

'Delivering some review copies of books for various programmes.' Francesca was glad the conversation was back on general lines. For several hormone-stirring moments she'd wanted to kiss her husband – and more. It was the first time she'd felt horny in a long time. And he'd felt it too. She'd seen it in his eyes.

'It sounds interesting,' he said slowly.

Her eyes lit up. 'Oh Mark, it is. I love the work. Ken and I get on extremely well. I feel alive again,' she enthused.

'It suits you. You look great.'

Francesca smiled. 'It's so ironic to hear you say that. I can't remember the last time you told me that I looked well when we were married. Familiarity and all that . . .'

'We stopped paying attention to each other,' Mark murmured.

'I suppose we did,' Francesca said sadly. In some ways she'd taken him for granted as much as he had her. The coffee came and she gulped it down. 'Mark, I have to rush,' she apologized. She took some notes out of her wallet. 'My share,' she said.

'Please, Francesca, just this once let me buy lunch. You can do it the next time,' Mark protested. He looked so earnest, she felt it would be churlish to refuse.

'OK. Thanks. I'll keep you informed about what's happening. And maybe you could think about what you're going to do about your stuff. Maybe Gerald might let you store it in his place,' she suggested.

'That's a thought, I suppose. I'll mention it to him and see what he says.' Mark stood up politely. 'See you, Francesca. Today was good.'

'Bye, Mark.' Their eyes met.

'This is strange,' he said.

'Us being civil?'

'You know what I mean.'

Her face grew sad. 'I know. I never thought it would be us. See you.'

She walked quickly out of the restaurant, overwhelmed with emotions. Because they had been civil to each other and had actually relaxed in each other's company it had felt almost like old times. And yet they were parting to go to completely separate lives. The most shocking realization had been that she still felt desire for Mark.

No, maybe it was desire for sex. After all, it's been a long time, she argued with herself as she sat in the car.

You could have had sex with Ralph if you'd wanted to. He'd certainly like to. It was Mark you wanted.

'Oh, shut up, Francesca,' she muttered as she indicated to get into the stream of traffic along the canal. Maybe the lunch hadn't been such a good idea after all. She was better able to cope with Mark when he was angry with her and she was angry with him. Today she'd felt herself softening towards him and that wasn't what she wanted.

She wanted the divorce, she reassured herself. Mark was only using her as an excuse not to have to make a commitment to Nikki. She was *not* going to be that excuse!

'You're getting a divorce? That's preposterous! Your dear mother would turn in her grave,' blustered Gerald. 'Cost you a damn fortune as well.'

'I know,' groaned Mark. 'Don't remind me.' He'd decided to get the bad news over and done with sooner rather than later. Now that Francesca was determined to sell up and divorce him he felt the need to know that his possessions would be somewhere secure until he had himself sorted out. Gerald was his usual cantankerous self, unfortunately.

'What does she want to sell that lovely house for? She won't get as good a property anywhere else. You'll be paying a packet for somewhere to live now.'

'I know. I don't want her to sell up but she sees it differently unfortunately and as I have books, paintings and bits and pieces to remove, I was wondering if you'd let me put them in the small bedroom for a while until I have myself sorted,' Mark said patiently.

'And when will that be?' demanded his father.

'Soon enough!'

'Are you still living with that other one?'

He tried to hide his irritation. 'Yes, Dad.'

'Why can't you put your stuff there?' Gerald demanded.

'Lack of space,' Mark said succinctly.

'Hrumph,' snorted his father.

'Can I put my stuff here or not, Dad? If not, fine, I'll arrange to put it in storage.' Mark laid it on the line.

'Storage would cost a fortune. You can have the spare room. But I hope it won't be for too long,' his father growled. 'Now that you're here you can cut the grass for me. My knees are aching something fierce. And another thing, I need to buy a new freezer – that one I have is on the way out. I want you to come around the electrical showrooms with me to help me pick one. We can do it tomorrow,' Gerald instructed.

It might be a hell of a lot cheaper in the long run to pay for storage, because one way or another his father would make him pay for the privilege of storing his bits and pieces. Mark shook his head as he went out to the shed to get the lawnmower. He plugged it in and began to cut the grass. He actually liked cutting grass. There was something calming about it. He strode up and down the garden, his mind meandering from subject to subject. It was going to be difficult dividing up the house contents. He and Francesca had accumulated a lot of *objets d'art*, especially when they'd travelled.

She was very set on getting a divorce. He'd never thought she'd go that far. He'd always known that she had a determined streak in her but the Francesca he'd met for lunch today was a far different woman to the one he'd been married to. There was a hard-edged assertiveness to her, a confidence, that was new. It had been bittersweet lunching with her today. He would have liked to spend longer with her. When he'd taken her hand something had happened between them. The old spark they'd had years ago had flared. It was like dating. He bet he could still turn her on too, if he wanted, Mark reflected as he emptied the grass cuttings. He'd seen the look in her eyes. He wondered if she was sleeping with the journalist. He couldn't be sure. He knew it was selfish of him but he hoped to hell that she wasn't. If she wasn't, eight months was a long time to go without sex. It would be good, he thought dreamily. Lying in bed with Francesca in their big bed suddenly seemed like the most desirable thing in the world.

He missed her, he missed family life, he missed his sons and he missed his house. Mark stood slack-jawed as it dawned on him what he was thinking. He wanted to go home. He wanted to be reconciled with his wife.

But what about Nikki? Mark chewed his lip. He loved Nikki's vibrancy and intelligence. She challenged him in every way: mentally, emotionally, sexually; but at the end of the day, he didn't want challenges any more. He'd had enough. He wanted familiarity, comfort, a shared history. If Francesca hadn't found out about Nikki and forced the issue, he often felt that the relationship would have run its course; he would have satisfied whatever need and want that was in him, got it out of his system and come to his senses.

Would Francesca take him back? he pondered. It would save so much hassle if she did. They could keep the house and get back to the way things were before and life would resume its smooth even tenor.

He thought about Nikki, about how much she loved him, and felt a stab of guilt. If he went back to Francesca she'd be gutted. She'd probably leave the bank. It would be difficult for her to continue working there. But she was relatively young, with a great career ahead of her. Her career was the most important thing in her life and she was going to go far, he thought proudly. Nikki would get over him. Their relationship had followed a far smoother course when they weren't living together. She'd find someone else.

Having finally faced what had been niggling at him for a long while, Mark felt as if a huge burden had lifted from his shoulders. Why hadn't he faced up to it sooner and not let things drag on to this extent? All he had to do now was to convince his wife to take him back and everything would slip right back into place, Mark thought with relief. He'd seen the look in her eyes when their hands touched. He'd woo her, he decided excitedly. He'd woo her like he had when he'd first met her and been crazy for her.

Whistling to himself, he put the lawnmower back in the shed. When she saw that he was serious about getting back together, and when she gave it some thought, she'd come to the same conclusion as he had. Mark was sure of it.

Chapter Forty-eight

'I know that you'll give out to me for saying so, but it was nice having lunch with Mark. Not fighting any more was such a huge relief,' Francesca explained earnestly. 'Listen to me!' she exclaimed. 'I shouldn't feel I have to justify having a civilized meal with my husband. Mind you, I do feel a bit confused. In one way it was easier when we were fighting, because I knew where I stood.' She folded another T-shirt and put it in the plastic bag Millie had set aside for them. She laid the full bag neatly in the middle of the suitcase. She was helping her sister pack for her vacation in France.

'I knew it!' Millie exclaimed. 'He buys you a half-decent lunch and you're crumbling already. I bet he asked you to reconsider the divorce and putting the house up for sale.'

'Yeah,' admitted Francesca as she matched socks together.

'Told you! He's so fucking manipulative, Francesca. Before you know it he'll be asking you to take him back,' Millie declared.

'Don't be silly!'

'Silly, am I? He doesn't want to marry your woman, he doesn't want you to sell the house. He's jealous of Ralph. He's being nice to you, treating you to lunch. Silly, am I? We'll see,' Millie retorted.

'Look, *I* asked him to lunch to talk about dividing up the contents of the house. Does that sound as though I'm planning on staying?'

'He's working on you,' Millie warned. 'Did Ralph get in touch yet?'

'No, actually,' Francesca said slowly. 'I thought I would have heard from him by now. He's probably up to his eyes.'

'A phone call doesn't take two minutes,' Millie snorted. 'One minute he's all over you, the next he's not calling. Bit of an enigma, isn't he?'

'Maybe he's giving me some space,' Francesca suggested hopefully.

'Maybe,' agreed Millie. 'But there's no need to go overboard.'

Francesca busied herself sorting out the girls' sundresses and shorts. She was disappointed that Ralph hadn't called. She'd hoped to see him over the weekend. Maybe her idiotic behaviour on the pier in Howth had been the last straw. But surely he could understand how she felt. He'd seemed OK about it. She might have been mixed up the night of their dinner date but she felt a damn sight more confused now after her little episode with Mark in the restaurant.

She paused, remembering the moment. Sadness darkened her eyes. Despite their little hand-holding incident, he'd gone home to Nikki and she'd gone home alone. He'd chosen Nikki over her a long time ago. Millie was mistaken. She couldn't be right about him wanting to come home. But did she want him to come back to her if that was the case? Francesca wondered. After all that had happened between them, did she want her husband back? *Don't be ridiculous, he doesn't want to come back, no matter what Millie says – and even if he does it's too late*, she thought, as she resumed packing her sister's big black case.

The following Sunday afternoon she drove to her parents' house. She couldn't put off telling them any longer. The house would be in the property pages in the next few days. She wanted to tell them about it first.

Maura sniffed as she opened the door to her daughter. 'Well, you're finally able to fit us in.'

'Don't be like that, Mam. Now that I'm working I don't have as much time to call as I used to,' Francesca protested.

'I don't know what you had to go out to work for,' grumbled her mother. 'You told me Mark gave you a generous allowance.'

'He does, but I want to earn my own money. I'm glad I'm working, Mam,' Francesca declared as she followed her mother into the kitchen and kissed her father on top of his bald head.

'There was no need for you to go out there killing yourself, sure there wasn't. Ray?' Maura looked to her husband for support.

Ray Johnson lowered his Sunday paper an inch or two. 'If she's enjoying it, what's the problem?'

'I do enjoy it. I enjoy it very much, as it happens,' Francesca said animatedly. 'For the first time *ever* in my life I'm standing on my own two feet and making all my own decisions and that's a sad confession to make when you look at it. I'm nearly forty-one and up until now I was someone's daughter, someone's mother, or someone's wife—'

'Well, your father and I make *joint* decisions and it suits us very well,' Maura said huffily as she filled the kettle.

'I know, Mother, and that's fine for you. I'm just saying that I like being my own woman.' Francesca paused, searching for words that would not offend her mother. 'Actually I've made other decisions about my future, some of which are going to take effect fairly soon. I've asked Mark for a divorce and we're putting the house up for sale. In fact it's going into the papers this week,' she said baldly. There really was no easy way to say it.

'Lord have mercy on us.' Her mother stood stock still in shock with the teapot in her hand. 'How can you get a divorce? The Church forbids it. Don't talk nonsense, child, I won't have the family name disgraced.' She turned to the counter top and busied herself with teabags.

'Mother, our marriage is over. Mark is with someone else and I want to have a life of my own and a place of my own and if the Church doesn't like that, I'm afraid there's nothing I can do about it. And as for the family name, if that's more important to you than my feelings and needs I'm sorry about that too,' Francesca said evenly.

'Ray, talk sense to her.' Maura was so flustered she

482

put sugar into the teapot. 'What about the boys? What about the relations? She won't be able to receive communion. I can't believe a daughter of mine, a daughter that I did my level best to rear as a good Catholic, would turn her back on God and the Church.'

'Mother! I haven't turned my back on God at all, although I did think that he had turned his back on me at one stage,' Francesca demurred. 'In a funny sort of way I feel that every step I take is being guided in some way. All this happened for a reason. What it is, I don't know but—'

'What kind of talk is that?' snapped Maura. 'It's blasphemy to say that God is guiding you towards divorce. I never heard the like. Ray, *speak* to her.'

Her father lowered his paper and his face took on an uncharacteristically stern look. 'Maura, leave Francesca alone. She's old enough to make her own decisions and have her own relationship with her Creator. And for what it's worth, I think she's right to sell up and get a place of her own and sort out her situation, financially and emotionally. And I'm proud of her the way she's come through all of this. God knows it can't have been easy, and neither of us have any idea or understanding of what it was like, so make the girl a cup of tea and stop nagging her. That's all I have to say on the matter.' He raised his paper again but before he did so he gave Francesca the tiniest wink. Her heart warmed in affection for her quiet, non-judgemental father.

Maura stared at her husband, opened her mouth to say something and shut it again. He was too soft with the girls and always had been, but she never thought that he would go so far as to countenance divorce. There was no point arguing with him once he made up his mind. He might be quiet and reserved and let her do all the talking but he was the most stubborn man she'd ever met and when he made a stand like that, there was no talking to him. Maura's mouth drew down in a thin line. The family name was going to be disgraced by divorce and it didn't matter a whit to either of them, it seemed. Obviously her novena to St Jude, that Francesca and that rip of a husband of hers would get back together again, hadn't worked. So much for being the patron saint of lost causes. She'd give St Rita a try instead, she decided as she carried the teapot to the table.

Francesca said nothing, but her father's support had given her heart. The worst was over now. She'd told her parents. Owen and Jonathan were backing her decision. There was nothing to stop her.

Maura slapped a cup down in front of her with a glare. *Tough, Mother, get over it*, Francesca thought unsympathetically as she reached over and took a chocolate goldgrain. All her mother had been concerned about was the Church, the relations' reactions and the disgrace to the family name. Francesca's feelings hadn't entered the equation. It was ridiculous to feel hurt, she told herself. She knew her mother of old. Why had she expected anything different? At least her father hadn't let her down; his stalwart support of her decision reinforced her determination to move on and make a fresh start.

'Don't let Ma get to you, Francesca. She'd be the same with me. It's not personal, you know. It's her conditioning, she's never learned to think for herself or work things out in her own head. Whatever the Church says goes,' Millie said later that night as they sipped a drink at Dublin Airport.

'I know. I'm not going to let it get to me. I wonder has Mark told Gerald yet?' Francesca said.

'What do you care whether he has or not? Neither of them are your responsibility any more. You just get on with your own stuff.'

'Yes, Millie. If you say so,' Francesca said agreeably.

'I do say so and I mean it,' Millie retorted.

'Yes, Millie.'

'Oh, go on, you! God knows what I'll come back to after a month away. Do you think you'll be able to visit us?'

'I don't think so. Even though August is quiet enough, Ken's taking a week off so I'll be holding the fort. Maybe the last week. I'll let you know.'

'Why on earth you'd want to visit bossy-boots is beyond me,' teased Aidan. 'I'd love you to come though. It would take the pressure off me. She's a terror to live with.'

'You have my sympathies, Aidan. I don't know how you survive it.' Francesca laughed as she got up from their table. 'I'm going to head off and get myself sorted for work tomorrow. Have a *brilliant* time.' She kissed them all and left in a flurry of good-byes, knowing that she'd miss them sorely for the month that they were away.

The following afternoon she'd mistakenly deleted a press release she'd keyed in and was cursing loudly when the buzzer rang.

'Yes?' she said in exasperation.

'InterFlora,' came the muffled response.

'Come on up,' she said, wondering whom the flowers were for. Hardly for Ken, she reasoned. He'd taken a client to lunch and had told her he'd be late back. Just as well if the flowers were for her, he'd tease the daylights out of her. She sat waiting in anticipation as she heard the delivery man's heavy tread up the stairs. The bouquet of yellow roses, blue irises and frothy gypsophila was enormous. Perhaps Ralph had sent them, she speculated with a little thrill of excitement as she signed the docket. The delivery man had barely left the office when she ripped open the envelope that came with the bouquet. Her jaw dropped when she read the note.

Lunch was lovely. It's great to be friends again.
Let's do it again soon,
Love, Mark
xxxx

Mark had sent the bouquet. This was totally unexpected. Francesca sat down at her desk and reread the note, stunned. It was his own handwriting too. He'd actually gone into the florist's and ordered the flowers personally. He hadn't done it over the phone or got his secretary to order them. She was impressed. He really was making the effort to end the bitterness between them. That was good. When he tried, Mark could be very charming and likeable. The flowers had cost a fortune. He wasn't at all mean, she thought fondly.

She wondered how Nikki would feel to know that Mark had had lunch with her and sent her flowers. It would probably drive her berserk. Pity she hadn't some way of letting her know, Francesca thought regretfully as she stuck the bouquet in the kitchen sink until it was time to go home.

She debated whether to phone Mark or e-mail him. Phoning was a little too intimate, she decided. Treating her to lunch and sending a bouquet of flowers was all very well, but she didn't want him to think that all was forgiven. He had a long way to go before she'd feel like that. She sat at her keyboard and e-mailed him.

Thanks for lunch and beautiful flowers. You shouldn't have.

She sent it off and waited for his reply. It came almost immediately.

You're very welcome. I wanted to.

I wanted to, she read over and over again. Why did he want to send her flowers all of a sudden? Why was he being so nice? Was Millie right, had he ulterior motives? What was going on in his head? It couldn't be because he was jealous of Ralph, she thought, confused. And if he were there was no need at all. Ralph, as far as she could see, had blown her out.

Chapter Forty-nine

'Let's go to the Galway races,' Nikki suggested brightly as she and Mark drove home from the office. He had been terribly subdued the past few days. It was disconcerting. She knew what was wrong with him. The estate agent's advert had appeared in the property supplement in full Technicolor. The accompanying piece had given a glowing description of the property. It would draw a lot of viewers. He'd gone very quiet when he'd seen it. She'd studied it intently, the pictures of the rooms especially, and couldn't help comparing it to her stylish but far smaller apartment. No wonder he didn't want to sell the house. He'd never be able to afford another property like it at today's prices.

'Ach, I'm not really in form for the races. It's been a tough couple of days,' Mark said wearily.

'Look, I'll sort out the accommodation—'

'Nikki, you're not going to get anywhere at such short notice, you can forget that. Everywhere will be booked out solidly,' Mark informed her.

'I've friends living in Galway, we don't need to book anywhere. Come on, we'll just stay one night. Let's go for Ladies' Day. I'll drive,' she wheedled.

'Ah, Nikki, I'm not in form,' Mark muttered.

'Please, Mark. Let's do something next weekend. We need to enjoy ourselves now and again. We haven't done anything nice for ages. It's getting to me,' Nikki said quietly.

Mark gave a sigh that came from his toes.

'Look, I know it's not easy seeing your former home for sale in the papers. I know it's not what you wanted. But it's happening. Let's go to Galway for the weekend to take your mind off things. Please don't shut me out, Mark.'

He was silent a long time.

'Mark, isn't there anything I can do to cheer you up?' she asked forlornly.

His expression softened. 'Sorry, Nikki. It's not your fault. I don't mean to be a grump. We'll go to Galway if that's what you want.'

'We'll have fun, I promise,' she assured him, hoping the change would bring him out of himself. He didn't say much for the rest of the evening and he went to bed early. Nikki sat mulling over a report she hadn't been able to concentrate on all day. She couldn't concentrate on it now either, she thought unhappily. She was at her wits' end. Mark had withdrawn into himself and there seemed to be no way of reaching him. Something was bothering him and no matter how hard she tried, she just couldn't get to the bottom of it. The sooner that damn house was sold the better. Maybe then Mark would finally realize that his marriage was well and truly over and that all debts to that nuisance of a wife were paid in full.

Francesca's mobile phone rang. She was swaying on the Dart as it trundled towards Landsdown Road. She rooted in her bag, trying to keep her balance. 'Hello?'

'Hi. Sorry I haven't been in touch. I was in Cork,' Ralph greeted her.

'Oh! Oh, hi, Ralph. I'm on the Dart. Can't hear you very well.'

'Where are you?'

'Coming into Landsdown Road.'

'Get off and come for a drink with me, I can pick you up in five minutes.'

'No, Ralph, I can't. The estate agent is calling by for a spare set of keys I got cut. I have to be at home.'

'Saw the house in the paper. It looks good. How about tomorrow?'

'OK,' she agreed.

'I'll pick you up at the office,' he suggested.

'No, I'm on the move tomorrow. Here and there. Ummm . . . how about the Herbert Park around six-thirty?'

'Excellent. Smashing place,' Ralph agreed. 'See you there.'

Francesca put her phone back in her bag. It was nice to hear his voice again, even if he had left it a while to call her. She'd seriously thought that he wasn't going to get in touch. She'd been disappointed. She was looking forward to seeing him again.

The first viewers were scheduled to call the following evening. It would be far easier if she weren't there. The thought of strangers trooping around her house, sticking their noses in her wardrobes and poking around her bedroom was daunting. She was absolutely dreading it.

A young man from the estate agent's called around seven-fifteen and Francesca gave him the spare keys. The house wasn't hers any longer, she thought a little sadly. Anyone who wanted to view it was at liberty to do so. It was thoroughly unsettling. She went to bed early but didn't sleep very well.

She spent the following afternoon with a printer, sorting out business cards and headed stationery, before calling on a client to deliver a presentation for a proposed PR campaign. It was her first presentation and she was nervous but Ken had insisted that she do it. 'Broaden your experience, Frannie. In case anything ever happens to me it will be good to know that I can rely on you to step into the breach.'

'I thought I was supposed to be doing mainly secretarial work and the odd jaunt here and there,' she pointed out.

'So did I but you've shown such a flair for the job it's a shame to waste you. Stop being a wussie, Francesca, and get in there and slay 'em. Wear that suit you wore when you were meeting hubby, it was cool.' Ken grinned. He was incorrigible. Because of Ken and his job offer, she'd become a different woman, she thought gratefully.

It went better than she'd expected, apart from the first nerve-racking minutes when she was sure that her voice was wobbly. It was a small knitwear company and the management seemed impressed by her presentation. She felt Ken Kennedy PR were in with a very good chance. She was tired but relieved when she walked into the cool, elegant foyer of the Herbert Park Hotel. She was looking forward to her drink with Ralph.

Although she was ten minutes late, he hadn't arrived either so she found a quiet corner and ordered a coffee and sat back and relaxed. She liked this hotel, she mused, looking around the stylish foyer. She liked the open plan design and honey-coloured façade, the attention to detail and the use of natural fabrics. She was proud to bring clients to the hotel, especially foreign guests. Katherine Kronskey had been very taken with the calm, minimalist setting and the marble reception area, enlivened with specially designed calligraphy rugs and a very good collection of modern Irish art.

She sipped her coffee and wondered what was keeping Ralph. He had such nice manners, he must have a good reason for his tardiness. When seven, and then seven-fifteen came with still no sign, she began to worry. She didn't have his number. It was on the Rolodex in the office but a fat lot of good that was to her, she thought crossly, annoyed with herself for not having the foresight to copy it into her own Filofax. She'd give him until half past, she decided, and then she'd go. An hour was long enough to wait for anybody. There was no point in hanging on. He'd hardly arrive that late. She was just about to leave ten minutes later when she saw him ramble across the foyer, gazing around, looking for her. She waved at him and a smile lit his face. As he drew closer and she saw him weaving his way between tables and chairs her jaw dropped in shock as she realized that he was quite drunk. He lurched onto the sofa beside her and before she realized what he was doing he leaned over, muttered, 'Hi sexy,' and kissed her passionately on the mouth, a wet, loose kiss that made her instinctively rub her mouth with the back of her hand when it was over.

'Ralph, stop it.' She pushed him away. 'You're drunk!'

'Just had a couple.' He grinned woozily. 'Oh Francesca, you're a gorgeous woman, let's go back to my place and ride each other ragged,' he leered. Francesca was so shocked she was speechless. He took her silence for assent and stood up, swaying and pulling her to her feet.

'Come on, beautiful, let Ralphie give you a night to remember. I can't wait to suck those magnificent tits. It gives me a stiffie just thinking about it,' he slurred.

Francesca couldn't believe her ears. She was horrified and disgusted. 'You *have* given me a night to remember, Ralph, believe me,' she said icily, pulling her arm free. With as much dignity as she could manage she crossed the foyer. He made to follow, protesting loudly, but tripped over the low coffee table. Her last sight was of him sprawled on the floor cursing as he struggled to get up. Once out of the hotel, she took to her heels and ran, afraid he would catch up with her. Running in a straight pencil skirt wasn't easy but she made it to the car and saw with relief that he wasn't following her. It was only when she was in the car driving towards the East Link turn-off that her breathing began to return to normal and her heart stopped racing.

'God Almighty!' she muttered. 'Thanks a million for that. Just what I needed.' She felt sick. It was impossible to believe that the suave, charming, mannerly man who had taken her out to dinner and been so kind to her after her row with Mark was the same man as the drunken, lewd, foul-mouthed boor she'd left sprawled on the floor in the foyer of the Herbert Park Hotel. Wait until Millie heard about 'Ravishing Ralph'. She'd phone her the minute she got home, she thought shakily. She was throwing her coins into the basket at the East Link when she suddenly remembered that Millie was on holiday in France. Inexplicably, Francesca burst into tears. Trust her to pick a dipso. She should have seen the warning signs. Mark would revel in it if he ever found out. Well, he never would find out from her, Francesca vowed as she wiped her eyes and blew her nose, trying to steer with one hand and coming perilously close to crashing into the roundabout at the East Wall Road.

She slept badly, unable to blot out the memory of his horrible remarks, and the following day at work she tensed whenever the phone rang in case it was Ralph. She didn't want to hear from him or see him ever again. Ken could deal with him from now on when business required it. But he didn't ring that day, nor the following, and by the weekend she decided that he'd be far too embarrassed ever to contact her again. That suited her fine. Maybe Mark wasn't so bad after all, she thought ruefully. He'd never dream of treating her so disrespectfully.

No, he just went off with another woman, her hateful little inner voice reminded her.

She was sitting at the breakfast counter the following Sunday morning flicking through the papers, drinking coffee and eating toast, when a photo in the social columns caught her eye. Her heart gave a lurch and her stomach twisted into a knot when she recognized Mark and Nikki smiling out at her. They were at the Galway races and they looked as though they were having a ball.

'Well, fuck you, Mark,' she swore. 'How could you bring her there? That was our place.' Millie was crazy to think that Mark wanted to get back with her. Right in front of her nose was the living proof that she was wrong.

She jumped off the stool and strode into the lounge, grabbed the yellow roses and irises out of the two large vases on either side of the fireplace and hurried into the kitchen and dumped them into the bin, pricking herself on the thorns as she did so.

'You can stick these up your arse, Mark Kirwan! Or better still, up your tart's!' she yelled. The phone rang. She flounced over to answer it.

'Hello,' she said sharply.

'Francesca, it's me,' a contrite voice said. 'I'm really terribly, terribly sorr—'

'Fuck off, Ralph!' Francesca roared, slamming down the phone.

Chapter Fifty

Ralph hung up the phone gingerly and rubbed his aching temples. There was no point in calling Francesca back right now. Experience had taught him never to try and explain anything to an angry woman, and she sounded rip-roaring angry, he conceded mournfully.

He couldn't remember a damn thing except arranging to meet her someplace. Where, he couldn't remember either, because shortly after he'd made the arrangement he'd bumped into an old mate and they'd gone on the tear. Either he'd stood her up or he'd met her sozzled. He dearly hoped it was the former. He wouldn't like a woman he so admired to see him out of control. His wife had told him often enough that he was a nasty drunk with a mean and vicious tongue. He could have done or said anything. He groaned. It was so frustrating not being able to remember.

'God! God! God!' He put his head in his hands. 'Why am I like this? I don't want to be like this. Why

496

don't you help me?' he demanded, raising his eyes to heaven. There was no answer. There never was. Ralph's head sank to his chest and he cried like a baby.

'Oh look, darling. Our photo's in the paper,' Nikki said gleefully as she folded the newspaper and passed it over to Mark. They'd arrived home from Galway an hour ago and were sitting relaxing, after the journey.

Oh shit! he thought. He hoped Francesca didn't see that. He hadn't said anything to her about going to the races. It was something they'd always done together and looking at the picture in front of him, of him and Nikki smiling happily at the camera, he knew if she saw it, she'd feel he was rubbing her nose in it.

'Very nice,' he murmured, handing back the paper. He should never have gone to the damn races. He might have been smiling in the photograph but that had been a façade. He'd only gone to please Nikki because he was feeling as guilty as hell about the way he was treating her.

If, by a miracle, Francesca took him back, he'd be dumping Nikki in the not-too-distant future and she had no idea what was going on in his head. He felt like a heel! He *was* a heel, he acknowledged uncomfortably. He'd never realized that he was capable of such duplicity. If he had any guts he'd finish with Nikki whether Francesca took him back or not. He was only using the girl. But he couldn't take that step, he thought miserably. If Francesca turned him down, he didn't want to be alone.

She's far braver than you are! The unwelcome thought intruded. Francesca had been alone for the past eight months – well, until gigolo journo arrived on the scene, he amended. She'd gone and got herself a job and made a new life for herself, and here he was clinging like a limpet to a woman he no longer felt the same about. He was pathetic, he admitted as he flicked through the *Sunday Business Post*. He couldn't concentrate. He stood up and went over to the french door and stared out of the window. The weather had turned bad again and rain battered against the windowpanes.

He'd want to make his move soon, he decided. The house was on the market. Offers would be coming in. Better to nip it all in the bud before things went too far. He'd call Francesca from work first thing in the morning and arrange a visit. What the outcome would be was anyone's guess; all he could do was hope. He stared out at the rain hopping off the balcony wishing he didn't have to hurt Nikki.

Nikki studied Mark surreptitiously as he stood with his back to her staring out of the balcony doors. The photo hadn't gone down well, she thought moodily. He was probably afraid his precious Francesca would see it and be offended. She'd been delighted to have it taken. Everyone who saw it would see that they truly were a couple. Mark had met many of his friends and acquaintances at the races and introduced her to them as his partner. It had all happened the way she wanted it to but it didn't make her feel any better.

He hadn't enjoyed the races, not that anyone who

didn't know him very well would have guessed it. He'd put on a very good front. But he was on auto-pilot, being charming to her friends, greeting his own, chatting, laughing, just as if he were enjoying himself. He did it all the time at work. She'd seen him work a room full of strangers superbly well and very few people actually realized that they weren't seeing the real Mark at all. Mark was an extremely deep, reserved man, she'd seen it straight away when she'd first met him. His reserve had challenged her. She'd been determined to get behind the façade. She wasn't having much luck at the moment. He might have fooled everyone else in Galway but not her. She knew him better than anyone, she assured herself. They might as well have gone to the moon for all the good the day at the races had done them. She was still back at square one and where to go from here was anybody's guess.

Christmas! she told herself for the umpteenth time. *Christmas is all I'll give it.* But even to her own ears, the threat was beginning to sound extremely hollow. She picked up one of the Sunday supplements and flicked through it, but she couldn't concentrate either.

'Coffee?' she asked with pretended cheerfulness. Mark was so deep in thought he never heard her. Disheartened beyond belief, Nikki wandered into the kitchen and made herself a cup of coffee. She might as well be living on her own than living with him for all the company he was at the moment, she mused sadly. And for the thousandth time she asked herself where it had all gone wrong.

* * *

Francesca had taken Trixie to the Bull Island for a walk. Several viewers were calling that afternoon and she didn't want to be in the house. They'd be gone by three-thirty, the estate agent assured her. The rain lashed down on the big golf umbrella she was holding, but she didn't mind. Sometimes she enjoyed walking in the rain. The sea surged and ebbed, roaring up against the shore. She could feel the taste of salt from the spray.

So Ralph had phoned to apologize. Big deal, she thought sourly. He could get lost. She had enough complications in her life without getting involved with a separated drunkard. She wasn't that desperate for a man. In fact, after seeing Mark's mug in the papers this morning with his arm proprietorially around that woman, Francesca decided that she was entirely better off without the species.

She walked briskly enjoying Trixie's antics. She was such a lovable little dog, she thought fondly. Buying an apartment would be out of the question, or even one of those outrageously priced egg boxes they called town houses. She'd had a look at a few of them and not been impressed. The mews had been lovely but the courtyard had been very small. Poor old Trixie would have been like a prisoner in it. Maybe it was as well that it had fallen through on her. Next weekend she would start serious house-hunting, she promised herself. She wondered if any of today's viewers would put in an offer, or if they were just coming to look out of curiosity. She knew there were people who spent weekends looking at houses for sale who had no intention whatsoever of buying.

She glanced at her watch. Three-twenty. She could start making tracks for home soon. The fire was lit in the lounge; she'd have a nice soak in the bath and then go downstairs and read the rest of the papers in front of the fire. She'd order an Indian or Chinese for dinner; she didn't feel like cooking.

The house was silent and empty when she got home. The estate agent had been as good as his word. She bathed and groomed Trixie and then poured herself a beer and filled her bath. The hot scented water infused heat into her body. It had been cold on the Bull Island. She lay in the bath reading a magazine and sipping her beer and felt completely relaxed. One of the nice things about living on her own was the freedom to do exactly as she pleased. Her bath refreshed her and after she'd dried her hair, she pulled on a tracksuit, settled down in front of the fire and immersed herself in the papers. The doorbell rang around five. If it was a potential buyer they could make an appointment for a viewing with the estate agent, she thought firmly. She wasn't inviting strangers into her house. She opened the door ready to politely tell the caller to go.

'Good evening, Francesca. I hope I'm not intruding. I wish to speak to you on a private matter,' her father-in-law said officiously as he stepped past her into the house.

'Hello, Gerald, how are you?' Francesca said half-heartedly as she closed the door behind him. *He* was the last thing she needed.

'Oh, well now, Francesca, I'm sure you're only asking out of politeness. You certainly made no effort to keep in touch once your marriage broke up,' Gerald accused bluntly, his little beady eyes cold and unfriendly.

'What can I do for you, Gerald?' Francesca said coolly, determined not to let him rile her.

'I've come here to tell you that you're making a big mistake putting this house up for sale. One you'll rue at the end of the day. That son of mine came to me asking if I could store his possessions in my spare bedroom and while I don't mind doing it for him, I feel strongly that someone should talk sense to the pair of you. I know Mark doesn't want to sell. It's all your doing. You're a fool if you sell this damn fine house,' Gerald blustered.

'Thank you for your input, Gerald, but basically it's none of your business. Your son left me for another woman and I had to pick up the pieces of my life and get on with things. And that's exactly what I did and will continue to do without any interference from you. Thank you for calling. Goodbye now.' She opened the door pointedly.

'Wait a minute, miss.' Gerald was affronted. 'You have a Wedgwood china set here belonging to my dear departed wife. If you're intent on selling up I want to have it back. I don't want Mark giving it to that other woman and I don't want you giving it to anyone either.'

'Mrs Kirwan gave us that china as a wedding gift, Gerald. You'd better see what Mark has to say about the matter. If he's agreeable I'll be perfectly happy to return it to you. Rest assured,' she said coldly. What a horrible little man he was. Thank God she was well rid of him. She opened the door even wider for him to leave.

'Well! Well, upon my word! The very least you could do is offer me a cup of tea,' Gerald huffed.

'Sorry! I'm busy. Good evening, Gerald. I'll get Mark to call you about the china,' Francesca said dismissively. Her father-in-law marched down the steps with bad grace but Francesca didn't wait for any parting shot, she closed the door firmly behind him.

'Bloody old rip,' she muttered. The nerve of him, calling on her unannounced looking for his china back and a cup of tea into the bargain! In spite of herself she had to laugh at his cheek. She didn't miss having him around constantly, that was for sure.

'You did what?' Mark asked incredulously.

'I went around and gave your wife some damn good advice and told her she was a damn fool to put that house up for sale. She was bloody rude to me,' Gerald snorted. 'Never offered me a cup of tea, a sherry or nothing. Extremely inhospitable. And I was always very good to her—'

'I don't believe I'm hearing this. You had no business doing such a thing. She'll think I was behind it. For God's sake, Dad, what did you want to go interfering for?'

'I wasn't interfering, Mark. I was giving the woman some fatherly advice. But she's pig-headed and stubborn. And what's more I told her I wanted the Wedgwood china your mother gave you back. That's an heirloom. I'm not letting it out of this family,' Gerald declared.

'My God!' muttered Mark. 'What are you going to do with it? Bury it in the coffin with you? I'm going. I need to phone Francesca and explain that this had nothing to do with me. Goodbye.' He slammed down the phone in a temper. His father had gone too far. Francesca was probably like a demon. Just when they'd got back on speaking terms, too. Trust his father to interfere.

He flicked through his diary and found her work number. She answered the phone almost immediately.

'Hi, it's me,' he said warily.

'Oh! Hello, Mark.' Was she frosty or just being extremely polite? He couldn't tell. He wondered if she had seen the picture of him and Nikki at the Galway races.

'Ah . . . um . . . I believe my father called over to see you last night,' he said delicately. 'I'm really terribly sorry, Francesca. I had no idea that he was going to pull a stunt like that.'

To his immense relief he heard his wife laugh. 'That's Gerald for you. What do you want to do with the Wedgwood?'

'I want you to have it,' Mark said decisively.

'No, Mark. Let your father have it. There's no point in upsetting him at this stage of his life,' Francesca replied.

'Well, if you're sure?'

'I am. The less clutter I have the better, when I get my own place.'

'Look, how about if I come over some evening and we sort out our bits and pieces,' he suggested. She was still clearly intent on moving. He *had* to persuade her to stay. It was best to play along though, for the time being.

'OK,' she agreed.

'What night suits you?' Mark asked. 'What time?'

'Wednesday or Thursday. Around seven?'

'Wednesday,' he said. 'I'm lucky this week, I've no business trips.'

'Fine,' Francesca said lightly. 'See you then.'

She was so self-possessed it was disturbing. She seemed to have her mind very firmly made up, he thought almost in panic.

'Ah . . . would you like to have dinner or anything?' he invited.

'No, Mark. I'll have something at lunchtime.'

'Oh, OK then,' he said, disappointed. 'See you on Wednesday.'

Chapter Fifty-one

'I'll be late home from work tonight, so we'll take our own cars,' Mark said offhandedly as he tied a knot in his tie and ran a brush through his hair.

'Oh! Where are you off to?' Nikki asked as she applied her eye shadow with practised ease.

'Ah ... just a golf-club meeting.' Mark flicked through his briefcase to make sure he had everything he needed for his day's work. 'Bye, hon.' He leaned down and gave her a peck on the cheek. And then he was gone.

Nikki put down her mascara and rested her chin on her hands. He'd been like a cat on a hot tin roof last night and this morning he'd spent at least ten minutes selecting the tie and shirt he was going to wear. He'd had his hair cut the previous day too, although it had been less than three weeks since he'd last visited the barber's.

Something wasn't right. That was the first time in all the months she'd known him that he'd ever gone to a golf-club meeting that she knew of. He was lying to her. Some instinct told her and she couldn't ignore it.

It niggled at her all day. What was he doing tonight that he didn't want her to know about? Who was he seeing? She began to get paranoid. Maybe he'd met someone else. Maybe he'd started an affair. That could be the reason for his moody behaviour these past few weeks. But who was it? Surely she'd know if it were someone at work. He was always pretty chatty to Sandra Daly in Treasury. And she was always pretty chatty to him. Nikki frowned.

'Is Sandra Daly in Treasury involved with anyone?' she asked Elaine when her secretary handed her some internal post. Elaine knew everyone's business. She was the world's greatest gossip.

Elaine's eyes widened at this uncharacteristic enquiry. Nikki pretended not to notice as she flicked through the mail.

'I don't know. I could find out,' her secretary replied helpfully.

'Oh, thanks,' Nikki murmured. 'A guy I know asked me to find out,' she fibbed.

'*Really?*' Elaine was thrilled with this bit of info. 'Who? Does he fancy her?'

'You don't know him,' Nikki said curtly, mentally kicking herself. Now it would be all over the office that a friend of hers was interested in Sandra. And if it got to Sandra's ears she could very well want to know who was asking about her. That would be extremely awkward. Nikki looked up coldly at Elaine. 'That's all, Elaine, thank you,' she said politely.

Snooty bitch, find out for yourself, Elaine fumed as

she walked into her own office. What a curious thing to ask though. As long as she'd worked with Nikki Langan, her boss had never asked her anything that didn't involve the job in hand. She wasn't into office gossip in the slightest. She'd caused enough of it though with her liaison with Mark Kirwan, Elaine thought smugly as she sat at her computer and began to type a memo for London.

Nikki sat staring into space. She was in turmoil. She had to go to London the following morning and she wasn't at all prepared. It was so difficult to concentrate when all this was going on. She'd never had trouble focusing on her work before. This was disastrous. She picked up the file that had lain untouched on her desk. It was important she was up to speed on all the information it contained.

'Concentrate!' she muttered. 'Concentrate!'

'Ken, I need to be home before the rush hour. Would you mind if I left around four-thirty?' Francesca asked her boss.

'Four-thirty *is* the rush,' Ken said sagely. 'Leave at four, things are slackening off anyway. August is always quiet enough. Go at three if you want, even.'

'Thanks, you're a pet. Maybe half-three.' Francesca smiled at him. She wanted to be showered and changed and totally in control and not rushing around like a blue-arsed fly when Mark came. He'd sounded a tad harassed on Monday. He'd clearly been mortified by his father's visit. He wasn't putting it on. She would have liked to have seen the look on his face when he found out about it. Gerald was such an interfering old busy-body. No wonder his daughter would have nothing to do with him. What her sister-in-law's relationship with Mark was now, Francesca had no idea. Nor did she really care. Letting go of Gerald and his attendant baggage had been one of the pluses of her marriage break-up.

The day flew. She was glad she knew Mark was coming. It was so much better than having him arrive unannounced. It was strange to be in a dither because her husband was coming to visit, she reflected as she drove home along the Dublin Road. It would be good to sort out who was having what. Fortunately their reading and music tastes were completely different so there'd be no rows about books and CDs.

There were a couple of paintings that she was especially fond of, particularly the *Herbaceous Border* by Angie Grimes. Mark liked it too. She'd like to keep it if he was agreeable, and also the Catherine MacLiam silk painting, *Omani Tribesmen*. She'd like to keep some of the sparkling crystal pieces they'd collected over the years. Thinking in those terms made it all seem very final, but in the long run these things had to be sorted, she assured herself as doubts began to set in.

Thanks to the mega clean-out she'd had, knowing that her house was going to be open to the public, the house was ship-shape. Her cleaner had been in that morning and the furniture shone and mirrors gleamed. All Francesca had to do was shower and change and decide what to wear.

'This is ridiculous,' she murmured as she stood flicking through the clothes in her wardrobe. She didn't want Mark to think that she was dressing up especially for him. Why on earth would she want to give him that impression? The sunny weather had returned after the wet, windy weather of the weekend; she'd slip into a sundress and sit out in the garden and give the impression of being oh so cool, she decided.

She showered, dried her hair and slipped the mint-green floral dress over her head. She'd bought it on holiday in Portugal. Its loose, easy lines flowed over her figure in a most flattering style. The spaghetti straps and low neckline showed off her tan. It was different to the more formal attire that she usually wore, but she was a different woman now, much more relaxed, and she was dressing to please herself. She'd just made herself a cup of tea when her mobile rang. She half expected it to be Mark cancelling. She was surprised at her feelings of disappointment. Fishing the phone out of her bag, she noted it was an unfamiliar number.

'Hello?'

'Mrs Kirwan, Stephen Boyle, we spoke about a mews in Monkstown that you were interested in a while back. A three-bedroom cottage in the same area has come on the market. Now, it needs some renovation but I think you might like it. I could send you out the details if you like.'

'Don't bother posting them, I can call in tomorrow and collect them. And thanks very much for phoning me,' Francesca said warmly.

'You're welcome, Mrs Kirwan. As I say I think it might suit your requirements and there's a very pretty garden at the back which is completely private.'

'Excellent,' Francesca said. 'See you tomorrow.'

How interesting to get Stephen Boyle's phone call just then. Perhaps because she was letting go of her old house, the door was opening for the new one to come in. She had the strangest feeling about the cottage, even though she hadn't seen it. Maybe this cottage was meant for her.

Mark put down the bottle of L'Air du Temps reluctantly. It was one of Francesca's favourite perfumes but he wasn't sure how she'd react if he bought it for her. Perfume was an intimate gift. They were no longer exactly what you'd call intimate. He wanted to bring her a present but he couldn't quite decide what. He'd bought a spray of blue irises and a bottle of Puligny Montrachet but he wanted some other little gift. Inspiration struck. She loved Leonidas handmade chocolates. He headed for the Royal Hibernian Way and spent five minutes choosing a selection of the rich, creamy chocolates and pralines. It was so ironic, he mused. He was on his lunch break buying gifts to woo his wife with, when once he'd spent lunchtimes buying gifts for Nikki. Life was very strange. It was almost as if it had come full circle.

He was as nervous as a schoolboy as he turned left into the driveway of the house. The sight of the 'For Sale' sign was like a physical blow to the solar plexus. This couldn't happen, he told himself as he looked at the big redbrick detached house with the ivy climbing up to the eaves and the sun glinting off the long Victorian windows. How could Francesca want to leave this place willingly? he asked himself as he studied the shrub-lined garden, hidden from the road with high evergreen hedges. She'd had them trimmed. They looked well. The whole place looked impressive, he reflected as he went to ring the door-bell. They'd have a buyer before long if she persisted with the idea of selling. He straightened his tie and cleared his throat. He could hear Trixie barking excitedly. He missed the little mutt, he thought fondly.

Francesca opened the door and his heart leaped. She looked lovely, he thought, shocked. She was wearing a filmy sundress and she was barefoot. He'd thought that she would have been all dressed up with the war paint on. She had a great colour. Her skin took the sun easily and she looked golden and healthy. A far cry from the dumpy, pale, pasty-faced woman of six months ago.

'Hi, Francesca, how are you? Just a little some-thing,' he said awkwardly, handing her the floral gift carrier bag and the spray of irises.

'Mark, what did you do that for? There was no need,' Francesca chided as she stepped back to let him in.

'I wanted to,' he said, closing the door behind him. The scent of fragrant pot-pourri and polish wafted under his nose. 'The house smells nice,' he said, for something to say. He felt remarkably ill at ease.

'Oh, well, they do say you should have the smell of bread baking or home cooking when you're showing a house,' Francesca said cheerfully as she led the way into the kitchen. 'But polish and pot-pourri will have to do because I don't have time to bake bread any more.'

'Are you busy these days?' he asked politely, following her into the bright, airy kitchen.

'Ah, it's not so bad this week. Things quieten down in August. Oh Mark! Leonidas!' she exclaimed with pleasure. 'They're my favourite.'

'I know.' He smiled at her. She smiled back.

'Would you like to sit out on the deck for a little while? It's a lovely evening,' she suggested impulsively. 'I've a bottle of wine chilling in the fridge. It's not as posh as the Montrachet though.'

'I'd love that, Francesca. I miss the garden.'

'It's a bit past its best, unfortunately. Everything always looks a bit worn out by the time August comes,' Francesca said as she uncorked the Chardonnay and poured the chilled wine into two glasses. 'Are you hungry? I could rustle up an omelette or something.' Francesca for some reason found herself reverting back to housewife mode.

'No, I'm fine, thanks. This is grand.' They strolled out to the deck. Francesca sat down while Mark wandered around the garden looking at favourite shrubs and flowers. Birdsong filled the air. It was peaceful. He knew he wanted to come home.

'Won't you miss this?' he asked hesitantly, rejoining Francesca on the deck.

'I suppose I will. But it's all too big for me to look after. And there're too many memories. I need a fresh start. Why don't you buy me out, Mark, if you have such strong feelings about the place?' Her grey eyes were wide and questioning.

'I wouldn't pay that amount of money for it, Francesca. It would be financial stupidity and I don't suppose you'd accept any less than what it's going for, if I was to continue paying you an allowance?' he suggested hopefully. Even if he could come back home and she moved out, he could woo her back, he thought excitedly.

Francesca shook her head. 'I don't want to be tied to your financial apron strings. I want to be free, Mark. I want to be my own boss.'

'It's not that bad, surely? I haven't made you feel under an obligation, have I?' he asked, hurt.

'Not really, no, Mark. You're a kind man. But it's not the way I want it to be. Not any more. A house has come up, a little cottage, and I'm going to look at it and if I like it, I'm buying it. So come on, let's go and sort out what's to be sorted,' she said briskly, standing up and holding out her hand to pull him up.

He took her hand. 'If that's what you want, Francesca,' he said, disappointed, as he followed her back into the house. 'So where do we start?' he asked as they stood in the kitchen.

'Here, I suppose,' Francesca said uncertainly. 'There's all the kitchenware and crystal. The Le Creuset pots, the—'

'For God's sake, Francesca, what on earth would I be doing with the pots and pans or any of this stuff?' Mark asked tetchily.

'Well, when you get a place of your own you'll need to equip it,' Francesca pointed out.

'No, you take what you want.'

'Come into the lounge and let's talk about the paintings and all the other bits and pieces we've managed to accumulate,' Francesca said easily.

'Let's have another glass of wine,' Mark suggested.

'OK, and maybe a couple of chocolates to go with it,' Francesca invited.

'I will if you will.' Mark laughed. He'd play along with dividing up their possessions but he was determined they were going to get back together again. This was his last chance and he wasn't going to blow it!

Chapter Fifty-two

Nikki drummed her fingers on the steering wheel. The traffic was chaotic, Ballsbridge was chock-a-block. She was on her way home from work and all she could think about was Mark and wonder if he was lying to her. She inched her way past the AIB headquarters and on impulse turned left and headed towards Sandymount. She was crazy, she knew, but she had to find out if Mark was lying to her. The only trouble was, Mark hadn't said what time the meeting was at. She could phone him and ask him if he was eating in town and suggest joining him. Damn! She should have thought of it while they were both at work. The traffic in Sandymount was as bad and she concentrated on negotiating the right turn for the East Link, before tapping in his number.

'*The person you are calling may be out of range or have their phone switched off. Please try later,*' was the infuriating response. Nikki's mouth drew down as anger ignited. Why had he switched his phone off? Why did he not want to be contactable? It was only six in the evening. His bloody meeting couldn't have started yet. She was almost screaming in frustration as the traffic crawled along Sean Moore Road towards the toll bridge. If any of her friends or colleagues knew what she was up to they'd say she'd really lost it, she acknowledged grimly as she gave the finger to a Ray-banned yuppie who tried to cut her up on the outside lane at the roundabout. 'Don't mess with me, buster,' she growled, not giving an inch.

She flung her coins into the basket and waited impatiently for the barriers to go up. A huge cruise liner was berthed up close to the bridge on the North Wall. The sun slanted onto the balconied staterooms. She could hear music coming from the decks. How she wished she was on it, instead of seedily following her lying lover. Tears smarted in her eyes. This was the worst thing that had ever happened to her. She had never before endured such misery. And all because of love. She drove past the ship and rounded the Point. A long line of traffic at a standstill ahead of her, right up to the Port entrance, made her heart sink. This was the craziest thing she had ever done but she wouldn't rest until she found out one way or another if Mark had been lying to her.

'I know you like them. I like them too,' groaned Francesca as they studied the paintings they both wanted. It was some time later. The Chardonnay was demolished and they'd started on the Montrachet. She was feeling a bit giddy. There was an air of unreality about the evening that made her feel reckless. 'I love the colouring and simplicity of Catherine MacLiam's painting. Look at the faces, hardly defined, yet you get such an impression of men who are at one with their environment. And look at the texture of the door behind them. She's a genius,' she observed, studying the painting that hung at the top of the stairs.

'I know. We should have bought more of hers,' Mark said ruefully. 'Let's have a look at the Angie Grimes one again. Remember we bought it to cheer ourselves up when Jonathan went away?'

'Yeah,' she said sadly. 'We were in bits.'

'Well, at least he's happy and I'm glad Owen's out there with him. It's good for them to be together.' He walked into the bedroom again and she followed him and stood beside him to examine the exquisitely detailed painting.

'I love the perspective and the texture and colour. Look at those daisies and the lupins. The work that went into them. I love that border,' Mark said admiringly.

'I know,' agreed Francesca as she looked at the painting afresh. 'It's the Herbaceous Border in the Botanic Gardens. Let's put the names in a hat and if you get that one I suppose I could always go to the Bots and take a photograph of it and frame it.' She giggled.

'Francesca, are you pissed?' Mark turned to look at her with a twinkle in his eye.

'I think I'm heading that way.' She smiled at him. One strap had fallen off her shoulder and she eased it back up. His eyes followed the movement of her fingers. He reached out and covered her hand with his thumb resting in the soft hollow of her breasts.

'I've missed you,' he murmured. They stared at each other, the air crackling with tension.

He took her face between his hands and slowly inclined his head until his mouth was inches from hers. 'I want to kiss you,' he said.

Francesca felt a surge of triumph. *Yes!* she thought. *I can have him if I want him. He's going to betray her like he betrayed me.*

She felt Mark's mouth on hers. Lightly at first, tender, moist, loving. His tongue explored the silky sweetness of her mouth, gently, skilfully, until she returned his kiss, opening to him until he kissed her hungrily and with passion, his hands sliding the straps of her dress off her shoulders, cupping her full hard breasts, his thumbs caressing her hardened nipples until she groaned with pleasure.

She drew away breathlessly. 'Are you sure about this?'

'Yes, I'm sure,' he muttered hoarsely, his eyes glittering into hers, his fingers gripping her arms.

'What about Nikki?' She had to say it. She had to hear him deny the bitch to her.

'It's you I want,' Mark said, pulling her back to him, thrusting against her, his hands moulding her to his body. They fell onto the bed, kissing wildly, passionately, pulling the clothes off each other.

'Oh Francesca, Francesca,' he whispered her name, frantic for her. His hands parted her thighs and he eased himself into her and felt her quiver beneath him, her breath coming in a long whispery sigh. *Thank God*, he thought with relief. *She wants me back. I'm home.*

* * *

Nikki sat for an hour and a half parked outside the clubhouse, her heart leaping in her chest every time a car drove in. There was no sign of Mark's BMW when she got there and she almost cried to think that the man she'd loved and respected had told her a downright lie. Finally, at her wits' end, she got out of the car and approached a golfer heading for the entrance.

'Excuse me, what time is the meeting at?' she asked politely.

'I don't think there's a meeting tonight. We had one last week, as a matter of fact. But I can double-check for you if you like,' the ruddy-faced man offered good naturedly.

'No, don't bother. My mistake,' Nikki said politely. He was only telling her what she knew all along. 'Thanks anyway.'

She walked back to the car. What did she do now? Where did she go? She drove blindly, unthinkingly, and found herself heading for Howth. She could go and throw herself off the end of the pier, she thought miserably. The last time she'd been on this road had been to confront that frump of a wife of his. The biggest mistake she'd ever made. He'd turned on her for that and they'd never really got back on track again.

A sickening thought occurred to her. He couldn't be. It was unthinkable. She accelerated and drove with mounting fear and anger until she came to the road that led to Francesca's house.

Did she really want to put herself through this? Nikki slowed down and stopped the car. She rubbed her eyes wearily. Whatever she did, she couldn't win.

If he was there, she'd die a thousand deaths. If he wasn't she'd be no wiser as to where he was and she'd still be miserable. She started the ignition and swallowed hard. The sun was setting. The nights were definitely starting to get shorter, she thought a little wildly. She indicated left and drove along slowly. Luxury houses well hidden from view lined the road. It was very rural with all the trees and hedges, she thought, trying to stave off her fear.

The large 'For Sale' sign signposted Francesca's house. It was because of her Francesca had put the house up for sale and it was because of that decision she was in danger of losing Mark. Nikki shook her head at the irony of it. The wrought-iron gates were open.

You can stop now, before it's too late, she told herself. The view of the driveway was still obstructed by the big oak tree at the end of the drive. Nikki eased her foot off the pedal.

'Coward!' she muttered and pressed down again. She turned to look in as she drove past and felt a sharp, stabbing pain of grief as she saw Mark's BMW side by side with his wife's car.

Chapter Fifty-three

'Oh Francesca, that was good!' Mark leaned on one elbow and looked down at his wife.

'At our age,' she giggled.

'What do you mean? We're in our prime!'

'Life begins at forty,' she quipped.

Mark lay down beside her and put his arm around her. 'I've been such a fool. I should have come home a long time ago and put us out of our misery. I was an idiot,' he murmured in her ear. 'Thank God we're together again, my love. The boys will be delighted and now we don't have to put the names of the paintings in a hat, we can share them for the rest of our lives.'

Francesca twisted around to face him. 'Wait a minute, Mark. What are you talking about?' she asked.

'Well . . . we're back together again, aren't we?' He looked perplexed.

'No, Mark, we're not!' Francesca said emphatically, sitting up.

'But, Francesca, we just made love. It was so good. We should be together.' Mark felt a niggle of unease.

'Mark, we just had sex.' Francesca slid out of bed and wrapped a robe around her.

'What!' Mark shot up in bed, aghast. 'You can't mean that.'

'Mean what? That we had sex? Grow up now, Mark. A passionate tumble in bed does not mean that all the past can be swept behind us and we go on to live happily ever after.'

'Why not? It's what I want!' he said truculently.

'It's always about what you want, Mark. Well, I'm sorry, but it's not what I want.' Francesca ran a comb through her hair and turned to face her husband. 'I was tempted,' she continued. 'But only for a second or two. You see, I like my life now, Mark. I'm still very fond of you—'

'*Fond!*' Mark spat the word. 'Fond? What the hell does that mean? That's the most wishy-washy word I ever heard. *Fond.* I don't want *fond*, I want you to love me the way you used to,' he said indignantly.

She looked at him sitting up in bed, his hair boyishly tousled, pouting with indignation, and had to suppress the urge to laugh. Her husband could be such a child sometimes. Did he really think it was all that easy? Did he think a bottle of expensive wine, handmade chocolates and a ten-minute roll in the hay was all it took? Was he truly that naïve? She remembered Millie's words about him wanting her back. They didn't seem so cynical now, she thought wryly. Millie had seen it all.

'Listen to yourself, Mark. It's all about what you

want. "*I* want to come back. *I* want you to love me the way you used to—" '

'I can't believe you're like this after what we just did, Francesca. Didn't it mean anything?' he demanded.

'Sure, Mark. It was good and I enjoyed it for what it was,' she explained patiently. 'But it doesn't change our situation—'

'Well, I think you're wrong. If you wanted to we could work it out,' he said sullenly.

'I care about you, Mark. You're the father of my sons and we had some very happy times but it's all different now. Everything's changed. *I've* changed.'

'You can say that again.' Her husband scowled. 'Is it because of that Ralph guy?'

'No, Mark, it isn't, it's got nothing to do with him. It's about me. Now, do you want to have a shower before you go? It might be an idea,' she said briskly. 'Call a taxi. You can't drive after the amount we drank. You can pick the car up tomorrow.'

'So you're throwing me out?' he said sulkily.

'Yes, love, I've a long day ahead of me tomorrow,' Francesca said cheerfully. 'You use the bathroom and I'll use the en suite.' Mark's face was a study as she walked into the en suite. He couldn't believe his ears.

Tough, she thought viciously. He'd never take her for granted again. His attitude was almost insulting. She stood under the hot spray and washed herself from head to toe. She felt invigorated. She'd been honest when she'd told him she was tempted to take him back but it had only lasted a minute or two and it was partly as a result of the wine she'd drunk. She did care for him, but in the eight months they'd been apart, she'd looked on their relationship with a fresh perspective and found it sadly wanting. It would always be about him. That was the way he was and he wasn't going to change at this stage of his life. That was his problem. She'd changed and that was his problem too. She grinned under the spray. She'd have to have breakfast, dinner and tea with Millie with all the news she had to tell her: Ralph's uncouth behaviour that had ended the relationship before it had started; and Mark's mistake in taking her for a doormat that he could wipe his size tens on.

She slathered body lotion onto her limbs, glad that the scent of it had removed all trace of Mark's musky smell. The sex had been good, but not anything spectacular. It had all happened too quickly, she could do as well herself, she mused as she massaged the lotion into her thighs. And it had proved to her that his fidelity to Nikki was nothing to be counted on. That had given her an enormous sense of satisfaction. She wished the superior bitch who'd stood in her house and lectured her had been here to see her precious Mark cast their relationship to the winds. If this, and the disaster with Ralph, had taught her anything, it was that she didn't need a man in her life. She was perfectly capable of existing happily enough without one. Francesca paused. 'How liberating,' she murmured. 'How very very liberating.'

She heard Mark showering as she walked downstairs. She put the kettle on; she was dying for a cup of tea. He joined her five minutes later. She was ironing a blouse for work.

'The taxi should be here soon,' he said awkwardly. He wouldn't look at her.

'Would you like a cup of tea?' she said easily. 'I made a pot.'

'No thanks.'

'I'll let you know what's going on about the sale. I suppose there's no need for you to take your stuff until there's a sale agreed. No point in cluttering up Gerald's spare room until you have to.' She ironed the sleeves expertly, ignoring the waves of resentment that were emanating from him. 'We've decided on everything except the two paintings. Which one would you like?' She felt she could afford to be magnanimous.

'I'll take the *Herbaceous Border*,' he said ungraciously.

'Fine,' Francesca said airily. The doorbell chimed. She felt relief flood her. 'I won't see you to the door as I'm in my dressing gown. I'll be in touch and thanks for a lovely evening, Mark.' Her heart softened at the sight of his woe.

'Are you sure that you don't want to change your mind?' he asked forcefully.

'No, Mark, I don't,' she said firmly.

'On your head be it then,' he reproached her and walked out of the house.

'No, Mark, not on mine, on yours,' she said determinedly, hanging her blouse on a hanger. 'Release, relax, GONE!'

Mark sat in the taxi as it sped along the Dublin Road. He was in absolute shock. He'd thought it was all going so well. When she'd returned his kisses and made no objection to making love – *sorry*, 'having sex', he corrected himself bitterly – he'd felt the most enormous sense of relief. He'd felt that the nightmare was over. But it was just beginning, he thought with dread. Francesca had blown him out. His house was going down the tubes. Deep down he'd always thought that Francesca would forgive him and take him back. And be glad to take him back. He'd really underestimated her. She'd been laughing at him back there in the bedroom. How dare she say she was 'fond' of him. He'd never felt so insulted in his life.

A dull throbbing at his temples reminded him of how much he'd drunk. How was he going to explain about the car to Nikki? Then he remembered she was off to London at the crack of dawn. He wouldn't have to. She'd hardly notice that it wasn't in the parking bay at that hour of the morning. Nikki loved him, he thought dolefully, but that didn't matter any more. He'd spend the rest of his life regretting the loss of his home and the loss of Francesca. His male colleagues envied him, he knew that. He saw the way they looked at Nikki lasciviously. He'd gloried in that once. Him and his stupid ego. If only they knew.

The taxi accelerated into the deepening night, on the road he had driven for so many years of his life. The road that led to his home. Now he was going in the opposite direction, unwillingly, fearfully. The lights of the city glimmered ahead of them. Mark sat looking out at familiar landmarks, his heart like lead.

Nikki lay in the bath reviewing her options. Was he going to come home to her tonight? And if he did what would she say to him? Would she straight out accuse him of being a lying bastard? If she did that he'd want to know what she was talking about.

Would she confess to spying on him? It was so pathetic she knew he'd lose all respect for her.

And hadn't she lost all respect for him? she argued. He'd come crashing down off his pedestal.

She couldn't tell him she'd been spying. She could tell him that she was unhappy and wanted to end the relationship. That would be the proper thing to do. The option that would give *her* back her self-respect. The alternative was to say nothing and suffer in silence until she absolutely couldn't take any more. To her consternation, she heard his key in the lock. She wasn't expecting him home *this* early. It was only nine-thirty. What on earth *was* going on over in Howth?

She lay still in the bath, her hands clenched by her side.

'Nikki? Nikki?' he called.

'I'm in the bath,' she called back. He poked his head around the door.

'Hi.'

'You're home early?' Her voice sounded admirably normal.

'The meeting was cancelled,' he told her. He looked ghastly. Grey and tired-looking.

'Are you OK?' she asked, concerned in spite of her anger.

'I've a migraine, Nikki. I'm going to sleep in the spare bed if you don't mind.'

'Oh,' she said. 'Give us a kiss then.'

He bent his head to kiss her and she inhaled the smell of his freshly washed hair. He'd very recently showered: she could smell the soap he'd used. A dead giveaway, she thought, sick to her stomach. 'See you when I get back from London,' she said as she raised her face for his Judas kiss.

He kissed her cheek. 'Have a good trip, Nikki,' he said.

No I won't, she wanted to shout. *It will be the worst trip of my life, thanks to you!* But she stayed silent. She heard him moving around the spare bedroom, heard the bed creak and she shivered in the lukewarm water. She stood up and stepped out of the bath and wrapped a large fluffy bath sheet around her but she couldn't get warm no matter how hard she tried. Her throat felt sore. She needed a sore throat like a hole in the head, she thought dispiritedly as she dried herself before slipping into bed. It seemed huge and empty. She missed the comfort of Mark's body. She missed his arms around her. She hated him for what he was doing to her and she hated herself for putting up with it. Tears rolled down her cheeks and a sob rose to her throat. She buried her face in the pillow to muffle the sound and cried her eyes out.

'We could pop around and have a look at it now if you like. It's vacant. The old lady who owned it died in a nursing home. The executors have put it up for sale,' the assistant in the estate agent's suggested helpfully. 'It's not far.'

'OK,' Francesca agreed.

'It needs work. New windows. New heating, re-decorating, but that's reflected in the price,' he explained as he picked up the house keys and opened the door for her. She sat beside him in his car and tried to keep her excitement under control.

Please let me like it, she prayed. After last night, she was more certain than ever that she was taking the right step. She wanted to get on with it.

The young man hadn't been exaggerating when he said that the untidy little cottage needed work. It had a stale, musty, uncared-for air and the wallpaper, curtains and carpets were tatty and dirty. The kitchen was dark and old-fashioned, far removed from her own airy modern fitted kitchen. The parlour with ancient sofas and antimacassars was of another era, as was the flock-papered dining room with its antique sideboard. The bathroom left much to be desired but the bedrooms were good sized. Bigger than the ones in the mews. She was daunted until she went out and stood in the back garden. A wilderness now, it had once been beautiful, she imagined, looking at roses growing wild along the creeper-lined walls and sweet pea and lavender wafting waves of perfume under her nose.

She could put in a dormer bedroom with en suite and break down the interior walls between the dining room and lounge to give more space. She could put down wooden floors, gut the kitchen and have a fitted one installed. She could put in french windows to lead out to a patio at the back, she thought excitedly. It could be beautiful.

She turned to the estate agent who was hovering hopefully in the background. 'It needs a lot of work but I like it. It has great possibilities. I want to buy it.' It could take £30,000 on top of the asking price, at least, to set the cottage to rights but a quick tot on her calculator assured her that she'd still have a very respectable lump sum behind her once she got her share of the house proceeds.

'That's great, Mrs Kirwan. You're sure?' he said.

'I'm certain. I've never been so certain of anything,' Francesca said happily. She had taken the first step on a great new adventure and she felt great.

Chapter Fifty-four

'I can't believe it.' Millie wandered through the cottage. It was the end of August, she was back from her holidays and she'd called around to Francesca's to catch up on all the news. The minute she'd heard about the cottage she'd wanted to go and see it. 'Cripes, Francesca, I go away for a measly four weeks and when I come back you've packed in enough dramas to last any normal person a lifetime – and now this. Look at the state of it!'

'I know.' Francesca grimaced. 'But I've had a builder look at the place and as soon as the sale is finalized he's going to make a start. I'll rent somewhere until I'm ready to move in.'

'You'll do no such thing,' Millie protested. 'You'll move in with us.'

'No, Millie. I'll have so much baggage, I'm better off renting,' Francesca argued.

'Look, we have a big garage, we won't park the car in it, you can pile your stuff in there and you can have the spare room and that's the end of it.'

'Millie, you haven't even spoken to Aidan about it.'

'As if I'd have to,' scoffed Millie. 'My little darling would be the first to suggest it, and you know it.'

'I know he's a pet. But I think it's an awful imposition,' Francesca said doubtfully.

'Oh, it is,' agreed Millie, straight-faced. 'Just think, you'll be in my debt for ever. You'll know not the day nor the hour when I decide to call in my marker.'

Francesca laughed. 'I'll live in terror.'

'And you've got a buyer for the house.' Millie walked out into the wild garden. 'It didn't take long. I told you it would be snapped up.'

'There were loads of viewers. It was down to three potential buyers in the end and they all really wanted it. And then last week one of them made the definitive offer. The papers were signed and it's all systems go,' Francesca explained.

'How does Mark feel? I *knew* he'd make a move on you, the sly bastard.' Millie couldn't contain her distaste.

'He's upset,' Francesca said quietly. 'I don't suppose I'll ever know if it was to keep the house or get back with me that he was the most keen on.'

'Is he still living with your woman?'

'Yep.'

'Doesn't say much for that relationship. If you'd taken him back he'd have dropped her like a hot potato.' Millie cupped a rose and inhaled the scent appreciatively.

'Yeah, well, that's their problem. I honestly don't care any more,' Francesca retorted.

'You wreaked a satisfying revenge,' Millie said slyly.

'What! I don't know what you mean.'

'Come on, Francesca,' Millie challenged. 'You let him believe he had a chance. You slept with him and let him be unfaithful to Nikki with you – and rightly so. You let him say it was you he wanted. And then you fucked him out on his ear. Dang, girl, I'm proud of ya!'

'It wasn't like that,' Francesca protested. 'I was a bit tiddly.'

'Not that tiddly, Francesca dearest. If he was swearing undying love to Nikki Langan you'd be spitting fire. But you don't care now because you know there's not only cracks but *crevices* in that relationship. Admit it.'

Francesca eyed her sister quizzically. 'What are you, some kind of a psychiatrist or something?'

'Nope. I'm a woman and that's *exactly* how I'd be feeling. I bet you enjoyed turfing him out having had your wicked way with him. No wonder he was in shock. Women don't do that kind of thing, especially sweet-natured wives who've been dumped and have the chance to get their husband back!' Millie laughed.

'Well, he had an awful nerve,' Francesca burst out. 'Just what did he think? He still doesn't get it. He thought right to the last minute that I was playing hard to get and that I would back down. As if.' She snorted. 'And I wonder if I hadn't put the house up for sale would he have been so quick to come back . . . if ever. That was one of the main reasons I didn't take him back,' she confessed. 'I didn't know the answer to that question.'

'Well, between him and Ralphie baby, you've had

a tough time. He was a major disappointment,' Millie remarked.

'Tell me about it, Millie. I couldn't believe my ears. I'm well shot of him.'

'And he only phoned the once?'

'No, I got a text message a while back that said, *Sorry, please get in touch*, but I ignored it. I don't want to renew our acquaintance, thanks very much. I want a simple life from now on,' Francesca declared.

'Is that right?' Her sister grinned, gazing around her. 'You certainly have a funny way of going about achieving it.'

'Just use your imagination, Millie,' Francesca urged. 'I'm telling you this place is going to be beautiful by the time I'm finished. Jim Donnelly is going to do the decorating so I'm in good hands.'

'He's excellent,' Millie agreed. 'He did a great job on my kitchen and bathroom.'

'There, you see, life's turning into a bed of roses,' Francesca declared optimistically, deadheading several roses that she already considered to be hers.

Nikki lay in bed, feeling absolutely ghastly. She was on her second dose of antibiotics but she couldn't shake the chest infection she'd caught earlier in the month. Mark was being kind in a distracted sort of a way. He'd brought her Lemsips and hot ports and insisted that she stay off work. She'd never been off work sick before and she was fretting about missed meetings and worrying about sneaky hot shots with their eye to the main chance muscling in on her territory.

Since that horrendous night when she'd caught Mark lying to her, he had immersed himself in work and travelled to three European cities plus New York. He had been too absorbed in his own little world to notice that she was edgy and distant from him. Or perhaps he noticed but didn't care. They'd been like ships that passed in the night for the past month. She felt as though her life was totally out of control.

Nikki frowned, remembering how she'd lain at home torturing herself when he'd gone on the New York trip in case 'the wife' had gone with him to see her precious sons. On one particularly soul-destroying night, when she'd drunk herself sick, she'd lifted the phone and dialled Francesca's number. She'd felt a faint sense of relief when the other woman answered and had hung up immediately. At least she wasn't in New York with Mark. But how often did she see him and what exactly was their relationship now? Nikki wondered anxiously.

The only time she felt she had Mark back was when they made love. At least he still turned to her in the dark some nights and for those few precious moments immediately after intercourse, when he lay in her arms, resting his head against her cheek, she felt he was hers again and all her fears receded for a little while, until he drew away from her and the barriers came back down.

He'd told her that the house was in the process of being sold. That was all. A bald statement of fact. She hadn't enquired further. She didn't care to. It was that damned house that had caused all the problems in the first place.

Mark picked up the phone and put it down again. He wanted to arrange with Francesca to pick up his belongings. He couldn't believe the house was almost sold. It made him ill to think about it. The thought of going there one last time was too daunting for words. There was no-one he felt he could ask to come and help him. He had dozens and dozens of acquaintances but very few real friends, he realized with a pang. Nikki was sick and besides he couldn't bring her out to Howth, it would be highly inappropriate to do so. In desperation he rang his father. 'Dad, I'm arranging for a bloke to bring a van around to the house to collect my stuff. I wonder, would you come with me?' he asked uncertainly.

'When?' his father said brusquely.

'I've to sort it out with Francesca.'

'Right. Just don't do it on Wednesday evening. It's my bridge night,' Gerald said gruffly.

'OK, Dad, thanks.' He put the phone down and felt a little less alone. He picked up some paperwork and tried to concentrate but the words danced up and down in front of his eyes. He picked up the phone again and dialled his wife's work number. The answering machine came on. It was obvious neither she nor her boss were in the office. He dialled her mobile.

She answered almost immediately. 'Hi, Mark. I'm sorry I can't talk for long, I'm heading into a meeting with a client,' she informed him. The irony of it struck him forcefully. How many times had he said precisely the same words to her?

'Look, I have a bloke lined up with a van to come

and collect my stuff. When suits you?' he said abruptly, annoyed at being given short shrift and inexplicably further annoyed at her confident, I'm-a-Busy-Woman air. She was getting just like Nikki, he thought with a faint sense of shock.

'I don't mind,' she said unhelpfully.

'How about Tuesday evening around six?'

'Perfect. Byeee.' She hung up. He stared at the phone. It wasn't knocking a damn feather out of the woman and here he was churned up about it all. He felt he didn't know her any more. She certainly wasn't the woman he'd married.

He was on the phone just after lunch on the Tuesday afternoon when his secretary came into his office with a brown envelope. 'These were left at reception for you, by Mrs Kirwan,' she said politely.

Mark didn't even wait until she'd left the room, he ripped open the envelope and stared at a set of keys that fell out onto the desk.

Sorry, Mark, I forgot I won't be at home this evening, I'm meeting Janet Dalton for a drink. I borrowed the spare set from the estate agent, just leave them on the hall table. Good luck. Enjoy the Herbaceous Border*!!*
All the best, Francesca

That was rich. That was really rich, leaving him to move his stuff on his own, he fumed. He'd hoped that the sight of him removing his belongings might finally make her see sense. She was such a softie he'd wanted to have her in tears. Then he'd have had one last go at persuading her to change her mind. He considered postponing his planned removal operation. But was there any point? he thought wearily. She'd put a deposit on a ramshackle cottage, she wasn't going to back out now. 'OK, Francesca, if that's the way you want it, fine,' he muttered crankily and flung the keys in the drawer.

Four hours later a white Hiace van crunched up the drive where he and his father were waiting. They'd made a start at bringing his stuff out to the hall. They worked in silence, his father puffing a little as he carried books and golfing trophies downstairs. Mark felt uncharacteristically grateful to him. They'd loaded everything into the van, except the painting that hung in the bedroom. Mark ran upstairs to lift it off the wall. There was a mark left behind it on the wallpaper when he took it down. The sight of it cut him to the quick. He sat on the bed, remembering the last night he'd spent in it with Francesca. And all the other good nights that had slipped by so swiftly he hadn't even noticed. Grief swamped him. A strangled sob rose to his throat. He tried to stop crying but he couldn't as a gut-wrenching, unbearable sadness enveloped him.

A self-conscious cough at the door startled him. His father stood looking at him in embarrassment. 'Are you all right, son?' he asked gruffly.

Mark shook his head. He couldn't speak. 'I'll tell the van driver to go on, we'll follow with the painting in the car,' Gerald said authoritatively and hurried down the stairs.

Mark sat alone crying. He heard his father coming upstairs again and made a huge effort to compose himself. 'Sorry about that, Dad,' he managed.

'That's all right, son. I'm sure this is very difficult for you, especially as it's all of your own making. We'd better get going. We don't want that van driver hanging around outside my house too long. He might take off with your things,' Gerald said anxiously.

'OK, Dad.' Mark knew his father was doing his best even if he wasn't being very tactful. He followed him downstairs carrying the painting. It was the last time he'd walk down the stairs. It was the last time he'd close the front door behind him. He laid the spare keys on the table. Grief overwhelmed him again.

'Come on, son, get it over and done with.' Gerald almost shoved him out of the door and he was the one who closed it behind him. 'I'll drive.' He held out his hands for the car keys.

Silently, Mark handed them over. He got in beside his father. 'Don't look back,' advised Gerald as he crashed the gears and lurched down the drive and shot out onto the road.

For a wild moment Mark hoped they'd crash into oblivion but as Gerald struggled with the car, he said unsteadily, 'Pull over, Dad. I'm OK now. I'll drive.'

'If you're sure.' Gerald couldn't hide his relief.

'I am. And, Dad' – he turned to his father – 'thanks for being there.'

'Hrumph.' Gerald went puce. He didn't like emotion, but some response was called for. 'I'm glad I was of some help, son, and I'm sorry it all came to this,' he managed, patting Mark awkwardly on the arm.

* * *

'Do you want me to come in with you?' Janet asked when they got home to Francesca's.

'Would you mind?' Francesca said shakily.

'Not at all. Give me the key,' Janet said kindly. She opened the door. Francesca saw the spare keys on the hall table and promptly burst into tears.

'Why don't you come and spend the night with me?' Janet suggested.

'No, no, I'll be OK. It's just I know how much Mark loved this house, and now I feel like a real heel,' she wept.

'Now stop that nonsense at once,' Janet declared. 'It was his doing in the first place that all this has come about. So don't you dare take that guilt on board.'

'I know, I know, I just wish it was all over and done with now. This part is going to be the pits.'

'Yes, it is, and that's why you're coming to spend the night with me and tomorrow evening we're going to start packing your stuff so you can be ready to go the minute the contract is signed, sealed and delivered,' Janet ordered. 'Get your clothes for tomorrow and let's go.'

Francesca was too upset to argue. Secretly she was relieved not to have to spend the night alone in the house. When she saw the bare wall in her bedroom where the *Herbaceous Border* had hung she broke down in tears again and sat sobbing her heart out in Janet's arms. If her friend hadn't been with her she was half sure she would have phoned Mark and told him that she'd changed her mind.

She cried many times over the following days as, with Janet and Millie's help, she packed away her and the boys' belongings.

'Am I making a big mistake?' she asked Janet one evening as they sipped coffee after a gruelling marathon pack.

'No, dear. You're not. And it's perfectly normal to go through what you're going through. You've lived here a long time and reared your family here. Of course you're going to be upset but it's much better to cry it out of your system than to hold on to it and make yourself ill. Cry all you want, dearie, but keep on packing,' Janet said wisely.

A week later, her solicitor rang to say a closing date had been agreed on. 'You don't have to be there if you don't want to,' she said. 'I can take care of it for you.' For a moment Francesca was tempted to agree but she had instigated the sale, it was only fair she was there to see it through, she decided reluctantly. The following day the removal men came to transfer her furniture and belongings to Millie's garage. It was the loneliest moment of her life. She'd asked Jonathan to defer his visit until she was moving into the cottage and he'd agreed but, as she stood surrounded by the clutter of moving, she was almost sorry he wasn't there with her. She walked around the half-empty house alone. Mark had had his beloved leather sofas and mahogany dining table put into storage. He'd decided to keep them at the last minute. Francesca wanted nothing. She planned to buy new furniture for the cottage.

In the event both she and Mark attended the closing. It went smoothly. They signed the necessary papers and cheques and handed over the keys and then she was given the keys to the cottage and it was all over.

'So,' said Mark as they walked away from the solicitor's office. 'Do I say congratulations?'

'No, Mark, I don't think so,' she said quietly. 'It wouldn't be appropriate.'

'I suppose not,' he muttered. 'It's a sad day for us.'

'Yes,' she said forlornly. 'It is.'

'I'm sorry about everything,' he said slowly as they came to Baggot Street bridge.

'Me too.' Her lip trembled.

'Oh, don't cry,' he said hastily.

'Sorry,' she whispered. He held her tight and she wrapped her arms around his neck. 'It's for the best, you'll see.'

No, he wanted to say, *it's not*, but he kept silent. It was too late for that now.

Francesca drew away from him. 'I have to go,' she said. 'Goodbye, Mark.'

'Goodbye, Francesca,' he said sadly and turned and walked away.

She didn't look back.

Chapter Fifty-five

December

'Well, Frannie, it was a long month's trial, and you're still with me.' Ken smiled at her as they sipped champagne at a Christmas bash in La Stampa.

Francesca laughed. 'I was so not what you were looking for. You oozed resentment. Poor Monica.'

'I owe her big time.'

'You do,' Francesca agreed straight-faced. 'We've had fun though, haven't we?'

'We've done well too,' Ken said. 'You know, I was thinking maybe sometime in the future we could employ someone else to look after the office and you could take on some accounts of your own. We could go into partnership. What do you think?'

'Are you serious?' Francesca was astonished.

'Very. Kennedy & Kirwan PR. Sounds good to me. We can expand much more, you know that!' Ken said earnestly.

'Kenneth, you're on,' Francesca declared.

'Right. We'll discuss the nitty-gritties in the new year. Right now I'm going over to brown-nose Danny Logan. He could put a lot of business our way if he were so inclined. I hear he's going into magazines. Taking on *Hello!*, *VIP* and the like.'

'Go for it! I'm going to have a chat with Linda Williams. She knows everything there is to know about PR. I really like her style.'

'Me too,' Ken grinned. 'Pity she's happily married.'

Francesca laughed as they parted and she was weaving her way through the glittering throng when a familiar voice said in her ear, 'Hello, Francesca.' Her stomach lurched.

'Ralph!' she spluttered. 'What on earth are you doing here?'

'I was invited,' he said sheepishly. 'Please can I talk to you for a moment?'

It was a shock to see him so unexpectedly. And a nuisance. She'd actually forgotten he existed. He looked tired. There was more grey at his temples than she remembered.

'OK, Ralph,' she said quietly, 'but I really have to go soon, there's someone I need to speak to.'

'I won't keep you long,' he assured her, steering her to a quiet corner. He cleared his throat and thrust his hands in his pockets. 'Francesca, did I show up that night I was to meet you or did I stand you up? I'm afraid I have no memory of it,' he confessed.

'You showed up,' she said flatly.

'Oh!' he said. 'I was drunk then. I'm sorry you saw me like that. Did I say anything to upset you?' he asked delicately.

'It wasn't very pleasant, Ralph, to be honest,' Francesca said uncomfortably. She certainly wasn't going to repeat all he'd said to her. 'But look, it's all water under the bridge now, let's wish each other well and forget it,' she suggested.

'I don't suppose I could prevail on you to put this behind us and to have dinner with me again?' He looked at her hopefully.

'No, Ralph, I think it's best all round if we leave things as they are,' Francesca said firmly. 'And now I really must go. Please don't think I'm rude but I have to speak to a few people. You know yourself. These things are work at the end of the day.'

'I know,' he sighed. 'You look very, very well, you know. Did you sell the house?'

'I did. I bought a cottage in Monkstown near the seafront. So I'm really close to the office, just a couple of streets away.'

'Is that the road that has a few cottages on it?' Ralph enquired. 'That's a smashing little place to live.'

'It is, yeah,' she agreed evenly, wishing he would move away. She had no desire to stay talking to him. She felt ill-at-ease, remembering his drunken suggestions. He seemed to be sober enough now, thankfully. He was drinking beer.

Ralph smiled at her. 'Well, I won't delay you, Francesca. The very best of luck with your new home. And once again, my apologies.'

'Forget it, Ralph. I have,' she said kindly, lying through her teeth. 'Happy Christmas.'

'And the same to you,' he said sadly as she moved away to talk to one of the best Sales and Marketing pros in the business.

Later that evening, as Francesca sat on the swaying commuter train, her thoughts wandered back to her meeting with Ralph. It had been a shock to bump into him so unexpectedly but she felt she'd handled it well. She was glad the meeting had occurred. She'd known that inevitably they'd meet at some function or another. Now it was done and there was a closure of sorts. She was relieved. She had no desire to resume their friendship. It was clear Ralph had a drink problem. She'd experienced a very dark side of him. It was not something she cared to repeat.

She smiled to herself, remembering the frightened, tense, insecure woman who had sat on a train several months ago silently repeating *release, relax, let go.* She had come on in leaps and bounds, she acknowledged matter-of-factly. Did she ever think that the desperate, uncertain woman who had scuttled out of Allen & Co.'s office with her tail between her legs would be considering a partnership offer in a PR company? Ken's suggestion made sense. She'd proved herself, proved that she was capable of handling her own accounts. They could really expand if they put their minds to it. They were a good team. Best of all, she had confidence in her own abilities.

She was a far stronger woman now than she'd ever been at any time of her life. She'd picked herself up and turned her life around and that was quite an achievement, she thought with satisfaction, smiling at her reflection in the window.

It wasn't the right place to have made his apologies, Ralph thought morosely as he ordered a double whiskey in the Horseshoe Bar in the Shelbourne. Francesca had looked so vibrant. Her eyes and skin were glowing and the well-cut black trouser suit she wore had not concealed her tall shapely figure. She was such a sexy woman and she had no awareness of it.

Maybe if he could get her on her own he could persuade her to come to dinner with him again. He knew where she lived now. At least that was a step in the right direction. Now that they'd made contact again and got over the initial awkwardness, their next encounter would be easier. He'd be on his very best behaviour with her from now on, he promised himself as he finished his whiskey and ordered another.

The Party

Chapter Fifty-six

Francesca studied her laden dining table and smiled broadly. Everything was almost ready. All she had to do was make the punch and have a bath and dress. A party in her new house. Who could believe it? she marvelled. This time last year she'd been a recluse, spending hours lying in bed crying her eyes out. Hating Mark, petrified to face the future. What a difference a year made. She poured herself a beer and sat down by the fire in her beautiful new lounge. Trixie snored delicately in her basket. The smell of fresh paint mingled with the scent of pine from the Christmas tree and the mouth-watering smells of cooking. A bough of pine and holly leaves along the mantelpiece sent forth the most glorious scent and festive red candles in shining brass candlesticks gave the room a very Christmassy air.

She looked around almost in disbelief. It was hard to imagine that this was the same shabby, uncared-for cottage that she'd walked into last August. Maple floors gleamed from beneath richly patterned rugs.

New double-glazed windows reflected the sparkling lights of the Christmas tree. Smooth, freshly plastered and painted walls in warm buttercup made the room bright and airy. Pelmeted chintz curtains that matched the material on her big, luxurious sofas lent a warm country cottage air. Small pine occasional tables held vases of roses and berried leaves. Her *Omani Tribesmen* hung over the fireplace and on either side of the hearth small recessed alcoves held shelves to display her sparkling collection of crystal and a few favourite ornamental pieces. White-painted louvre doors folded back to lead into the dining room that was dominated by the large pine table and chairs and the beautiful pine dresser on which reposed her collection of china. It shone under the recessed lights and Francesca smiled at the sight of it. This house was so completely different from her old home, in décor and atmosphere. She loved it, she really did. It was a house of joy to her. And she'd only been in it ten days. It was hard to believe. She'd moved in the week before Christmas and the most wonderful thing of all, her sons had spent Christmas with her. The boys had approved mightily of the cottage. That had been her great concern, that they wouldn't like it after the grandeur they'd been used to in Howth. She need not have worried. They followed her down the hall to their respective bedrooms and pronounced themselves more than happy.

'And you kept all my gear, Ma. You're the best.' Owen enveloped her in a bear hug when he saw his precious guitar and CD player. It had been a joy to see them both. They'd spent hours talking and reminiscing, laughing and teasing just like they'd used to.

She studied the table critically once more. She'd eschewed caterers. This was *her* party. She'd cooked all the food herself. A pale pink salmon lay on a bed of lollo rosso, olives and lemons. Platters of honey-roast ham, cider beef, turkey and salamis stood on either side. Dishes of salads and dips lent a variety of colour. Baskets of breads – tomato, onion, nutty brown – were at one end. Dishes of sliced tomato, cucumber and olives drizzled with oil and herbs at the other. A pot of creamy, herb-seasoned pasta in a carbonara sauce sat on her hob ready to be popped into the microwave. A pile of plates and napkin-wrapped cutlery lay on the dresser beside the wine and champagne glasses.

She strolled into the kitchen that led off a small archway from the dining room. It was a peach of a kitchen, she thought, happily gazing around, still quite unable to believe that this was her new home. Fitted pine presses covered every wall. An eye-level state-of-the-art oven and a gleaming hob delighted her housewifely heart. The big fridge-freezer groaned under the weight of chilled beer, wine and champagne. A colourful trifle, plum pudding and brandy butter, cinnamon pears and blueberry and raspberry sorbets took up two shelves, for afters. But still she wondered if she had enough food. The kitchen was spotless, all dishes cleared away. One thing about living with Mark all these years, she'd learned to be organized when throwing a party.

But this was a different party, she mused as she stood looking out onto the garden that had been tamed somewhat. This was a party where she was inviting friends that mattered. Her nearest and dearest. This wasn't about impressing colleagues at work. This was about fun and showing appreciation and giving thanks to all her stalwarts who had got her through the most difficult yet exhilarating year of her life: especially the boys, Millie and Aidan and their girls, Janet, Monica and Bart, Ken and Carla. Some of her book-club friends and two of her old neighbours in Howth who'd been especially kind. Viv Cassidy had *not* been invited. Her parents had gone to Galway for a holiday break; she was glad she didn't have to invite them, even though that was an awful admission to make, she acknowledged guiltily. Her mother was still cool with her. Her presence would have put a damper on things. But she would have liked her father to be there.

The phone rang. 'Hi,' she said cheerfully, expecting it to be Millie.

'Hello, Francesca,' Mark's deep voice came down the line. 'I was wondering if Jonathan was there. I can't get him on his mobile.'

'No, Mark, he and Owen spent last night with the O'Reillys. I'm not expecting them home until later. I'll get him to give you a call.'

'I was hoping he'd come out for a drink and that perhaps Owen would come too, I know they're going back to the States in a few days.'

'They can't go drinking with you tonight, Mark, I'm having a party and they're the guests of honour!' Francesca laughed.

'Oh! Oh, very nice. I hope it all goes well for you,' he said politely.

'Thanks,' she said warmly. On impulse she heard herself say, 'Why don't you drop in for an hour or two if you're free? It might be a perfect way of breaking the ice with Owen. If he saw that we were civil with each other he might thaw out a bit.'

'Oh, I wouldn't like to impose,' Mark demurred.

'Don't be silly, Mark, I'd like you to come. You'll know everyone, except Ken and his girlfriend. What do you say? I'd like you to see the house.'

'Are you sure?'

'I'm certain,' she assured him. 'Any time after seven. It's off the coast road, second turn on your right after the garage. You can't miss it, my car will be parked outside. It's the only newly done-up cottage on the street.'

'OK then,' Mark agreed. 'I'll see you. Thanks, Francesca.'

'You're welcome,' she said, putting down the receiver.

People would get a surprise to see Mark arrive, especially Owen and Millie, but if she could put the past behind her so could they, she thought. Part of her was longing to show off too. To say to Mark: *Look what I achieved without you. See what you're missing, you idiot.* She smiled. 'Vindictive bitch,' she muttered. But she was entitled, she told herself happily. Tonight was going to be a great night and if Owen and Mark could be reconciled that would be the icing on the cake.

Mark stared out of the lounge window. Francesca sounded so happy and carefree, he thought enviously. How he'd missed having Christmas dinner with her and the boys. Nikki had been as sick as a dog, unable to keep her food down. He was worried about her. She hadn't been well since catching that terrible dose at the end of the summer. She didn't seem to be able to shake off whatever was afflicting her. He'd insisted that she go to the doctor later today. He'd offered to come with her but she'd refused his offer. She'd lost weight and was terribly wishy-washy looking. They'd had a very quiet Christmas. It had suited him, he thought glumly. He wasn't in the humour for socializing. They'd both gone into work for a few hours that morning, he'd left to play a round of golf but she'd stayed and assured him that she was going to the doctor on her way home. They were supposed to be going to the Inchidoney in Cork for New Year but if she wasn't feeling up to it there wasn't much point.

He wondered how Owen would react to his presence at the party tonight. He had to give it to Francesca, she'd done her best to sort out the bad feeling between him and his son. He was curious to see what she'd done with the cottage. He'd gone up to have a sneaky look at it one evening and had peered in the grimy windows and wondered if she had gone off her rocker. But Jonathan had told him that she'd done a magnificent renovation on it.

It had been a joy to see his son and he'd held him close on their first meeting, glad to feel some connection with his family again. He'd invited Jonathan and Owen out to dinner with his father, but Owen had declined. He'd hoped time, and the fact that Francesca was happy, would have helped to heal the rift but Owen was being as bull-headed as ever. A trait Owen had obviously inherited from him, Mark admitted. Gerald had been delighted with the invitation to dinner. They'd gone to Shanahan's on the Green. It was ironic that his relationship with his own father had improved as a result of the dreadful episode when Mark had left his home for the last time, a sad and sorry man.

Mark sighed. He wouldn't say anything to Nikki about dropping into Francesca's. He wasn't in the mood for a snit. She was terribly edgy lately. Life was not a barrel of laughs in the Langan/Kirwan household, he thought glumly as he went to the off licence to buy a bottle of champagne for Francesca's party.

Nikki sat in her doctor's surgery, flicking through a magazine. Even though she'd made an appointment, he was running an hour late as a steady stream of coughing and snuffling, well-heeled, well-dressed patients shuffled in and out. It was almost six. It was probably to be expected, she thought sourly. He'd been closed all over Christmas and apart from today and tomorrow would no doubt be closed over the New Year break as well. A wave of nausea overtook her and she swallowed hard. She'd had to take another dose of antibiotics at the end of November, her third prescription in four months for that damned chest infection that kept recurring and ever since she'd been feeling atrocious. She, who'd never been sick in her life, had turned into a complete crock. At first she'd blamed the effects of the antibiotics for her malaise, now she'd wondered if she'd developed an ulcer with all the stress she'd been under.

It had been terribly difficult working when she'd been feeling below par, but at least her work hadn't suffered. She was in line for her biggest bonus ever and there was talk of promotion. That gave her some small comfort. She was going to ask the doctor to send her for some tests to nip all this illness in the bud once and for all, she decided as the receptionist called her name. But first she wanted something to effect an immediate cure of this damned ulcer or stomach bug or whatever it was. She wanted her trip to Cork to be a fresh start for her and Mark. A fresh start for a new year. Things had to get better than they were now. It was all so different from last Christmas, she thought unhappily as she walked down the carpeted corridor. She'd been so happy and optimistic then. Life had never looked so good. She'd felt vibrant, and full of life. Now she felt like a wet rag. She switched off her mobile. She didn't want any calls while she was being examined.

'Hello, Nikki, how are you?' Dr Morris said kindly when she entered the surgery. 'What's the trouble?' To her absolute mortification, Nikki burst into tears.

'I don't know what's wrong with me, doctor. I feel rotten. It's one thing after another lately,' she wept.

'Sit down there and we'll have a look and a listen,' Dr Morris said calmly as he patted her arm paternally and handed her a tissue.

The doorbell rang while Francesca's punch was simmering on the hob. She hurried out to answer it. The boys had keys, so it couldn't be them. She opened the door and stood rooted to the spot.

558

'Ralph!' she stammered. 'What on earth are you doing here?'

'Hello, Francesca,' he said cheerfully. 'You were easy to find. Your cottage is the only one on the street with fresh paint. I figured it was yours. Journalistic instincts and all of that. Happy New Year.' He thrust a bouquet of red and white carnations at her. 'I thought perhaps that we could make a fresh start, if only you'd give me the chance.'

She cursed herself for telling him where she'd bought the house. 'Oh Ralph,' she groaned. 'Why did you do this? Wasn't it better to leave things as they were? I'd much prefer it.'

'Please, Francesca,' he pleaded. 'I've changed. Honestly. Let me prove it to you.'

'Ralph, I'm having a party tonight and I'm rather busy. Could we talk about it another time perhaps?' She couldn't believe he was standing on her doorstep.

'Oh!' he said crestfallen. 'I suppose so.'

'Well, it's not really a huge party as such,' she explained hastily, thinking that he might expect an invite. 'It's for the boys before they go back to America,' she prattled. 'I want to give them a little family send-off. And now I really must go. Please don't think I'm rude but I've a lot to do.'

'Oh, OK,' he said dejectedly. 'The house looks lovely. Again, the best of luck with it. Goodbye, Francesca, and once more, I'm extremely sorry for upsetting you. I hope we can meet in the New Year. Sorry for interrupting your preparations.'

'That's OK, Ralph. Have a very happy New Year,' she said politely as he turned away and walked down the path. She felt a little sorry for him. She'd liked him, but after her experience that night, she felt she could never be comfortable with him again.

She closed the door and walked back into the kitchen inhaling the aromatic scent of the punch. She added some port and swirled some cinnamon sticks around the ruby mixture. It smelled delicious. She took a sip and was satisfied with the taste. Excitement started to bubble; she was so looking forward to entertaining her guests. She nibbled on a glacé cherry and promptly forgot all about Ralph.

Ten minutes later she heard a key jiggle in the front door. 'Mega smell, Ma.' Owen burst into the kitchen followed by his brother.

'Hi, did you have a good time?' She kissed them both, delighted to have them with her.

'Too good,' Jonathan declared.

Owen sloped into the dining room and snaffled a slice of salami.

'Hands off,' warned Francesca.

'But I love this stuff, Ma.' Owen chomped away happily.

'Don't touch another thing, Owen. Go and change your clothes and get ready for tonight,' she ordered.

He lifted her off the floor and swung her around. 'Make me,' he teased.

Francesca squealed. 'Put me down, you brat. Jonathan, tell him to stop,' she pleaded. 'You'll hurt your back, Owen. I weigh a ton.'

'Ah no, not a ton, Ma, half a ton maybe,' Owen said cheekily as he put her down.

'You're brazen impudent.' She laughed. 'Go on and get ready.'

'You've done a great job, Mam.' Jonathan followed her back into the kitchen. 'I'm looking forward to tonight.'

'Your dad's coming,' she murmured. 'How do you think Owen will react?'

Jonathan looked surprised. 'Is he?'

'Well, he wanted to meet you for a drink and I told him that I was having a party and suggested that he call in for an hour or two,' Francesca explained.

'That's cool, Mam, really cool. I'm glad that you felt you could do that. I'm really proud of you, you came out of this amazingly together, as the Yanks would say.' He hugged her warmly.

'I had good support, love. That's what tonight is all about. It's to say thanks and to show that I've made it and I'm fine. And I'm glad Mark's coming. It's much better than fighting and rowing. So when your dad comes, will you have a word with Owen and tell him to put the past behind him?'

'OK, Mam. Don't worry,' her eldest son reassured her.

'Right. I'm going up to have a bath. See you shortly,' Francesca twinkled. She was feeling light-hearted and exhilarated. She'd never looked forward to a party as much.

She climbed the wooden spiral staircase at the end of the hall that led to her newly built dormer bedroom. It was a most peaceful room. A big pine double bed lay under a Velux window and at night she could see the sky overhead. A pine dressing table and pine wardrobes filled one wall. A rocking chair and small coffee table positioned beside the small dormer window gave her a view of her back garden. She had such plans for that garden, she thought happily as she pulled the pale green curtains shut and began to undress. The en suite was decorated in peach and green with pine accessories. Pot-pourri and scented candles were dotted here and there. She loved lingering in a scented bath with the candles lit listening to soothing music wafting in from the bedroom. It was a warm, snug little haven. And best of all, it was *her* little haven, she thought happily as she ran the bath and poured a liberal amount of bath oil into it.

'So here I am, an independent woman,' she congratulated herself as she lay soaking in the fragrant water. Selling the house had been the best move she could have made. She didn't miss it. She felt far less lonely here and she loved the security of knowing that this was her house and Mark had no say in any of her affairs now.

She was glad that he was coming tonight. Her anger and bitterness had lessened to an enormous degree. Yet she had to admit that nothing would give her greater satisfaction than to know that his relationship with that woman was over. It was a petty attitude, she knew, but the hurt had gone deep.

She could hear the boys moving around their respective bedrooms. She was going to miss them when they were gone but at least she knew that she was well prepared and capable of living on her own and it held no fears for her.

An hour later, dressed in an elegant black cocktail dress, she sipped a glass of champagne with her sons. Soft music played in the background, candles flickered in the subdued lamplight and the

Christmas tree, the focal point of the lounge, twinkled and sparkled, the lights reflected in the sheen of the wooden floor and the glass of the windowpanes.

'The place is really nice, Mam,' Owen approved as he sneaked an hors-d'oeuvre.

'Stop stuffing your face, there'll be nothing left.' Francesca marvelled at her younger son's prodigious appetite. The doorbell rang. She jumped up, eager to greet her first guest. It was Millie and Aidan and the girls and there was a flurry of hugs and kisses as everyone was welcomed with a glass of punch.

Ten minutes later, Janet, Monica and Bart arrived within moments of each other and before long Ken and Carla had arrived. It was the first time they had seen the house and Francesca gave the guided tour amid much oohing and aahing and admiring comments.

Afterwards she stood in the lounge in the centre of a circle of her friends, offering canapés while her sons took care of the drinks, and felt a moment of happiness. The woman who had collapsed in a heap a year ago was gone. A far stronger, confident woman stood in her place. She'd survived.

Ralph sat in his apartment feeling very sorry for himself. He was absolutely alone, he told himself as he poured himself a generous whiskey. His wife and daughters had gone down the country to visit his in-laws, without a thought as to how he'd feel. He'd been so hopeful that Francesca would take pity on him and let bygones be bygones. After all, it hadn't been easy knocking on her door and apologizing yet again for whatever he had to apologize for. She could have shown him some mercy instead of leaving him standing on the doorstep like a pariah. It was a bit much. Her manners left a lot to be desired. The least she could have done was invite him to the party. He drained his tumbler and refilled it. He'd have another drink and think about his options, he decided as the whiskey began to kick in and he felt himself relaxing.

Nikki lay tensely as the doctor examined her gently. He was being extremely thorough but she wished it was over. She wanted to be at home with Mark. She could see a puzzled look on the doctor's face. 'So you were on antibiotics at the end of November and it was after that that you started to feel off-colour, even though it did its work on the chest infection?' he probed.

'Yes, doctor.' She tried to keep the impatience out of her voice. He'd been through this already.

'I see. Come and sit down, Nikki, and we'll have a little chat,' he said, helping her up off the couch.

I don't want a little chat. I want to go home. I just want to feel well again, she wailed silently as she fastened the buttons on her blouse and straightened up her skirt.

'Mark, I've a favour to ask you, could you drop me over to the Nelsons' right away? I know it's short notice but the bloody battery's gone flat and I'm supposed to be going over for my tea. Could you give me a lift?' Gerald asked expectantly.

'Yeah, yeah sure, Dad. I'll be right over,' Mark

said. He hung up and dialled Nikki's mobile number. Her phone was switched off. He went into the bathroom and freshened up. By the time he collected his father and delivered him to Rathfarnham where the Nelsons lived it would be after seven. He might as well carry straight on to Francesca's. Nikki was late. The doctor must be busy, he thought, surprised, as he dialled her number again and left a message on her answering service.

His father was waiting, red-cheeked and impatient. 'Come on, son, let's go. I don't want to delay these people. I phoned them to let them know that I'd be late. And I've ordered a taxi to take me home so you won't have to come back out to Rathfarnham for me. It's a bit of a trek.'

'It is,' agreed Mark. 'Here's the keys of the car. Get in. I just want to collect something upstairs.' He ran upstairs to the spare room. It was piled high with boxes and black sacks. He hadn't done anything about his belongings. Come the new year he'd make a decision on his future. He saw what he was looking for, tucked it under his arm and hurried downstairs. He didn't want his father to blow a fuse.

'Right, Dad, let's move it,' he said briskly as he closed the boot. He was a little apprehensive about going to Francesca's party. In fact he was sorry he'd told her he'd go and was tempted to phone her and cry off. What if Owen caused a scene? It could be awkward. But Owen wouldn't make a show of his mother, surely, he reassured himself. Perhaps it would be OK. They might even take the first steps towards friendship again and that would be the best thing that could happen.

Of course the Nelsons insisted he stop and have a drink and he couldn't be rude. They were old family friends and they were delighted to see him. But Mark was anxious to get going. It was almost eight when he finally pulled up on Francesca's road. He had to park several doors away. Her place was chock-a-block. He could hear the sounds of music and laughter as he walked up the garden path. It looked so different from the first time he'd seen it, he thought in admiration as he noted the new windows and door and the fresh paintwork. The garden had been replanted and a new wooden gate hung prettily to give a true cottagey effect. It was nice, he admitted and, typical Francesca, he thought fondly, she had a real Christmas tree. She'd never had any time for artificial trees no matter how realistic. She liked the fresh sweet smell of pine permeating the rooms and the dropped pine needles had been a small price to pay.

He swallowed, ran his fingers through his hair and rang the doorbell. He could see through the glass door a tall shape loping out into the hall. His heart started to pound. He hoped it was Jonathan.

It was. He'd obviously been primed by his mother to be on the lookout for Mark. 'Hi, Dad,' he greeted him. 'Come in. The place is hopping.'

'So I see.' Mark smiled. 'Here.' He handed Jonathan the champagne. 'Stick that in the fridge. I want to give this to your mother. Where is she?'

'Somewhere in the throng.' Jonathan laughed. 'Come on, I'll walk in with you.'

'Thank you, son,' his father said gratefully as he followed him into the lounge. It was a lovely house, he thought in surprise. Small, of course, but beautifully decorated. He liked the softness of it all. The room was full. He smiled at Bart and Monica and stopped to talk to them for a brief moment and then he saw Francesca. She was laughing at something a young man was saying. He had his arm around her shoulder. 'Now, Frannie!' he was teasing.

Mark felt a momentary surge of indignation. Who was that young whippersnapper calling his wife Frannie? She looked radiant in her chic black dress, with her hair pulled back from her face, emphasizing her cheekbones. Her eyes sparkled in the candlelight and she looked so at ease and happy that he could only stand and stare at her in shock. She wasn't missing him at all, he realized. Her life seemed to have improved immeasurably since they'd split up. She turned in his direction and saw him. Her eyes lit up, she excused herself to the whippersnapper and took the few steps over to him. 'Mark!' she exclaimed. 'You made it. I wasn't sure if you'd come.'

'This is for you,' he said awkwardly, handing her a painting. 'I'd like you to have it in your new home. You've done a lovely job with the house.'

'Oh Mark, it's the *Border*. I can't take this,' she said. 'This is the one you wanted.'

'Of course you can. I want you to have it, honestly, Francesca,' he assured her.

'Mark, thank you, that's so kind of you.' She flung an arm around him and kissed him on the cheek, the other arm holding the painting to her. He handed the painting over to Jonathan and hugged her back warmly and they smiled at each other in the midst of the guests, much to Millie's and Janet's astonishment.

Owen's eyes widened as he saw his parents embracing. Francesca saw him and took Mark by the hand and led him to where Owen was standing. Her son flushed a dull red, but he stood his ground. Mark held out his hand.

'Hello, son,' he said firmly. Owen's gaze flickered to Francesca.

'Please, Owen, if I can forgive your father, surely you can too. Please make up and let us be a family tonight.'

Owen's jaw worked as a myriad of emotions flickered in his eyes. 'Hi, Dad,' he said gruffly as Mark stepped forward and hugged the daylights out of him.

'I love you, Owen. I'm sorry for everything,' Mark whispered. 'I'm so proud of the way you stood up for your mother.'

Francesca felt a lump threaten to choke her. 'Oh Mark, stop or I'll start blubbing.' It was wonderful to see father and son reunited. 'Owen, take your father's jacket and get him a drink, I think it's time we started eating.'

'I'll drink to that,' Owen said shakily, his eyes suspiciously bright.

'Come on, son, get me that drink and tell me all about life in America,' Mark said firmly, happier than he'd been in a long long while.

'Millie, will you come and give me a hand in the kitchen? I've garlic bread and pasta to serve up,' Francesca murmured to her sister.

'You never told me that you'd invited Mark,' Millie hissed. 'And kissing him like a long-lost friend – what's going on?'

'Peace and reconciliation,' murmured Francesca happily. 'Goodwill to men.'

'Well, at least he and Owen are talking. That's something, I suppose, but don't expect me to fall all over him,' Millie said forthrightly as she slipped on a pair of oven gloves and opened the oven door, letting the rich, tantalizing smell of homemade garlic bread waft out into the kitchen.

The guests dived on the food with gusto and Francesca looked on with satisfaction as she served up dishes of creamy pasta. It was so satisfying to watch people eating heartily instead of nibbling and it was good to have cooked the food herself. She'd found there could be a sameness about catered parties, especially when the same few caterers were used on the circuit.

It was a jolly, buzzy party. Mark relaxed and began to enjoy himself, much to his wife's genuine delight. She'd thought he looked strained and tired. Not at all laid back and carefree as she was.

'Auntie Francesca, can I go and lie down in your bed, 'cos I'm tired?' her five-year-old niece asked.

'Of course you can, pet, come on with me,' Francesca said, leading the little girl by the hand up the spiral staircase. Sarah was enchanted with the bedroom and sat in the rocking chair looking out of the dormer window.

'This is cool,' she enthused.

'It sure is,' agreed her aunt gaily.

Downstairs, the doorbell rang. Bart was nearest so he answered it. 'Hello, is this Francesca's party?' a tall man asked, waving a bottle.

'It sure is, come on in,' Bart invited politely. The

tall man stepped past him. Bart's nose wrinkled. This chap had had a few already, he noted as fumes of alcohol drifted past him.

Ralph made his way into the lounge and stared bleary-eyed around but he couldn't see Francesca. He ambled out to the kitchen and saw an open bottle of red wine. He poured himself a glass and drank it in one go.

Nikki tried Mark's mobile again but it was switched off. She was shaking. Mark had left a message earlier and she'd felt like crying when she heard him say that he'd gone to give his father a lift to Rathfarnham and then he was meeting Jonathan for a drink. There'd been no talk about lifts or going for drinks earlier in the day. When had all this come up? And just when she needed him most. She got into her car and gunned the engine. She didn't want to go back to the empty apartment. She'd spent the last hour wandering around a shopping mall. She felt sick to her stomach.

The apartment was dark and unwelcoming. He could at least have left a light on, she thought resentfully as she let herself in. She went into the bedroom and lay down on the bed. She'd just rest there for a minute and hope that her swirling, racing thoughts would calm down. Her eyelids drooped. She'd never felt so utterly exhausted in her life.

The shrill ring of the phone woke her and she shivered. She glanced at the clock and saw that she'd been asleep for over two and a half hours. She was shocked. It was almost ten-thirty.

Hoping against hope that it was Mark, she lifted the receiver.

'Nikki, hi, how are you, babe?' Her heart sank. It was Karen Regan, a friend of hers. She sounded pissed.

'I'm OK,' she said brightly.

'Are you doing anything tonight? I just thought you might be at a loose end like me and you might like to pop over for a drink. I saw Mark driving through Monkstown earlier and guessed you might be fancy free for a few hours.'

Nikki felt weak and dizzy. What was Mark doing driving through Monkstown? Karen must be mistaken. He'd told her that he was driving his father to Rathfarnham and going for a drink with his son.

'Aah . . . sorry, Karen, I'm actually on my way out myself. A work thing. I'll call you in the New Year,' she lied desperately.

'Oh OK, just rang on the off chance, babe. No probs,' Karen slurred. 'Cheers.'

Nikki hung up and sank into a chair. Maybe Karen was mistaken. It was obvious she'd been drinking. But then she'd said that she'd seen Mark earlier. Was that before she'd started to drink? Nikki shook her head in despair. He'd lied to her again. He was going to see his wife. Going to play happy families. Well, she'd had enough of his crap. How dare he play fast and loose with her. She grabbed her car keys. It was time that Mark Kirwan learned a few home truths, she raged. She'd taken as much as she could take. He'd made a fool of her once too often. It couldn't be too hard to find the bloody house. It was a cottage, Mark had told her. It was off the coast road. She'd look for Mark's parked car and knock on every damn door until she got the right one.

Ralph edged his way to the buffet. He was hungry. He hadn't eaten all day. He jerked the arm of a vaguely familiar-looking man as he walked past. The man stared at him and recognition dawned in his eyes.

'Oh, it's the cruddy husband,' he muttered.

'I beg your pardon?' Mark said aggressively, staring at him.

'I said, "It's the cruddy husband,"' Ralph enunciated carefully. 'What are you doing here? I thought the magnificent Francesca hated your guts.'

'You're drunk,' Mark accused him.

'So what?' scoffed Ralph woozily. 'It won't stop me riding the ass off your beautiful, voluptuous wif—'

Mark's blow connected with his jaw and was followed swiftly by one to the nose. He vaguely heard a woman scream as he crumpled to the floor.

'God Almighty, Mark!' exclaimed Millie. 'Was that absolutely necessary? Don't you dare ruin Francesca's party!'

'Yes it damn well was,' said Mark through gritted teeth. 'He insulted my wife.'

Ralph groaned at his feet.

'What's going on?' demanded Francesca, coming into the room in a panic. She saw Ralph at Mark's feet, blood spurting from his nose. 'God Almighty! What's he doing here?' she demanded, horrified.

'Insulting you,' fumed Mark.

'Oh, for God's sake, did you have to hit him on the nose as well? How macho of you, Mark. Look at my good rug!'

Millie tittered. 'I like your style, dear,' she murmured.

The doorbell rang. Ken answered it. He was thoroughly enjoying the scene. A wild-eyed, pale woman stood at the door. 'Francesca Kirwan's?' she demanded. Ken nodded, taken aback at her rudeness.

The woman brushed past him and raced into the lounge. She saw a group standing around a man lying on the floor and then she saw Mark.

'You bastard!' she swore, lunging at him and slapping him around the face. 'You lousy, lying, fucking bastard,' she screamed hysterically as he tried to grasp her wrists. 'How can you want to be with her after all the things you've said about her? It's me you love. Me. How can you do this to me, Mark? How can you treat me like this? Well, don't think that you're playing happy families here any more because there's going to be another little addition to your family. I'm pregnant, do you hear me, *darling*! I'm pregnant,' she yelled.

A horrified gasp went around the room. The colour drained from Mark's face. Francesca's hand flew to her mouth in shock. A pin could be heard drop as Nikki went as white as a sheet and dropped gracefully on top of Ralph in a dead faint.

Another communal gasp rippled through the onlookers.

Ralph lay dazed beneath Nikki.

Millie's mouth was a round O.

'I'd better bring her home,' Mark said uncertainly, bending to assist her.

'You'd better,' Francesca said and threw a glass of water over the woman lying prone at her feet.

'*Francesca!*' remonstrated Mark. 'There was no need for that.'

'No, there wasn't!' slurred Ralph indignantly. Some of the water had landed on him.

'Wasn't there?' Francesca said icily. 'I disagree. I didn't ask her to come here and cause a scene and faint. Please leave.'

Nikki spluttered and came to. Mark carefully helped her to her feet. He was shaken to the core. 'Come on, we're going home.' Nikki looked dazed. She clung to his arm.

Francesca marched out to the front door and opened it wide. 'Sorry, Francesca,' Mark muttered as he supported Nikki out of the door, her face dripping with water.

The two women stared at each other.

'I don't want you ever to set foot in any house of mine again,' Francesca warned.

'Don't worry. I wouldn't contaminate myself,' Nikki raged.

'Out!' snapped Francesca and closed the door with a resounding bang behind them.

Ralph was struggling to his feet as she came back into the lounge. 'I'll take care of him,' Ken offered, man-handling him out of the room. Ralph was too far gone to protest.

Everyone looked at Francesca. She looked back at her guests and gave a shaky smile. 'Entertainment laid on specially for your pleasure. Sorry about that. Anyone like a drink? I know I could do with one.'

People laughed and the tension eased as Aidan and Owen promptly began to refill glasses. *I might as well enjoy myself*, Francesca thought shakily, taking a slug of red wine as her party got into full swing again.

Après Party

Chapter Fifty-seven

'Well, you certainly know how to throw a party, girl,' Millie said drily.

'Oh, don't remind me,' groaned Francesca. 'It was a disaster.'

'On the contrary, it was highly entertaining,' Millie said wickedly.

'Millie!' Francesca glared at her. It was the following afternoon, her sister had dropped over to have a post-mortem on the party and catch up on developments.

'Sorry,' said Millie. 'But you have to admit, it was far from boring, and once Ken hauled Ralph into a taxi and Mark took Fecund Mother home, things revived and a good night was had by all.'

'I know. I still have the hangover to prove it,' Francesca moaned.

'Have you been talking to Mark this morning?' Millie asked as she plonked a cup of coffee in front of her sister.

'Yeah. He's in bits. Total shock. I can't believe it myself.'

'How do you feel about it?' Millie eyed her sister.

'As shocked as he is. I can't imagine Mark into feeding and nappies and all the rest of it. He never wanted any more children with me. I know you'll think this is horrible of me but I really hope they don't have a little girl. I could cope with a boy, but a girl would be difficult. I always wanted a daughter.'

Millie reached out and took her hand. 'It's not horrible at all. But you'll cope whatever it is. I'll tell you one thing, though. That pair aren't going to last. Child or no child. That relationship is on the ropes.'

'Don't say that,' Francesca said.

'It's the truth. You heard her last night.'

'She was hysterical,' Francesca murmured.

'Hysterical or not, she's had it with him. He'll be back on your doorstep yet.'

'No he won't,' Francesca said firmly. 'I'm nobody's back-up system any more. He can stand on his own two feet just as I had to stand on mine.'

'That's ma girl!' Millie grinned. 'Did the stain come out of the rug?'

'Yeah. Bart, bless him, did a great job on it.' Francesca sighed. 'That Ralph is something else. Can you believe him coming back here?'

'I don't think he'll venture back after getting his nose bloodied,' Millie declared. 'You have to admire Mark defending your honour.'

'Bloody idiot,' snapped Francesca. 'Making a show of me and ruining my party. Men! They're pathetic.'

'But where would we be without them?' giggled the irrepressible Millie. 'How boring our parties would be otherwise.'

Francesca caught her sister's eye and started to giggle too. They laughed and laughed until she was gasping.

'I was so looking forward to my party,' she confessed. 'I'll be the talk of Howth.'

'Who cares? It was good fun. And isn't Ken a poppet? He really livened the place up and got us all on track again after the little hiccup.'

'I know, he's a dote. Owen and Jonathan got on like a house on fire with him and they all teased me unmercifully. I felt sorry for the boys hearing that they were going to have another sibling the way they did.'

'Ah, don't fret about them, they're fine. And besides, they'll be across the ocean so it's not going to impact too much on them. Don't you take it all on board now,' Millie warned. 'It's not your problem. And don't let Mark cry on your shoulder every five minutes. He's dipped his wick, he has to deal with it.'

'Yes, Millie.' It was easier to agree.

Millie looked around her. 'I came to help you tidy up and there isn't a thing to be done.'

'The lads were great. They told me to stay in bed and they did it all this morning. They've gone to a match this afternoon. Come on in and we'll sit by the fire,' Francesca suggested.

'OK. I'll have a root in the fridge if you don't mind, I'm starving,' Millie announced.

'Me too,' Francesca said, feeling suddenly peckish.

'We'll have a picnic,' decided Millie. 'Grab a plate.'

'Look, I'm sorry,' Mark said wretchedly. 'I *did* go to Rathfarnham with Dad and I *was* going to meet

Jonathan for a drink but Francesca was having a party and he couldn't make it so she suggested I call in for an hour or so. She wanted Owen and me to make our peace. She thought it would be a good opportunity. I just didn't say it to you because I thought you'd be annoyed. You're always very touchy where Francesca is concerned.'

'You slept with her last August, didn't you?' Nikki accused.

He turned away from her. 'Don't be daft,' he muttered, shocked at her perception.

'Look me in the eye and say you didn't,' Nikki challenged him.

He turned to face her and the contempt he saw in her eyes made him lower his.

'Bastard!' she swore. She was lying in bed, as white as a ghost. He'd taken her home last night and she'd closed the bedroom door in his face and refused to talk to him until ten minutes ago. He hadn't slept a wink all night. He didn't want another child. He felt totally trapped. 'How did you get pregnant? I thought you were on the pill,' he said sullenly.

'I am. It's so bizarre. I actually once thought of stopping it to get pregnant in an effort to bind you close to me. I decided against it. Thought it was too drastic a step to take even for love. Mother Nature seemingly had other ideas.' She gave an unamused laugh. 'The antibiotics interfered with the pill and I lost protection. I'm about six weeks' pregnant. The test was well and truly positive, darling.'

'What do you want to do?'

'Do you mean do I want to have an abortion?'

'It's up to you, Nikki, I wouldn't presume to interfere in any decision you make,' Mark said flatly.

'It's your baby, Mark.'

'I know.'

'Why didn't you have more children with
Francesca?'

He stood up and jammed his hands in his pockets.
'She had something called endometriosis, she
couldn't have any more. I was glad. I felt two were
enough.'

'You're a selfish bastard, Mark.' Nikki sat up in
the bed and glared at him.

'You're not the first woman to tell me that,' he
growled.

'So you don't want it?'

'No.'

She took a deep breath. 'I'm keeping the baby. I
always shoulder my responsibilities and I won't shirk
this one.'

'Fine. I'll support you.' Mark stared out of the
window.

'You don't have to support *me*, Mark. You can pay
your share towards the baby's upkeep, of course. But
I can support myself, I always have done and I always
will,' she said coldly. She pulled back the sheets and
got out of bed. She opened the wardrobe doors and
took out an armful of his clothes.

'What are you doing?' he asked in surprise.

'Helping you pack,' she said calmly. 'I always said
I'd give it until Christmas. Well, Christmas has come
and gone and I want to make a fresh start for the new
year. And that fresh start doesn't include you.'

'Don't be stupid, Nikki. I can't leave you like this.'

'Yes you can. It's over,' she said harshly.

'But where will I go?' He was horrified.

'I really don't care, Mark. Go back to your precious Francesca. You don't seem to be able to stay away from her. All I know is that you're not staying here. I've had it with you. I want you out, now.'

Francesca's phone rang. 'Hello?'

'Hi, it's me. Look, I'm in a spot. Nikki and I have broken up and I need a bed for a little while until I get myself sorted. I know it's short notice and I've a cheek to ask but could I bunk on your sofa for a couple of days?' Mark sounded frantic.

Francesca's heart lurched. Millie was right. They were *finito*. He and Nikki were over. And he was coming running back to her. She took a deep breath. 'Sorry, Mark, I don't think that's such a good idea, if you don't mind. I'm sure Gerald will put you up. I'm sorry.'

'Oh!' There was stunned silence at the other end. Then, 'I just took the chance. Sorry for bothering you.' Mark gave a poor me sigh that came from his toes.

'I'll let you go then, Mark, to sort things out. Talk soon,' Francesca said calmly. 'Bye.'

'Bye.' Mark hung up and Francesca stared into the fire. She didn't regret her action. She was not Mark's doormat any longer. Funny though, she'd longed for the day when her husband and that woman would break up. Now it had come and somehow it didn't feel half as good as she thought it would.

* * *

Mark dialled Gerald's number. The phone rang and rang. Mark began to feel panicky. He was homeless, with all his worldly goods packed into his BMW. What the fuck was he going to do? He'd have to rent a place and then go and buy somewhere, but he couldn't get anywhere tonight. He could end up stuck in a hotel the way things were going. He couldn't believe that Francesca had refused him.

He felt enormous relief as he heard his father answer the phone with a hint of breathlessness.

'Hello, Dad.'

'I was in the shed, that's why it took me so long,' Gerald wheezed.

'Dad, I'm asking a favour. I need a bed for a couple of nights until I get a place of my own. Can I come home?'

'Has that other one thrown you out?' Gerald demanded bluntly.

'Yes.'

'I see. Well, you can't sleep on the side of the road. You'd better come home then, but don't expect haute cuisine and gold-star hotel treatment,' Gerald declared and hung up.

Mark smiled in spite of himself. His father was, as ever, true to form. He shook his head and started the engine. He was forty-six years old and going home to live with Daddy, his marriage and relationship in tatters. Was there anything more pathetic?

Nikki watched Mark drive out of the parking bay. She felt very calm. Queasy, but calm, she acknowledged wryly. Now that she'd finally made a decision she knew what she was dealing with. That was a start.

It was funny but she felt huge relief. No more paranoia, no more fretting about whether Mark loved her or not. No more having to feel jealous of that Francesca cow. A sadness enveloped her. She'd really loved Mark. But it wasn't enough. It was too one-sided. A totally unequal relationship. She'd never get involved in one like that again, she vowed. It had wrecked her emotionally and physically. Mark had been the worst thing that ever happened to her.

From now on she'd be totally in control of her life again. Her career would flourish. She was going to actively seek a new position. She'd have no problem getting a new job. She looked down at her flat belly and slid her hand along it. There was a baby in there. It was hard to believe. *I won't think about that right now*, she decided. If she started thinking about this baby and how it was going to affect her future she'd crack up altogether. She had to deal with her heartache first. She caught sight of a picture of herself and Mark. It had been taken early in their relationship. They'd been happy then. Tears welled in her eyes. It had all gone so badly wrong. She loved him but she couldn't live with him any more. It was affecting her emotional stability too badly. She *had* to get her life sorted and get going again. Nikki lay on the bed and wiped her eyes. No more tears. She'd shed enough to last a lifetime. It was time to move on.

Ralph studied his reflection in the mirror. He had a black eye and a bruised nose and jaw and he couldn't remember a thing about it. Fear gripped him. It was getting worse and worse. He was losing days at a time now. New Year was coming up. He hated New Year.

He had two options, he thought calmly. He could kill himself. Take the tablets here and now and wash them down with a load of booze, or he could take the harder option. It frightened him.

He picked up his car keys, dismayed at how much his hands shook. He drove cautiously until he came to the high-walled iron-gated building. He drove into the tree-lined drive; the branches were bare and stark against the gunmetal sky.

He smiled at the girl in reception. 'I'd like to sign myself in for treatment but could I do it quickly because I'm afraid I'll take to my heels and run out of here. And if I do that I'm dead,' he informed her, handing her his car keys.

'Hey, Mam, what do you want for the last supper?' Jonathan called from the kitchen. It was their last night at home.

'I think I'd like a toasted cheese sandwich,' Francesca said. She wanted something simple after all the rich food over Christmas. She was ironing Owen's shirts. She finished the last one and carried the neat pile into her youngest son's bedroom, slid them into a plastic bag and placed them in the open case on the bed.

'Are you going to be OK, Mam?' Owen put his arms around her.

'I'm going to be fine,' she assured him and meant it. 'It's not like when you were leaving the last time. I didn't know what I was going to do with myself. I could have ended up the world's greatest potterer.'

'I won't be half as worried about you this time.'

Owen smiled at her and kissed the top of her head. 'I'm more worried about Dad. Imagine ending up living with Granddad at this stage of his life.'

'Your father will be fine, Owen. He just needs to shift his ass and buy a place for himself, but the thing is he doesn't like hassle. He likes the easy life and life's not easy. So it will be interesting to see how long he sticks it at Gerald's.' She grinned. 'I think that I can guarantee you your father will have a place of his own in the not-too-distant future.'

'I love you, Mam.'

'I love you too.' She hugged him tightly.

They wouldn't let her take them to the airport.

'Two of us going! Could you imagine the bawl factor? No way, Ma. Under no circumstances,' Jonathan said firmly. 'We'll take a taxi.'

'Definitely,' agreed his sibling.

'Well, if that's what you want.'

'It is,' they assured her very emphatically.

To tell the truth she was relieved. It would have been hard to keep her composure at the airport. And she didn't feel so bad knowing that they were together. Besides, she planned on going out to visit them at Easter so that was something to look forward to.

The following morning their farewells were short and sweet. She could see them laughing at her and at the tears sliding down her cheeks as she waved her goodbyes. She laughed in spite of herself at their antics in the taxi and waved after them until the car turned onto the coast road.

She closed the door behind her and wiped her eyes. It was dark and cold and the crack of dawn and her warm cosy bed beckoned. She climbed her spiral staircase and slid back into her bed and snuggled down under the quilt. The cottage was silent, but it was a calm, serene silence and she felt peaceful. She would help Mark find a place of his own. She was now the stronger one in the relationship, she thought in surprise. It felt good. She was looking forward to going into partnership with Ken. And then at Easter she would fly out to the States to holiday with her sons. Mark could join them if he wanted to. They could spend time as a family and then she could come home to her gorgeous little house. *Her* house. Oh yes, she had an awful lot to look forward to, Francesca thought drowsily as her eyes closed and she fell into a deep, untroubled sleep.

THE END

APARTMENT 3B
by Patricia Scanlan

'The perfect book for those moments when you need to escape' *Woman's Realm*

Behind her, along the cliff's edge, house-lights were starting to twinkle, delicate pinks and yellows and whites, depending on the colours of the curtains and lampshades. Ahead of her the pier curved protectively around the bay, its high storm-wall seeming almost impenetrable.

This is the backwater world of Moncas Bay that still represents home to businesswoman Lainey Conroy as she embarks on a new life to try to forget her past. So when the apartment of her dreams comes on the market in the city, she's determined to buy it. But bidding against her for artist Liz Lacey's luxurious penthouse apartment are the world and his wife. Including Lainey's own sister-in-law and jealous rival, Cecily, who seeks the ultimate escape from her two-up, two-down origins back in Moncas Bay, and who will stop at nothing to prevent Lainey from acquiring it.

Behind the dreams, behind the ambitions of those who have set their hearts on Apartment 3B lies a hidden landscape; of girlhood rivalries; of local daughters made good; of being the talk of the Bay; and, all too often, of disappointment . . . and exciting new beginnings.

1-85371-136-5

CITY LIVES
by Patricia Scanlan

'A page-turner . . . for incurable romantics who love a fairytale ending' *Ireland on Sunday*

Devlin, Caroline and Maggie. Women in their prime. They have it all. Careers. Success. Marriage. They are the envy of their peers. But at what price?

Just when Devlin has everything she ever dreamed of, a callous betrayal shows her that there's no room for friendship and loyalty in business. Can she be as tough as she needs to be in a world of deceit and double-dealing, where honesty and integrity are rare commodities?

Caroline, fed up being a victim, is no longer shy, unsure and needy. She's about to take a step that will change her life. Then tragedy strikes, and her plans change completely. But as one door closes . . . another opens.

And Maggie, alone, unsupported and unhappy in her marriage, has to make a choice that will put her children's needs before her own. Has she the strength to do what she has to do?

City Lives is the story of three women who have one great certainty in their lives. Their friendship. The enduring bonds of loyalty and love will carry them through the worst of times and the best of times.

1-84223-007-7

PROMISES, PROMISES
by Patricia Scanlan

'Love, laughter and tears' *Candis*

The village of Glenree is home to the Munroe women: from the glamorous new in-law, Emma, to dogsbody Miriam and 'Airs-and-Graces' Sheila, who is forced to watch her own daughter Ellen become the talk of the county.

The saying 'love is blind' could have been invented for the wayward Ellen, whose life changes for ever when she leaves the ebony darkness and winding country roads of Glenree for the bright lights of the city. It is there she falls in love with Chris Wallace, a skunk of the highest order.

Promises, Promises covers a decade in the lives of the four Munroe women – and the charming philanderer who leaves a trail of emotional destruction in his wake. A tale of love and heartbreak, laughter and tears, that will strike a chord with all women . . . especially those who have loved a rotter!

1-85371-736-3

MIRROR, MIRROR
by Patricia Scanlan

'This is perfect summer reading: hearty, humorous, and romantic. Be prepared to be bad company, though – it's a compulsive page-turner which keeps you guessing until the very end' *Home & Country*

When Chris Wallace looks in the mirror he sees a deep and complex man. He is, in fact, selfish, shallow and very, very devious. A master of deceit. Successful, charismatic and sexy, women love him.

Suzy Wallace, a woman scorned, wreaks havoc and revenge on her husband's mistress, once her best friend, now her sworn enemy. She will never forgive and never forget.

Alexandra Johnston, ambitious, talented and seductive, uses every trick she can to get what she wants . . . and then finds out that having is not quite the same as wanting.

Ellen Munroe, the mother of Chris's child, the woman he has used and abused over and over, finally has the chance for happiness with an honest, decent, steadfast man . . . until Chris lies his way into her heart again.

Can Ellen finally see that he is a callous, persuasive manipulator without conscience, who uses lies and false promises to destroy the lives of women who love him? Will she have the strength to walk away?

Mirror, Mirror is the story of women who have had enough. A tale of delicious revenge and glorious vindictiveness, as Chris Wallace tastes the bitter fruits of his deceits and finally gets what's been coming to him.

1-85371-832-7